Darkness Falls

A RAVENWOOD MYSTERY

MIA JAMES

Indigo

Copyright © Mia James 2011

First published in Great Britain in 2011 by
Indigo
An imprint of the Orion Publishing Group
Orion House, 5 Upper St Martin's Lane, London WC2H 9EA
An Hachette UK Company

This edition published in Great Britain in 2012 by Indigo

1 3 5 7 9 10 8 6 4 2

A CIP catalogue record for this book
is available from the British Library

ISBN 978 1 78062 043 5

Typeset by Deltatype Ltd, Birkenhead, Merseyside

Printed in Great Britain by Clays Ltd, St Ives plc

The Orion Publishing Group's policy is to use papers
that are natural, renewable and recyclable products and
made from wood grown in sustainable forests. The logging
and manufacturing processes are expected to conform to
the environmental regulations of the country of origin.

www.orionbooks.co.uk

For Margaret and Ray

Prologue

Whitechapel, 1888

He stalked her. Keeping to the shadows, slipping from doorway to doorway, he followed the girl, never losing sight of her, never losing her scent. He increased his pace, falling in behind her. She swayed as she walked, stumbling here and there, but he matched her step for step, his feet sliding across the cobbles, carefully skirting the puddles. He didn't want to leave footprints, didn't want to leave any trace. The fog helped: thick, swirling. The fog was his cloak, his accomplice, it wrapped around him and kept him hidden. Hidden was good. Hidden was safe.

He sniffed the air and turned his head. An open window, some sort of roasting meat. He was hungry, God he was hungry. *Not long, not long now*, he thought. Soon he would touch her skin, soon he would feel his hands on her throat.

There was a sudden swell of noise as a tavern door opened and two men stumbled out, reeling into the road. He quickly slipped out of sight, unseen in a swirl of fog beyond the cone of gaslight, just a shadow, nothing more.

Come on, he thought, watching as the girl flirted with the men, *leave those fools alone.* He hated waiting, hated this gnawing need. The need to eat, to feed. For a moment, he closed his eyes and tried to recall a time when he wasn't shackled to this craving, this huge open furnace that roared for fuel. He had been happy then – or had he? There had been something back there, something he wanted to forget. He glanced over his shoulder.

He knew he was being hunted too, by creatures who enjoyed the sport. And they wanted him dead – of course they did. He was a failure, an experiment, a plaything to be discarded. But he hadn't gone away, he couldn't. He had to feed. They had made him this way – and one day they would pay for it. But not now. He had one purpose this night and that was to hunt. And to do that, he needed to stay hidden.

He pulled further back into the shadows as a carriage clattered past. Not that he would raise an eyebrow on these streets. Just another down-at-heel gentleman taking a stroll, perhaps looking for some company. He was careful; that was how he survived.

With a curse towards the laughing men, the woman moved off again. Down Flower Street, weaving in and out of the gaslight. He was getting closer, closer. He could see her clearly now. When he sniffed the air he could almost taste her, a half-smile spreading across his mouth. He had her now. He knew every twist and turn of this cramped, crumpled quarter of the city, where the buildings lolled over towards the road, teetering like drunks at the bar. Closer, his boot-heels whispering over the cobbles, reaching out a gloved hand …

'Oof, have a bleedin' care!' said the woman. 'Oh, 'ello kind sir, you looking for a lady to have a warm?'

She was younger than he had thought. Pretty, under that worn face. God, she looked like … her. Suddenly he was flooded with doubts. What he was doing was wrong, wasn't it? Or was it? He wasn't sure any more. It had become an addiction, a necessity he had stopped questioning long ago. The woman must have seen his hesitation and assumed he was feeling guilty, thoughts of a wife or a sweetheart perhaps.

'Don't worry, darlin', there's no harm in having a little fun is there? Say a few Hail Marys come Sunday and you'll be all square with the boss,' she said, reaching up to finger his lapel. He pulled back from her, jerking away at her touch.

'Oi, no need to play so hard to get, dearie,' said the woman. 'If you've a shilling, I should think we can be friends.'

A shilling? A girl in this part of town would be lucky to get tuppence. She was trying to trick him, manipulate him, just like everyone else around him. He could feel the anger rising in him again. That blind, tearing rage he couldn't control, the one that made him do ... terrible things. The girl saw his face harden and shrugged.

'Awright, awright,' she said, putting her hands on her hips, 'You can't blame a girl for trying can yer? Don't s'pose you've anywhere to go 'ave yer?'

He took a deep breath, trying to compose himself – not yet, not here. He shook his head.

'No, a nice gentleman like you ain't gonna have lodgings around here, are you?' She cackled with laughter at the thought. 'Don't worry, I know a place, nice and cosy.'

She beckoned to him with one grubby finger and he followed, turning into a narrow cobbled lane, then another and through a doorway into a paved backyard full of crates and junk. This was perfect. They were hidden here and the darkness could flow out of him. No one would see anything. Not until he wanted them to, anyway. Then everyone would see what he had done. *Everyone*. He reached for her, pulling her into the shadows.

''Ere, you're keen incha?' laughed the woman, leaning against the wall in what she imagined was a seductive manner. 'Come on then.'

'I tried to fight it,' he whispered, pinning her against the wall. 'But it was too strong.'

'That's right lover,' she said, doubt creeping into her voice. 'No sense denying yourself, is there?'

She flinched a little as his hands found her throat.

'Ooh, that's how you like it, eh?' She smiled. 'You're a naughty one incha? What should I call you?'

He stopped for a moment. Who *was* he, after all? Did he even have a name? It had been so long since she had called to him, so long since he had felt whole. Now he was simply a part of the dark, at one with the shadows and the fog, his body melting into these streets.

'My name?' he whispered, tilting her neck backwards, exposing her flesh to him. He felt powerful, invincible. The urge was so seductive, so consuming. He bent his head, taking in

3

her smell, her warmth. He brushed his lips against her skin in one final kiss.

'You can call me ... Jack.'

PART ONE

Chapter One

North London, February 13th, Present Day.

It was growing dark as April walked towards the cemetery. It had been one of those bright, crisp winter days and as the sun dipped behind the trees, long shadows fell across Swain's Lane. She pulled her coat tighter around her as she walked towards the gate. It wasn't just the cold; she hated this part, walking past the cemetery office, seeing their thin smiles and the pity in their eyes. Highgate Cemetery was home to 150,000 souls, but most of them were long forgotten, their headstones overgrown and the names choked by moss and weeds. No one came to visit them save the occasional tour party drawn to the Gothic splendour of the tombs.

But April Dunne was different. Her father was William Dunne, the renowned journalist and author of supernatural books, who had become one of the very few people to have been buried in Highgate's West Cemetery in recent years, interred in the family vault perched halfway up the steep hill. And that made April a celebrity here; the one mourner in Highgate visiting a family grave. Of course, April had celebrity of her own. She was the poor girl who had stumbled into a murder right here in the cemetery, only to have to face another tragedy a few weeks later when she saw her father die in front of her, his throat torn out, his blood soaking into the hall carpet. That was enough, enough for any sixteen-year-old to have to bear. But April had almost died too. Just across the road in the East Cemetery, a maniac had tried to rip her arm off, strangled her and left her to die on a broken tombstone. April Dunne was the girl death couldn't seem to leave alone.

Maybe that's what they'll carve on my headstone, April thought as she hurried through the black iron gates and waved at Miss Leicester, the grey-haired guardian of the cemetery office. At least Miss Leicester wouldn't want to chat or offer her sympathy. She never seemed to move from behind her desk in the converted chapel, and she never, ever seemed to smile. And as April had become the cemetery's most frequent visitor – she had been visiting most days since she was discharged from hospital a week ago – no one needed to ask her business. Miss Leicester merely nodded at her and looked meaningfully up at the large clock on the wall. The cemetery closed at five on the dot and woe betide anyone who lingered. April shivered at the notion; she had no desire to be on the receiving end of a telling-off from Miss Leicester and she certainly didn't want to be trapped here after dark.

Passing through a stone archway and walking up the steps, April was struck by how beautiful the place was. No, beautiful wasn't quite the word, not given the haunting, mournful nature of the place. It was *proud*, like a once-elegant face riddled with lines and wrinkles or like an old house full of secrets. But it wasn't creepy – not until after dark, anyway, and even then, April could remember the romantic night she had spent here, walking hand in hand in the moonlight with a mysterious boy she barely knew. She smiled at the memory, but still hurried up the winding path towards the family vault. She hadn't quite been able to get used to the faces of the carved angels watching her as she passed. Alone in Highgate Cemetery as the light dimmed, it was easy to see things out of the corner of your eye – a face or a figure that disappeared as soon as you looked again.

'Stop jumping at shadows,' she whispered to herself. 'Everyone here's dead, remember?'

Yeah, like that makes me feel better, she thought. As she turned left a gap opened up in the trees and April could see far beyond the darkening headstones to the London skyline to the south, the city lights just blinking on. It looked like a mirage, a sketchy outline of something she could spend her life running towards but never reach. Civilisation seemed a long way away.

April pulled her phone from her pocket and checked the screen – a reflex action, a desire to feel in touch with someone. There was a picture on the screen: her best friend Fiona and her newest school friend Caro, the two girls who had kept her sane since she'd moved to Highgate a year ago. They were hugging each other and pulling faces for April's camera. She smiled, then felt a stab of sadness, remembering that the snap had been taken at her dad's funeral. It was nice to know you had friends, and that people cared for you – loved you – but at that precise moment, seeing them made April feel even more alone.

That's the problem with being hunted by blood-sucking killers, she thought with a grim smile. *You never really know who's on your side*.

April reached up and rubbed her neck. It was still tender and bruised where Marcus had tried to strangle her. Marcus Brent, who had seemed just another schoolmate, and who turned out to be a vicious vampire. Who had tried to kill her. Considering the ferocity of his attack, April supposed she had recovered fairly well. Two months of hospital care and intense physiotherapy meant that her arm was fully functional again, with just a long raised scar as a reminder. But nothing would heal the memory of those open jaws lunging at her. There was no medicine for that.

Wrapped up in her thoughts, April almost stumbled into the tomb, a tall stone building jutting from the south side of the path. At first, April had felt weird about her father being buried above ground – it seemed wrong somehow. But since she had started visiting her father's resting place, it actually felt better that he wasn't under six feet of soil. If you were buried, it was all over, right? There was no clawing your way back out. But here, April felt she could swing open the iron door and her dad would be there, exactly as she remembered him: kind, happy, wittering on about how mermaids were real or how the pyramids were actually landing lights for UFOs. She walked over to the steps and crouched down, taking the wilting flowers from the vase and replacing them with the small bunch of yellow daisies she had brought with her.

'Hi, Daddy,' she said quietly, 'how's things?'

She'd been coming to chat to her father every day, telling him the mundane details of her life: who she'd been talking to, what was in the news, all the latest gossip exactly as if they were having a cup of tea in the kitchen.

'Mum's been winding me up again today,' she said. 'We had another fight. I go back to Ravenwood tomorrow and she said I should get my hair done first. I mean, after all that's happened, she thinks how I look at school is important? I know she's only being herself, but sometimes I can't stand her ...'

Sitting on those steps, April could imagine William Dunne sitting behind the door, listening to her, smiling, nodding. She supposed it was her version of therapy. Of course, she should probably have been going to real therapy, the kind where you lie on a leather couch and talk about your pain. God knows she had enough of that to go around. But then the whole point of therapy was that you were honest with the psychiatrist, wasn't it? And April really couldn't do that. She smiled to herself as she imagined the conversation:

'Well, Doctor, it all started when I discovered that Highgate – and my whole school – was infested with vampires. Then I fell in love with a boy called Gabriel and it turns out that he's a vampire too. Yes, vampires are real, they're everywhere! Ha-ha! No, I haven't considered medication.'

Gabriel. She gave a little shiver as she thought of him, his tall outline, strong shoulders and those moody, darkly intense eyes. Your regular common-or-garden vampire heart-throb. It had taken a lot to convince her that Gabriel was really a vampire, an undead blood-drinking killer. She'd buried a knife in his chest and seen the wound heal before her eyes before she accepted it was true. It seemed vampires had always lived among humans, hiding in plain sight, infected with some disease that kept them at the point of death, allowing them to be constantly rejuvenated. That was why they didn't age and why they looked so good. And Gabriel looked good. *God, he looked good.* But her stomach lurched as she realised she was using the past tense to describe him. Because Gabriel was dying – and all because or her. She had infected him with a sort of vampiric anti-virus she carried in her body, and if they didn't find an antidote to it he would die.

'God, what a mess,' April whispered to herself, thinking that that was the understatement of the century. The vampires were recruiting converts through her school, they had killed her father and now the boy she loved was perhaps days away from a horrible painful death – and she had no one to talk to about it. Gabriel was too wrapped up in his own problems – not least his own impending death – and besides, when they were together, meeting secretly after dark at Gabriel's insistence, they didn't waste much time talking. So who did that leave? Her mother seemed more interested in her blow-drys and even her best friends Fee and Caro had been out partying with the vampire girls they called the 'Suckers': could she trust them? So April was here, huddled on the cold stone steps of a tomb, talking to a dead man. And tomorrow was her seventeenth birthday.

'Dammit', she whispered as she realised she was crying. 'Not again,' she said, brushing the tears away. 'Sorry, Daddy. I keep doing this, don't I?'

She knew she didn't need to apologise. William Dunne would have been thrilled to hear that April had found real-life vampires on their doorstep. And of course *he* would have believed her. He would have just given her a big hug and said 'Come on, we'll sort this out.' He was such a great dad. *Had* been a great dad.

Until someone ripped out his throat.

She shook her head angrily. This was happening all too often lately. She tried to get everything straight in her head, then a self-destructive part of her mind would pop up and mock her. But *was* the voice in her head? Or had someone actually said it? She glanced around. No one there. Of course there wasn't. God, she was getting paranoid.

Was it just paranoia? The truth was, the vampires *were* after her – or they would be when they realised who she was – because April Dunne was a Fury. That was the vamps' term for someone who carried the anti-virus in their blood. And if they figured out her secret, they'd stop at nothing to wipe her from the face of the earth. She took a deep breath and picked up one of the yellow daisies, absently pulling off its petals one by one as she spoke.

'I'm dreading going back to Ravenwood, Daddy,' she said, 'Everyone tells me I'll feel better once I get back into a routine, but I'm not sure I want to, you know? So much weird stuff has happened since we moved to Highgate, it seems wrong to sweep it all under the carpet. And until I get to the bottom of what happened with you, I don't feel I can move on, have a future. And with Gabriel ...'

What was that?

April stood up, looking around her.

She was sure she had heard a – *what was that?* – a laugh?

'Who's there?' she said as evenly as she could. Was there someone in the bushes listening to her? Was someone laughing at her? No one else would be in the cemetery at this time would they?

'Is someone there?'

There it was again: a giggle, and not a light-hearted one. There was evil in that laugh. But where was it coming from? The trees? The tomb?

'Hello?' she whispered under her breath – and she heard real laughter this time, echoing around the cemetery. She whirled around, scanning the trees, but in the dimming light every statue and bush looked like a crouching figure ready to leap. Her mind flashed back to that terrible night in the snow when Marcus Brent had tried to break every bone in her body before choking her half to death.

'Who's there?' she shouted.

And then, behind a tomb, she saw a dark figure. It was just standing there, like a statue. *Was* it a statue? Or was it a vampire?

'You're next.'

This time April was sure she had heard it: a real whisper, low and dripping with spite.

Screw this, she thought. She dropped the flower and ran, sprinting down the path as fast as she could go, the graves passing in a blur, the angels and statues seeming to lean in, reaching out to her. Turning a corner, she slipped on some leaves and almost went down, skidding, catching the edge of a tomb and grazing her elbow.

Dammit. Dammit. Run. She didn't dare look behind her, not knowing who or what was following her. Now she could see the top of the steps and she took them three at a time, tearing across the wide courtyard and through the gates onto Swain's Lane without stopping. Just as she thought she was free a dark figure stepped out in front of her, arms spread wide, grabbing her. She wanted to scream but she couldn't, she couldn't even draw breath.

'Hey, hey! Calm down!' said a familiar voice. 'What's going on?'

She looked up – Gabriel! It was *Gabriel*!

'Oh thank God, it's you,' she breathed clinging to him and hugging him tight. 'It's you, it's *you*.'

'It's me,' he said in an amused voice.

April stepped back and slapped him on the arm.

'Hey! What was that for?'

'You scared the life out of me! I thought you were …' she glanced around, 'You know, one of *them*. They were chasing me!'

His eyes narrowed and he looked behind her, back through the iron gates and up the darkening path.

'What happened? Tell me quickly.'

'I thought I heard – saw – something up by my dad's … by the tomb.'

Gabriel's eyes locked with hers, intense.

'What exactly did you see?'

'I saw someone behind one of the graves. Well, I think I did.'

'And they spoke?'

'I think so. They were laughing, whispering,' she said, knowing how lame it sounded. 'It was horrible.'

He paused, looking through the gates again.

'Are you sure it wasn't the gardeners or ...'

'I *heard* someone, Gabriel,' she said.

He looked at her, then looked up towards the dark path again. 'Wait here, I'll take a look.'

'Oh no,' said April, holding on to him. 'You're not leaving me here alone.'

He seemed about to say something, then changed his mind and pulled her into a hug.

'Whatever happens, I won't let anyone hurt you, do you understand?' His eyes met hers. 'Do you understand?'

April knew she was letting down a generation of feminists, but she couldn't help but smile. *He's lovely when he gets all macho.*

'Okay, Ironman,' she said, 'but let's get away from here, just in case, okay?'

'Sure,' he said, putting his arm around her protectively and steering her up Swain's Lane. His tone was reassuring, but she could feel he was alert for danger, peering through the black railings of the East Cemetery looking for the enemy. Looking for his kind.

'Listen, I know you like to visit your dad alone, but next time maybe I should come with you, rather than meet you here afterwards. And maybe we could visit in the daytime,' he said.

'Hey, I thought the time of day didn't matter to you Suckers.'

Gabriel looked annoyed and April inwardly winced. She knew he hated it when she talked about vampires as if they were a species in the zoo.

'Vampires will kill you in the middle of the day if they have to,' he said. 'But they're more likely to wait until darkness falls. It's easier.'

'Wow, you're really putting my mind at rest,' she said, although the truth was, being here with Gabriel, she almost felt silly for imagining things up there in the cemetery.

He reached out and tucked her into another hug. 'Don't worry, I'll look after you.'

'I know you would, but I don't think Miss Leicester would approve of my having a chaperone. She'd think we were up to some sort of shenanigans.'

He tilted her chin upwards and kissed her softly.

'Well maybe she'd be right.'

April giggled and kissed him back, slipping her hands inside Gabriel's coat. The intensity of her kiss was short-lived, however, as she felt his bones through his clothes. He had lost an awful lot of weight and the power and vitality he had exuded only weeks ago was diminishing. If you didn't know he was ill, of course, you wouldn't suspect a thing. His skin was a little less luminous, there were slight dark rings under his eyes, but a stranger would simply think he was tired. April knew better.

God, please don't die, she thought, looking into his eyes as they broke apart. *Not yet*.

April had promised she wouldn't hassle him about his condition, but she found it hard, especially knowing she was responsible.

'How are you feeling, old man?' she asked, trying to make a joke of it.

He smiled. 'I'm fine, April. I feel good. I know you're worried I'm going to keel over, but I'm all right. I have aches and pains, but that's just being human again.'

'Are you sure? I can't stop thinking about Milo.'

Milo was a boy she had kissed at a party before April had known she had the Fury virus inside her.

'I only kissed him once and I didn't know he was a …' she lowered her voice '… a vampire. This Fury virus or whatever the hell it is I've got inside me had killed him in a matter of weeks, Gabe. I can't stand to think the same thing is going to happen to you.'

'Well maybe I'm stronger than Milo,' said Gabriel. 'Or maybe I have some resistance to the virus. I think – I hope

– I've been kissing you more than Milo, so I'm guessing I've been more exposed to the virus.'

April frowned.

'Hey, don't laugh about it,' she said. 'This is serious.'

He stopped and stroked her hair back.

'I know it's serious, April. I'm the one living with this, remember? I'm just saying that these things aren't predictable. Some people can survive lung cancer for years while others succumb within days.'

'I'm not sure you're reassuring me,' said April.

'Well how about I prove it?' He linked hands with April, and whirled her around in a mad parody of the waltz. 'Could a dying man dance like this?'

'Hey, stop! I feel sick!' She laughed, throwing her arms around his neck. They kissed, her lips against his, savouring the taste, the touch, her lips tingling. *I'm going to miss this*, she thought, *I'm going to miss you.* It was a cruel irony that the kiss which brought them together was the same kiss which would take him away – unless she could find a cure. And there was one: a potion called the Dragon's Breath, whose recipe was hidden away in a book called the *Albus Libre*. It was supposed to reverse the effects of the Fury virus in a vampire … and it could make Gabriel a fully-fledged Sucker again. Not an ideal solution, but at least he would be alive. The problem was that the *Albus Libre* – never mind the Dragon's Breath – was a legend: she'd spent days scouring the internet and there wasn't one mention of it anywhere. It didn't seem to exist. And there was something else: wherever it was, she wasn't entirely sure Gabriel wanted her to find it. She had tried to get him involved, tried to discuss her search for the book with him, but he had repeatedly changed the subject or had pulled her in for another kiss, which had made her forget all about it. Maybe it was more of that paranoia, but something was setting off alarm bells for April; it was as if he didn't *want* to find the book.

'Gabriel, can I ask you a question?'

'You can ask, but I'm not sure I'll be able to answer.'

'Do you know anything about the *Albus Libre*?'

'Like what's in it?'

'No … more like where it is?'

He shook his head slowly. 'Don't you think I'd have said something if I did?'

'I'll be honest,' she said softly, squeezing his hand. 'I'm not sure you would.'

There had been something about Gabriel since their kiss on the snowy lawns at the Winter Ball all those weeks ago, something that had changed which she just didn't understand. He seemed to be enjoying the prospect of death.

'Don't you want to get well?'

'Of course I do.' But he looked away as he said it.

'Gabriel …'

He touched his hand gently to her face.

'I know you're trying to help, but think what this is like for me. Whatever I do, I lose you. I can't be with you if I die and I can't be with you if I go back to being a vampire. And faced with that, just being dead almost seems preferable.'

'Gabriel, no!' she gasped. 'You can't say that!'

His face hardened.

'April, I know this is hard for you to understand, impossible in fact. But think about what you're asking me to do; you're asking me to become a monster. I know I'm dying and now I've found you it hurts to think of losing you, but you have to understand what it's like to be … in the grip of the dark. It's so hard to control.'

There was something in his eyes April didn't think she'd seen before. Fear. He wasn't afraid of death or pain or never-ending maths lessons, but he was scared of becoming a vampire again.

'I'm sorry. I didn't know.'

'It's like being trapped in a black tunnel,' he said quietly. 'All you think about is feeding, everyone around you is a potential victim; every day offers temptation after temptation. You can smell it, see it – I look at someone on the tube, I can almost

17

taste the blood rushing through them. All I have to do is reach out and sometimes ...'

He trailed off. 'It's hell, April. Truly. Every day was hell until your kiss set me free, and now you're asking me to go back to it.'

She pulled him closer.

'But it's the only way we can be together. And remember it's not for ever, you just have to stay alive long enough to find the vampire who turned you into that "monster". Then we can kiss for as long as we like.'

He smiled sadly.

'I know.'

They walked across Pond Square toward April's house, their steps slowing as they got closer.

'I'll see you tomorrow?' she said, wondering if he knew it was her birthday. Probably not, why would he? April hadn't mentioned it to anyone, and it seemed a bit trivial after all that had happened. *It's enough that I can be with you*, she thought, turning her face up for a kiss. He smiled but put a finger to her lips, nodding towards the police car parked just down from April's front door.

'Not with all eyes on us.'

The police had been there since the attack. Partly for re-assurance and protection, and partly to discourage the press from knocking on the door.

'I don't think the police will care,' she said, winding her arms around his neck.

'Well what about your mum?' He smiled.

'Oh she'd want us to kiss. She's very modern that way.'

He looked around the square, then pulled her behind a tree. 'It's not that,' he said seriously. 'We've got to be careful. We can't act too much as if we're going out. I think we need to cool it a bit.'

April felt her stomach turn over.

'Cool it? Why?' she said. Was he dumping her?

'Because I want to protect you. We don't know how this

virus is going to affect me. If people see us as an item, going around kissing, and then I suddenly get ill ...'

'But everyone saw you kissing me at the Winter Ball,' she protested.

'Yes, but just once – and they also saw you pushing me away. We need to keep that distance between us, make the vamps think I'm the last person you'd want to kiss. That's why I've been careful to only meet when there's no one else around.'

'But Gabe ...' she said, her heart hammering.

'No, April,' he said, 'it's the only way. Vampires are careful, paranoid creatures, they have to be. Some of them must suspect there's a Fury out there. Milo's death was a big clue – and if they've made that connection, they'll guess that the Fury is someone at the school. If I do suddenly get sick and we're together, you'll be Public Enemy Number One.'

April wished she could protest, but she knew he was right. She touched the scar on her neck again; she had barely survived the attack of one monster, if they all turned on her, she wouldn't stand a chance. And it was only for a while, wasn't it? Until they could find a way out of this mess.

Seeing her dismay, he cupped her chin and turned her face up to his. 'Are you scared they'll find you?'

'Not as scared as I am of losing you.'

He smiled.

'You won't lose me. We just have to pretend for a while.'

'So what's the point? Why are we together if we can't *be* together?'

'Why?' he said, backing her up against the tree and kissing her, his body pressed against hers. '*That's* why. I'm only saying in public, April. Otherwise we can be together whenever, and wherever we can. I'm very good at sneaking about in the dark.'

'I don't think my mum's liberal attitude will stretch that far.'

He kissed her again, his lips soft, his arms strong. She wished they could stay that way for ever, his heat against her, addicted to each other, yearning for more. There had to be a way. She had to find it.

*

April's mother was sitting in the kitchen, her head in her hands, her blonde hair sticking up in tufts between her fingers.

'Is is really necessary to slam the door so loudly?' she said without looking up.

'Good to see you too, Mum,' said April. She opened the fridge, took out some juice and closed the door with a thump.

'April!'

'Sorry,' said April. 'Just getting a drink. Looks like you've been helping yourself too.'

There was a glass of dark red liquid in front of her mother. A Bloody Mary, April guessed, with more vodka than tomato in it if she knew Silvia. In her head, April always used her mother's first name. That way it felt as if she was just some friend of the family. April couldn't stand the idea of being tied to her for ever.

'Sarcasm is the lowest form of wit, darling,' said Silvia, squinting up at April. 'Anyway, why are you in such a chirpy mood? I thought you were all depressed about going back to school. That "Mum, I can't get my hair done", "Mum, you don't understand my pain" routine.'

'Obviously you don't understand my pain, Mother,' said April, sipping her juice. 'Or you wouldn't be making fun of it. Life has moved on from when you were my age, we have telephones and cars now.'

'I'm not that old, darling. I had my moments.'

'So Gramps is always telling me.'

Silvia rolled her eyes. 'Pass me the paracetamol from the cupboard? I think I'm coming down with something.'

'White wine, I should think.'

April passed the tub across and watched as Silvia shook some pills out.

'So what are we going to do for the big day tomorrow?' her mother asked.

'Nothing. I just want to forget all about it. If Dad can't be here, then … well, you know.'

Silvia reached out to her and squeezed her hand.

'I know, but I think we should be celebrating life while we're here, don't you?'

April shook her head.

'Seriously, Mum, I don't want to make a fuss. Please?'

Silvia held up a hand. 'Okay, okay, it's your choice.' She gave April a sideways glance. 'So where have you been this afternoon?'

'I could ask you the same thing.'

April wasn't sure where her mother was going at night, but she was coming home drunk and spending the whole morning in bed. There had been a couple of nights when she hadn't come home at all. It sickened her to think it, given that her father had only been dead a matter of weeks, but April half-suspected that Silvia was dating already. The very idea made her feel sick.

'Me?' said Silvia. 'I've been seeing friends if you must know. Do I have to clear it with you first? Anyway, don't avoid the question. Where were you?'

'Seeing Dad.'

Silvia paused. April knew she didn't like her going to the cemetery, not after the business with Marcus Brent, but she couldn't very well ban her from visiting her father's tomb.

'Don't worry. I was careful,' she sighed. 'Miss Leicester wouldn't let anyone bad into her domain.'

'This is serious, April. Don't make light of it.'

'I'm not making light of it! I was there with Gabriel if you must know.'

Not quite the truth, but not quite a lie either. He *had* been there at the end.

'So how come you never bring this mysterious Gabriel home? I'm a modern mother, I understand a young girl's needs – you do remember that talk we had about the birds and the bees … ? I can always make myself scarce.'

'Mum!' said April. 'I don't think we should be talking about this.'

'Why not? I'm a woman of the world, I know a thing or two about—'

'Enough, Mum! And you wonder why I never bring him home.'

'I'm only looking out for you, darling. Men can be such shits sometimes.'

'Well, not this one. He saved my life, remember?'

'Yes, well I'd at least like to thank him for that, but he disappeared the moment you were taken to hospital.'

April closed her eyes at the memory. Gabriel had saved her with the kiss of life, and willingly signed his own death sentence when he did. She was still struggling to come to terms with the cruel irony of that one gesture of love.

'What's the matter?'

April looked up to find her mother staring at her.

'What do you mean? Nothing's wrong,' stuttered April, avoiding her mother's gaze. 'A minute ago you were complaining that I was too happy.'

'I know you, April,' said Silvia. 'You get that look when something's troubling you. Has something happened? Is it this boy?'

'No, Mother. He's fine,' said April, irritated. It was disconcerting how her mother could switch between vacuousness and mad protectiveness in a heartbeat – and it was spooky how well she could read April's moods.

'Since when have you been such an expert on my inner thoughts?' asked April. 'Have you been reading my diary again?'

'Oh please, I don't need to. Whenever something serious happens, you start looking like Ophelia after she drowned. You had it back in Edinburgh whenever that spotty boy Neil Stevenson was mentioned.'

April almost gasped. Neil had been her first major crush; she hadn't told anyone except her best friend Fiona. It was mortifying to discover her mother had known all along.

'You knew about that?'

Silvia laughed. 'I should think everyone knew about it, including poor Neil. You used to moon about around him as if you were composing sonnets in your head. I always knew you could do better though. I was so pleased to find your Gabriel is good-looking.'

'God, Mum, you're so shallow!'

'Oh, and those posters on your walls are all of ugly boys? An active inner life is all very well, but a girl still needs to get butterflies in her tummy when he walks in the room. I know I do.'

'Is that why you've been going out every evening? Trying to find a new man?'

April knew she was overstepping the mark, but she was furious at the idea of her mother thinking about other men – perhaps even seeking them out – when her dad was barely cold in the ground.

'April,' warned Silvia. 'What I do is none of your business.'

'Isn't it? Well how do you think it makes me feel? How would Dad feel if he knew you were out drinking and God knows what only weeks after he was murdered?'

'It's hard for me too, April. There are things you don't know about your father and I, things in our relationship that we were trying to work out.'

'Things he had to put up with, more like.'

Silvia pursed her lips, trying to keep her temper in check.

'I know you've always put your dad on a pedestal, but he had his faults too.'

'Like what?'

'Oh, I don't know – like his crazy plan to move down here? If we'd stayed in Scotland, we'd have been fine. He'd be alive!'

'I didn't think we had much choice,' said April, looking away. She had found a letter to her father offering him a job in Glasgow, so she could only assume he had chosen to come down to Highgate to investigate the vampires. But it wasn't a detail she could very well discuss with her mother.

Silvia took a sip of her Bloody Mary.

'Like I say, you don't know everything.'

'What the hell is that supposed to mean?' said April, frowning.

'There are some things you don't need to know, April,'

said Silvia. 'We were married for twenty years and adults have some things they don't necessarily want to discuss with their children.'

April looked at her mother. Did Silvia know about the job offer? Did she know about the Ravenwood investigation? No, she *couldn't* have, there was no way she would have stood for it.

'But I ought to know, if it's why we came to London. I'm not a child. I can understand these things.'

Silvia gave a hollow laugh.

'Don't be so sure.'

'Don't patronise me!'

'If you want to be treated like an adult, you'd better start behaving like one.'

'Like you, you mean? Drinking vodka and picking men up in bars?'

'How dare you!' yelled Silvia, slamming her glass down on the counter. 'Get up to your room!'

April pushed her chair back.

'Don't worry, I don't want to stay here,' she said, storming out of the kitchen and up the stairs, slamming her bedroom door. Safely inside, she threw herself across the bed and grabbed her phone. *God, she was insufferable!* How could they have the same DNA? She must have got all hers from her dad. Stabbing at the keys, April called Fiona.

'Come on, Fee,' she whispered. Her friend always knew what to do, partly because she was sensible and level-headed and partly because Fiona's parents had been through a particularly nasty divorce a few years ago. April groaned when Fee's mobile went to answerphone.

'It's Fee, you know what to do ...'

April threw the phone down, smashing it against the bed-side table. *Oh bugger*, she thought, scrabbling to pick it up. She felt a wave of relief when it still worked. *God, I'm getting so angry these days*, she thought. Is it the Fury thing? She'd been told that being a Fury equipped her to combat vampires: not only was her blood like poison to them, she would also be able to face them in a fight.

Yes, but which vampires, exactly? Gabriel had told her that vampires who were born as vampires were far more powerful than vampires who were 'turned' by having their blood infected by a vampire bite. What if she came up against one of those super-vamps? April certainly didn't feel much like an action hero – she cried at romantic comedies and dreaded the dentist. But she had certainly been feeling angrier and angrier since she and Gabriel had found the Fury birthmark behind her ear.

She went across to her mirror and pulled back her hair, looking for the mark. For a moment, April dared to hope it wasn't there, but then she saw it and her stomach sank. A sort of blobby star shape. She'd scoured the internet for some mention of it – Fury, vampire virus, anything – but there was nothing apart from various theories about why there was a star on the flag of the Ottoman Empire. She wished she'd paid more attention in history, then she might have an idea what it all meant.

What it means is you're a freak, thought April. *And you've just called your mother a slut.*

'God, I did, didn't I?' April whispered to herself. She felt her cheeks burn with shame and embarrassment. *I really should go and apologise*, she thought, wondering how she could ever have said such a thing. She looked at herself in the mirror, seeing the hollow eyes, the tired rings beneath them – and, God, were those frown lines on her forehead? *Who are you?* she wondered as she peered closer. April knew she had changed – who wouldn't after everything she'd been through in the past few months? – but she wasn't entirely sure she liked her reflection. *I've got old, that's what's happened*, she thought.

She walked over to the window, looking out at the dark square. Drizzle was falling, throwing a haze over the yellow street lights. She reached up to rub the scar on her arm. April remembered the first time she had looked out onto the square the day they had moved in. It seemed so long ago. Her heart turned over as she thought of her dad that night, lighting a fire in the living room and trying to make this stuffy old house cosy and welcoming. *I miss you, Dad,* she thought. *I'd never have been so angry at Mum if you were still here.*

April's eye was caught as she saw movement in the square. *Gabriel?* No, it couldn't be him. But there was definitely someone standing in the shadows, looking up at the house.

'Who is that?' she whispered, drawing back into the shadows herself.

Were they really being watched? She looked for the police car, but couldn't see it from her window. Where *were* they? She looked back at the figure and immediately jumped back, her hand flying to her mouth. He was closer – and he was staring directly up at her.

Was it a Sucker? The police? The man was standing in the shadow of a tree, so she couldn't see his face, but she knew – she was absolutely sure – that he was staring at her.

She jumped as she heard her mother slam a door downstairs, only glancing away for a second – and suddenly the square was empty. April leaned into the window, looking left and right, but the figure had gone. Vanished. That certainly didn't make her feel any better. Who the hell was that? Was it the thing she'd heard whispering in the cemetery? She sat down on her bed, far too jumpy to relax. A blazing row and a creepy stalker would do that for you. She wondered for a moment if she should tell her mother about the figure in the square, but dismissed the idea. What had she seen, exactly? And anyway, it didn't sound as if Silvia was in the mood to talk.

Instead, April grabbed her phone and tried calling Gabriel's number, but all she got was a 'This phone is currently unavailable' message. Typical. Why was there never anyone around when you needed them? Sighing, she stood up and walked over to the wardrobe. Back to Ravenwood tomorrow. She really should pick out some clothes for the morning. What *was* appropriate dress when you were returning to school after you'd been half-killed by a maniac? She pulled out a few things and threw them on the bed, but nothing seemed right. She looked towards her bedroom door; this was the sort of thing her mother was great at. Maybe now would be a good time to go and beg forgiveness for being a cow. Taking a deep breath, April walked down the stairs, mentally rehearsing her excuses: 'Under a lot of pressure', 'Worried about school', 'Missing Dad' – all true, of course, but none of them really made up for calling her mum a slut. At the bottom of the stairs, she stopped as she heard Siliva's voice. She was talking on the phone.

Curious, April held her breath, listening.

'So when, then?' said Silvia, her voice low. 'You're not being fair.' Silvia sounded upset, as if she had been crying. *God, was that because of me?*

'I know, I know,' continued Silvia. 'But I can't keep on like this.'

Keep on like what, exactly? thought April, intrigued now. Who was Silvia talking to?

'I want to see you. I *need* to see you.'

April could feel her heart jump. Was she talking to some man? One of those guys she'd been picking up on her drunken nights out. Suddenly all thoughts of apologising evaporated.

'Same place? You'd better be there.'

April heard Silvia bang the receiver back into the cradle and she carefully tip-toed back into her room, closing the door behind her.

Who had she been talking to? Who did her mother *need* to see? Was it something to do with their fight? Something to do with Dad? Or was she really having an affair? She *couldn't* be, could she? Another loud slam: the front door. April jumped up and ran to the window, just in time to see Silvia's figure crossing the square. Where was she going? And what was so important that she would leave her vulnerable daughter all alone in this dark creepy house? God, why couldn't she have a normal mother? April turned back to the room, saw the clothes lying on the bed and began to laugh. Tomorrow she would be going back to Ravenwood, a school riddled with vampires, every single one of whom would tear her throat out if they knew her secret. Her boyfriend was dying and had told her they had to pretend they hated each other and on top of all that, she had to find out who had killed her father – and why. Oh, and she had no idea who she could trust.

'Bugger the wardrobe,' she said, scooping up the clothes and chucking them onto a chair. She'd work it out in the morning.

Tonight, she had bigger problems to worry about.

Chapter Two

As she walked down the path and across the road, the wind clanging the garden gate shut behind her, April idly wondered how far off spring was. Jesus, it was cold. Some start to her seventeenth year. She hoisted a beautiful leather satchel over her shoulder – a surprise birthday present from her mother, it had been waiting for her outside her bedroom door when she woke up – and pushed her hands deep into her pockets. She glanced around the square, but there was no sign of the dark figure from the night before. Try as she might, April had not been able to sleep last night, getting up to peek out the window every now and then, but the square had been empty. April had almost managed to convince herself it was just some random dog-walker, but it never hurt to be careful, did it? 'They'll attack you in the daytime,' wasn't that what Gabriel had said? A cheery thought to match the gloomy mood of the day. She looked up at the grey clouds and tried to remember when she had last seen the sun. She should be used to it, of course; she'd lived in Edinburgh long enough, but somehow she'd never learned to love the cold. Wasn't it supposed to be warmer down south? For a moment, she pictured herself in a floaty summer dress, running through a meadow hand in hand with Gabriel, laughing together. Wouldn't it be wonderful to be so free, without worries and pressures and prophecies. *Do most girls have to worry about prophecies on their birthday?*

Her stomach rumbled. April had deliberately skipped breakfast that morning to avoid her mother, not that she had expected her to be up so early. She would be lying in bed until noon, an empty wine glass standing by the bed, smeared with lipstick. She didn't know why Silvia was lying to her – or, what was that phrase? 'Being economical with the truth' – but she knew that she didn't want to get into a screaming match before her first day back at school. So April had gone straight downstairs and out the front door, not looking back. As she passed the church and walked down the hill, April noticed a car parked in the road and her heart sank. Standing there, leaning against the door, was Detective Inspector Ian Reece.

Oh no, what does he want now?

DI Reece was nice enough for a policeman, but the last thing she wanted on her first morning back at school was to be asked a load of difficult questions.

'Hello, April, I believe congratulations are in order,' he said as she approached.

'Thanks,' she said. 'Doesn't feel as though there's much worth celebrating today.'

'No. Can't be much fun going back to school on your birthday.'

She shrugged.

'It's not going to be much fun going back full stop.'

Reece smiled sympathetically.

'You think everyone's going to be looking at you?'

'Think it? I know it. It's not every day the school has a pupil savaged by a fellow student. They'll be gathering around wanting to see the scar.'

Reece snorted.

'Well, I won't keep you long. Just wanted to give you an update on the case.'

'Which case? Mine or my dad's?'

He pulled a face.

'Nothing on your dad's murder at the moment.'

Meaning: the trail is as cold as a polar bear's bum, thought April.

'It's regarding Marcus Brent. It doesn't look like he's left the country after all,' said Reece. 'We've been through all the passport records and checked hours of CCTV footage at airports and ferry terminals.'

'So you're saying he's still nearby?' said April, thinking of the laughter in the cemetery and the figure outside her window last night. 'Is that supposed to make me feel better?'

'I think it's best you have all the information, April. You're safer that way.'

'Well I don't feel very safe,' said April, winding her satchel strap around her fingers. 'I've been seeing things.'

'Things? What sort of things?'

April shrugged. What could she say, really? Vampires, murderers, maniacs?

'I don't know, just things,' she sighed. 'I thought I saw someone in the square last night. I mean, it might have been someone out for a walk or something, but ...'

DI Reece nodded.

'Listen, that's understandable after what you've been through, but honestly, there's no need to worry. We're watching the house and there's no way Marcus is going to come back.'

'Don't be so sure, Inspector Reece,' said April. 'I looked into his eyes. He was insane. I really don't think a police car parked outside my house would be much of a deterrent. Anyway, it's not just Marcus I'm worried about. There's been a lot of weird things happening in Highgate since I got here.'

'You said it.'

'What's that supposed to mean?' April frowned. 'That this is my fault?'

'Not at all, April, don't be so jumpy. I'm just agreeing with you. There have been some strange goings on and you're right to be worried – no one knows that better than you. But you simply need to be careful. Don't wander off on your own, tell people where you're going, come straight home after school. All the usual stuff: look both ways before you cross the road.'

'Now you're starting to sound like my mum.'

'I hope not,' he smiled, then gestured towards the car. 'Do you want a lift?'

'No, I don't think turning up in a police car is a good idea this morning. Thank you. Besides, I'm not in any hurry. All that stuff people tell you about your school days being the happiest of your life? I hope they're lying.'

She left DI Reece and walked on down the hill, feeling the butterflies in her stomach as she got closer to Ravenwood. It was a different kind of apprehension to last term's, when all April had to worry about was being the new girl and fitting in with the brain-boxes and rich kids pulling up in their posh cars. She almost laughed. It was hard to remember a time when she had such ordinary problems: what to wear, who to speak to, would there be any cute boys there? Now she had real problems, problems which could end up with someone dead – and not just Gabriel.

April slowed as she saw the school gates. Who deliberately walks into a building they know is full of mythical killers? No one sane. But April had to. DI Reece might not have any leads, but she did. Her father had been investigating the school before he was killed. Either he had got too close to whoever was behind Ravenwood, or he had been murdered by a vampire. Either way, April knew the truth about his death was wrapped up in whatever was going on at Ravenwood. And it wasn't just for her dad; she had to find the Vampire Regent, the vamp king-pin behind the Ravenwood plot, because the blood-sucking Regent had turned Gabriel into a vampire all those years ago. Legend had it that if Gabriel killed the vampire who made him, he would return to being human. And they could finally, properly, be together. Of course, it was only a legend. Pulling her satchel higher up on her shoulder, she walked up the steps and into Ravenwood. Right now, legends were all she had.

'April, could I have a word?'

April groaned inwardly. She had been the first out of her seat at the end of her philosophy lesson, hoping to make it to the door without having to speak to Mr Sheldon.

'Don't worry, it's not a lecture,' said the teacher, beckoning to her. 'I just wanted to have a quiet chat when everyone's gone.'

She watched as he ushered the rest of the students out of the room and closed the door.

'So how are you feeling?' he asked, gesturing that she should sit. 'First day back, it must be a little strange.'

April knew what he was getting at. Mr Sheldon wasn't just April's philosophy teacher, he was Ravenwood's headmaster. And no headmaster wanted his school to attract the sort of headlines April made. *Highgate schoolgirl attacked in cemetery. Maniac tries to eat student.* The press had lapped it up of course, especially with her dad's death. They had camped outside the house, desperate to make some connection between the two attacks. Had Marcus killed her father too? Had they been victims of the same serial killer? And then there was the juicy addition of it all happening in Nicholas Osbourne's grounds, one of the most prominent and controversial businessmen in the country.

'I'm okay,' said April, 'I'm feeling much better, anyway.'

'That's good. Your wounds all healed and so forth?'

He looked at her with those strangely piercing eyes which had earned him the nickname 'Hawk'.

'Yes, well, I still have pain in my arm,' she said, 'and I have to go for physio for my neck, but …'

'Good, splendid. I want you to know everyone here feels terrible that you were attacked by Marcus Brent, even if it wasn't on school property. He was a Ravenwood student after all, and we feel a certain responsibility.' He paused to cough.

'And I feel some responsibility personally. You will remember I was there when the boy attacked you in the lavatories …?'

How could April forget? Hawk had walked in just as April had been cornered by Marcus. If he hadn't …

'I disciplined the boy of course, but I can't help feeling that I should have taken greater steps to ensure your safety.'

Just then a light went on above April's head: Mr Sheldon was worried she might sue the school – or even worse, him personally – for negligence. He had clearly known Marcus was unhinged and a lawyer could have argued that the school should have protected her. She almost laughed out loud. Here she was, planning to expose Ravenwood as a nest of vampires, and all the headmaster was worried about was a lawsuit.

'Well, I hope we both understand each other?' said Mr Sheldon.

Oh yes, I understand you perfectly, thought April.

'You do know that my door is always open, don't you, April?'

April nodded, although she was thinking: *There's no way I'm going into your lair.* She had no idea if Mr Sheldon was a vampire, but these days she found herself assuming the worst. In actual fact, April had spent most of the lesson looking at her fellow students, wondering which of them were Suckers and which of them were being recruited. Gabriel had told her to look out for sleek hair and flawless skin, but that covered almost everyone at Ravenwood. And you could hardly go around staking people because they'd had a shower that morning.

She looked up at Mr Sheldon's white hair. It would certainly make sense for the man in charge of a school recruiting vampires to be a vampire. But she and Caro had thought that about Nicholas Osbourne and they had been wrong. And anyway, would a high-ranking vampire really be worried about bad PR?

'We're always here, whatever you need,' said Mr Sheldon.

Yeah, right, thought April. *As long as what I need serves the vampire cause.*

'Of course,' said April, gathering up her bag and heading for the door. 'And thank you.'

'Cheeky buggers,' said Caro as they sat at their usual table in the refectory at break. 'I can't believe they were trying to manipulate a poor injured teenager into dropping a civil suit against the school. It's immoral!'

'I think manipulation is what they do here,' said April, lowering her voice. 'And assuming we're right about Ravenwood being full of Suckers, immoral is sort of the point, isn't it?'

'*Assuming* we're right?' hissed Caro, 'A bloody great vampire tried to rip your arm off and beat you to death with it! Isn't that proof enough?'

April had to smile. Caro was the odd one out at Ravenwood, a rare individual at a school where you were either a straight-A geek or a super-rich Barbie doll. Caro was clever, but she dyed her hair, painted her nails and wore too much eye make-up.

'Sorry,' said April, 'I'm just a bit out of it. I've got so much on my mind: my father, Gabriel and this whole Fury thing, the school ... I don't know which way's up any more.'

Caro's expression softened and she touched April's hand.

'I'm sorry. I know it's hard. You've just got to focus on one thing at a time.'

April sighed.

'Okay, so which "thing" do we start with?'

'I think we use the opportunity we have: everyone will want to talk to you about your ordeal; I think it's a perfect opportunity to get in with the Faces.'

The Faces were the super-groomed, over-styled girls who ruled Ravenwood with their icy stares and withering put-downs. Davina Osbourne was their leader and April was pretty sure they were at the centre of Ravenwood's vampire recruitment, thus April needed to get their confidence if she was ever going to find out what was going on.

'So what do you think I should do? Show them my scars and hope they look hungry?'

Caro laughed. 'No, but they're going to want to be best mates with you now you're a school celebrity, so I say make the most of it. And I've got a plan to help you get in with Davina.'

'What plan?' said April suspiciously.

Caro tapped the side of her nose. 'Ask me no questions ... Anyway, speak of the devil,' she said, nodding towards a girl approaching them. She was beautiful with high cheekbones and long glossy blonde hair complemented by a purple Chanel shift dress and patent pumps way higher than the school dress code allowed. Davina Osbourne, Queen of the Ravenwood Faces – and more than likely, head of the vampire nest.

'Darling, how are you?' said Davina, dipping in to air-kiss April. 'I've been sick with worry.'

'I'm okay,' said April. She knew everyone in the refectory was watching them and could feel her cheeks flush. Davina stepped back and gazed sincerely into April's eyes.

'Are you sure you're fit enough to come back so soon? I mean, given what Marcus Brent did to you. Personally, I'd have taken the whole term off.'

'Thanks, but I'm fine. I've been out of hospital for a week now and there's no reason to stay off school. Anyway, it's not much fun staying at home with my mum.'

'God, I know what you mean. I'd rather jump off a bridge than be cooped up with my family. Christmas was bad enough.'

Davina looked at April again, her hand over her mouth.

'I've put my foot in it again, haven't I? It can't have been very festive for you this year, can it?'

'Funnily enough, it wasn't too bad.'

In fact, April had found Christmas easier to cope with than she had expected. The hospital had let her go home for the night and for once her mother and grandfather had put some effort in, decorating the house with a tree and presents. It looked like a picture-perfect Hollywood set of a family Christmas. April had made it as far as the Christmas meal – called in from a caterers, naturally. Silvia was never the most domestic of women – before she finally broke down and cried. The sight of the turkey had set her off: it had always been her dad's job to carve.

At that point her grandfather had laid down his knife and fork. 'Come on,' he'd said and, wrapped up in scarves and hats, they had walked down to the cemetery and laid a bough of holly on the steps of the tomb. Sadly, as most Christmas Days she could remember had descended into screaming rows, it had turned out to be one of April's favourite Christmases.

'Well, it's a new year now,' said Davina. 'We must be positive and put all that behind us.'

'Hark at Gandhi,' muttered Caro, before April elbowed her in the ribs to silence her.

'Anyway, it's Valentine's Day!' she said, clapping her hands with excitement. 'You should see all the cards Chessy got.

36

Come on over,' said Davina, beckoning April across to the other side of the refectory where the Faces and the rugby boys were lounging. 'Besides, there's someone who wants to see you.'

April glanced at Caro who pulled a face. 'Don't mind me,' she said, holding up a trashy gossip magazine, 'I've got some homework to be getting on with.'

April followed Davina to the far side of the hall and her heart jumped as she spotted Gabriel sitting on the edge of a table, his dark hair flopping over his face. *God, he's beautiful*, thought April, before reminding herself that she was supposed to hate him. *It's only pretend, remember?*

April made a point of turning away from him, her chin raised, a gesture Davina picked up on.

'Not speaking to Boy Wonder?' She smiled. 'I thought you might be all hot and heavy after his big hero act.'

April pulled a face. 'I'm grateful to him for helping and everything, but that doesn't change the fact he's a self-obsessed idiot.'

Davina nodded, clearly loving the drama.

'Couldn't agree more,' she whispered. 'You can do much better. And on that subject, I said someone wanted to see you.'

'Who?'

'Hi, April,' said Benjamin, stepping forward and pushing his hair out of his eyes. If Gabriel was beautiful, Benjamin Osbourne wasn't far behind. His shaggy blond hair and blue eyes looked like they came straight off a catwalk. 'You're looking great.'

'Oh, thanks,' said April, slightly embarrassed. It felt weird being complimented by another boy within earshot of Gabriel, but she knew she had to keep up the pretence.

'You're, erm, not too bad yourself,' she said, wincing at how lame she sounded, but Benjamin didn't seem to notice. He took her by the elbow and led her to one side.

'Listen, April, I just wanted to say how sorry I was about Marcus,' he said.

'What? Don't be silly, it wasn't your fault.'

'Well, I feel bad about it. I should have seen the signs.

He always had something against you for some reason, but I thought he was just jealous.'

'Jealous?' she asked. 'Jealous of what?'

Benjamin smiled, but not his usual confident smile. This was timid, he was unsure of himself. 'You must know,' he said quietly.

April was amazed. She had guessed that Benjamin liked her a bit, but she assumed he was just flirting with her because that's what he did with all the girls. Maybe he really *liked* her. Then again, maybe it was this damn Fury thing. April had good reason to suspect Benjamin Osbourne was a vampire – why wouldn't he be? He was gorgeous and his sister was pure evil – and the Fury was designed to attract vampires to her, like some twisted Venus fly-trap.

Ben looked as if he was about to speak, then glanced away.

'Sorry. I shouldn't have said anything. You and Gabe have a thing going on.'

'Had. Past tense,' said April, resisting the urge to look back at Gabriel. 'I mean I'm grateful for what he did, but we're not married or anything.'

Play the game, she said to herself. *You've got to distance yourself from Gabriel.* She turned to Ben and touched his hand.

'Thanks for checking on me though, that was sweet,' she said, 'I know this must have been hard for you too, Ben. Marcus was your friend, wasn't he?'

Ben shrugged.

'Only because I clearly misjudged him.'

'He hasn't been in touch?'

'I don't think I'd be the first person he'd call, not when he went crazy at my Christmas party and almost killed someone I ... someone ... well, he knew I thought highly of you.'

April raised her eyebrows.

'I didn't think boys talked about girls like that. I thought you spent all your time talking about football and cars.'

Ben smiled.

'We make an exception every now and then.'

She touched his arm again and flashed him a small smile, wondering if Gabriel would see.

'Thank you for your concern, Ben. It's sweet.'

She walked back to her table, head held high, deliberately ignoring Gabriel as she passed him.

'You'll never believe what just happened,' she whispered to Caro. 'Benjamin Osbourne just …' but April could see her friend wasn't listening. She was staring at the other side of the room, her face like thunder.

'What's the matter?'

'Look at the new king and queen of the Faces.'

Across the room a dark, handsome boy and a Chinese girl with long hair were holding court, surrounded by amused onlookers. The girl was Ling Po, who had been the archetypal nerd just a few months ago, with thick glasses and clumpy shoes. Then she'd been adopted by Davina and her friends, and now she was one of them: shiny hair, perfect make-up and designer clothes. She was talking to Simon, one of Caro's oldest friends. All through school, Simon had been a rebel and an outsider just like Caro, but in the past few weeks he had started hanging out with the Faces and rugby boys and now he dressed and spoke just like them.

'Look at Little Miss Hilarious. You wouldn't know she had been the geekiest girl in school before she got all vamped up.'

'Shhh!' said April. She pulled Caro up and dragged her outside, banging through a fire door and out into the playground where they wouldn't be overheard.

'Caro, you've got to be more careful! You can't go around saying things like that.'

'Well,' said Caro sulkily, 'it annoys me, her swanking around showing off like she's some sort of diva.'

'Look, I know Simon was your friend, but you have to remember the vamps have seduced both of them. Don't underestimate the Suckers' power.'

'What power?' snapped Caro. 'I mean, it's not like those old Dracula movies where the evil vampire hypnotises the virgin and bites her against her will, is it? We're always talking about how the Suckers have this terrible supernatural power, but it's not supernatural at all, is it? They're just giving them makeovers. Come and join our gang, be as cool as us. Dress like us and talk like us and you too can have what we have. It's pathetic.'

'But you can't blame them for that, they just want to fit in.'

'Who cares about fitting in?' snapped Caro. 'Simon was cool without those scum-suckers. He was cool because he was Simon. *That's* what upsets me. He's decided that being The Same is better than being Him.'

April gave a rueful smile and stroked Caro's arm.

'Sorry, honey. You really love him, don't you?'

Caro's cheeks immediately flamed red. 'Shut up, April, that's not what this is about! It's a matter of principle. I'm asking you if these people are worth saving.'

'Yes!' shouted April, surprised by how passionate she felt. 'Yes they are. I know you're angry with Simon, but everyone's worth saving. It's one thing to be angry with someone, but it's another to abandon them to some horrible fate. No, we don't know exactly what the Suckers are up to, but we can be fairly sure they're not arranging a tea party. Simon could have his throat torn out – do you want that?'

Caro glanced at her, then looked down at her hands.

'No ... I suppose not.'

'So don't be so hard on him. It's not all fun for him either – remember when I found poor geeky Ling crying in the toilets after they sucked the blood out of her? You can't blame her for wanting to be one of them rather than being prey. It's those kids we have to save.'

'Okay. Sorry. But sometimes I wish we didn't have to do this.'

April smiled.

'Who else is going to save the universe?'

Caro shivered, wrapping her arms around herself. 'Well neither of us, if we freeze to death out here talking about it.'

'Come on, let's go back in,' said April, linking her arm through Caro's.

Just before the doors, Caro stopped.

'Listen, don't be mad,' she began.

'What is it?'

'You know how I said I had a plan ... how to get in with the Suckers a bit more?'

'Yessss ... ?' April said suspiciously.

'Well, um, I've arranged something. A party. A sort of coming-out party for you to celebrate your recovery. And your birthday.'

April gaped at her. She had no idea anyone knew it was her birthday.

'Where? When?'

'It's tonight. At Davina's. She was going to have some sort of Valentine's Ball anyway and she loved the idea of turning it into a surprise birthday party for you.'

April's heart sank. The last thing she felt like doing was having a party, especially at the place she had almost been killed.

'I'm so sorry A, I know you won't want to go back there so soon,' Caro said in a rush, 'but we need to get closer to the Suckers, to infiltrate and play them at their own game. I even thought we might be able to find the *Albus Libre* there, seeing as they have a big library and everything ...' She trailed off.

'It seemed like a good idea a few days ago, but now you're here, I wish I'd never suggested it.'

April forced a smile.

'It's okay. It's fine. We'll have a great time playing pin the tail on the monster.'

Caro laughed with relief.

'Well, it's funny you should say that ...'

Chapter Three

April was pretty sure she'd never have a career as a Hollywood star. She spent the next lesson feeling completely sick after her debut performance playing the part of a girl who didn't care about Gabriel Swift. She knew that it was necessary to protect both of them, but that didn't mean she had to like it – and she certainly hadn't liked the way Gabriel was throwing himself into it. While she'd been talking to Ben, he'd been flirting with other girls. But April trusted him – she *had* to. They were both in danger here, literally surrounded by undead monsters who would tear them apart if they suspected anything. God, but it hurt to do. She had hoped for some shared smile across the room, but she had barely dared look in his direction. *Be strong, April*, she scolded herself. *It's only a game.* But it was a game with the highest possible stakes and she wasn't completely sure she could take the pressure.

As she doodled in her notebook, too preoccupied to tune in to the lesson at all, April found herself looking across at Benjamin. Did he really like her? He had certainly seemed sincere. *But he's a vampire, April* – he could easily be playing his own elaborate game, couldn't he? She watched him as took notes, his blue eyes cast down, unaware that she was staring at him. There was something knowing, beautiful, even frightening about Ben. He was certainly pretty cocky most of the time, but he could also be vulnerable. Which wasn't something you could say about Gabriel, who was always so strong and reserved ... until now, of course. Now it killed April to see him struggling with pain and illness, frightened to go back to a way of life he hated, too proud to admit he was suffering.

The moment the bell rang, April grabbed her satchel and was up and out of the classroom. She knew what she had to do; she was going to find Gabriel. Okay, so they needed to play their roles in public, but if she couldn't see him in secret, feel him in her arms, kiss him, she thought she might snap. *He might be dead soon*, she thought, *why should we be spending what little time we have apart? Screw the danger.*

April was striding down the corridor, determined to get to the school gates before Gabriel had a chance to leave. She turned the corner towards the main entrance and was suddenly grabbed from behind.

'Hey, what—' she said, but before she had time to protest she was pulled sideways into an empty classroom, stumbling into a desk. As she whirled around, April immediately saw her abductor: Layla, her arch enemy, the Face who had been dating Milo, the vampire who died. Not that Milo had told her he was seeing Layla when he kissed her, the blood-sucking rat. Layla had never had any proof that April and Milo had kissed, but she had always hated April – maybe she had some sixth sense about what had really happened. Certainly she was now glaring at April with undisguised spite. No, it wasn't spite, it was something else.

'What do you want?' demanded April. 'Let me go.'

'Shut up,' hissed Layla pushing the door closed behind them and locking it. 'I don't want any of them hearing.'

'Any of who?' Layla looked agitated and edgy, not quite in control of herself. April took a step away from the girl, out of reach of her talons, but Layla made no move towards her. In fact, April noticed that Layla's nails were all bitten right down. Somehow that detail was more disturbing than being cornered by a girl she knew hated her. Layla was one of the top Faces; Hell would freeze over before they let their manicure regimes slip. What the hell was going on?

'What do you want, Layla?' asked April. 'If this is about Milo ...'

'It's not about Milo,' said Layla. She had expected anger, but Layla just sounded miserable. Close to tears in fact. 'It's about me. It's *me* they're after.'

'After you? Who's after you?'

'*They* are. You know who I mean. They think I—'

There came a sharp rapping on the door.

'Who's in there? Open this door at once!' They both recognised Miss Holden's voice.

'Please, I haven't got much time,' said Layla, jumping forward and clutching April's hand. 'They can't see me talking to you. You've got to help me, April, please. You don't know what they're capable of.'

'Who? How do you think I can help?'

'Don't play the innocent!' she snapped, tightening her grip on April's hand, 'You *know*, I've seen it in your face. They'll tear me apart, like those foxes in the woods.'

'Foxes? What foxes?'

'You know. You of all people must know!'

There was another rap on the door.

'Open this door right now!'

Layla clutched at April's arm, making her wince. Her eyes were wild, she looked terrified.

'Layla, listen to me …' said April.

'No, you listen,' said Layla, pulling her forward and whispering urgently in her ear. Then, just as suddenly, she turned away and unlocked the door.

'Sorry Miss Holden, we were just having a little chat,' she said as the teacher burst in. 'You know, about losing people and stuff.'

Miss Holden looked suspiciously from one girl to the other.

'Is this true, April? Are you okay?'

'Yes, yes,' said April, flustered. 'We were just talking, like Layla says.'

The teacher looked at them, a sceptical expression on her face.

'All right, get moving. The bell's gone.'

April was glad to get away, thinking about what Layla had whispered in her ear.

'They're going to kill me.'

Chapter Four

'But I don't want a party.'

'Of course you do, darling. Everyone wants a party. It's what civilised women live for.'

Silvia was sliding dresses down her wardrobe rail, the wooden hangers clacking against each other. 'Not this, no ...' she muttered to herself. 'Too sheer ... too formal ... too frou-frou ...'

After their fight the night before April had assumed her mother would ground her for a month, but at the mention of a party at Davina's, she had immediately forgotten all about it. *God, she's so shallow*, April thought. *All she wants for me is rich friends*. Friends like Layla, presumably. April thought back over their strange encounter in the locked classroom and remembered Layla's terrified face. She had never been very fond of the girl, but she'd seen how scared she was. Of what, though? Had someone threatened her? It couldn't have been the Faces – Layla was one of the top dogs in that particular pack. And who else could frighten someone like Layla? The vampires? But if she was friends with all the Suckers, why would they want to hurt her?

'Can't I just wear something of my own?' asked April, sitting on the edge of her mother's bed. 'I'm not going to a masked ball. Anyway, all your dresses make me look fat.'

Silvia looked at her sharply.

'You do not *look* fat, April, because you *aren't* fat. We just have to choose something flattering, that's all. If we'd had a bit of notice ...'

'Well I can't help it if I get a bloody party foisted on me,' she said sulkily.

45

Silvia turned and held a bottle-green dress up against herself. 'It is not a "bloody party", my sweet, it is a golden opportunity for you to show people how lovely you are. And you will look fabulous in this. Put it on.'

'Mum ...'

'Put it on.'

Sighing, April pulled it on. It was a soft jersey wrap dress. Not too formal, very flattering.

'See?' said Silvia, standing behind April as she looked in the full-length mirror. 'You look beautiful.'

It was almost true. There was no doubt the dress was a perfect match for her figure, but April wasn't about to admit that. She wished Gabriel was here to see her looking so nice, but then immediately remembered how they were supposed to be acting like strangers. She had no idea if he'd even be at the party and if he was, would he even look at her?

'So why don't you tell me what the real problem is?' said Silvia softly. 'You've been in a terrible mood for days.'

How about 'my vampire boyfriend is pretending to hate me' and 'my mother's keeping secrets from me'? she thought, but decided not to say it out loud. She had no desire for a replay of last night's fireworks.

'I just hate everyone looking at me,' said April. 'They do it anyway, because of Dad and the Marcus thing, but throwing this party isn't for me, it's an excuse for them. And I don't ... I really don't want to go back to that house, Mum. I was almost killed there, remember?' She shivered. 'It's horrible to even think about it.'

'I know, darling, but you know what they say about falling off a horse: you've just got to get back on.'

'It's not the same as riding a horse, Mother.'

'I know, but the Osbournes were very good to you and it never does any harm to be polite. I think they feel a bit responsible for what happened.'

Yeah, and you don't want Davina's mum to stop inviting you round for cocktails, thought April, but she held her tongue. After all, April really didn't have much choice. First, Caro was right, they needed to get in with the Faces, make them believe they were potential recruits; it was their only chance of getting information about the Vampire Regent. And second, if she was going to save Gabriel, she had to find that book. Admittedly, the Osbournes' library was a long shot, but it was the only lead they had at the moment.

'Be back by midnight, it's a school night, remember?'

April sighed. She knew her mum was being nice, but she was still disturbed about the conversation she'd overheard the night before. There was something her mother wasn't telling her.

'So what did you do today?' April asked.

Silvia hesitated, then stood up, putting dresses back on their hangers.

'Oh, not much. Just went to that lovely little deli in Hampstead, the one that does those little olives? Then I had coffee with Barbara, you know, Davina's mum? No gossip though.'

April went cold. She distinctly remembered Davina saying her mother was out of town. Why would Silvia lie? The sad truth was April was never that sure about her mother. She should have been her rock, the one person she could rely on, but Silvia had always been flaky and evasive. She didn't even know where her mother had been when her father was killed. She had some story about being on her way back from Grandpa Thomas's house, but something about it didn't ring true.

'Mum, can I ask you something?'

'What?'

'Why were you at Grandpa's the day Dad was killed?'

Silvia met her gaze.

'I had to speak to him about something. Family business.'

'But what family business?'

'Something about Grandpa's will.'

'Why? What's wrong with Grandpa? Is he ill?'

'No darling, he's strong as a horse. But – and I know this is hard to face, especially right now – he's not going to live for ever and we need to plan for the future.'

'Why didn't you tell me?'

'Well, the timing was pretty bad, to say the least, wasn't it? I was worried you'd react like this, assume that Grandpa was going to die. It's not what you needed to hear.'

The doorbell rang.

'In fact, that will be him now.'

'Gramps is here?'

'We've a few things to sort out, legal stuff about your dad,' Silvia called over her shoulder as she ran down the stairs to open the door. 'But I think he mainly wants to see the birthday girl.'

April followed her down and laughed as Grandpa Thomas swept in, his wild white hair sticking out of a big fur hat. 'Princess!' he boomed, catching April in his arms. 'Give your old granddad a hug. It's so cold outside.'

'Careful, Dad,' said Silvia, 'she's only just out of hospital, remember?'

'I'm sorry, Princess,' said Thomas, letting her go. 'I just wanted to hug my beautiful girl. But your mother's right, shouldn't you be sitting down?'

'I'm not an invalid, Gramps.'

'You got a hug for me too?' It was only then that April realised there was someone else, standing behind her granddad.

'Uncle Luke!' she said, pleased. April didn't know her mother's brother very well, but there was something reassuring and solid about him.

'Here, we got you a little something,' he said, handing April a small box wrapped in gold paper. 'Don't worry, your mother told us what to buy,' he added in a whisper.

April tore it open and found a beautiful pair of toffee-coloured cashmere mittens inside. They were perfect: they even matched her new bag. She glanced at her mother – sometimes she did get things right.

'Oh they're lovely,' she said, hugging the men. 'Thank you.'

They hung up their coats and moved into the living room.

'So are you in London permanently now?' April asked Luke.

48

'He has some swish flat in Chelsea when he could be staying with me,' said Thomas. 'Helping out his old dad.'

'You don't need anyone to look after you,' said Luke. 'You'll outlast us all.'

April wasn't sure that was true. Despite her mother's reassurances, her grandfather looked older, more frail than he had last time she saw him. He'd always had a face like wrinkled leather, but he seemed paler now, less solid.

'Well, you look all grown up, Princess,' said Thomas. 'My little girl has flowered into a beautiful woman.'

'Gramps ...'

'April's having a birthday party at her friend Davina's.'

Thomas frowned. 'You're going back there?' He glanced at Silvia, his concern obvious.

'It's okay Gramps, really. I can't keep hiding from things. I'm not exactly jumping for joy going to that house, but you can't blame bricks and mortar for the way some loony behaves. I just want to get it over with and move on.'

'But it's not safe in this neighbourhood. That's why I've come to see you. Someone needs to watch over you both.'

'I don't need looking after,' said Silvia.

'Yes you do, everyone does. Someone is out there, and who knows what they're planning?'

'They never caught this Marcus guy, did they?' asked Luke.

'No,' said Silvia, glaring at her brother. 'But there's no need to worry April about that. The police are outside.'

'One car? Pah! How will that stop a killer?' said Thomas.

'Yeah, thanks, you've really made me feel safer,' said April.

'Come on, let's get you to this party before they scare us both to death,' said Silvia, grabbing their coats and steering April towards the front door.

'You watch out for those boys,' shouted Thomas after them. 'You never know what they're up to.'

Yes, Gramps, thought April sadly. *You're absolutely right.*

April didn't want to go in. She hadn't been sulking when she had said she didn't want a party – she was genuinely afraid of going back to the Osbournes' mansion. All those nights lying in the hospital, she would close her eyes and see freeze-frame moments of that horrible Winter Ball, like a series of overexposed photographs she couldn't erase. The tears in her mother's eyes as they toasted April's dad, Gabriel standing across the dance floor looking amazing, the heat of Ben's desk lamp as her face was pushed towards it. And then the terror of running through the cemetery, her blood dripping onto the snow, the chilling feeling of being hunted, cowering behind a headstone trying not to breathe, believing that she would never see her family or friends again. And then that wonder-ful, terrible final image of Gabriel smiling down at her, his lips descending, their amazing kiss as the snowflakes drifted down.

April shut her eyes and took a deep breath.

'April?' asked her mother. 'Are you okay?' She was grateful that Silvia was dropping her off in the car. The nights were short and dark and the Osbournes' drive was long and creepy; she wouldn't have wanted to walk along it alone.

'Yes, it's just … there are so many bad memories here. I was almost killed here. It's great that my friends want to help me get over it. But I still … I'm afraid to go back in there.'

Silvia reached over and squeezed her hand. 'It's only natural you're feeling apprehensive, darling, but honestly, I think you're going to have a great time. If you're not, or if you feel sick or ill or anything else, just give me a call and I'll be straight over, okay?'

'Thanks, Mum. You can be human sometimes after all.'

'I'll take that as a compliment,' said Silvia with a wry smile, opening the door. 'You have a fabulous time. And no kissing!'

'Mum … !'

'Okay, okay, I'm going …'

They were all waiting for her in the dining room.

'HAP-PY BIRTH-DAY!' they shouted, sending party poppers and streamers into the air. All of the Faces, and all of their louche floppy-haired boyfriends, were standing on chairs, cheering and clapping. April didn't know when she had felt more embarrassed.

'Thanks everyone,' she said lamely as the girls ran up squealing to give her hugs.

'You look amazing,' said Chessy without, for once, a shred of irony. *Good old Mum strikes again.*

The house had been given over to the Valentine's Day theme, with hundreds of heart-shaped balloons suspended from the ceiling, huge vases of red roses and strings of fairy lights hanging in twinkling garlands over the windows. In one corner, there was a big silver banner reading 'Happy Birthday, April', covered in tacky glitter and streamers. *That will be Caro's contribution*, thought April with a small smile. *I bet she enjoyed undermining Davina's careful interior design.*

'Thanks so much for doing this for me,' said April, nodding towards the banner as Davina came over to air-kiss her.

'Don't thank me,' said Davina, 'Thank Caro, this is all her idea. I just provided the space. Although I bet Daddy could have pulled a few strings to get us a room at the Savoy for you.'

'Well, it's lovely anyway.'

'Can I get you a drink?' said Caro with a little too much enthusiasm. 'We have cherryade or cream soda. Or I could mix the two for a cocktail.'

'No martinis?' asked Ling.

'Not on a school night,' said Layla.

April looked at her with surprise. She hadn't expected to see Layla at the party, especially not after she'd given the impression that she was terrified of the Faces. *The Faces, or someone else.* But Layla seemed to be back to her usual sarcastic self. April made a mental note to try and get Layla on her own and ask about her strange performance earlier in the day.

'I don't think it'd be a good idea for me to drink anything anyway,' said April. 'I'm still taking about six different types of pills.'

'Ah yes, we mustn't forget poor April's condition, must we?' said Layla with barely concealed sarcasm. 'The poor lamb must be suffering.'

Davina shot an angry look at her, but April tried to step in.

'Oh don't worry, I'm feeling fine,' she said, hastily changing the subject. 'Just a bit hungry.'

'Well I can help you with that,' said Caro, leading April over to the dining table, which was spread with paper plates holding sandwiches, crisps, chocolate fingers and sausages on sticks. Davina looked as if she was going to faint.

'I did offer to fix Caro up with Mummy's caterers – they do some wonderful canapés and finger food – but Caro – um – Caro wanted to go with her theme.'

'It's ironic!' said Caro proudly.

'It's revolting,' said Layla under her breath, taking a swig of her drink. April caught her eye and when she looked back defiantly April guessed it wasn't just cherryade in Layla's cup. She looked around for Gabriel and her heart leapt when she saw him standing in a corner talking intently to Simon. She caught his eye, and he nodded and turned back to his conversation.

It's only a game, she repeated to herself. Maybe she'd be able to get him alone later on. It was killing her not being able to speak to him properly. April picked up a sausage roll, but realised she didn't feel at all hungry.

'What can I get you, Davina?' asked Caro, clearly enjoying herself.

'Nothing for me,' said Davina patting her flat stomach. 'On a bit of a complicated diet. No carbs or protein, definitely no artificial additives.'

As Caro explained that it was the additives that gave crisps their taste, April excused herself to go to the bathroom. Partly because she really didn't like all the attention she was receiving, and partly because she was on a mission. Somehow, she had to find her way to the library. She walked out into the entrance hall, past people sitting on the stairs, kissing and drinking. The door to a sitting room was open and there was a group gathered around a glass table – whatever they were doing, she wouldn't be able to snoop in there.

'You lost?'

'Oh, hi, Simon,' said April. 'No, just looking for the loo.'

'It's all a bit much, I guess? You must be feeling a bit fragile after what happened.'

April smiled gratefully.

'Yes, it's partly that. Plus I'm not the best at these social things.'

'Neither was I, I have to admit, but you learn to love it.'

She looked at him. With his slick new haircut and designer clothes he was barely recognisable from last term. *But then we've all changed a lot since then, haven't we?* thought April.

'Are you okay, though?'

'What do you mean?' asked Simon.

'Well, we don't see much of you any more.'

'You mean, "what the hell am I doing hanging out with these phoneys?"'

April laughed.

'Well, maybe. You never seemed to like them.'

'That rebel thing was all a pose. Inside every kid in a leather jacket and eyeliner is someone who really just wants to fit in. Yes, I know they're a bit … well, strait-laced, but when you get to know them they're pretty cool. Why shouldn't I be the cool kid, when I've been the outsider all my life? They accept me, they like me.'

'We accepted you and liked you.'

'But you and Caro, you're different, April.'

'Different good or different bad?'

'Just … different. I'm sick of being different. It wears you down.'

There was a bang behind them as the bathroom door opened.

'Bloody locks,' said Layla, reeling out into the corridor.

'What are you two looking at?' she sneered as she saw April and Simon. 'Seen something interesting?'

'Are you okay, Layla?' said Simon.

'Yes, of course,' she said, her chin raised. 'Why shouldn't I be?'

April gave Simon a meaningful look and he took his cue.

'Gotta pee,' he said and disappeared into the toilet, locking the door.

'Having a little reunion were we?' said Layla.

'Layla, what's the matter? Yesterday you said ...'

'Nothing,' said Layla quickly, cutting her eyes left and right. 'I didn't say anything. And there's nothing wrong,' she said taking a swig of her drink. 'Nothing that this can't fix, anyway.'

'But I might be able to help.'

'Oh yes, the heroic Miss Dunne, the brave girl who rises above it all, you'd love to fix my problems wouldn't you? Well let me tell you' – she barked out a bitter laugh – 'you can't help me now. I think this is a long way beyond your capabilities.'

'But what's going on?'

'Who said anything was? I'm fine. I'm among friends, aren't I? Not like you. *You're* the odd one out here.'

'Layla, you're not making sense.'

'I'm making perfect sense. You'll see. Now if you'll excuse me, I've got to have another of these delicious cream sodas.'

April walked back into the main party room, wondering what Layla had been trying to say to her. 'You're the odd one out?' What did that mean? She shook her head. Maybe Layla was drunk, and it was as simple as that. Maybe she'd been drunk at school too.

'Hey, Beautiful,' said Ben ambling over, stuffing some crisps in his mouth and smiling at April. 'Do you like the new look for the old place?'

'It's great,' said April distractedly.

'You all right? Are you feeling okay? I mean, your first day out and all that.'

'I'm fine,' she said forcing a smile, aware that she needed to snap back into her role.

'Well in that case, would you like to dance?'

Ben gave a little bow and put out his hand like some Regency gentleman. April smiled and nodded. 'Thank you, Mr Darcy,' she said.

As it turned out, Ben was a pretty good dancer and with Caro waving her arms around and making her laugh, April soon found she was genuinely enjoying herself. Everyone was dancing. All the sausages on sticks had gone. It seemed that everyone, even vampires, liked to let their hair down once in a while. Benjamin leant in and whispered in her ear.

'See? You look so much better when you smile.'

'Oh thanks,' said April. 'Nice to hear you think I'm usually a misery.'

'I meant you haven't been well, it's good to see you better.'

'Sorry, I'm not good at accepting compliments. Thank you.'

'You're welcome,' he smiled. 'I'll see you later on, okay?' he said, kissing her hand.

'Ooh, I think someone's sweet on you,' said Davina as they all walked out to the terrace.

'Oh no, he's just being friendly.' April blushed.

'No. I know my brother and he doesn't look at other girls the way he does at you.'

'Really? How does he look at me?'

'Like he's a puppy who just wants to play.'

'Oh.'

'I think he's a bit worried about you and Gabe, though.'

'Well, I don't think he needs to be.'

'Well that's good because I just saw him heading upstairs with Chessy,' said Davina with a little too much relish. 'I'm not sure there's much future in that one.'

April turned towards the garden, trying not to let Davina see her reaction. Gabriel was sneaking off with another girl? Just how seriously was he taking this cooling-off idea? April dug her fingernails into her palm, struggling to control her temper. How *could* he? Was he just using her to get the Dragon's Breath? She just didn't know what to think any more – but she couldn't let Davina know how hurt she was. She blinked back her tears, concentrating on the line of trees and the dark slab of wall at the end of the Osbournes' garden. Beyond that was the cemetery, the place Marcus had hunted her. Then Gabriel had come and given his life for hers, an act of pure love. Yet here he was, ignoring her and finding opportunities to go off with other girls. It just didn't make sense, any of it. Davina put a hand on her arm.

'You okay honey?' she said, following April's gaze. 'I didn't know whether I'd done the right thing having the party here, but Caro said it was better if you faced up to it.'

April nodded, relieved that Davina had misread her misery.

'No, Caro's right,' she said. 'I can't spend the rest of my life being scared of the dark. It was horrible, but I need to move on.'

'Why did he do it? Why was he so angry?'

April looked at Davina. She was fairly sure the girl was a vampire – did Davina know Marcus was a Sucker too? She must have done, she was head of recruiting at the school and Marcus was her brother's best friend. Even if she hadn't known before, Marcus's attack on April would have convinced her. April wondered how Davina felt about it. Angry, probably. Gabriel had told her again and again that vampires were hunters and, as such, tried their best to blend in with their surroundings. Anyone being so blatant in their desire for blood risked exposing all of them.

'Maybe I annoyed him. Ben thinks he was jealous,' said April with a laugh. 'Either way he's gone now, thank God. Where do you think he is?'

'I don't know, but I'd certainly advise him not to come anywhere near me ever again,' said Davina. A casual observer would have thought she was being protective of her friends and family when she said that, a sort of 'I'll give him a piece of my mind' statement, but the look of hatred on Davina's face was chilling. April didn't need to wonder what Davina's feelings were any more. It was clear she wanted Marcus dead.

April rubbed her bare arms, feeling goosebumps. 'Ooh, I'm suddenly feeling cold, can we go inside?'

'Of course,' said Davina, 'I should have thought. You can't be a hundred per cent yet, can you? Anyway, Caro had a great thought about how to warm us all up.'

They walked back in and Davina stood on a chair. The party goers gathered around in front of her.

'Okay everyone, we're going to play sardines. For those of you who have forgotten your childhoods, it's like hide and seek in reverse; one person goes to hide and the rest of us try to find them. The difference is, when you find their hiding place, you have to get in with them, until we're all hiding together.'

'Mmm ... cosy,' said Layla with a hint of sarcasm. Davina ignored her.

'As it's April's party, I think she should be first to hide. April, we'll give you a five-minute head start, then the search begins.'

There were hoots and cheering. As April moved towards the door, Caro whispered 'library' in her ear. April immediately understood; this was an ideal time to look for the book. She had explored the house a little at the previous party and she knew that the southern part held a study and some other rooms. That was the most likely location for the library, so she headed down the corridor to the side of the stairs. As she did so, all the lights in the house went out. There were theatrical screams from the living room.

'Don't panic,' she could hear Davina calling, 'we're just making it a little more interesting.'

Interesting is right, thought April, feeling her way down a corridor. *Tactless might be another word, considering the last time I was here, I was hunted through the dark by a maniac.* Luckily, April didn't have time to dwell on it as she knew she wouldn't have much time to search the library before the 'hunters' got there – and she still didn't know where it was. In the dark, the house took on a sinister feel, with creaky floorboards and half-open doors leading into rooms full of shadows. *Doesn't help that the place is full of vampires, either*, she thought, peering around another corner.

'That's got to be it,' she whispered to herself as she spotted a door wider than the rest. She pushed it open and sure enough, there was the library, a large room with French windows at one end and an old walnut desk at the other, the walls covered with floor-to-ceiling shelves, crammed with serious-looking leather-bound books. April closed the door quietly and clicked on the desk lamp. *God, there's got to be thousands of books*, she thought. *How the hell am I going to find anything in here?*

'Psst!' Caro put her head round the door and April jumped.

'You scared me!' she hissed angrily. 'And what the hell are you doing coming up with this stunt? It's hard enough to come back to the scene of the crime without you saying "let's terrify the birthday girl".'

'Sorry A,' said Caro, 'but it was the only way I could think of getting everyone out of the way while we looked for the book.'

April shook her head. 'No, I'm sorry too. I'm just a bit on edge. Davina said she saw Gabriel going off with Chessy.'

'Oh, don't worry about that,' said Caro soothingly. 'It's probably just part of his plan to throw everyone off your scent. He's not going to be interested in that fat cow, is he?'

April giggled despite herself. 'I suppose not.'

'So come on, let's see if we can find your Superman his anti-kryptonite spell.'

It was still dark in the library, so they both used their phones to light up the shelves.

'Bloody hell,' said April, scanning the spines, 'where do we start?'

'I'll go left, you go right. Look for something old and dusty.'

'Why?'

Caro tutted.

'Old because it *is* old, dummy. And dusty because if the Suckers knew they had it, they wouldn't have just left it on the shelf, would they? If it's here, no one will have touched it for years.'

April set to work, quickly scanning the shelves. Most of the books fitted into the 'old' category, being bound in leather or linen. There were a few shelves with more colourful books in modern dust jackets, but they all seemed to be about art or photography.

'Hey, check this one out,' whispered Caro, holding up a hardback with a slightly yellowed white cover. '*The Joy of Sex*. You wouldn't have thought it to look at Ma and Pa Osbourne, would you?'

'Put it back,' hissed April, glancing towards the door. 'We shouldn't be taking books out unless we have to – we don't want to leave fingerprints, do we?'

'Ooh, hark at Miss Marple,' muttered Caro, doing as she was told.

April was beginning to despair of ever finding anything in the library. There were too many books and most of their titles were written in small or faded type. She was feeling both the fear of being discovered and the pressure to find a cure for Gabriel – while he was off canoodling with Chessy, for all she knew.

'Why are we doing this?' she snapped finally. 'It's not like Gabriel cares one way or the other.'

'Hey, I know it's hard for you, but think how he must be feeling. He has to pretend to be one of them, to be part of the conspiracy, otherwise he's dead. Plus he's trying to protect you. I'm sure he'd rather be in here making out with you, but we don't live in that world any more.'

April pulled a face.

'Fine. Let's just find the bloody thing and get out of here.'

'Hello! Have a look at this,' said Caro. She was standing in front of an ornate Oriental-looking cabinet. 'Locked!' she said with annoyance, trying to peer through the crack between the doors. 'If it's going to be anywhere, it'll be in here …' She reached up on tip-toe, running her fingers along the top edge of the cabinet.

'What are you doing?'

'Well, if it were me, I would put the key … ah!'

She brought her hand down holding a small brass key.

'Bingo. Watch the corridor, I'll see if I can get it open.'

Gingerly, April pulled the door open and peered outside. Her heart leapt as Layla came around the corner, and she ducked back inside.

She could hear a countdown being shouted out in the distance.

'Hurry, Caro!'

'Come and look.'

'Have you found it?'

'Maybe,' said Caro.

'Maybe?' April hurried over.

'I mean maybe it was there, but it isn't now.'

April looked. The cabinet was empty. But from all the disturbed dust, it certainly looked as though whatever books had been in there had been moved very recently.

'Shh!' said April. 'Someone's coming!'

Caro ducked behind the desk and April jumped behind the door. Her heart sank when she saw Layla walk into the room and tip-toe to the drinks cabinet. Carefully opening the door, she poured herself a brandy and prepared to knock it back. Just then she spotted April and spilled the liquid down her front.

'God,' she spat, brushing the drink off her kingfisher-blue dress. 'This is silk, that's going to stain now! What the hell were you doing there?'

'Hiding, of course.'

She glared at April. 'And is that the best you can do?' she asked. 'Hiding behind a door?'

'I haven't found a decent hiding place yet,' said April, stepping out of the room. She didn't want Layla to spot Caro too.

'Well you'd better hurry up,' said Layla, her annoyance plain. 'The rest of them will be here in a minute and Davina will hit the roof if he knows you were in here. Her dad is very protective of his books.'

'I should think he's pretty protective of his booze too,' said April, nodding towards the glass in Layla's hand. 'Maybe we'd both better keep quiet about where we've been, eh?'

April doubled back towards the lounge. She could hear the sound of trampling feet and laughter coming from the upstairs rooms and some shouting coming from the direction of the kitchen. She guessed they had already searched this part of the house. She turned into the entrance hall and pulled open a door; it was a small walk-in closet crammed with coats. Perfect. She pushed the jackets to one side and got inside, closing the door behind her. It was cosy enough in there, but

April couldn't relax. She kept thinking of one thing: where was Gabriel right now? Was he looking for her, hoping to find her on her own, snatch a few words or kisses, as she was? Or was he looking under the bed with some slut, pretending she didn't exist. April knew she had agreed to this and yes, it made sense they pretend to dislike one another. But did he have to pretend so *well*?

She froze as the door opened and a blond head ducked inside. It was Ben.

'Aha! My superior detective skills pay off!' he whispered. 'So now I have to get inside too?'

'Um, yes, I think so,' said April as Ben closed the door, wriggled between the coats and sat down next to her, being careful not to spill the glass of red liquid he was carrying.

'You okay?' he said. 'I did tell my idiot sister that you might not be too happy creeping around in the dark, but she insisted it would be "fun".'

'Oh, don't worry, I'm fine,' said April forcing a smile. 'Just thinking about ... you know.'

In actual fact she was thinking about how she could feel his thigh pressed up against hers and how warm it felt. She knew she shouldn't be thinking about anyone but Gabriel, but where was he?

'Well, maybe this will help,' he said, handing her the drink. April took a glug and grimaced.

'Bit strong?' he smiled. 'I'm not that keen either. Actually, I think Caro might have hit on something with this party food. I think I actually prefer her cherryade to these cocktail things. And I never saw any of Davina's fancy catered canapés disappear as fast as Caro's sausage rolls.'

'Maybe we're not as old as we'd like to think,' said April, immediately seeing the irony in what she had said. For all she knew, Ben could be two hundred years old. Still, he certainly looked good. *Stop it, April,* she scolded herself. *Remember he's a vampire.*

'One thing's for sure,' said Ben. 'We're all a lot better off since you came along, April Dunne.'

April looked away.

'I'm not sure everyone would agree.'

Ben raised his eyebrows.

'You mean Gabe?'

'I was thinking about Layla, actually. We just had another run-in. In fact none of that crowd have ever really warmed to me. You must have noticed.'

He shrugged. 'I don't think the likes of Layla and Chessy warm up at all. But some of us are glad you're here, me especially.'

April looked at him. He was cute, but was this all an act? Was he really saying he liked her, or was this all part of the vampire honey trap?

'Well, thanks,' she said lamely.

'Listen, can we talk?' said Ben. 'Seriously, I mean?'

'I ... I suppose,' said April warily.

'Not here, I don't want any other sardines coming in and interrupting us.'

He pushed open the closet door and, checking the coast was clear, led April towards the front of the house.

'Well, I'm not sure I should leave the party ...' said April as he opened the front door, glancing back over her shoulder and hoping Caro had seen them.

'Don't worry, I promise not to keep you long, I just want to say something to you. I think it's time I did.'

April was excited and frightened at the same time. She liked Ben, whatever he was; after all, wasn't Gabriel a vampire too and she loved – liked – him. And why shouldn't she flirt with other boys if he was doing exactly the same thing? It's all part of our cover story, isn't it? If Gabriel can go off with Chessy, why shouldn't I go off with Ben? And anyway, could you really cheat on someone who had vanished upstairs with another girl? If Gabriel was really in love with her, where was he now when she was risking her neck – literally – trying to save him? Outside, Ben pulled her to one side, their breath steaming in the cold air, their feet crunching on the gravel.

'April, you know I like you,' he said, his intense blue eyes searching hers.

She smiled. 'I have an idea.'

'And you say Gabriel's not in the picture any more? Because he is still my friend.'

'I'm not sure how much Gabriel Swift ever was in the picture,' April said quietly.

'Then maybe you and I ...' he said, reaching out a hand to hold hers.

'You and I ... ?' said April, unsure what he wanted, unsure of what she wanted herself.

He pushed a strand of hair out of her eyes, an intimate gesture that made April's heart beat faster.

'Ben, I'm not sure ...' she said, 'I ...'

'Well I am,' he said, stepping forward, his body against hers. 'I'm sure I want to do this.'

He bent his head, kissing her softly on the neck. It was so gentle and so unexpected that April actually groaned with pleasure.

'What are you doing?' she murmured, half-hoping he'd do it again.

'What does it look like?' said Ben, kissing her cheek. 'I'm kissing you. Don't you want me to?'

'Yes ... No, I ... I don't know,' said April feeling his arms around her, an electricity between them, every part of her alive with longing and desire.

'Oh God,' she moaned. It was so wrong, but she couldn't stop. Ben leant in again, his lips coming down towards hers this time. April felt her lips part, then heard a gasp and saw Ben jerk out of her sight. There was a thud and a grunt as he landed on his back. She whirled around to see Gabriel standing over him.

'Gabe!' she shouted. 'Don't! I didn't ...' but he wasn't listening, he was glaring down at Ben.

'Get out of here, Ben, I'm warning you,' he growled, his fists bunched at his sides.

'Come on, Gabe, you made it clear you weren't interested

in her,' said Ben, getting up and dusting his hands off. 'Don't make this into a big deal.'

'It is a big deal,' said Gabriel, taking a step forward.

'Well, if that's the way you want it ...' said Ben. April was shocked at the speed with which he moved, hurling himself forward, his shoulder slamming into Gabriel's stomach. Gabriel tried to side-step, but he was too slow and they both landed on the drive in a shower of gravel.

'Stop!' she shouted. 'Enough! Both of you!'

Heedlessly, Gabriel rolled to his feet and flipped Ben over, sending him flying into the wall with a thud.

'Back off, Ben, I'm warning you.'

Ben wiped a dark trickle of blood from the side of his mouth, looked at it, then launched himself forwards, swinging a lightning-fast punch at Gabriel which knocked him backwards, stumbling into a car. Seizing the opportunity, Ben jumped forward and grabbed Gabriel's shirt, but April caught his arm.

'Stop! Right now,' shouted April, 'I'm serious, Ben.'

'He's asking for it ...' Ben began, but before he could say anything more, April turned on him, her teeth bared.

'Get off him!' she hissed. 'I won't tell you again.'

Her eyes were blazing and her words full of authority. For a moment, Ben stopped and looked at her, his mouth open.

'Hey, come on,' he said, putting up his hands. 'I didn't start this. He's been treating you like dirt, he deserves this ...' he said, making a lunge for Gabriel. April stepped forward and swung a punch that thumped into Ben's shoulder.

'Ow!' he cried, stepping back and rubbing it. 'That hurt!'

Suddenly April felt herself lifted and thrown to the side. 'Stay the hell out of this,' Gabriel yelled. 'This is between me and Ben.'

'Hey, don't speak to her like that,' said Ben.

'She's just a stupid little slut, what do you care?'

'*Slut?*' April screamed, turning towards Gabriel, unable to believe what she was hearing. 'How *dare* you?'

'Oh and I suppose you came out here to do some bird-watching, did you?'

'Screw you, Gabriel,' hissed April. 'That's it! I've had enough of your two-faced crap. You can't make up your mind about me, you go off with *Chessy* at every opportunity, and then when someone else decides I'm worth bothering with, you suddenly coming running back. Is that supposed to be attractive?'

Ben looked from April to Gabriel and back again.

'Okay,' he said, holding up his hands and backing towards the front door. 'It looks as if you two have a few things to sort out.' He turned towards Gabriel. 'I'll sort *you* out later.'

Gabriel just sneered.

'And I'll be here whenever you need me, okay?' said Ben to April.

'Thanks,' said April quietly as Ben closed the door behind him. As soon as he was gone, Gabriel grabbed April's arm and marched her around to the side of the house.

'Hey! Slow down!' she cried. 'I'm wearing heels!'

'Bugger your heels. What the hell were you doing?' said Gabriel angrily.

'What was I doing? What were *you* doing? And I'm a slut now?'

He threw his hands in the air in frustration.

'Don't be so bloody stupid, April. I saw Ben pulling you outside and I knew he wasn't planning on showing you the roses.'

'So now you're jealous? After you've gone upstairs with some other girl?'

'Oh, grow up, April. If you'd kissed Ben and he'd keeled over with the virus, how long do you think it would take the vamps to join the dots? I was *protecting* you.'

'Oh, not this again. You're always protecting me, aren't you? Well I don't want to be protected, I want to be loved!'

His face softened and he put out a hand to touch her cheek.

'I do love you—' he began, but April slapped his hand away.

'Calling me a slut doesn't really sound like someone who loves me.'

'I had to stop you! You didn't know what you were doing!'

'Don't be so bloody patronising! You might be four hundred years old, but that doesn't make you my dad.'

He looked at her, searching her face.

'You really don't know, do you?'

April suddenly felt cold. What was he talking about?

'What?'

'Didn't you see Ben's reaction when you told him to back off? He was genuinely worried. Just for a moment there, April, you were a Fury.'

'What? No!'

April turned and tried to walk away, but Gabriel followed her.

'You can't avoid it, April. You might not like it, but it's who you are.'

'It is not! I am not a murderer!' But her voice wobbled. She wasn't sure of anything. Was he right? Had she lost control? She didn't feel like a killer, she didn't want to hurt anyone. But it was true that her temper had been getting the better of her recently. But that was just the stress and the grief, wasn't it? Or was it something more than that?

'That's why I pushed you aside and tried to distract you,' said Gabriel. 'I needed to stop you before you did something serious. You cannot reveal who you are to anyone. They'll hunt you down and I won't be able to save you, April.'

'Like you'd want to!'

'Listen to me! Stop acting like a spoilt schoolgirl; this is serious! They will torture and murder you without a thought.'

April burst into tears.

'Why? What have I done? Why me?'

Gabriel took her in his arms. She resisted for a moment, then sank into his embrace.

'I didn't mean to hurt you, April,' he said, stroking her hair. 'But I needed to throw Ben and the rest of the clan off the scent, make them think I'm not interested in you.'

'Well that's how it's feeling to me,' said April sulkily. 'Okay, you ignore me at school and flirt with other girls in front of me … but to go off with Chessy and then get all jealous when anyone so much as looks at me …?'

'It's an *act*, honey,' he said, his eyes searching hers. 'We talked about this. I love you with all my heart, I feel it to the bones of me. You must know that?'

She smiled reluctantly. 'Maybe. But it still kills me when you're cold and distant and when I see you with other girls.'

Gabriel didn't say anything more, he just pulled her close and kissed her. Long, hard, lovingly. She felt the tingle spread from her lips, through her body and out to her fingertips.

'But why do we have to pretend?' she sighed, looking up at him. 'Why can't we just be together, especially after this evening? I can't take it, Gabriel.'

'Because …'

He passed a hand across his forehead, stumbled back a pace, then dropped to the ground.

'Gabriel! What's the matter?' she gasped, kneeling down beside him. 'Gabriel!'

His eyes had rolled up in his head and his skin was burning hot. Oh God, they were too late. He was dying, just like Milo.

'Gabriel! Don't you die on me,' she said, slapping his cheek harder than she meant to. 'Come on, Gabriel!'

April turned as she heard footsteps coming down the side of the house. It was Caro running towards them.

'Caro, help me!' she cried, trying to lift Gabriel's head.

'What's going on? Did you punch him out?'

'He just collapsed! Help me, please!'

They managed to get Gabriel into a sitting position and finally he opened his eyes.

'Thank God! Are you okay? Can you stand?'

'I think so,' said Gabriel, climbing unsteadily to his feet.

'What happened?' asked Caro, supporting him from the other side.

'It's the virus,' said Gabriel. 'It's been making me weaker. I obviously wasn't up to fighting with a full-blood vampire,' he said, trying to smile. 'Listen, leave me here. I'll get home all right.'

'I'm not leaving you,' said April.

'You have to,' said Gabriel. 'Caro, tell them I was trying to win April back, but she told me where to get off. Keep her safe; keep this secret. I can't let anyone know I'm weak – we'll all be in danger if they realise.'

'He's right,' said Caro, pulling April away. 'We need to get back inside.'

'No, I'm not leaving you.'

'Please,' said Gabriel, fixing her with an intense stare. 'You *have* to. We all have to be strong now.'

April threw her arms around him and squeezed tight.

'We're going to fix you, okay?' she said fiercely. 'I won't let you go, not now.'

Gabriel smiled and bent to give her a last lingering kiss, then turned and moved off down the drive. April stood and watched for as long as she dared, then allowed Caro to lead her inside.

'Oh God, Caro,' said April when they were back in the hall. 'He's *dying*. What am I going to do?'

'I'll tell you what *we're* going to do. We're going to find that white book and get him fit again. It's the only thing we can do.'

'But what if he dies? I can't handle him flirting with some-one else, I don't think I could stand losing him.'

'He won't die, honey. We're going to crack this thing, okay?'

April wiped her eyes and nodded. 'Okay.'

They walked back into the party and Davina immediately strode over.

'Ben told me all about it, April. Was Gabe a total pig?'

April glanced at Caro, gathering her resolve to lie and lie well. Now they had started down this road, they had to pull it off – they *had* to.

'Worse than a pig,' said April. 'He had the gall to call me some awful names, and then he tried to kiss me.'

'Ben told me, but I couldn't believe it!'

'Well, you should have heard the language that came out of her mouth when she blew him off,' said Caro.

68

'I can imagine. You just wait until I see him,' said Davina. 'No boy does that to a friend of mine and gets away with it.'

'Thanks, Davina, I should have listened to you in the first place. You were right about him.'

'Well, you're better off without him. Why can't boys control themselves? They're pathetic.'

April sat down at the table and Ben walked over

'You okay?' he asked. 'Listen, I didn't mean for any of that to happen ...'

'I know,' said April with a weak smile. 'I just want to go home.'

'Sure. I'll call you a cab.'

She touched his arm. 'Thanks.'

'Look, I just didn't like the way he was taking you for granted. I've seen him do this before – I hope you can see what he's like now.'

'Yes, I think so. Thanks for looking out for me.'

'Can I call you during the week? Just to check you're okay.'

'You'll see me in class tomorrow, Ben,' she smiled, hoping that it looked genuine.

'I know, but just to make sure.'

'I'd like that.'

'So what does it mean, Fee?'

April had called Fiona the minute she got home.

'It means that boys are all the same,' said Fiona, 'even if they are a hundred and forty years old. Vampires, humans, they all seem to be here to screw us up.'

April was glad she still had her best friend to share things with. Caro always seized on the craziest angle, but Fiona was the direct opposite, finding the calm logic in any situation. Fiona had come down from Edinburgh when she was in hospital and having her there to talk to for a few days had been better than a year of therapy.

'So do you think Gabe's still interested?'

'Of *course* he is, you nincompoop, why wouldn't he be? You're gorgeous.'

April laughed; she could always rely on Fiona for a spot of ego-boosting when she was feeling down.

'Listen, I don't know why you're making this so complicated. So he's a vampire – so what? He says he loves you and that he wants to protect you, and that seems to be what he's doing, so why not believe him? He's got a point – if you are this Fury thing, the bad vampires are going to want to get rid of you.'

'Wow, thanks.'

'It stands to reason. I think Gabriel's being quite sensible. Unfortunately, it seems you've got to find that cure pretty sharpish though.'

'You make it sound so simple.'

'Well it is – find the *Albus Libre*; cook up the potion; he's back to drinking blood.'

April clucked her tongue.

'Not ideal.'

'Yeah, but at least then you have the chance to find the Regent and get the whole thing reversed. If he dies first, you've got nothing. In fact, worse than nothing, because then they'll be after you.'

'But we didn't find anything in the Osbournes' library. And it looked like they'd just moved some books.'

'It could have been their priceless collection of *Harry Potter* novels for all you know. Just because you didn't find it in the first place you looked, it doesn't follow that you never will, does it?'

'S'pose not.'

'Listen, April, keep in mind what's most important right now. Forget finding your dad's killer for the moment, nothing will bring him back. But you can save Gabriel.'

'But *how*, Fee?'

'You have to keep looking – and look fast. Gabriel might be an idiot sometimes, but he's right when he says this isn't a game. You could end up dead.'

'Thanks for that,' said April sarcastically.

'Well, you know what they say, live fast die young, leave a great-looking corpse.'

April stared out of the window, her reflection in the glass skeletal, her eyes hollow.

'It's the corpse part I'm worried about.'

Chapter Five

The early morning fog was still clinging to the trees when April turned into the little lane. *Seven thirty*, thought April. *The morning after a party too; I must be mad.* In truth she'd been awake for hours, her mind going round and round with questions and problems, most pressingly how to help Gabriel. She couldn't get that image out of her mind: Gabriel falling over on the path, lying still and lifeless. For one heart-stopping moment, April really had thought he was dying. *He is*, she reminded herself. *And I have no idea how long he has.* Still, April had been reassured by her reunion with Gabriel, hearing him using the 'L-word', feeling his arms around her. It was still maddening to have to pretend they weren't together, but she had to trust him, didn't she? Yes, she had to believe that what they were doing was right and stick to the plan: find the book, get the cure and save Gabriel. Whatever came after that, they'd have to work out when it happened. Because if nothing else, the party last night had proven one thing – without Gabriel, she had nothing.

Which was why she was walking up to Miss Holden's house, tucked away in a tiny hidden lane on the outskirts of the village. A little cottage with bow windows and ivy running up the side, it had a charming English country garden that, even in winter, looked neat and tidy, with clipped box hedges and shiny green shrubs. It reminded April of the gingerbread house from her Hansel and Gretel storybook as a child. *Dad used to read that to me*, she thought with a sudden jolt of pain. She stood still on the pavement across the road from the teacher's house, pressing a hand to her chest. This was happening more and more – suddenly she would think of her dad and burst into tears or want to throw herself under a train. Maybe the numbness and shock of the first few months since his death was wearing off, but the wound seemed more raw and painful as the days passed, not less. But she didn't want to stop the pain, however much it hurt, because doing so would mean letting him go somehow.

Try and remember the good things, hold onto all the great things he did, she told herself, trying to breathe evenly. Remember the stories.

She remembered how he used to embellish the stories, weaving in characters from other fairy tales. 'It doesn't say that, Daddy!' April would laugh as Goldilocks or Sneezy from Snow White appeared to save Hansel from the witch's oven. *I wish he was still here to give this story a happy ending*, she thought, looking up at Miss Holden's cottage. Taking one final deep breath, she crossed the road, unlatched the wooden gate and walked nervously up the flagstone path. She had no idea how Miss Holden was going to respond to her turning up at her door at seven thirty in the morning. The teacher had given April her numbers to 'call any time', but she hadn't wanted to call ahead in case Miss Holden tried to put her off. She needed to talk right now. So Fiona, with her computer wizardry, had managed to track her address down from a social networking website.

'Well, she did say "my door is always open",' April whispered to herself as she knocked on the sky-blue door. She waited, expecting to get the biggest telling-off of her life. After all, if April was in Miss Holden's shoes, having students appearing on her front step was the last thing she'd want. *Oh no, what if she has a boyfriend? What if he answers the door?*

But no strangers came; in fact there was no movement inside of any kind. She knocked again and waited, but the house was silent.

April stepped back and looked up at the windows. Miss Holden's bedroom window, perhaps? The curtains were still drawn. She was now imagining all sorts of things going on behind those drapes. *Calm down, April*, she scolded herself. *She's most likely just asleep.* She wouldn't be pleased to be woken up by some schoolgirl, though. She glanced back at the garden gate and considered running away, but she couldn't back out now. Besides, Miss Holden had been the one who had told her to get in touch, who had told her how important she was. April glanced at her watch – seven forty-five. Teachers at Ravenwood were always in school before the students turned up at eight thirty – she must be up. Maybe she was in the kitchen – it was worth a try, wasn't it? She followed the stone path around the house to the left and ducked under the branches of a tree, moving along the side of the house and into the back garden. It was just as neat and tidy here, with flower-beds, a small lawn and a large patch which had obviously been given over to growing vegetables. April felt uncomfortable here, trespassing. It was too private and personal back here, as if she was going through her teacher's handbag or something. Nervously, April peered in though the back window – it was indeed the kitchen. She could see the old-fashioned Aga and a big wooden table spread with the papers and a cup of coffee; she could even see the steam rising from the mug.

'Hello, April.'

April almost jumped in the air, turning around with her hand clutched to her chest. Miss Holden was walking down the garden path towards her, carrying a basket.

'Miss Holden! You scared me!'

'I could say the same thing to you,' said the teacher. 'What are you doing here?'

'Sorry, I just needed to talk to you, to … to … someone,' she stammered. 'I knocked at the front door, but there was no answer and I didn't want to wake you, but …' April realised she was babbling and trailed off. 'Sorry,' she repeated.

'It's okay,' said Miss Holden. 'I was in the greenhouse and I thought you were a burglar, but then I suppose even burglars like a lie-in.'

'Sorry, I …'

'Don't worry, I'm glad you came, actually. Why don't you come inside, I've just made coffee.'

The kitchen was warm and cosy, decorated in a traditional style with wooden worktops and tiled walls. She immediately felt safe and at home there. Something soft brushed against her leg and she looked down to see a Siamese cat rubbing its tail against her.

'Don't mind Jasper, he's just hoping you'll feed him.'

April bent over to give the cat a stroke, but he trotted away, then jumped up onto the counter, fixing April with an imperious gaze.

Miss Holden laughed. 'That's cats for you. Fickle.'

April sat down at the table and Miss Holden put a mug of coffee in front of her.

'Toast?'

April wrinkled her nose.

'I'm not very hungry these days.'

'I can imagine,' said the teacher, sitting opposite her. 'These past few weeks can't have been easy for you.'

'No, they haven't. That's why I'm here so early, really. I've got all these things going around in my head, all these things I need to do, but I don't know how to make them happen so I end up just worrying more.'

'What's worrying you?'

April laughed, thinking, *Where do I start?*, but Miss Holden didn't smile.

'That I can't trust anyone, I suppose.'

'Well that's a good thing. A strong instinct. You can't tell who's a vampire, who's a recruit and who has their own agendas, not even the people closest to you.'

'You mean Gabriel?'

'I didn't say that, but it can't be easy for you to be … dating? Is that what you say these days? It can't be easy dating a vampire.'

It was still strange hearing Miss Holden say 'vampire' in such a matter-of-fact way, like it was entirely natural to find them hanging about the neighbourhood.

'It's not that I don't trust him,' said April. 'I do. It's just that – well, I'm the Fury, aren't I? I'm supposed to be super-attractive to vampires, to draw them in and whatnot. So I worry that maybe Gabriel likes me because I'm like some sort of vampire catnip, not because he actually likes me.'

April hadn't even been aware it was bothering her until she had said it out loud.

Miss Holden smiled.

'That, I can't help you with. But from what I know about him, he doesn't enter any relationship lightly. But I will add: he is a vampire, and vampires are not in control of themselves. You saw what that catnip can do to them.'

April knew Miss Holden was trying to warn her, telling her that Gabriel was only one step away from becoming like Marcus – that a vampire could turn on you at any moment. In fact, Gabriel had said the same thing. She knew she should be scared, but instead she simply felt a huge surge of relief. Her mind had latched onto one vital piece of information: Gabriel didn't play the field and therefore he must be serious about her.

'And this Fury thing, it's starting to worry me. Last night …'

'What? What happened last night?'

What *did* happen? What could she say? *I went a bit mental?* And then April realised Miss Holden would be angry if she thought she'd exposed her abilities to the Suckers.

'Nothing, it's just when I get angry, I don't feel I can control it, it's like I've … it's like I've turned into my mother.'

Miss Holden gave a half-smile.

'I can see why you might say that. But the truth is, you're not in control of it right now, and especially not if you get emotional. It's like anything, learning the piano or learning to drive: it takes practice to perfect.'

'I wish I was just learning to drive. Then I could get away from all this.'

The older woman nodded sympathetically.

'I wish I could tell you not to worry, that you can run away from it, but I can't.'

'Oh.'

'There's no point pretending, April, as much as we all might want to. We are surrounded by vampires and they're on the move. They've killed at least three people in Highgate and they've tried to kill you – if they find out what you are, they'll try again. Which is why it's vital you learn to control your abilities.'

'And how am I supposed to do that?'

'Well, that's where I come in. I can help you understand what's happening to you and learn how to use it effectively, but that's going to take time and that's why we can't allow the vampires to discover you're a Fury.'

April felt a little bad, remembering how she'd reacted when Gabriel said the same thing.

'And do you really think they're everywhere? I thought maybe I was paranoid to think they were watching me.'

'Not paranoid, no. Even if they don't know you're a Fury, the vampires will still be drawn to you. And anyway, you were there when Isabelle was killed, your father was murdered and you've been attacked by some sort of rogue vampire; it would be strange if they weren't watching you already.'

April took a deep breath, struggling not to panic. Here was a woman who seemed to understand the vampires telling her that she *was* being followed, she *was* being watched – that the shadowy figures in the cemetery and the square the other night probably *were* vampires. *When will it all end*, she thought miserably, *don't I have enough to deal with already?* Master some sort of 'abilities', hide them from the vampires, find and kill the Vampire Regent, save her dying boyfriend and avenge her father. Tears began to roll down her face.

'Sorry, April. I wish I could give you more good news, but you have to understand that the stakes are about as high as they can get. If we don't stop the vampires, if we don't bring down Ravenwood, there's a good chance our cosy world could turn into a living hell overnight – and I'm afraid it has fallen to you to fight back. But you're not on your own. I'm here to help you. So are the rest of the Guardians – we will do our best to stop them together.'

'What do you want to stop, and who are the Guardians? How many of you are there? What do you do?'

Miss Holden glanced at the clock.

'I'm sorry, April, we don't have time now. We've both got to get to school. All you need to know is that there are more of us than you think, and that we're here to help.'

Her disappointment and fear must have shown on April's face because Miss Holden reached out and touched her hand.

'Okay, I can see that this is all getting to you. Why don't you tell me what you need from us – from me – right now.'

April looked across at Jasper, who seemed to be looking back with one eyebrow raised. *Do cats even have eyebrows?* April didn't know where to start. Her dad's death? Saving Gabriel? What was going on at Ravenwood and who was behind it?

'I want to find that book and save Gabriel.' That was the truth – Gabriel was dying and her heart was dying with him. She had to do everything in her power to help him.

Miss Holden took a moment to sip her coffee.

'And then what?'

'What do you mean?'

'What will you do when you've saved Gabriel?'

'Well, then we have to find the Regent and …'

'And what? Hand them over to the police?'

'I, uh, I hadn't really thought about it …'

'Bullshit.'

April looked at her teacher, her eyes wide.

'I'm sorry, April, but you're telling me you watched your father die, sitting in a pool of his blood, and the thought of avenging him has never crossed your mind?'

'Well, of course I've had moments where I …'

'Where you what?'

'I don't know …'

'What, April?' said Miss Holden, leaning towards her, her face severe. 'What would you do if you found the Regent? What would you do if you found the animals who killed your dad?'

'I'd tear their throats out!' yelled April, jumping to her feet. 'I'd make them suffer like he suffered!'

Miss Holden sat back, her face serious.

'And that's the truth,' she said quietly. 'The truth is you couldn't hand them over to the authorities. It's very unlikely we'd ever get any evidence you could use in a court of law and, even then, I doubt any prison could hold a vampire for very long.'

'So you're telling me I'll never get justice for my father's murder?' said April incredulously. 'You're saying they'll get away with it?'

'Well, that depends on you.'

April felt cold. She had a sneaking suspicion she wasn't going to like what came next.

'What do you mean, on me?'

'You, a Fury. The vampires' nemesis. I want to be sure you understand exactly what we're talking about here, April. You have to kill them. We're not investigating a mystery, you are a soldier going to war. Make no mistake, they will kill you without a thought – and they will enjoy it – so you had better be prepared to kill them.'

April felt her skin prickle. She felt sick and hot at the thought.

'Kill them? You mean I have to hammer a stake through their hearts or ...'

Miss Holden shook her head sadly.

'I know you're only seventeen and would rather be worrying about shoes and kissing boys, but that's all gone. You need to grow up, toughen up – and fast. Your life and your friends' and family's lives are at stake.'

'But I don't want any of this.'

'Tough.'

Miss Holden sat back and folded her hands. 'Your father is dead, April. Murdered. A vampire tried to kill you; it's real, it's happening. Yes, you could ignore it, but I doubt you'd make it to eighteen and you would take a lot of innocent people down with you. The only way to save Caro, Fiona, your mother and even Gabriel, is to embrace it. The only way you can save them is to stop the killers who are coming for you all.'

In a rush, April realised her teacher was right. She hated her for it, but there was an undeniable truth in what she said. It wasn't about her any more. It never had been. 'All right then, tell me what to do!'

Miss Holden spread her hands.

'Find that book.'

April gaped at her.

'"Find that book?",' she repeated, struggling to control her temper. 'Is that all you've got to say? Miss Holden, I came here for advice. You're supposed to have all this amazing knowledge to give me and you're saying "Find that book"? At least tell me where it is!'

'You know I can't do that, April.'

April curled her hands into fists under the table. *Is it okay to use my Fury powers to kill bloody Guardians?* she wondered, gritting her teeth.

'Let me guess, it's against the rules?' said April, her voice shaking.

'April, you have to understand – I should never have even told you about the *Albus Libre*, I can't help you find it too. Yes, there are rules ...'

'Well screw your rules and screw your war!' shouted April, standing up again. 'If you won't help me, you're not much use, are you?'

She picked up her bag and strode over to the door.

'You know what? I'll ask my friends. They'll help me, however dangerous it is – because we look out for each other.'

'April, please ...'

'I'll see you in school,' she said, closing the door behind her.

Chapter Six

April didn't feel like going to school, but she knew she had to. She could probably get away with skipping a few days on compassionate grounds, but after her meeting with Miss Holden, she was filled with a new sense of purpose. The woman was maddening, with her riddles and her ridiculous rules, but she was right about one thing: April couldn't waste time wishing this whole mess away, she had to roll up her sleeves and get to work. She needed to find the book, and then she would have the means to save Gabriel; she had to track down the Regent, somewhere in the shadows behind Ravenwood, and make him release Gabriel – then they could be together at last. And she needed to find out who had killed her dad, and then she would have peace of mind. She had spent far too long being a silly little girl. It was time to grow up and accept that none of this was going to go away. Yes, she wished her dad would come back, she wished she and Gabriel could run away and leave it all behind and, more than anything, she wished she didn't have this bloody Fury thing hanging over her, making her even more unsure of herself. As she walked up the steps to the school's main entrance, she decided she was going to do whatever was necessary to bring this to a conclusion. It was the helplessness, the sense of being overwhelmed that was crippling her. If she was honest with herself, she had wanted Miss Holden to just say, 'Okay, April, I'll make it all stop. No vampires, no Fury, just you and Gabriel – oh, and look – your father has come back.' But she hadn't – she couldn't. April had to face up to the fact that she was a natural anomaly, like those kids who could play chess at three or who could do back flips. She was what she was, it was that simple. 'Get on with it', that's what her dad would have said. 'You don't have to like it, but you do have to finish the job.'

Right then, thought April, *let's get this sorted*. Infiltrate the Faces, see what I can learn about Ravenwood, and turn Gabriel back into a vamp. If I don't start doing something, I'll go mad.

She found Caro after her English lesson and pulled her into the girls' toilets. After checking they were alone, she laid it out for her.

'It's time to get serious. I'm going to find that book and I'm going to find the Regent.'

'Brilliant. I'm with you all the way.'

'No you're not. Not any more.'

Caro frowned.

'Why not?'

'Because we're being naïve about this. We're assuming the Suckers are stupid, but that's the last thing they are. They've remained hidden for centuries, they've set up this school to recruit new vamps and heaven only knows what else they're up to.'

'Okay ... so how are we being naïve?'

'Because if Suckers are anything, they're suspicious and paranoid. One of their own has been killed by a weird disease. Vampires don't get sick – so that's going to make them jumpy at the very least. My dad's been killed and I've been attacked – that makes me exactly the sort of person who would get nosy, maybe put two and two together. And that's why I want to keep you out of this.'

'That's very noble of you but ...'

'I'm serious, Caro. I've realised I have to take this seriously, and the more we dig into this the more we're going to put ourselves in danger. So I don't want you getting into all this Vampire Regent and stuff with the Faces. I have to do it, you don't.'

'But you can't do everything on your own.'

'Don't worry, I've got a job for you. Dig into the governors of Ravenwood.'

'I've tried that, but ...'

'Well try harder! Someone must have put their name to something. Remember when we broke into Sheldon's office? I found an invoice for some weird windows they'd put into the science block. That must have been expensive, someone will have had to sign that off. And something else – I want to know why the vamps don't come out in photos.'

Caro grinned.

'Okay boss, you're in charge,' she said.

April nodded. For the first time in ages, she felt as if she was in control of what was happening.

'Yes I am,' she said. 'And I'm not going to forget it.'

Chapter Seven

For once, Mr Gill wasn't asleep. Usually April startled him out of a doze when she pushed through the door of Griffin's bookshop, making his little bell jangle. The strange, dusty little store didn't attract many customers and April got the impression Mr Gill preferred to be left alone with his books and memories, all stacked up in teetering piles. Of course, she didn't think he'd just have a copy of the *Albus Libre* sitting on his desk, but it was a good place to start. But today, Mr Gill was different. For a start, he was wearing a clean tie with pink spots.

'My dear girl!' said the shopkeeper as April walked in, 'Splendid to see you. How have you been keeping?'

'I've been a little under the weather, to be honest,' said April.

'Of course, of course, I had heard. A terrible business.' He moved a pile of brochures from a stool. 'Sit down, please, and tell me to what I owe this happy visit.'

April saw that the brochures were for holidays and that there were stacks of old travel books piled on his desk.

'Are you going somewhere?' she asked.

'Ah, well that's the question. Where to go when the world is your oyster?'

April laughed.

'You seem, well, quite upbeat?'

'I am, I am. And I have you to thank for that, my dear.'

'Me? Why?'

'Because you reminded me of what is important in life. I have been sitting here surrounded by these dusty old books,

84

cataloguing, listing, alphabetising, never looking out of the window. And then in you come and say one magic word. Well, no, you didn't exactly say the word, but you let it pop into my head.'

'And what was the word?'

'Marjorie,' he said wistfully.

'The school librarian?'

'The very same. She had somehow managed to slip out of my life, but I'm delighted that we are now courting.'

'That's wonderful,' said April. 'Are you whisking her away for a mini-break?'

'I have no idea what a mini-break is, but yes I was hoping to rekindle the flame of our passion on some sunny boulevard. And it's permanent – I'm selling up this one-man gaol. One of those coffee chains you young people seem so fond of has made me a very generous offer.'

April felt sick. Yet another adult walking out of her life. One of the few people she felt would never change was doing exactly that. Why can't anyone stand still for two seconds? she thought. Her face must have betrayed her disappointment.

'Don't take it so hard, dear girl, I had no idea these dusty tomes were so important to you.'

April shook her head.

'I'm sorry, I'm being selfish. It's great that you're getting out there and finding happiness, genuinely, that's brilliant. I just hope you have more luck with love than I'm having.'

Mr Gill picked up his tartan flask and poured April a cup of tea.

'Yes, I can see that something is troubling you. Is it an affair of the heart?'

April found her eyes were filling with tears.

'Sorry,' she said, taking the tissue Mr Gill offered. 'It's just that someone I care about is in a great deal of danger.'

'And how can I help?'

'I need to find a book. A rare book. It's called the *Albus Libre*.'

Mr Gill immediately looked troubled.

'Are you sure? Are you sure that's the title of the book you're looking for?'

'Yes. Why?'

'Well, it's a very rare tome indeed. There are many who think it's just a myth, one of those books people wish existed, but never did.'

April blew her nose.

'But it *has* to exist, Mr Gill. It's my only hope.'

'It's none of my business of course, but why would you want such a thing? The *Albus Libre* is a book of the occult.'

'I know, but it's very important I find it.'

'I can see that, my dear. But I'm not sure I can help you. It's one of those books which have become legendary. No one has ever seen a copy, but there are always rumours. A dealer I once worked with in Munich has a client who claims to have met someone with a copy in their private collection. But I've never met anyone who has seen it themselves. All we know is that it is wrong.'

'Wrong? That's a curious thing to say about a book.'

'Not wrong as in "not right", but as in dangerous. Evil, perhaps.'

'Because of the spells?'

Mr Gill sipped his tea and sat back.

'Oh, I doubt that any of them work, my dear. There are plenty of old spell-books on the market, many of them genuinely very old, but most of them are fragments of something. Like someone's trying to clutch at the last rays of sunshine and trap them between parchment leaves. No, I'm not worried by the spells. It's the sort of person they attract that concerns me.'

'So you have no idea where I'd find a copy?'

'Turin, perhaps? Or Jordan. They have quite a brisk trade in the exotic out there.'

April gaped at him.

'Jordan in the Middle East?'

'Quite so. In fact …' He rummaged through his pile of brochures and pulled one out, entitled 'The Seven Wonders

Tour'. 'See?' he said, pointing at photos inside. 'They do trips to Luxor, Petra and the site of Babylon.'

'But I can't go there,' said April in despair. 'I need the book right away.'

Mr Gill looked at her sympathetically.

'I'd love to help you, but it's dangerous to venture down that path.'

'You think I might do some bad magic?'

'No, I think it's nonsense myself. But the people who do believe in it, they are dangerous. And I think they are on the rise.'

'What?'

'Oh, I may be an old man, but I've been here long enough to see this happen before. I heard what happened to you. And your father, of course. It's a pattern, I'm afraid. I don't think your father will be the last.'

'But we can't just let it happen, Mr Gill.'

Mr Gill put down his tea and nodded thoughtfully. 'Quite so, quite so.'

'So what can I do?'

Mr Gill stood up and turned April to look out of the window. From where they stood, they could see the steeple of St Michael's, the fox weather vane just visible, turning lazily in the wind.

'When darkness falls,' he said, 'look to the light, my dear.'

April thanked Mr Gill and left him leafing through a book of European canal maps. She had wanted the old man to give her more answers, but she knew she'd have to dig deeper than that. So why not follow his hint and try at the church? St Michael's overlooked the cemetery after all – and whether it was coincidence or not, the cemetery had been the centre of everything bad which had happened in the village. Certainly easier to get to than the Middle East, anyway. She was walking along South Grove, staring up at the black spire, when she turned and saw another police car parked across the road from her house.

Oh God, not again, she thought. *Don't let it be more bad news.* She ran across the square and burst through the front door to find DI Reece sitting in the front room, perched awkwardly on the edge of his chair, a cup and saucer held in both hands. The way Silvia was glaring at him, April knew Reece hadn't had a comfortable wait.

'What's up?' said April eagerly. 'Is there news about Dad's case?'

'No,' said Silvia with undisguised anger. 'We've just been discussing the Inspector's so-called detective work. It seems he has run out of ideas.'

'Now that's not what I said, Mrs Dunne,' said Reece. 'I said our current leads have failed to return the results we would have liked. That doesn't mean we have given up on the case by any means ...'

Silvia narrowed her eyes. 'It seems to me, Inspector ...' she began, but April cut her off.

'What is it, Mr Reece? Have you found Marcus?'

'No, I'm afraid not,' said DI Reece, glancing nervously at April's mother, clearly expecting another outburst.

'Don't give him a hard time, Mum,' said April. 'He's doing his best.'

'Well his best isn't good enough! My husband has been killed and my daughter attacked, forgive me if I expect the police to come up with a little more than "we don't know".'

'I can understand your frustrations, Mrs Dunne ...'

'Can you? Can you really? Have you ever had to bury a loved one?'

Reece paused, looking at her.

'Yes, I have.'

'Well, then I'm sure you appreciate my need to find answers. Like: what exactly are the police doing to prevent any further attacks on this family?'

'The house is still being watched, of course.'

'That silly little police car parked in the square? You really think that's going to stop this maniac?'

'Mum! Please!'

'Well excuse me for feeling protective of my only daughter...'

'Please! At least until the inspector has told me why he's here.'

'Well actually it's a missing persons case. I wouldn't usually be given this, but considering the circumstances, it's been brought to my attention.'

April looked from Reece to her mother.

'Who's missing?'

'Your little friend Layla, darling,' said Silvia. 'She's disappeared.'

Chapter Eight

Layla had disappeared without trace. She had left the party at Davina's house and had not been seen since. It was as if the moment she stepped onto the street, she had been swallowed up by the city.

'According to her mother, Layla went to the party promising to be home by ten,' said DI Reece. 'But she never made it. Layla's seventeen and by all accounts is pretty self-sufficient. Usually we wait forty-eight hours before we raise the alarm, but given everything that's been going on in the area, we're taking this seriously.'

Reece explained that Davina had waved Layla off at about nine-thirty, just after April had left, and according to Davina she'd insisted on walking home. It was only a five-minute walk to her house, but when she hadn't returned by eleven, her mother had called Davina, who had raised the alarm.

'Why wait forty-eight hours, Inspector? These are children we're talking about here. Anything could happen in that time,' said April's mother, still clearly spoiling for a fight.

Reece shrugged wearily. 'It's the twenty-first century, Mrs Dunne. In most of these cases, the missing person has gone to an all-night party without mentioning it, met up with a new boyfriend or is just sleeping off too much drink at a friend's house. Kids these days get themselves into more trouble than they used to, but I'm afraid we find they're no more likely to confide in their parents.'

April saw her mother bristle at the implication, but she knew the policeman was correct. April reckoned she had managed to get herself into more trouble than any teenager in history and she still had no intention of telling her mother about it. She could hardly just drop it into conversation: 'Mum, I've discovered a nest of bloodthirsty vampires at my school and I suspect they may be behind Dad's murder. Oh, I should have mentioned that I have some sort of super powers to kill them.' She'd land in the local loony bin so fast her feet wouldn't touch the ground.

DI Reece turned to April.

'Do you know anything about this, April? Does Layla have a boyfriend she might have gone to stay with?'

April shook her head.

'No, as far as I know she was still cut up about Milo.'

'That's the boy who died?' said Silvia. 'She was involved with him?'

Reece nodded. 'Another of the reasons we're concerned. She might well have been feeling emotional last night – I understand the boy fell ill at a similar party a few months ago.'

April felt her stomach turn over. *He fell ill because of me, because I poisoned him with my kiss*, she thought.

The detective's sharp eyes caught the change in April's expression.

'What is it, April? Do you know something about it?'

'No, not really. Layla did seem a little bit upset at school yesterday, but she seemed back to her old self at the party. I think she might have been drinking though …'

'Are you sure that's all? This is important, April. You won't be getting Layla into any trouble if that's what you're worrying about. All we want to do is make sure she's safe.'

'I didn't – I don't – really know Layla that well.'

'Really?' said Reece, raising one eyebrow. 'Your teacher said she found you two talking yesterday …' He flipped open his notebook and read a line. '… "deep in conversation" was how she put it.'

'Well, if you must know we were just talking about losing people,' said April, blushing at the lie. 'You know, my dad's just died and she had Milo pass away …'

Reece looked at her sceptically.

'That doesn't sound like someone you barely knew.'

'I suppose we had a few things in common, but I wouldn't have called her a close friend.'

'And was one of these things in common this boy Milo?' asked Reece.

'What are you implying?' snapped April. 'I didn't have anything to do with Milo.'

'April, I'm just trying to get a handle on Layla's state of mind.'

April shook her head.

'I told you, we talked about people around us dying. That does seem to be happening a lot, despite all the stuff the police keep saying about how safe we all are.'

Reece didn't rise to the bait. 'We are sympathetic to your loss, April. If you need to talk about it, we can arrange for a counsellor if you'd like?'

'Oh yes, and what would I say?' said April angrily, 'Oh, my dad had his throat torn out by some mad psycho and bled to death in my arms? Are they going to have similar stories to share?'

Silvia cleared her throat.

'I think what April's saying is that she'd rather talk to me about it.'

'No I'm not, Mum!' said April. 'How could I talk to you about it? You weren't here, were you?'

'I can't help that I wasn't here, darling,' said Silvia, looking shocked.

'But you're never here, are you? You've always got something better to do, you don't want to hear about my problems . . .' she looked over at DI Reece and trailed off. 'Sorry, Mr Reece, you came here to talk about Layla, didn't you?'

Reece nodded and stood up.

'Don't worry, if anything occurs to you, you've got my number. I know you appreciate how concerned we are about Layla.'

April walked out with Reece. In the hallway, she stopped.

'Do you really think Layla going missing has anything to do

with my dad and all the other stuff?' she asked quietly.

Reece looked at her for a long moment. 'If I was saying this to anyone else, April,' he said, 'I'd give you the usual police line of "don't worry, I'm sure she'll turn up", but I'm really not convinced. We've been to her house. It doesn't look as though she has taken anything. No bag or clothes are missing. She didn't plan to disappear, that's for sure. And no one has heard from her. In today's world, that's the most worrying thing. A seventeen-year-old girl who hasn't so much as texted a friend in almost twenty-four hours? That's a worry.'

April opened the front door for the detective.

'Much as I hate to admit it, April, I think your mother's right about the car.' He nodded towards the police car parked in the square. 'Whoever or whatever we're dealing with here is not going to let that stop him.'

April nodded solemnly. 'I'll be careful.'

He smiled. 'You see that you do.'

'Oh and Mr Reece? Why did you say "If it was anyone else"? Why did you tell me the truth about this?'

The smile faded from Reece's face.

'Partly because you lost your dad and that business with Marcus Brent – you understand the stakes, but also …'

'But what?'

'Because I think you know more about what's going on here than you're telling me.'

'Honestly, I don't …'

Reece held up a hand to stifle her protests.

'That's fine, April, I know you must have your reasons. But twenty years in this job has taught me one thing: secrets are like wounds. The longer you ignore them, hide them away and pretend they're not bothering you, the longer they have to fester. Eventually, they make you ill. You can't keep secrets for ever, April.'

Chapter Nine

St Michael's was taller than she remembered. It sat overlooking the cemetery like a disapproving aunt. There was always something about churches that made her think of Miss Batty, her old headmistress in Edinburgh, a pinched-faced old harridan who looked down her nose at you, whether you were misbehaving or not. *Houses of worship should be just that*, thought April, *somewhere you come to celebrate and rejoice.* But big churches like this always made her feel as if she had done something wrong. *Or maybe I've got something to confess*, she thought to herself. Her conversation with DI Reece had unsettled her. Without saying as much, he seemed to be implying something similar to Miss Holden, earlier that day. That unless April pulled her finger out and did something, more people were going to die. People she cared about. *People I love*, she thought with a blush as she pushed open the door and saw the aisle ahead of her. God, April, what are you doing thinking about marriage at a time like this? She cast her eyes upwards, nervous that God might be looking down, tutting and shaking his head. *What? What have I done? I only want to love him, be with him*, she thought. *I thought you were all about love.*

April sat down on the edge of a pew, not entirely sure what she was doing there and feeling small and insignificant. Everyone seemed to be telling her she was super important, but April certainly didn't feel that way. She thought about Layla, hoping she was okay. That was the other thing about being in church: it made you want the best for people – at least while you were there.

Looking up, her eyes were drawn to the stained-glass window. Scenes from the Bible, Jesus feeding the five thousand, Jesus healing the sick. But there was one detail that didn't quite fit. A fox resting at Jesus' feet. It had red eyes and one foot rested on a sword. What the hell was that all about? Admittedly April hadn't spent a huge amount of time studying the Bible – in fact she and Fiona had pretty much used their RE lessons as a free period in which to pass notes back and forth, giggling – but she didn't remember there being any foxes in the New Testament. Wasn't it all set in, like, Israel and Egypt? She wasn't sure, but she didn't think they had foxes out there.

She walked down towards the altar, remembering how she had felt seeing her dad's coffin right there, covered with flowers. It was still raw and she had to force herself not to start crying.

Under her feet she saw a carved slab reading, 'Beneath this stone lies the body of Samuel Taylor Coleridge', followed by a strange verse:

Stop, Christian Passer-by! – Stop, child of God,
And read with gentle breast. Beneath this sod
A poet lies, or that which once seem'd he.
O, lift one thought in prayer for S.T.C.;
That he who many a year with toil of breath
Found death in life, may here find life in death!
Mercy for praise – to be forgiven for fame
He asked, and hoped, through Christ. Do thou the same!

Coleridge? Hadn't he been mentioned in English? What's he doing buried in the middle of the floor? The squeak of a rubber sole on the stone floor made April look up. The vicar, Mr Gordon, was approaching. He had red cheeks and young, kind eyes. He'd done a good job at her dad's funeral and she'd felt safe with him. She only hoped he could help her now.

'Our most distinguished resident,' said the vicar, nodding towards the plaque.

'Is Coleridge actually buried under here?' asked April.

'Yes, he is. But only for the last fifty years or so.'

April looked at him curiously.

'But wasn't he ancient? I mean, didn't he live in seventeen something?'

The vicar laughed.

'Yes, born 1772, died 1834. He was originally buried in the graveyard of the Old Chapel next to the boys' school, but there was some falling out with the trustees in the sixties and he was moved here.'

April pulled a face. 'I wouldn't like that. I mean, aren't you supposed to be allowed to rest in peace?'

The vicar nodded. 'I rather agree with you. When I'm gone, I want to stay wherever I'm put. It didn't do anything to help all the rumours about vampires in the area at the time, either.'

She looked at him, her eyes wide. Maybe Mr Gill had been right to point her in this direction after all,

'Vampires?'

He shook his head.

'A lot of silliness of course. Samuel Taylor Coleridge wrote the first vampire tale, a poem called *Cristabel* about a young woman who encounters, or perhaps is a vampire. So obviously when the author rose from the grave, so to speak, some people's imaginations ran away with them.'

'So that must have been the same time there were all those rumours about the cemetery?'

The vicar's smile dimmed slightly.

'Ah, well that was something different. St Michael's may back onto the cemetery, but it isn't ours. As you are aware, we do hold services for the departed souls who are to be interred there, but only rarely.'

'Why's that?'

The vicar chuckled, but there was an edge to his laugh, as if it was a question he didn't want to answer.

'Well, the cemetery has its own chapel of course, and more to the point, very few people are buried there nowadays.'

'But surely …'

'My, you are inquisitive, aren't you?' he said, walking to the entrance and closing the door. 'I shouldn't be surprised, knowing your father.'

'How did you know my dad?'

He gestured back towards the altar. 'Do you have time for a cup of tea? One of the ladies from the choir will insist on making me these enormous cakes and' – he patted his belly – 'I really could do with a little help.'

He led her to the left, down the line of pews and through a small door to one side of the aisle, then along a corridor into what April assumed was the rectory.

'Have a seat,' said the vicar, showing her into a comfortable sitting room with chintzy sofas and polished oak furniture as he went off to prepare the tea. The walls were lined with glass-fronted cupboards, most of which were stuffed with books, and April wasted no time in looking at them. They all seemed quite old, but they were mostly maps and novels, nothing like what she was looking for. She turned her attention to the other most striking aspect of the décor: a number of glass cases containing stuffed animals. There was a weasel, two pigeons and a coiled snake. And in pride of place on the sideboard was a fox with a slightly wonky eye. April went over to examine it.

'Are these yours?' she asked as the vicar came back in carrying a tray.

'Well, they're not to my taste, but the rooms came furnished and I didn't have the heart to throw them out. So they stayed and I've come to rather like having them around.'

'What's the deal with the foxes anyway?' April asked. 'They seem to be a theme in the church, what with the weathervane on the spire and the fox in the window.'

'Oh, it's one of those visual jokes the artist put in. You know how the people who built cathedrals used to base the gargoyles on real people? People often ask me about it. The fox represents the hunter, which is why his foot is on the sword.'

'Someone once told me foxes represent witches.'

'Oh no, not at all,' said the vicar, waving a hand to dismiss the idea. 'I think people like to read too much into these things. There are all sorts of local superstitions based on the idea that there is some ancient evil buried under the hill here and, because they live underground, that foxes must somehow be touched by it.'

April held her breath. That was one of her father's ideas: that there was some sort of disease which had come from underground and was being spread the same way.

'There's evil underground?' she said.

'Merely local legend, my dear. Given that Highgate is dominated by a huge cemetery, it's only natural people would dream up such fantasies from time to time.'

'Seems a little hard on the poor foxes.'

'Indeed. Anyway, it's likely much more straightforward: the artist probably just saw a lot of foxes in the area at the time – this was almost two hundred years ago, remember, when this part of London was out in the country.'

He turned to the tray of tea things and began cutting into a huge sponge cake, jam and cream oozing from the sides.

'Anyway, why don't you tell me how I can help?'

How *could* he help? Mr Gill had suggested a visit, but now she suspected he was trying to get her to seek religious advice, which wasn't exactly what she'd been hoping for. Not that she didn't believe in God, well not exactly. She was certainly starting to believe in the devil – how could she not, after all she had seen? But what could the vicar tell her that might help her find the White Book? The books in his cupboards weren't that old.

'I wondered how you knew my father?' she finally asked. 'You said you were old friends, but we'd only been in Highgate a few weeks.'

The vicar smiled indulgently and poured the tea.

'Hard for you to imagine, I know, but I wasn't always the vicar here. I met your dad at university.'

'Really? Wow,' said April, wondering if her dad had really looked as old as the vicar did. As if reading her thoughts, the vicar laughed.

'No need to be so coy – yes, I am older than him. I was working there on my doctorate and spending some time as the chaplain of his college. That's like a university in-house vicar, if you like. But as you can imagine, excitable young teenagers don't have much interest in going to church.'

'But my dad wasn't a church-goer, was he?'

He paused.

'Not really. But young people often have a crisis when they're away from home for the first time. Nowadays, I'm sure they have counsellors to turn to, but back then it was the chaplain or nothing if you got yourself into a pickle.'

'What sort of pickle?'

'Ah. There is a certain confidentiality to these conversations. But let's just say he had a crisis of faith.'

'Faith? I didn't think he was religious.'

'Not in such a straightforward way, no. But you've seen the books he wrote – your father was a man who wanted to believe in things, who was looking for answers. Who was always hoping to prove the myths true. When we first met, he was … well, he wasn't sure which side to choose.'

April was feeling more confused than she had when she came in.

'You mean my mum? I know my granddad didn't approve of him. I always got the feeling they only got married to annoy Gramps.'

The vicar shook his head, frowning. 'Oh no, I can assure you there was much more to it than that. Your parents were, and remained, very much in love.'

April shrugged.

'It didn't feel that way at the end. They were always arguing.'

'Well I can't comment on that. Adults always seem to find a way of buggering things up for themselves, don't they?'

April laughed. She liked Mr Gordon. Most adults wouldn't speak to a teenager so frankly.

'So when did you last see my dad? Before he died.'

Mr Gordon glanced at the stuffed fox, seeming to gather his thoughts before he spoke.

'It was about a week before he died. He came to see me just after that poor girl was found in the cemetery. It was partly a social call as you'd just arrived in the village, but he also had his journalist's hat on too. Wanted to know what I knew, especially as Isabelle ...'

April leant forward. 'You knew her?'

'Oh yes, she was in the choir as a younger girl, and then in the girl guides in the village and so on. Always used to say hello. Until that funny business with the book.'

'The book?'

'All very curious. She had stopped coming to church, she'd fallen in with quite a bad crowd, I think. Some sort of nastiness involving drugs of some kind, and a few people died. After that, she moved away. University in Central London, I think. Anyway, out of the blue, she came to see me, asking about some book or other she was looking for. We have quite a collection of books here, as you can see. I'm no expert though, they were all here when I arrived. I'm rather afraid I prefer John Grisham myself.'

'What was it? What was the book, I mean?'

He shook his head. 'Some sort of mythology or magical thing, as I recall. I felt a bit uncomfortable talking to her about it, to be honest.'

'Why? Do you think she was a witch?'

The vicar laughed.

'No, my dear. I was concerned for her. As I said, she had fallen in with the wrong crowd and I was worried she was turning down a rather dark road. It seems I was right. It broke my heart to hear that she had been murdered, and so close by, too.'

April nodded. She wasn't about to tell him she had been there and had almost stumbled over Isabelle's body.

'Well, thanks for the tea and cake,' she said, getting up. 'It was nice to talk too.'

The vicar put a hand on her knee.

'I think I've disappointed you, April,' he said. 'Perhaps if you told me what you wanted to find out?'

April hesitated for a second. Could she trust him? He was a friend of her father's and a vicar to boot. But she could hardly lay the whole vampires, Fury, Dragon's Breath thing on him, could she?

'I was just hoping I might find out what he was investigating before his death,' she said, feeling bad for lying inside a church, 'If I can work that out, maybe I can find out why he was killed.'

'But surely the police ...'

'I know, I should leave it to them, but the police don't seem to be getting anywhere and I feel I'll go mad if I can't make some sense out of it.'

The vicar looked thoughtful for a moment, then crossed to the sideboard, rummaging in a drawer underneath the fox.

'I can see you're going to pursue this, so perhaps this might be some help.'

He handed her a small business card.

Redfearne's Books
Specialists in the Occult and Witchcraft,
12 Everard Street, Covent Garden

'Isabelle gave this to me in case I needed to contact her. I think she was working here. She may even have found what she was looking for. But please April, be careful?'

'I will,' said April, holding the card tightly, as if her – and Gabriel's – life depended on it. 'I will, you can count on that.'

Chapter Ten

Gabriel was waiting for her outside the church. He was leaning against the wall, his hands thrust into his pockets and his collar turned up against the cold. As April walked over, she could see his skin was pale and waxy and he seemed to be shivering. She longed to run to him, throw her arms around him and kiss the warmth back into him. To check, after his collapse last night, that he was okay. But she reminded herself of his instructions. *People might be watching.*

'Are you waiting for me?' she asked casually.

'We need to talk.'

'Yes, we do,' said April in a low voice. 'I think I've got a real lead on the *Albus Libre* ...'

'Not here,' snapped Gabriel, taking her arm and leading her down the hill.

April frowned, a little hurt and angry that he was being so short with her, plus she was concerned that he was blowing so hot and cold all the time – maybe it was something to do with the illness? She glanced at his face – he didn't look good, that was for sure. She had hoped that last night's dramatic collapse had been down to the fight, but seeing his grey pallor and the way he had started coughing, it was time to stop fooling herself: he really was sick.

'I was so worried about you at the party,' she said. 'You haven't been answering your phone – didn't you get my messages?'

Gabriel coughed again and shrugged. April balled her hands into fists, trying to control her irritation. She knew he was trying to maintain his facade of strength, but she was only trying to help him, couldn't he see that? Maybe he was still angry about the Ben thing – she couldn't blame him, really. Sighing, she tried to change the subject.

'Did you hear about Layla?' she asked. 'She's gone missing.' Gabriel nodded.

'I saw the police car. She'll be fine.'

'What makes you so sure?'

'I saw her with half a dozen different guys last night, and I'm pretty sure she'll be with one of them. My guess is she's been looking for someone to fill the hole Milo left in her life.'

'But she told me someone was going to kill her, Gabriel! Maybe she wasn't looking for a boyfriend, just someone to protect her.'

He shrugged again. God, he was impossible sometimes.

They had reached the Ponds now and Gabriel led them to a bench. It was too cold to do much more than perch on the edge, hands in pockets.

'So what did you want to talk about?' asked April nervously, looking up at him. Was he going to break up with her properly now? After all, she had been about to kiss another boy when he caught them yesterday – and he did seem unusually grumpy.

'I saw where you went this morning.'

'To school?'

'No, April,' he said impatiently, 'earlier.'

Her eyes widened as the penny dropped. He had followed her to Miss Holden's. Had he been trailing her all along? Had those scary figures she'd been spotting in the corner of her eye been Gabriel?

'You've been following me?'

'Of course. I have to protect you, keep you safe ...'

'For how long?'

'Ever since you got out of hospital, I just wanted ...'

'You just wanted what?' she gasped. 'I thought I was losing my *mind*, Gabriel! I thought I had another vampire stalker out there trying to kill me, when it was you all along? Jesus! You won't even answer my phone calls, but you're creeping me out by stalking me every night?'

'You don't understand: the vampires will stop at nothing.'

'Yes, I know, Gabriel! But why does everything have to be so bloody secret with you? If you could have just told me, I might not have spent the last week thinking I was about to be killed – and I might not have been scared off from visiting my dad! Why can't you just tell me these things?'

April didn't know why she was so angry with him. Maybe it was the way he was treating her like a child, like someone who couldn't be trusted with information. Or maybe it was the way he kept pushing her away. Last night he had keeled over in front of her and she was desperate to wrap herself in his arms, promise him she was finding the cure, and be told that it was going to be all right. Instead he'd dragged her out in the cold to lecture her. God, he really was Victorian, wasn't he?

'So what's wrong with my visiting Miss Holden, anyway?'

'She's a Guardian, April. She's sworn to destroy all vampires. That includes me. Can't you see that I might find that a little bit worrying? Why do you have to go to her for help?'

'Because *you* won't help me!' she cried. 'I was asking her about the *Albus Libre* – not that she was any use – but it's not like I've had any help or enthusiasm for finding it from you.'

'And have you wondered why she really wants to get hold of it?' said Gabriel.

'I don't care, Gabriel! All I care about is getting you healthy again. And do I need to remind you that it was Miss Holden who told us about the Dragon's Breath in the first place? She's risked the wrath of the other Guardians to help us, and she's prepared to help me save your life. Without her, you'd be on death row.'

'And she did that out of the goodness of her heart? You don't think she and her council might have some ulterior motive?'

'Like what?'

'They want you to trust them, they want you to see them as the good guys. "Here, take this and you can save your boyfriend." It's a con, April, and I'm their bait. They're trying to recruit you just as much as the Faces are.'

'So what are you trying to tell me? That the Guardians aren't good guys?'

'I don't think there's anything I can tell you – you seem to have it all worked out already.'

'Well I have to, don't I?' she shouted, her anger rising again. 'Because the one person who knows what's going on won't tell me.'

'The Guardians aren't as they seem. They're not all like Miss Holden. That's all you need to know.'

'All I *need to know*?' she repeated incredulously. 'Who the hell do you think you are? My life is in danger, I'm risking everything to save you, and you're treating me like a child.'

'So what do you want to know, April?'

'Well how about telling me exactly who I'm up against. Who at Ravenwood is a vampire? It's information like that which might just save me from getting eaten alive.'

'Yes, and it might also get you killed. If I give you a list of vamps at school, you *will* behave differently towards them and maybe even give yourself away. It's more important – and useful – if you behave as if you have no idea they even exist.'

April was about to object, but she could see the logic of it. If Gabriel said 'Mrs Bagley is a killer, she's murdered five people,' the next time the school secretary called her name she might jump in the air. Even so, it was still deeply irritating to have Gabriel pick and choose what she was allowed to know. She flinched as rain began to fall on them, fat droplets dimpling the pond's surface.

'All right then,' she said, crossing her arms against the cold. 'Tell me about Isabelle. The vicar said she was conducting her own investigation. What do you know about that?'

'Isabelle?'

'Yes, Isabelle. Every time I ask you about her, you give me a different story. You were there the night she died – tell me what happened.'

Gabriel stared out at the rain.

'I don't know,' he said quietly.

'You don't know? What do you mean you "don't know"? I'm asking you for honesty and that's what I get?'

'That is honesty, April!' he snapped, suddenly angry. 'If you're determined to ask about these things, you might get answers you don't want to hear. There are times when I'm … not myself, when I'm not in control. It's like I'm a character in a story I'm not a part of. The darkness takes over and things happen, bad things.'

She looked at him, searching his face.

'What sort of bad things? Are you saying you had something to do with Isabelle's—' April didn't get to finish her sentence as suddenly Gabriel doubled over, hugging his stomach, pain etched on his face. She reached out for him, her arm around his shoulders. *Oh Christ, not now, give me more time, please.*

'What is it?' she said. 'Gabriel, what's wrong?'

'I'm sorry,' he gasped. 'I love you so much, but I can't protect you. You're everything to me and I'm too weak. You're right, I should do more and I know I'm letting you down. But you can't imagine how this feels to me.'

She put a hand on his back, stroking, soothing.

'Tell me. Make me understand.'

'It's like I've been … given a gift,' he said slowly. 'The gift of death.'

April gaped at him, her mind stunned for a moment.

'The gift of death?' she said, 'the *gift* of death?'

She jumped to her feet, unable to believe her ears.

'How dare you? How *dare* you!' She could feel her concern and frustration becoming anger, the rage rising and getting the better of her again, exactly as it had when she had faced up to Benjamin. It was like red mist coming over her eyes.

'My father is dead and I would do anything, *anything*, to bring him back. His life was precious, he didn't want to leave us. And you're telling me you're happy to let it all slip away. You selfish bastard!'

'April, you don't understand what I'm going through,' he said, his face shiny with rain – or were those tears? April was too angry to care, her own tears of frustration rolling down her cheeks.

'Screw you! What about *me*? What about anyone who cares for you? We're the ones left behind in pain, we live in hell. If you die, I'll spend every moment wondering if there was something more I could have done, if I should have been quicker or smarter or fought harder. Is that what you want to condemn me to? Do I mean that little to you?'

'This isn't about you.'

'Oh grow up! You're a hundred bloody years old and that's the best you can come up with?'

She pulled her wet hair back to show him her birthmark.

'You see this? You think I want this, you think I like having this curse? And having you look at me like I have "poison" tattooed on my forehead? I hate it. It's keeping us apart; it's my death sentence as much as it's yours if anyone else finds out. But I'm not going to lie down and die, I'm going to *fight*.'

'April—' he said, reaching out a hand towards her, but she stepped away.

'*Of course* this is about me, you selfish bastard! You don't exist in isolation, I'm connected to you. I *won't* live without you.'

She stared at him for a moment, then screamed at the sky, curling her hands into claws.

'God! Men!' she yelled, then turned and stormed off.

'April!' he called, running after her, still holding onto his stomach.

'No, forget it, Gabriel. You're so wrapped up in your own feelings, you can't even consider mine. Go on then, crawl away and die if that's what you want. I've got surviving of my own to do.'

'But I'm experiencing things I'd never imagined,' he said. 'Hot, cold, pain, discomfort. It's like I can see the world in colour again.'

She stopped and turned, about to yell at him again, until she saw the pain and despair on his face and relented.

'Look, I'm sorry,' she said more softly. 'I do think that's

great, but I want it to be *permanent*, Gabe. I want you to feel like that every day ... but to do it we need to make you a vampire again and then find the Regent.'

Gabriel hesitated for a moment.

'I'm not even sure there is a Regent,' he said, despair in his voice.

'Don't you want to live?' she said, losing her patience again. 'Don't you want to be with me? I thought you loved me.'

'I do, April, and I want to be with you so badly. But I'm so tired. I can't go back to that existence. You don't know what it's like; the endless urge, the darkness sucking you down like quicksand. The horror of staring at death, wanting to be part of it. Wanting to be swallowed by the blackness.'

April shook her head.

'I don't understand what you're saying.'

He glanced at her, his eyes hollow and flat.

'Isabelle ...' he croaked. 'You asked about Isabelle. You wanted to know what really happened? I killed her.'

April's stomach clenched. 'You ... killed her?'

Gabriel hung his head. 'I stood there and I let her die. She was injured, wounded when I found her, crying, begging for life. I knew she was in danger, I could feel ... whatever was out there in the dark, just waiting to finish her. And I wanted ... '

'You wanted what?'

'I wanted to kill her myself!' shouted Gabriel, his face creased in pain. 'I wanted to drink her blood, to tear her apart. Every fibre of my being was willing me to do it, to become that animal, to be *possessed* by the darkness. It was all I could do to fight it.'

'But you rescued me, you got me away.'

He nodded sadly.

'Yes, I couldn't let whoever – *what*ever – it was take you too. But I should have saved Isabelle.'

April put her arms around his neck. 'You can't save everyone, Gabriel. But you can fight back and you can resist – you proved that by pulling me away. Now you need to *keep* fighting, you need to be strong for me ... you need to stay alive. *Stay alive for me, Gabriel.*'

Finally she broke down, sobbing into his shoulder 'I can't have someone else die on me. I didn't think I'd be able to stand my dad leaving me, but if *you* died, what would I do then? You can't leave me, please.'

Gabriel wrapped her in his arms and held her tight.

'All right,' he whispered fiercely. 'All right, my love: for you. I'll do it for you.'

Chapter Eleven

April couldn't believe she hadn't seen the shop before. Now she stood peering in the window, it seemed so obvious. Redfearne's bookshop was such a contrast to all the trinket shops and sandwich bars and fancy boutiques that populated this touristy end of Covent Garden. It was like a lone sapling growing in a flower bed. Once you knew it was there it stood out, but otherwise somehow your eye managed to skip over it.

The frontage was a dark stone and the door was painted purple. The window was crowded with books, candles, decks of cards and all sorts of gothic paraphernalia. Honestly, April was now feeling a little reluctant to find the *Albus Libre* after everything Gabriel had said. Plus she never felt confident going into little shops like that. There was nowhere to hide when someone said, 'Can I help you?' or 'Are you looking for something in particular?'

What was she going to say? 'I'm looking for a powerful spell book, which may only exist in legend'? Come to think of it, they probably had that sort of request every day.

She took a deep breath. *It's now or never. Do you want to save Gabriel or not?* For a moment, she wasn't entirely sure. Before his terrible confession about Isabelle, April hadn't really understood the hell Gabriel was going through. All he wanted was to be human again, to live a normal life, to love and marry and have kids: all the mundane things we take for granted. But instead he had spent a hundred years trapped in a cage, forced to do and see terrible things, racked with guilt, struggling with his desires on a daily basis – and then along came April, desperate to push him back into that horrible prison. Maybe the kindest thing was to let him go. But she couldn't, not while there was hope. Yes, he would become a vampire again, but if they could just find the Regent and – *one thing at a time*, she reminded herself. *One thing at a time.*

She heard chimes as she pushed open the thickly-painted door. *Of course*, she thought. *Of course they'd have chimes.*

Inside, the shop had a low ceiling and a velvet sofa in the centre of the room, but apart from that it looked like any other small independent bookshop. *What were you expecting? Skulls hanging from the roof?* A pretty woman behind the counter looked up from a book and smiled, but didn't hassle her, so April walked among the shelves, trying to look natural. There were lots of surprisingly modern books on ghosts and tarot reading and 'paranormal romance'. April allowed herself a smile. *Pity my love story isn't working out the way it does in the books.* There was even a chalkboard by the till advertising coffee and cake; it was more like an internet café than a scary witches' coven. April suddenly realised that this would be exactly the kind of shop which stocked her father's books. She walked around to the section marked 'Conspiracy' and sure enough, there was the whole collection: William Dunne's name running down the spines. She reached up and pulled out *Beneath the Dark Waves*, her dad's book about the Loch Ness monster, realising with a flutter that it was the book she had discussed with Gabriel the morning he had told her about the birthmark behind her ear, the one which proved she was a Fury. April heard footsteps and quickly put the book back, turning around and picking up a book about dreams. She didn't want to get into discussing her dad with the shop-keeper.

'That's a pretty good one if you're looking for the meanings of dreams,' said the woman as she approached. 'In fact, I consulted it myself the other day. I had the strangest dream about Robert Pattinson.'

'I think I've had that dream too,' said April.

The woman laughed.

'Probably not quite the same,' she said. 'In mine he was running a carousel at the fairground, but wouldn't let me on the ride.' She nodded towards the book, 'Apparently it means I'm scared of rejection.'

'Ah, I see,' muttered April, not sure if the woman wanted a chat or was just being helpful. This was exactly why she avoided shops like this. You never had these problems in Asda.

'I haven't seen you in here before,' said the woman.

'No, my first visit. Do I stand out?'

The woman rolled her eyes. 'As you might imagine, we have a lot of regular customers. Some very interesting individuals.' She dropped her voice to a conspiratorial whisper. 'So it's always nice to see a human being in here. I'm Jessica, by the way. I run the shop.'

'I'm April. I'm not surprised you get some special customers given the kind of stuff you stock here.'

Jessica frowned and April quickly added, 'That came out wrong. I mean there's a lot of stuff on magic. I guess if you wanted more normal customers you'd have to stock golf books or something on knitting.'

'Yes, but what fun would that be?'

Just then something caught her eye and she crossed to a wall where there was a picture of someone she recognised. It was a photograph of Alix Graves.

'Ah, you've spotted our celebrity customer,' said the woman. 'Alix used to come in from time to time. I think he was just looking for titles for his songs.'

April looked at Jessica for a moment. She was pretty, maybe in her early twenties, her long brown hair pulled up into an untidy bun and a sheer cardigan over her dress – one of those boho-chic looks that seem completely thrown together but are really hard to pull off. She was cool and sexy and confident. April wished she could just sit in the corner of her own bookshop sipping lattes and reading. What a wonderful life to lead. No worries about vampires or destiny or anything. Just restock the books about fairies and keep the hobnobs coming. April felt a wave of jealousy.

'Is there anything you were particularly after?' asked Jessica. 'You don't …'

'What?'

'Well you don't look like my usual customers, put it that way. It takes all sorts, of course, but you don't look as if you've got a natural interest in the occult.'

April chuckled.

'No, you're right. But ... well, I've got a project.'

'I see. What's it about?'

April looked about her to check the shop was empty.

'Vampires.'

Jessica nodded. Clearly not an unusual choice of subject matter in this shop.

'What sort?'

'Are there different sorts?'

Jessica smiled ruefully. 'Step this way,' she said, leading April to the back of the shop. 'This is the vampire section.'

'Wow,' said April. There were books on Eastern European vampires, Hammer Horror vampires, vampires as representations of addiction or sexuality, psychic vampires, people who believe themselves to be vampires, genuine blood-drinking serial killers and endless fiction – almost all set in American small towns. April could only shake her head and laugh.

'I went to the library to look for books on vampires and I could only find about three.'

'That's why we've been here since 1892. There are always people who believe in these things.'

'Don't you?'

Jessica paused, holding April's gaze.

'I believe in things I've seen with my own eyes, which does rule out a lot of what I stock. In here there is inevitably a lot of nonsense and wishful thinking, but there is a lot of truth too. And it's that truth that keeps me running this shop, otherwise you're right, I might as well be selling knitting patterns.'

'Well, the truth is what I'm looking for,' said April. 'Actually I need to find a specific book, called the *Albus Libre*.'

Jessica's expression hardened.

'You've heard of it, then?'

'Of course I've heard of it,' said Jessica, all her initial

friendliness gone. 'Now if you're just going to waste my time, I think I'd better ask you to leave.' She pointed towards the door. 'It's that way.'

April frowned. 'I'm sorry, I didn't mean to upset you, but I assure you I'm serious about finding this book and this shop is the only lead I have.'

The woman shook her head in irritation, taking April's arm and leading her towards the exit.

'There are plenty of other bookshops in London, you know. Why don't you go and play your silly schoolgirl pranks on them?' She opened the door and gestured towards the street. April could see she had angered this woman but had no idea why.

'Please,' she said desperately, 'this isn't a joke. I don't know what I've said, but really, it's so important to me to find that book.'

The woman crossed her arms.

'Oh yes? And why is that?' she said sceptically.

'Because my friend is going to die if I don't.'

Jessica looked at April for a long moment, then closed the door again.

'All right,' she said. 'Tell me why you really want that book.'

April hesitated. She needed information badly and here was a woman who knew this world inside out, but she was confronted with the same dilemma which had dogged her search all along: could she trust her?

The truth was she had to start taking chances otherwise she was going to get nowhere. And more than anything she needed allies.

'I need the book because ... sorry, it all sounds insane.'

Jessica gave a half smile. 'Look at where you are. I can't imagine it's going to be any crazier than half the things I've heard within these walls.'

'Okay, how about this?' said April. 'My father has been murdered, my school is overrun by real-life vampires and my boyfriend is going to die of a supernatural virus unless I find this book.'

April could feel her eyes filling with tears again.

God, I've got to stop doing this, she thought, *some bloody Fury I am.*

'Come on,' said Jessica, putting a hand on April's shoulder and leading her to the velvet sofa. 'Come and sit down.'

She handed April a tissue.

'So this is about Highgate? The murdered journalist was your father?'

'You know about that?'

'Please – some of my customers spend half their lives wandering around that cemetery. It's all anyone has been talking about for months. I'm sorry about your dad,' she added softly. 'It can't have been easy to lose him.'

April shook her head. She hesitated for a moment, but for some reason had an intuition that Jessica was the sort of woman who would understand.

'It's almost as if he hasn't gone, you know? Like he's still just sitting in the next room. Maybe it's because I want that to be the case, but he still feels real to me.'

Jessica tilted her head sympathetically.

'I know a bit about that. Love is a powerful thing. Sometimes when you lose someone, they stay with you. Sometimes it can feel real, physical. Sometimes it might be.'

'What do you mean?'

She smiled. 'Most religions believe in some form of life after death and I think that's because the power of the human spirit to endure is much, much stronger than anyone really understands. Maybe the poets and the swamis are right, and you do live on after death.'

April didn't know what to make of Jessica, but she liked the way she spoke, the way she put things. It was reassuring, somehow. Or maybe this was how everyone who came into the shop spoke.

'And what about the vampires?'

'Doesn't this sound mad to you? Someone coming in and saying their school is full of vampires?'

'Well you're clearly not a natural believer in anything

supernatural – to be honest, I doubt you even recycle. So if someone like you comes in and tells me their neighbourhood is full of vampires, I'm inclined to take it seriously. You don't strike me as the hysterical type. And you say your boyfriend is in danger? The same way your father was?'

'No. Yes … Sort of. I think it's related. But I know that book is the only thing which will save him.'

Jessica looked at April for a long moment.

'He must be someone very special.'

'He is,' said April, looking at the floor.

'Then I should find a way to help you, shouldn't I?'

She went over to her desk and unlocked it. She held up a card.

'This will get you where you need to go.'

'What is it?'

'It's a library card. To the best library of its kind in the world. You'll see what I mean.' She wrote down a name and address on a pad and tore the sheet of paper off.

'In the Victoria and Albert museum?'

Jessica nodded.

'Queen Victoria had a particular interest in this subject, from the moment Albert died. The museum houses her library, and this card will get you in. Ask for the special collection, everything you need should be there.'

'Thank you, thank you so much,' said April, looking at the card. 'But … are you sure? I mean, you have no idea who I am – why would you trust me?'

Jessica smiled.

'When you've been around as long as me, you get a sense for these things.' The smile faded from her lips. 'But be aware, April, this isn't something you can take lightly. This is deadly serious. If that book exists and if it has the knowledge you need, then it isn't information you want to be sharing with anyone else, do you understand me?'

April nodded. 'Of course, I just want to find this spell called the Drag—'

Jessica held up a hand.

'I don't want to know, it's better that way. It's your business and the risks are yours.'

April looked at her.

'Risks?'

'If what you're telling me is true and the information is life or death to you, then there's a very good chance there are others who will feel the same way.'

'So if the book is there, why haven't the vampires broken in and grabbed it before now?'

'Vampires cannot enter the library,' said Jessica.

'What, do they have garlic hanging from the roof?'

Jessica smiled and shook her head. 'More straightforward than that. You'll see. But be careful, okay? And promise me you'll get what you need and only that? The last thing we need is real spells flying around the internet.'

April nodded. 'I promise,' she said as Jessica walked her to the door.

'One visit, look for what you need, then bring the card straight back. Are we clear?'

'Absolutely,' said April, 'and thank you again. You don't know what this means to me.'

'I think I might. Anyway, good luck. I hope you find what you're looking for. I never did.'

Chapter Twelve

'So what do you think?'

April and Caro were dodging between backpackers and day trippers on the escalator at Monument, heading for the District line.

'What do I think? I think all tourists should be given a piece of paper at passport control with the words "Stand on the right" written in big letters,' said Caro with irritation. 'Is it too much to ask? Everyone else is standing on that side for a reason, you idiots!'

April was glad she had back-pedalled on her policy of keeping Caro out of the investigation for the visit to the V&A. Partly because no one knew this conspiracy stuff better than Caro, but mostly because Caro's inability to take anything seriously took the pressure off April a little. She knew time was running out for Gabriel and that she needed all the help she could get, whatever the risks.

'No, I mean all this about Queen Victoria?' said April. 'I mean, could she really have collected a huge library about the occult and paranormal stuff?'

'Ah well, now you've got me on home turf,' said Caro. 'This is a classic conspiracy. It was well known that Queen Vic was into all sorts of alternative medicine. She made homeopathy popular. She was also rumoured to be getting tarot readings and holding séances in the palace, all to contact Prince Albert. Gold-plated Ouija board in there, probably.'

'But where's the conspiracy?' said April. 'She was grief-stricken and ahead of her time, that's all.'

'Ah, well it goes deeper than that. The conspiracy angle is

that Victoria's interest in the supernatural wasn't just based on grief and hope. It was like she *knew* – not just believed – it had some foundation. There's all sorts of theories linking the Royal Family with the Freemasons, suggestions that there was something odd going on with their East European roots, but it seems that the Windsors – or the Saxe-Coburg Gothas, back then – have always been aware of the vamps.'

They ran across the platform and jumped onto a train as the doors swished closed. As they sat down, April's mind vaguely recalled something from her last history lesson.

'Weren't the Royal Family connected with Jack the Ripper somehow, too?'

'One of her grandsons was a suspect. Didn't you see that Johnny Depp film? They argued the Ripper was the queen's surgeon. Whoever he was, he had some knowledge of anatomy; he managed to remove his victim's internal organs whole.' Caro held up her hands as if she were holding a beating heart. April held up a hand to stop her.

'All right, you can spare me the details.'

'Anyway, whether the Ripper was royalty or not, the theory goes that Queen Victoria put her foot down – she wasn't having that sort of nonsense upsetting her subjects – and ol' Jack suddenly disappeared.'

'Wow,' said April. 'If Miss Holden put all that in her history lessons I'd have spent less time gazing at Benjamin.'

'You've been gazing at Benjamin?' said Caro. 'What, in a romantic way? Are you mental – he's a Sucker!'

'So's Gabriel, remember?'

'Yeah, but Gabe's an outsider, a lone wolf. Ben's in the inner circle of Suckers. I thought all that stuff at the party was just an act to get in with them – wasn't it? Anything else, it'd be like sleeping with the enemy.'

'I was only *looking* at him, Caro, when Gabriel wasn't available. And anyway, he's not like that. Really, he's much nicer when you get to know him.'

Caro raised her eyebrows.

'I know all the glossy magazines say "make him jealous",

but I think you're playing with fire there. I thought it was all sorted out between you and Gabriel, anyway.'

'It is. I think. Anyway, let's talk about something else,' said April uncomfortably. She wasn't happy talking about this with Caro, at least not until she could work it all out in her own mind first. Gabriel's erratic boiling-hot, icy-cold mood swings were starting to unsettle her, especially when he didn't seem to want to recover. But she wasn't ready to face her fear that his behaviour could be undermining feelings she had been so sure of in her hospital bed only a few weeks ago.

'Okay then,' said Caro, lowering her voice and glancing at the other people in the carriage to make sure they weren't overheard. 'That stuff about vampires not appearing in photos? I delegated it to Fiona.'

'Caro! I—'

'Hold your horses! I thought it made sense since Fee's a computer whizz and she'll be able to figure it out better than I can. Anyway, she gave me some sort of techno-babble answer. It was something about how the vampires are sort of dead, but they're also super-alive so they give out a magnetic wave. It was something to do with bees dying, too.'

'Come on, Caro, focus. I want to understand this. It might be important.'

Caro took a deep breath.

'Okay … apparently honeybees are hugely sensitive to the earth's magnetic waves: if you put a magnet next to a beehive, they build it as a cylinder instead of as a honeycomb.'

April made a 'whooshing' gesture above her head. 'That's fascinating. What's it got to do with vampires?'

'Exactly. This is why I delegated. Fee said all this to me and it was like she was talking Swahili.'

'I thought you were studying biology.'

'Plants I understand. Well, their molecular structure anyway. I've killed every pot plant we've ever had in the house. Anyway, Fee's theory is that vamps let off these magnetic waves … and not only do they confuse bees, they also disrupt cameras, like when you see news footage of some office full of computer screens – and the camera can't capture the screens properly. It's the same idea. But the interesting thing is how Ravenwood is wrapped up in all this.'

They had arrived at South Kensington and jumped off the train.

'Ravenwood?' April prompted as they got on the escalator.

Caro smiled. 'Ah yes. Remember how all the teachers here are ludicrously over-qualified, they're all from Harvard and MIT? Fiona did a search on Mr Langdon, head of science. Before he came here he was some mega-bucks consultant in Silicon Valley. He's a world leader in the field of digital imagery.'

'So? Why would they want him here?'

'Well our Mr Langdon has just done a deal with one of the big Japanese camera firms. He's come up with a new sensor for cameras that captures things which were previously invisible. In the press release, he said he owed the idea to one of his students at Ravenwood.'

'Things that were invisible …? You think he means vampires?'

'Maybe. It would make sense if one of the reasons the vamps are recruiting all these big brains was for specific purposes, wouldn't it? Remember all that stuff Miss Holden was saying about how they used to be hidden, but now they're coming out of the shadows? If they can have their photos taken and appear on film, they can do all sorts of things. Become politicians, celebrities, everything. Even Davina could get married to some billionaire and appear in *Hello!*'

'God.'

They clunked through the barriers and up the steps, crossing onto Exhibition Road and walking past the Natural History Museum, its roof lined with carvings of weird and exotic animals, the high arched windows framed by curly seaside-rock pillars of stone. They walked up the wide steps of the V&A and in through the entrance, taking a minute to admire the entrance hall before exploring some of the dark, polished corridors, peering into the glass cabinets, while their shoes squeaked on the stone floors. 'Reminds me of Ravenwood,' whispered April. 'Like someone's going to jump out at any moment.'

'Shhh! Here it is,' said Caro.

The library had heavy double doors with polished brass handles. Through the glass panels in the door, they could see the library itself.

'It's like looking into the past isn't it?' said Caro. The shelves ran down two walls and were double height with a gallery running around the top. The centre of the room held reading desks. Everything was dark wood. No one would have to remind you to be quiet in there. They walked inside with trepidation; it was intimidating and April suppsed that was the point. There were only two people inside the big room – an old man in half-moon spectacles hunched over a large book and a very thin woman with white hair who immediately approached them waving her hands.

'I'm sorry ladies, no school parties in here. This is for members only.'

'Yes, we're members,' said April as confidently as she could, pulling out the card like it was an FBI badge.

'Miss ... Mueller?' said the woman dubiously, reading the name on the card and looking them both up and down.

'We're here to visit the special collection, please,' said April with what she hoped was a charming smile.

'The special collection?' said the woman, as if startled.

'Yes, the special collection,' said Caro, pointing to the pass.

The woman glanced around and lowered her voice. 'This is all very irregular. I'm going to have to make a telephone call.'

She walked over to a desk and quickly dialled a number.

'Hello, this is Mrs Franks, I'm sorry to disturb you ... no, I am aware of that sir, but ... I'm sorry, but I have two young ladies here who wish to visit the special collection.' April noticed that she said the words 'special collection' in a hushed voice. 'Yes, it all seems in order ... I believe Philips is down there. Very well. Thank you, sir.'

The woman put the phone down with some force, clearly

unhappy, and walked back to April and Caro.

'You'd better come with me,' she said, moving towards the back of the room. She produced a bunch of keys and opened a door. 'Through here.'

They found themselves in a dark corridor. It looked as if it was being used to store old exhibits from the museum. As they followed Mrs Franks, they passed tables of fossils, a sculpture of a horse, and jars full of what looked like baby animals suspended in an unpleasant-looking green-tinged liquid. At the end of the corridor, the woman unlocked another door which opened onto a narrow staircase. They walked down two flights and, from the change in temperature, realised they were underground.

'Along here,' said Mrs Franks, indicating another dark corridor. As they turned the corner, there was a roar and both April and Caro leapt back. There was a huge black Alsatian dog rearing up at them, barking and snapping, white foam dripping from his jaws. Behind the dog, a squat man in a blue uniform was struggling to hold onto the beast's lead.

'Don't worry, ladies,' said the man, raising his voice to be heard over the barking. 'He's very friendly once he's got used to you. Hold out your hands, let him have a sniff of yers.'

April glanced over at Mrs Franks, but her expression hadn't changed, as if this was a normal day in the library. Perhaps it was.

Nervously, the two girls offered their hands to the dog, who immediately whined and sat down, wagging his tail. April and Caro exchanged a look; evidently they had passed the test.

'Come along,' said Mrs Franks, turning towards a large door and making a big show of choosing the correct key. She handed April some white cotton gloves. 'These must be worn at all times,' she said as she rattled the key in the lock and pushed the door inwards. 'No eating or drinking. Strictly one book from the shelf at a time and' – she fixed Caro with a glare – 'no books are to be removed from the room at any time under any circumstances.'

'Of course,' said April politely.

'When you have finished,' said the librarian, indicating a buzzer by the door, 'ring this bell. I will see you out.'

'Thank you,' said April. 'We'll be as quick as we can.'

The woman made a humphing noise and disappeared, clicking the door closed behind her.

'Bloody hell!' said Caro. 'What was all that about?'

'I guess that was the anti-vamp alarm Jessica was talking about.'

'Well, I'm glad Rover didn't smell death on me. I've never seen teeth that big before.' She turned her attention to the room they were in, a huge cellar brimming with books, animal skeletons, stuffed specimens and weird plaster models, all carefully preserved by the thrumming air-conditioning units along the walls.

'Wow, look at this place!' said Caro. 'It's amazing.'

'In a creepy sort of way,' said April walking over to examine the shelves. The books were all stored in cupboards with ornate wire fronts that didn't look as though they'd been opened in years. Putting her gloves on, April pulled a cupboard door open and removed a large book with a leather binding. She put it on the wide table in the centre of the room and opened it. It made a cracking sound, incredibly loud in the quiet cellar, and she winced. 'It's like it's brand-new.'

'Maybe they are,' said Caro. 'Queen Victoria was pretty rich, maybe she bought every book published and no one ever got around to reading them all.'

April shook her head.

'You'd need a warehouse the size of a town for that. This is the special collection, remember? Someone chose these books for their importance.'

'Just look at them!' gushed Caro, going from case to case. 'There's something on every unexplained phenomenon in history. Ghosts, mind-reading, synchronicity … God! It could really be here, A! I mean, the British Empire covered about two thirds of the globe at the time, Victoria could have got any book from anywhere in the world.'

April nodded.

'It's here somewhere, I can feel it.'

'Yes, but where?'

'Well don't just stand there, get some dust on your gloves!'

Over an hour later, though, April was beginning to despair. Caro was having the time of her life; she had found books on time travel, ghosts and even prehistoric monsters in the Thames, but April had only one purpose: to find the White Book. They'd searched half the cases already and while there were many, many books on witchcraft and creaky tomes filled with what looked like ancient spells, none of them were *the* book. Sighing, she opened another cabinet and began to run a gloved finger along the spines, determined not to go so fast that she missed the book, but also painfully aware that she might be wrong – perhaps the book wasn't here and all this was a monstrous waste of time neither she nor Gabriel had. 'Listen, we're going to find this book,' said Caro, giving April a hug, carefully keeping her dusty hands away from her back. 'It's going to be okay. Think positively.'

'I'm trying ... but there's so much to worry about it's crushing me. So we find the book, then what? If it works, Gabriel goes back to being a vampire ... is that supposed to be a good thing?'

'This is what you're fighting for, honey. Yes he'll be a vampire, but an *alive* vampire. If that's possible. If he's still kicking, then you've got a chance to fix it all, haven't you? We've got a chance to find the Regent and get him completely cured.'

'I guess so,' said April, wearily turning back to the shelf. 'It's just ... sometimes it seems he doesn't want to, like I'm forcing him to do it.'

'I'm sure that wasn't what he meant,' said Caro over her shoulder.

'You should have heard him by the pond, Caro ...' she began, but her voice slowly trailed off. April was aware that she had stopped breathing.

She was staring at a small book, the size of a slim notebook, although it was bound with thick leather, some sort of pale skin. When she slid it from the shelf she could see the pages were yellow and uneven, and it looked incredibly ancient and fragile.

'Is that it?' Caro's voice had sunk to a whisper.

April opened it, then gasped as she read the title page, hand-written in ink in an elaborate curly style.

Albus Libre:
Spells and potions for the conjuring of evyll and witchcraft.

'I think it is.'

'I sort of imagined it would be bigger.'

'Paper was expensive when this was written,' said April. 'They'd have used as little of it as possible.'

Carefully, she carried the small book over to the table and gently began leafing through it, not wanting to damage the pages. It was all beautifully hand-written, filled with symbols and diagrams she didn't understand.

'There it is!' hissed Caro. The top of the page was titled:

The Breath of The Dragyne
being an elyxir to reverse the foul contaygion
known as the Blood of the Fury and restore the Vampyre
to the dark lyght.

Below it was a list of ingredients along with their quantities: Lief Bark, Mandrake, Black Mossleaf and others.

'We've got it! We've got it!' cried Caro, grabbing April and jumping up and down. They were both laughing and squealing with delight.

'But how are we going to get it out?' said April suddenly. 'We're not allowed to take the books out.'

Caro smiled.

'The rules were made long before they invented this,' she said, pulling out her mobile phone. 'We can take photos on the highest resolution, then download and print them out.'

'Brilliant!'

Caro gave a little bow.

'But of course.'

'Come on then, quickly, before Miss Icy-Face comes back and turfs us out.'

April held the book open while Caro took photos from every angle.

'Right, let's get out of here,' said April. 'This place is starting to creep me out. I swear some of the stuffed animals are watching me.'

Caro looked around at the room longingly. 'Can't we stay just a little longer? The stuff in here, it would blow their minds on trueconspiracy.com.'

April shook her head sadly. 'Sorry, honey, I know this is your dream come true, but remember why we're here. Gabriel's barely hanging on by his fingernails. I'm worried that if we even delay by a minute, we might be too late.'

Caro sighed and gave April a wan smile. 'Okay, just let me take a few more snaps from the spell book,' she said, turning over random pages and snapping away.

'Hey, no!' said April, 'Jessica said to only take the Dragon's Breath spell and nothing more.'

'Sorry A,' said Caro sheepishly. 'It's just that it's a spellbook and maybe there's something in here to make me gorgeous and famous and rich.'

'You're already gorgeous and clever, Caro.'

'Well rich couldn't hurt then, could it?'

Chapter Thirteen

'It's funny,' said Caro as she pressed the bell on the bus. 'I've been past Queen's Wood so many times, but I've never seen anything but trees.'

'That's all there is,' said Gabriel as they stepped down and watched the bus pull away.

'But they're not "just trees", are they?' said Caro miserably. 'It's like a creepy enchanted forest where the trees start trying to kill people.'

'Lovely thought, Caro, just what we need when we're about to step into a spooky wood,' said April. She was in a bad mood because, despite his promise to be strong for her, April had practically had to drag Gabriel along tonight. Still torn between being with her and accepting his so-called gift of death, no doubt. Added to which, the more real it became, the unhappier she felt about the idea of Gabriel becoming a vampire again. But as Caro said, at least he would be alive. That was something, wasn't it?

They waited until the bus had disappeared, then walked down a path and into the trees.

'See?' whispered Caro. 'Can't you just imagine these branches being fingers reaching out to you?' She turned to April. 'And what about your little speech about keeping me out of all this? Now would be the perfect time to put your foot down.'

'It would, but I need your expertise again,' said April.

'What expertise?'

'You study biology, don't you?'

'Biology, not botany. There's a big difference.'

Gabriel stopped, seeming to sniff the air.

'What?' said April.

'It's not safe here,' he said quietly, his dark eyes darting around the woodland.

'I was only joking about the trees ...' said Caro.

'Quiet,' hissed Gabriel. His body was tense, his head cocked, listening.

'What is it?' whispered April, but he didn't answer.

April strained her ears to hear what he was hearing, but there was nothing except a whisper of wind and the occasional rush as a car passed on the road.

Then Gabriel shook his head, frowning. 'Maybe it was nothing ...'

'You can't freeze in your tracks like a bloodhound and then say it was nothing!' said Caro, badly spooked.

'I just thought I smelled ...'

'What?' asked April softly. She could see what Caro hadn't noticed: that Gabriel was scared. For a hundred years, he had been invincible, walking through the world like some kind of superman. But now, since her kiss, he was weak, vulnerable. Suddenly things he would normally brush aside made him jump, and he didn't know how to process all this new information. He looked at her with wide eyes.

'Death,' he said, 'I smelled death.'

She squeezed his arm. 'It's okay,' she said lamely. 'I was reading up on this place. It used to be called Churchyard Bottom. During the Black Death it was used as a plague pit.'

'Plague pit?' said Caro, looking even more spooked.

'So many people were dying, so they dug a mass grave and piled them in. That's why nothing's ever been built here and why it's so overgrown. Maybe that's what you're picking up on,' she said to Gabriel.

'Perhaps,' said Gabriel. The look on his face – bleak, lost, so unsure – almost broke her heart. She wanted to hug him, he looked so lonely, but they had a job to do. And she was annoyed, she reminded herself.

'Let's keep going.'

As Gabriel walked ahead, Caro pulled at April's arm.

'Look, if vampboy smells death then I'm not going anywhere. I've seen enough slasher movies to know this is exactly when someone gets decapitated.'

'Look at him,' April whispered urgently in Caro's ear. 'He's not coping well.'

'Him? *I'm* the one who's not coping.'

She paused as she saw April was genuinely worried. 'All right, so what's wrong with him?'

'It's like he still has all his vampire instincts, but his protective layer's been stripped away. I think he's still sensing everything way more than the rest of us. Smells are more stinky, noises are louder ... but suddenly they're all threatening. I don't think he knows how to deal with it.'

'Well what use is he to us, then? I thought he was here to protect us.'

'Caro, he's dy*ing*!'

Her friend shrugged then sighed. 'Okay, but if we all get sliced up like bagels, don't say I didn't warn you.'

They walked on, following the path deeper into the trees. The light had been fading as they had stepped off the bus, and here, where the bare branches were reaching across the trail forming a tunnel, it was incredibly grey and gloomy.

'What are we looking for, exactly?' said Caro huffily. 'And why have we come at night?'

'According to the *Albus*, some of the plants have to be picked at night to be effective.'

April pulled out a torch and her notebook. With Gabriel's aid, plus a Latin dictionary, an online translator and a pile of books about native woodland plant life, she and Caro had assembled a shopping list of ingredients complete with diagrams and photographs so they could identify the correct plants. She had expected them to be super-rare, but many were listed as 'common' or 'habitat: English woodland'. In the end, Mr Gill had provided her with an old *Guide to British Flora* which had listed them all.

'First we need *Spineroa nervosa* or Blackfern,' said April, finding a page marked by a fluorescent-pink sticky note. She flicked her torch on and showed Caro the picture.

'Hmm … looks like a normal fern to me,' said Caro, 'only black.'

'Apparently, it likes damp conditions and shade,' April said.

'It'll be right at home here then,' said Caro, skirting around a muddy patch and ducking under a branch. 'What about this?' she pulled up a plant.

'That's a dandelion, Caro,' said April.

'Well, how am I supposed to know?'

'Yeah, I'm *so* glad I brought you along,' said April sarcastically.

'The feeling's mutual, darling.'

It was darker now as they walked deeper into the woods, the undergrowth thicker, but that also meant there were more plants. With help from Gabriel's sharp eyes and nose, they found three of the ingredients quickly.

'And there!' said Caro. 'Black ferns!' She was right. They waded through the waist-high plants growing a few yards from the path, selecting the healthiest-looking leaves.

'Right,' said April, 'now all we need is …'

Gabriel put his hand over her mouth and pulled both of the girls to the ground.

'Be still,' he murmured into their ears.

The girls both froze. Slowly they heard footsteps approaching. They were light and nimble, more like a child's than a man's, but from where April was lying, she could see the white flash of trainers as they passed.

'This way,' said a low voice. 'We can't let them get away.'

The feet paused for a moment, then moved off at speed, deeper into the woods. After waiting in silence for another tense minute Gabriel finally let them up.

'Who the hell was that?' hissed Caro.

'Were they vamps? Looking for us?' breathed April.

Gabriel nodded gravely. 'We don't have much time. At the moment, they'll probably assume we're out having a little party, but if they find us with these leaves, they may make a guess in the right direction.'

Caro raised her eyebrows meaningfully, but April shook her head.

'No, we can't leave until we have everything on the list. We haven't come this far to let a few nosy vampires put us off.'

'It's all right for you, Ms Fury,' said Caro. 'All I've got to defend myself is a book on plants.' She looked back and forth between April and Gabriel, then sighed. 'Okay, what's left?'

April peered at her notebook.

'Mandrake.'

'I know that plant,' said Gabriel. He closed his eyes, as if in concentration.

They stood silently for a while.

'Ahem, the Suckers?' hissed Caro. 'I don't like to suggest they're planning to bury us in the plague pits, but it's a real possibility.'

'Quiet,' said April, her eyes on Gabriel.

'We have to go north,' he said and began to move up a path.

'Hey! Where are we going?' hissed Caro, but Gabriel was gone. She turned to April. 'Where's he going?' April just shrugged and set off after him. Gabriel moved fast, plunging through the gaps between the trees, taking paths across open fields, skirting housing developments, as sure-footed in the dark as he was in full daylight.

'He sure doesn't move like someone who's dying,' complained Caro.

Finally they came to the edge of another thickly wooded area. Gabriel hesitated, looking around and sniffing the air. Finally he walked in and the trees swallowed them up again. 'More woods? Where are we?'

'This is Coldfall Wood,' said Gabriel. 'We're on the edge of the Islington and St Pancras cemetery.

'Another graveyard? That's great,' said Caro.

'No, this place is different,' said April. 'Can't you feel it?'

There was something different about it. It was just as dark, if not darker than Queen's Wood, but it didn't have the same oppressive feel to it. Maybe she had been sensing the death back there too. Even Caro seemed happier among these trees.

'What about your spiky-toothed friends?' she asked Gabriel.

He shook his head, examining the ground. 'They won't come here.'

Gabriel strode ahead and Caro turned to April.

'Next time we go on a nature ramble, remind me not to invite your boyfriend. He's not big on the giggles, is he?'

April flicked her torch on and peered at the book.

'Mandrake is a root that grows under trees,' she read. 'Apparently it got its name because it's shaped like a man. Legend has it, it grows under the trees wherever someone's been hanged.'

'Better and better,' sighed Caro. 'I take it back. It's creepy here too. But aren't roots under the ground? How are we going to find them?'

Gabriel walked back. 'Hand me the trowel.'

Bending down under a tall tree, he dug a small trench then scrabbled with his hands, finally pulling out a soil-covered lump that looked for all the world like a grubby version of the fresh ginger on sale in the supermarket.

'How did you know it was there?'

He held the orange root up to Caro's nose.

'I smelled it.'

Caro took a tentative sniff, then recoiled, pulling a face. 'Just smells like dirt to me.'

'That's the point, I think you'll find.'

They whirled around. An elderly woman was standing behind them in a small clearing, holding the leads of two huge Rottweilers. The way they were baring their teeth, April got the impression they weren't too happy to have visitors. Gabriel stepped out, putting himself between the woman and the girls.

'Leave us alone,' he said quietly. April was surprised to see the aggression on Gabriel's face.

One of the dogs reared up snarling, his sharp fangs exposed and snapping at him. Gabriel stopped, but he didn't give ground. It looked as if he and the dogs were in a staring contest.

'I'm surprised at you, Gabriel,' said the woman. She was small, with grey hair drawn back into a bun. She was dressed in a padded jacket and green wellies, as if she had just been out walking her dogs.

'And why would that be?' said Gabriel, never taking his eyes from the dog in front of him. 'Old age catching up with you?'

The woman gave a hollow laugh.

'Don't insult me,' she said with unconcealed threat. 'I know why you're here. The question is why you would take such a risk.'

April looked between them.

'What are you talking about? Gabriel, do you know her?'

The woman looked at April.

'So you're the one. You're prettier than I had heard. I can see why he's so—'

'Don't speak to her!' snapped Gabriel. He took two steps towards her and the dog barked, a clear warning.

'Tell your mutts to back off,' growled Gabriel. 'Or you know what will happen.'

'Do I?' asked the woman. 'Your aura is not what it was, Gabriel. You're weak. Now why is that?'

'Don't underestimate me, old woman.'

'And do not threaten me!' she snapped. 'You know the rules.'

'Don't speak to me of rules, witch!' growled Gabriel. 'There are no rules any more. They are going to rise up and swallow this place like a wave.'

The woman laughed. '"They"? Do you *still* speak of yourself as if you are somehow different? I think we both know that's not true. What about the one in Hanbury Street? Or Mitre Square?'

'Do you still listen to gossip?' shouted Gabriel. 'Are you really so blinkered—'

'Oh for God's sake, what's going on?' April demanded. 'What's all this about?'

The woman looked at April and the anger clouding her face seemed to clear.

'Your friend is not welcome in these woods,' she said softly. 'It is a clean place, a good place. We do not allow the darkness to enter here.'

'You will have no choice, you stupid old woman!' shouted Gabriel. 'Nothing will stop them. Nothing. The darkness is coming, even you must see that!'

'Is that a threat?'

'Oh for God's sake, you sound like a pair of children,' said April. 'Look, I don't know why he's upset you, but clearly you don't like vampires coming here.'

The woman looked at her sharply.

'Yes, he's a vampire. Yes, we knew it, yes, he's helping us. So what?'

'It is forbidden for them to come here. It's against the ancient lore—'

April surprised herself by laughing out loud.

'Oh just listen to yourself,' she said. '"Ancient lore"? You sound like something from some old film. You're not Gandalf and this isn't the Shire.'

The woman blinked at her, a look of astonishment on her face. Gabriel seemed equally awestruck.

'Look, I'm sorry we had to come here,' said April more evenly. 'But it was important. Something's happening with the vampires out there. I don't know what it is, if it's this darkness Gabriel's talking about, but he's right: it's breaking all the rules, vampire or otherwise. If you're really some kind of witch, I doubt your magic circle or your ancient lore is going to protect you. It didn't stop us entering your woods.'

The woman's face betrayed a ghost of a smile.

'She has spirit. And wisdom, too,' said the woman. 'You have chosen well, Gabriel.'

'I think you'll find I chose him,' said April. 'But thank you.'

The woman gave a low whistle and the two dogs whimpered and lay down on the ground. She stepped forward. 'May I?' she asked gently.

April nodded. The woman lifted a hand, pulling April's hair back behind her ear.

'I understand. Child, you have the weight of the world on your shoulders, I need not add to your burden. Take your herbs and go in peace.'

She touched April on the shoulder and leant in to whisper in her ear.

'And take an old lady's advice: don't let him see how much you care.'

When April turned to ask her more, the woman had gone. As if on a command, the dogs leapt to their feet and ran off in opposite directions.

'Whoo ... That was one crazy lady,' said Caro. 'And she didn't seem to like you, eh, big guy?'

'I shouldn't have brought you here,' said Gabriel, clearly still furious. 'I should have known she would find us.'

'But who was she?' asked April.

Gabriel didn't seem to hear her question, instead muttering to himself, 'Those stupid, stubborn, blinkered, bigoted ...'

'Gabriel!'

'Witches, April. She was a witch.'

'I thought witches wore pointy hats,' said Caro. 'Not Barbour jackets.'

'Vampires are scared of witches?' asked April. 'Why?'

'That's why,' said Gabriel, pointing to their bag. 'Because they still have knowledge which can undermine all that we are. Even when nothing else can touch us, they can find a way.'

'Well thank God for that,' said Caro. 'No offence.'

Gabriel gave a grim smile. 'None taken, Caro. And perhaps you're right, after all. Maybe it is good to know someone's standing in the way.'

April looked around, still frightened that the vampire trackers would catch them.

'I only hope they are.'

Chapter Fourteen

April stood at Miss Holden's back door, holding up an orange plastic carrier bag. She felt like a homeless person begging for shelter. Which, she supposed, she was in a way.

'What have you got there?' asked the teacher.

'I think you can guess, Miss.'

'Been on a nature trail, April?' she asked with a hint of irony. 'Listen, I'm glad I could be of some help, but if you'll excuse me, I have some marking to do.' Miss Holden began to close the door, but April put her foot in the gap.

'I need help, Miss,' she said firmly. 'Help me make it. Please.'

Miss Holden looked at her for a long moment, then opened the door.

'Come in.'

The teacher bolted the door behind them, then walked over to the sink and began filling her copper kettle.

'I appreciate your position, April,' she said, 'but I can't help you with this. You have no idea how difficult it's been to help you as much as I have.'

'Difficult for *you*? My dad was killed, Miss! My whole world has fallen apart and without Gabriel I have nothing left! How is this harder for *you*?'

'I don't make the rules, April. I can't simply decide to help just because you ask.'

'Rules? That's what this is about? Why is everyone talking to me about rules all of a sudden? My mum's become some sort of moral beacon – so's Gabriel and that old woman, now you.'

'What old woman?'

'It doesn't matter. The point is: there are no rules any more. The Suckers aren't toeing the line, or haven't you noticed? "By midnight"? "No children"? "No celebrities"?'

Miss Holden looked startled.

'Oh, I'm learning – that's what I came to Ravenwood for, isn't it? But all those rules have been broken, so what makes you think you should stick to your narrow code, especially when it's *wrong*?'

'Even if I agreed with you …'

'Forget it, then. Just forget about it. I thought you were going to help me.'

'I did, April! I told you about the book – what more do you want?'

April stood up and walked towards the door.

'Sit down, April.'

'No—'

'SIT DOWN, damn you!'

Miss Holden grabbed April's arm and pulled her into a chair.

'All right, listen to me. I know you're angry and confused – God knows you have a right to be. But this isn't all about you, however much it may feel like it. I didn't make the rules, I learned them from my father, as all Guardians do, and I grew up believing them. At first I thought they were just fairy tales, something to scare the children with and keep them in bed at night, but when I was old enough, he showed me that his stories were true.'

'Where's your dad now?' asked April.

'He's dead, April. Being a Guardian is a bit like being a bomb-disposal expert. You have to learn a lot, and if you get one detail wrong then it's all over very quickly.'

'I'm sorry.'

'Don't be. Unlike you, Guardians get to choose. It was the life he always wanted. He believed in our cause the same way that I believe in it … but it's not my private crusade. The Guardians are a huge organisation. They're in every country on

earth, present at every level of society. And like any organisation, there is a hierarchy. I can't decide to change the way we
do things. There are consequences if I choose to break the
rules.'

'But you have a choice: you can decide to change the way
you do things.'

'Yes, I can. I also have to decide if I think doing so is worth
the consequences.'

'They're bad consequences?'

She sighed and nodded.

'I'm sorry about that, Miss, but this is a matter of life or
death. If someone appeared on your doorstep, bleeding to
death, would you just shut the door and make a cup of tea?'

'No, I suppose not.'

'What would you do?'

'I'd do something about it.'

April picked up her bag and plonked it on the table.

'Well, let's do something about it then.'

Making the Dragon's Breath was a long process and April
knew she would never have managed it alone. Miss Holden
worked through the night, preparing the plants, grinding
them down using a pestle and mortar, then boiling them to a
paste. The kitchen was full of steam, piles of chopped leaves
and pots and pans. It all made April think of her dad. Every
birthday, he would insist on making her a cake. Both he and
April would end up covered in flour, with butter in their hair,
and hundreds and thousands stuck to their clothes. Silvia
would hover around, moaning that they should have gone to
Fortnum and Mason, but she'd still gobble up the wonky old
cake at the end and declare it the most delicious thing she'd
ever tasted. Her dad would give her a kiss and say, 'That's
because it was made with love.' There were none of those old
Dunne family traditions on her last birthday of course, but
then the Dunne family was hardly the same any more, was
it? And now here April was, in a very different kitchen, making a woman she hardly knew create a magic potion to save

someone she had every reason to hate – and probably ruining her life in the process. It was a different kind of love, but April could see there was love here nonetheless.

'You okay?'

April looked up, snapped out of her trance and blushed.

'Sorry, I was just thinking of my dad,' she stuttered. 'We, er, we used to make cakes in the kitchen … don't worry, it's stupid.'

'No, it's not stupid, April. You should remember your dad. As long as you do, there's always a little piece of him in the world.'

'You really believe that?'

'I know that, April. It's something I've lived through.'

'Sorry,' said April. 'Sometimes I forget that I'm not the only person in the world who has lost their dad.'

'It does that to you,' said Miss Holden.

She gestured that April should come over to the stove where the potion was simmering in a small copper saucepan.

'Okay, give me your thumb,' she said.

'My … my thumb?' stuttered April, but before she could object, the teacher had seized her hand and pricked the ball of her thumb with a knife.

'Ow!' cried April, trying to pull away, but Miss Holden held tight, squeezing the wound until a couple of drops of blood plopped into the mixture,

'Sorry, April,' she said, releasing her and handing her a square of kitchen towel. 'There are plasters over there in the cabinet.'

'Why the hell did you put my blood in there? I didn't see anything about that in the recipe.'

'No, that's one of those things passed down father to daughter, a Guardian's secret. The Dragon's Breath is a spell of evil, remember? But my father taught me that adding a Fury's blood purifies the potion, makes it a weapon for good. Now only Gabriel can use it.'

'I don't understand, why only Gabriel?'

'Because Gabriel is different, April. Whatever the other

Guardians think, I know they're not all the same. He's infected by the darkness, but his heart is pure. He *wants* to be good, he wants to escape from the fog that surrounds him. Remember that when a vampire turns, he has to want to live, he has to will his body to fight for eternal life. There's no science to it, or at least no science we understand yet, but it's to do with the human soul. Your blood in the potion will help him find his way back. That's the best way I can explain it.'

April watched as she poured a thick brown liquid from the small saucepan and filtered it through some gauze into a small glass bottle.

She stuck a little cork in the top, then carefully sealed it with wax.

'There you go,' she said, handing April the bottle. April held it up to the light. 'Is that it? It looks horrible,' she said.

'Probably tastes horrible, too,' said the teacher. 'But it will do the trick, I'm pretty sure of that.'

'How can it, though? How can a load of ferns and muddy roots and boiled up blood cure Gabriel of some deadly virus?'

'It's not a deadly virus, and this formula will counteract the effect of whatever it is in your body which stops the vampire disease and is preventing Gabriel from regenerating.'

'But how?' April frowned, shaking the bottle.

Miss Holden laughed.

'If it was in a pill, would you think it would work?'

April blushed. 'Yes, I suppose I would.'

'It's exactly like antibiotics. They work by helping your body fight off bacteria. Alexander Fleming discovered penicillin by watching how bread mould attacked bacteria, and people had been using the same stuff in natural remedies for years. Spider's webs have a type of penicillin in them, believe it or not. So is it so strange that that bag of stuff you found in a wood can cure Gabriel?'

'If you put it like that, it makes sense, but' – she gestured around the kitchen – 'it does seem a bit weird to me. I'm used to Lemsip.'

'Well, if you have a cold, drinking honey and lemon would do you just as much good.'

'Really? I guess I assume because it comes in a packet it will work better.'

'Belief is a strong healer too.'

'Thanks, Miss. I know this was a big thing for you to do.'

'Sometimes it takes someone to tell you what was right in front of your nose. My every instinct is that I should do nothing to help a vampire, any vampire. But I think there's something different about your vampire. I hope I'm right. And your little speech was true – all the rules we used to play by have changed. As a history teacher, I should remember the Romans.'

'What do you mean?'

'The Romans built their empire by military force. Their soldiers weren't any braver or more fearsome than their opponents, but their generals were smarter. The barbarians would always fight in a certain way, but the Romans kept changing their tactics, searching for the enemy's weakness.'

'But where are they now?'

'You're looking at them. We are the Romans, April. They forgot what made them great. They became bloated and arrogant and failed to move with the times. All those people walking down the high street to get their paper or getting the bus to work, they have no idea how close they are to total destruction.'

'Well, I can't imagine they want to, either …'

'The truth is humans are creatures of habit and have a huge capacity for self-delusion. We deliberately limit ourselves. Shop in the same place, wear the same clothes, have the same job for life, go on holiday to the same place every year. It's as if people think they have for ever – oh, I'll go to China when I retire.'

April was shocked at her tone.

'But that's just the way people are,' frowned April. 'You can't blame them for that. They're just getting on with their lives.'

'But they are lives which are hanging by a thread,' said Miss

Holden. 'They have no idea how easily all that cosy ordinariness could just disappear and their lives – if they manage to stay alive – will become a living hell.'

April didn't like what she was hearing.

'Do you really think that? Are the vampires really planning to take over the world?'

'That's one of the things you need to find out, April. We know they're on the move. We know they're starting to surface. Yes, maybe Marcus had gone rogue when he acted, but the rest of them are behaving differently too.

'It's as if they're preparing to come out, to go public.'

'What? So everyone will know they're real?' said April, thinking of Fiona's discovery about the camera technology developed at Ravenwood: *making things which were invisible visible*, that's what she had said wasn't it?

'I don't know what they're planning, April,' said the teacher. 'It's just a feeling. They used to be so careful about staying hidden, but now it's like they almost want to get caught.'

'What happens then?'

'I wish I knew.'

April stood up and walked to the door. 'Thanks for doing this, Miss. I know it breaks the rules, but it means a lot to me.'

'Just make sure he understands how important it is.'

'Oh, I'll tell him, don't you worry.'

Chapter Fifteen

It was a lovely sunny morning, but it was cold. April and Miss Holden had worked through the night and well into the morning but the temperature didn't seem to have risen since dawn. Gabriel was wearing his navy peacoat with the collar up and a green scarf wrapped around his neck. The pink spots in his cheeks only highlighted how pale his skin had become – almost translucent. He walked slowly as if it gave him pain and occasionally he would cough. If April hadn't known better, she would have thought he just had a bad cold. But she did know better. She was killing him. The man she loved had kissed her and given up his life for her. She had infected him with something, something that was eating him from the inside. Normally, that thought would have made her gloomy and depressed, but this morning she felt happy and light. This morning she had a cure, right there in her pocket. She curled her fingers around the bottle. It was a bittersweet victory of course. Right now they could be together but Gabriel was dying. Once he took the elixir he'd live, but they wouldn't be able to kiss, maybe not even be close to each other again for – well, she didn't for how long. She glanced up at him, wondering if they would ever be as close as they were right now, walking through Regent's Park. She hooked her arm through his, gently tugged him to a stop and snuggled closer, giving him a long kiss.

'What was that for?' he said with a smile.

'Just because.'

They walked on, passing the sign with the monkeys, following the arrows towards the zoo. It had been Gabriel's idea that they had a last date before he took the potion. She had wanted him to drink it straight away, but he said he wanted to savour the moment and take this final morning to be together. April wondered if he really wanted to savour being human just for one more day. Everything would be different after this. But there would be hope. Yes, he would be a vampire again, but he would have a chance. If – when – they found the Regent, he could be free. They could be together again, without worrying about his health, without any fear that other people would discover his secret. *Their* secret.

Paying at the booth, they pushed through the turnstiles and went inside. They were in a large open space, a sort of crossroads with signposts pointing in every direction. In the distance, they could hear the calls of the birds and apes and there were strange scents in the air. It was still early, but April didn't imagine that the zoo got very busy this time of year. Just a few elderly tourists and a few families with children in buggies.

'What do you want to see first?' asked Gabriel.

'The lions,' said April decisively. They followed the signs along the path, passing the otters, the rhinos, strange birds with crazy hair-like feathers, at least that was what it said on the cages. Most of the enclosures were empty, or seemed to be. Perhaps the creatures liked their privacy.

'I hope the lions are there,' said April, cuddling closer to Gabriel as they walked. 'I was obsessed with lions when I was little, I had loads of books about them.'

'Did you have a cuddly lion?'

April nodded.

'Leo. Not terribly original, I know, but I took him everywhere with me. My mum was always complaining about how filthy he was.'

'And where's Leo now?'

April frowned.

'Come to think of it, I don't actually know. I assumed he had been put in a suitcase in the loft. But then, we don't have the same loft any more ...'

For some reason, this made April more sad than it should. 'Poor Leo, I hope he's okay.'

'I'm sure he's having a party with all the other lions,' said Gabriel. 'Come on, let's go and see.'

They walked up to the lion enclosure, but it too seemed empty. Just a wide open space of flat-topped rocks and bare vegetation.

'Don't worry,' said Gabriel, 'they're here.' They walked down a ramp through a concrete archway into a large room. In front of them, behind a thick Plexiglas window, was the lions' winter shelter. It was much like the outdoor one: just rocks with a few plants, but at least it was covered over. There was one male with a shaggy mane lying on a rock and a female pacing up and down right behind the glass. As they walked in, the male lifted his head, as if to say 'What are you doing in my room?', while the female began to pace faster. She seemed agitated, peering at them through the glass.

'What's the matter with her?'

Gabriel frowned, shook his head slightly as a couple walked in pushing a baby in a pram.

'Hey, look at the big lion, Max!' cried the mother. 'She's looking for food.'

It didn't look to April as if the lion was hungry. She was growling now, her head dipping back and forth. She seemed to be searching for something. Suddenly the male stood up and roared.

'Gosh!' said the father, looking slightly concerned. 'He's feisty, isn't he?'

'I think we'd better go,' said Gabriel quietly, backing towards the door.

The male had moved to the edge of the platform and was shaking his head violently. He roared again and the baby began to howl.

'Christ,' muttered the mother, pulling the buggy backwards and heading towards the exit, glancing at April and Gabriel as she went.

'Come on,' said Gabriel, but April hung back. The female

was growling now, whipping her head from side to side, bashing it against the glass.

'Come *on*,' said Gabriel, taking her arm.

'What the hell was that all about?' she asked when they were a safe distance from the enclosure. She could see the young couple standing with a keeper, pointing towards the lions. April didn't want to be accused of anything, so they kept moving.

'What was wrong with them?'

'Take a guess,' snapped Gabriel.

'Hey, don't take it out on me.'

'I'm sorry. I thought it would be different. I shouldn't have come here. I've been fooling myself.'

'Fooling yourself? What about?'

'That I was becoming human again. I'd hoped, against all the evidence, but the truth is I'm just a sick vampire.'

'You think they knew what you are?'

Gabriel nodded, sitting on a bench, hands thrust in pockets.

'If there's one thing that will upset a predator, it's having another predator on their territory. It's only natural. They must have caught my scent.'

She reached out and stroked his forehead. He was burning hot, soaked with sweat.

'Don't take it so hard. It's not your fault.'

'Why shouldn't I take it hard?' he replied. 'If you really think this magic potion is going to save me, you don't know anything.'

He jumped up and strode towards the exit. April ran to catch up with him. As Gabriel passed the zebras, they shied and ran and as he crossed the path in front of the spider monkey enclosure, all hell broke loose. They all began to screech at once, running back and forth along their branches, rattling the bars of their cages. It was as if an entire street of car alarms had been triggered at once. Keepers and public alike came running and shouting, bewildered at this sudden cacophony, but no one was looking beyond the cage to see what had startled them in the first place. April covered her ears, but Gabriel just kept walking, his head down, his eyes dark. They pushed through the exit and across the road, into the park.

'Gabriel,' called April, catching his arm, trying to slow his pace. 'Stop. Talk to me.'

As he turned, she could see he was beyond exhaustion. His face was white and his lips were pressed together in a thin blue line. Sweat was beading on his forehead and running down his temple.

'I don't want this any more, April,' he said, his voice barely a croak. 'I know you're doing what you can to save me, but I'm not sure I can go back. I know it sounds insane to you that death is preferable, but you saw how those other creatures reacted to me.'

'They were only animals, they didn't know what they were doing.'

'But they do! And they're just the tip of the iceberg!' said Gabriel, his cheeks flaring a dull pink. 'They were right to be scared – I'm a killer. And ... and God knows, I don't want to be.'

'Listen to me, Gabriel,' she said, taking his hands in hers. 'You're not a killer. Not to me. You know what I see when I look in your face? Gabriel. My Gabriel, the man I love. And that's who I'm trying to save. No one else. Forget all this "save the world" stuff, forget the Fury thing, forget being a vampire for the moment. None of this is about that. This is about making my boyfriend better. This is about saving your *life*. And it's about you choosing to live so you can protect *mine*.'

She pulled out the bottle and held it up to him.

'Here, take it. Please. For me?'

Reluctantly, he took it from her. Seeing it there in his big hand, it looked terribly amateur and ineffectual, like the tiny bottle Alice drank from in Wonderland. Would it make Gabriel shrink or grow? Would it do anything at all? Maybe this was the Guardians' idea of a joke: give the hated vampire some hope, then laugh as he died in agony. But April didn't think so. For some reason, she was convinced it was going to work. Gabriel looked at the murky liquid inside and smiled wryly. 'You're sure there're no side effects?'

'None. Well, it might turn you into one of the living dead. Oh, and it smells like poo.'

'Ah. Well that's okay, then.'

They walked up to the top of Primrose Hill silently, hand in hand. April could hear the catch and wheeze in Gabriel's lungs by the time they reached the bench at the abandoned summit, but he didn't complain. The time for that had passed; they were high above London, the early morning fog still lying over the buildings, the sun leaking through the clouds here and there making office windows shine like jewels. April wondered how he was feeling, if he was looking at the world through human eyes for the last time. But then, as he had said, he really wasn't human, just a watch winding down. He was taking a lot on faith – that they would be able to find the Regent. That he wouldn't be doomed to carry on drinking blood for another thousand years. But then belief was a very powerful thing, wasn't that what Miss Holden had said? April looked at the boy – the man – she loved in a sideways glance, feeling warm tears running down her face.

'You have to come back to me,' she croaked. 'Don't leave me here alone.'

'Hey,' said Gabriel softly, brushing her tears away. 'I couldn't stay away from you. If I had to cross the widest desert to reach you, I'd be there.'

He paused for a moment, looking out to Big Ben and the London Eye in the distance. 'We'll come back here. When it's all over? This will be our place.'

He kissed her then, holding her face, his palms wet with her tears, and as he pulled away April could still feel the kiss lingering on her lips.

'To you,' said Gabriel and, breaking the wax and pulling the cork out with a soft pop, he tipped the liquid down his throat. April didn't know what to do, what to expect. Would he clutch his throat the way TV villains did when they were poisoned? Would it be slow and gentle like taking headache pills?

'How d'you feel?'

'I'm not sure I'll feel anything … oh, God.'

Suddenly he doubled over. 'Christ,' he said through gritted teeth, hugging his stomach. 'Urggh …'

April put her arm around him.

'Gabe, what is it? What can I do?'

'Nothing,' he gasped, 'nothing, I …'

Then he let out a terrible scream, like a wounded animal.

'Gabriel,' she said, trying to hold him, but he pushed her hands away.

'You have … to … go …' he managed.

'I can't leave you—' she said.

But then he turned to her, his teeth bared, his eyes bloodshot and red. He looked like the killer she had seen that night on the Embankment. He looked like a vampire.

'Leave!' he growled, spittle flying from his mouth. 'I'm not sure … not sure I can control myself, April. It's … not safe for you here … go!'

'Gabriel …'

'Go!' he roared. She stepped back and ran, running down the hill without looking back. When she turned at the bottom, he had gone.

PART TWO

Chapter Sixteen

A million pounds. It was a ridiculous amount of money. It was something you saw on a TV drama about a kidnap plot, not in real life. In her mind, April saw a forklift truck bringing her a load of gold bars and leaving them in the front garden. That was how crazy it seemed.

'But how?' asked April suspiciously. 'How can there suddenly be a million pounds in my account?'

The solicitor leant back in his chair and smiled condescendingly.

'Well, you can't actually go to a bank and have them fill a suitcase with it, if that's what you're thinking.'

No, right now I'm thinking about pushing you backwards off your chair, thought April. *That would wipe the smug look off your face.*

April's already short temper had been on a hair-trigger since she had watched Gabriel take the Dragon's Breath two days ago. He hadn't called, hadn't texted, hadn't replied to any of her messages, hadn't given her any indication at all that he had even survived the process, and April was about ready to bite someone's head off as a result. Or push them off their chair.

'No, many years ago – just after you were born, in fact – your father took out a life insurance plan,' continued the solicitor. 'A very generous life insurance plan. He arranged that in the event of his death, your mother would never have to work again and, well, I suppose the same applies to you. I know it's not going to bring your dad back, but it shows he was thinking of you, doesn't it?'

'My daughter doesn't need a life insurance policy to prove

her father loved her, Mr Jones,' said Silvia.

'No, no of course not. But, well, these policies aren't cheap. It must have taken considerable sacrifices to pay the premium every month.'

'And is that any of your business, Mr Jones?'

'Well in actual fact, yes it is. The size of the policy is the reason I'm talking to you instead of to your family lawyer. My department specialises in questionable claims.'

'Questionable?' said Silvia, her eyes narrowing. 'If you're implying ...'

He held up a hand.

'Not at all, not at all. This simply came across my desk because it is unusual that a man should choose to pay a quarter of his wages on a life insurance policy. Yes, he was a journalist, but even so, it's a lot of money. I wonder: was your husband a careful man?'

Silvia snorted. 'Not really. He would hardly have spent his days investigating drug cartels if he was, would he?'

'Then I don't see ... did he believe he had a disease we didn't know about?'

'Oh I see,' said Silvia. 'Typical insurance company, you're trying to wriggle out of paying. Well let me tell you—'

'No, no, you misunderstand me, Mrs Dunne. The payment has been authorised. The money is yours and your daughter's. Your husband paid his premium to us on the dot every month and, especially given the manner of his death, we have no reason to think this is in any way suspicious. No one could have predicted that.'

'Then what are you implying?'

'Nothing, Mrs Dunne, I am just intrigued. Why did your husband have such a large life insurance policy? It doesn't make a great deal of sense.'

'He was probably mis-sold the policy when he contacted you. No doubt your salesman sold him the most expensive package. Maybe he didn't shop around, I don't know. You'll appreciate I can't ask him because he was murdered.'

The solicitor turned bright red.

'Yes, indeed, and we would like to extend our sincerest condolences to you at this difficult time.'

'Really. Sincere is not a word I'm entirely sure you know the meaning of, Mr Jones.'

She could be insufferable and irritating, but there were still times when April really loved her mother.

They left the building and walked down the busy London street, their breath steaming in front of them.

'So what was all that about?' asked April. 'Why was that man asking all those questions about Dad?'

Silvia sighed. 'It's his job to be a little toad, darling.'

'No, I don't mean that. I mean what he was saying: was it true? Dad spent a fortune on life insurance?'

Silvia shook her head. 'Finance has never been my strong point. I always let you dad sort out paying the bills. You don't think I'd have let him spend all that money on something so unnecessary, do you? Even now, that man has the power to drive me mad.'

April looked at her mother.

'What do we do now?'

Silvia shrugged. 'We have a party.'

'A party? You *are* joking?'

'I don't see why not. Your father obviously meant to provide for us, so we should make use of it.'

'What, go on a shopping spree?' said April sarcastically.

'He knew me well, darling. What do you think he'd expect me to do with all that money? What else are we going to do? Put it into bonds? Give it away to charity?'

'I don't know, but having a party … it's as if we're happy he's dead.'

But why did he leave all that money? Wondered April. *Did he expect to be killed?* Obviously he had run the risks of upsetting the wrong people in his work as an investigative reporter. That was true. But this seemed something more than that. Mr Jones was right: no one expects to get their throat torn out by a vampire, do they? It might have made sense if her dad had taken the insurance out a week before his death, but he'd done it seventeen years ago. It just didn't add up. Like almost everything in her life right now. She suddenly thought of Gabriel and the terrible, hungry look on his face when he'd taken the potion. She had been calling and texting him, but his phone was switched off. Where was he? Had he gone on a blood-sucking rampage? Was he dead in a ditch? She had no idea.

'Anyway, the upshot is that your dad provided for us and for that, at least, we should be grateful.'

'At least? What's that supposed to mean?'

'Nothing.'

'What's the matter? Why all these snide references to Dad all the time?'

Silvia's attitude toward April's father was seriously beginning to upset her. Weren't you supposed to cut someone a bit of slack when they'd died? Don't speak ill of the dead and all that? April had the distinct impression that Silvia wasn't just angry, she actually resented William for dying. Like he had any choice about it, and now they knew about the insurance, it wasn't as if they were left in the lurch either. What was her problem?

'Snide? I didn't say anything about your father.'

'Well maybe you should. Aren't you supposed to be his grieving widow? It was bad enough you gave him such a hard time when he was with us, without you making him out a bad father now he's gone.'

'It's only natural I should feel angry at your father. Robert says ...'

'Robert? Who's Robert?'

'Mr Sheldon.'

'You've been seeing Mr Sheldon?' April said incredulously.

'He's a friend.'

'A friend? What kind of friend?'

'I can choose my own friends, April. I don't need your approval. I have issues I need to talk through and I've known Robert a long time.'

'Longer than Dad? Or maybe only since he died?'

'What are you implying?'

'Whatever you think I'm implying!' April shouted. 'What difference does it make what I think? You're going to go out and do whatever you— oh, forget it!'

April stalked off in disgust.

'April! Come back here!'

'No!' yelled April. 'I'm old enough to choose my own company too.'

She ran off down the street, bumping into people as she struggled to get away. She ignored their protests and ploughed on, needing to put distance between her and her mother. Turning a corner, she saw a taxi and flagged it down, hoping she could scrape together enough change from her purse for the fare back to Highgate.

I've got a million quid in the bank, she thought as she told the driver: 'Highgate Cemetery, Swain's Lane.' *I can afford it.*

April waited until the taxi's red tail-lights had disappeared up the hill before she approached the gates. She rapped timidly on the cemetery office window, half hoping that Miss Leicester had already gone home, half hoping her disapproving face would appear at the glass. It was only quarter-past six, but it was already as dark as it ever got. And April wasn't entirely sure she wanted to be in the cemetery alone, not after hearing the whispers and laughter the last time she came here in the dark. She cupped her hands around her eyes to peer in through the latticework windows. No, the office was empty. Everyone had gone for the night.

Right then, no excuses, she thought, looking up at the gates. The original architects had obviously anticipated this moment, having made the wrought iron gates fit the stone arch perfectly, so April skirted around the building and looked at the railings surrounding the courtyard where the funeral vehicles pulled in. Clearly there had been crowd-control issues at some point in the cemetery's history – the tall iron fence was topped with revolving spikes which had been reinforced with rather more modern-looking razor wire.

'Screw that,' said April, turning and striding up the hill, keeping the high cemetery wall to her left until she came to the North Gate, the place she had first met Gabriel Swift, the place it had all started. She tried not to think about that night as she wedged her foot into the fence and pulled herself up, scrabbling for a hand-hold in the crumbling wall to the left of the gate. She had been terrified that night and had run home covered in what she had assumed was fox-blood. She couldn't afford to be so squeamish any more. Or so naïve.

Grimacing, groaning, she hauled herself up, the pointy tops of the gate digging into her hands and thighs as she rolled over them. 'Dammit,' she whispered as she snagged her tights and felt them rip. *Better than an artery I suppose*, she thought, landing awkwardly in the mud and rotting leaves on the far side. She ran into the cemetery, barely giving the little white building just inside the gate a glance, letting the darkness separate her from the living world. She knew Gabriel had warned her not to go into the cemetery after dark, but today was special. She needed to talk to someone or she would burst. She still had her torch from the night in the woods and she flicked it on, shining it into the faces and the closed eyes of the stone angels as she walked along the path, through the shadows, her torch beam waving back and forth. She knew the way well enough by now and it didn't take her long to find the tomb: a glowering black slab in the darkness.

'Hi, Daddy,' she said, huddling down next to the door. 'I've just come from your solicitors. Apparently you've made me a rich woman. I suppose I should say thank you.'

The truth was, April didn't really want to have anything to do with the money. Of course, like everyone else, she had occasionally wondered what she would do with a million pounds if she had somehow won the lottery, but this was different. The money seemed tainted somehow. Blood money, quite literally. And the mystery surrounding it only made things worse. That horrid man at the law firm had been quite right: they had been poor when April was born. April didn't know much about journalism, but she did know that it wasn't a huge money-spinner, especially not for a junior writer working his way up. How could he have afforded such huge premiums? And more to the point: *why* had he? Had he expected to die? It was all so strange.

'Daddy, why did you leave us all that money?' she asked quietly. 'Did you know you were in danger? But how could you have known so long ago? Was it because I was a baby and you were worried how mum would cope if you died?'

April's questions were met with silence. *Well, what else were you expecting, genius? A reasoned argument? A note slipped under the door?* April stood up and brushed the dried leaves off. For the first time since her father's death, visiting his tomb gave her no comfort. Maybe it was the late hour or the fact that her thoughts were directed elsewhere. *Or maybe I'm growing up*, her mind countered and perhaps there was some truth in that. Maybe it was time to stop relying on someone who was so patently, so undeniably dead.

'You're not coming back, are you, Daddy?' she whispered, running her fingertips over the cold metal of the door.

'Don't be so sure,' said a voice and April literally jumped into the air, falling back against the door, whirling her torch out into the darkness as if it could defend her.

'Who's there?' she gasped. 'Who the hell is that?'

'Relax,' came the reply. 'It's me.'

'Gabriel?' she whispered as her beam caught a figure standing ten yards away. His white teeth glinted in the torchlight – he was laughing.

'Damn you, Gabriel Swift,' she yelled as she ran towards him, jumping into his arms and hugging and squeezing him tight, breathing in his smell, wishing she never had to let him go. Laughing, he squeezed her back, swinging her around and kissing the top of her head.

'You're okay, you're okay,' she said. 'I thought I'd lost you for ever.'

'Never,' he said fiercely, brushing her hair back and looking into her eyes. 'I will never leave you again.'

Even in this darkness she could tell he was better, although he still looked as if he had been up for two days straight. His sparkling eyes were red-rimmed, his hair sleek but out of place.

'Where have you been?' she said, slapping his arm. 'I was worried sick. I thought you were dying up there!'

'I'm sorry, but I couldn't risk your staying. It felt as if I was going through the change all over again.'

There was pain in his eyes at the memory.

'Sorry,' she said. 'Sorry I hit you, I mean. And sorry that you went through all that for me.'

He laughed.

'Not just for you. You were right, April. This isn't just about me. There are other people relying on me – on us. And I have things to do before I can lie down and die. I've searched for the Regent for so long, I can't just slip away and let him carry on corrupting the world.'

April nodded, but looked a little put out.

'And there's you, of course,' he grinned. 'I couldn't leave you.'

She smiled, looking into his eyes, overjoyed to see the life there. He was alive! *Alive!*

April threw her arms around his neck again, grinning. 'I'm so glad you're back.'

'So am I,' he said, cupping her face gently. 'I felt so far away, so lost. And yet I knew I had to get back to you.'

April lifted her chin and he leant in, his lips coming down towards hers, so close she could feel his breath …

'No!' she cried suddenly, jerking away from him. 'We can't!'

Gabriel stepped away from her, all the colour drained from his face.

'Oh God, I'm sorry!' he breathed. 'That's so stupid. I'm just so used to being able to kiss you whenever I like.'

April gave a sad smile.

'Me too,' she said softly, pulling him into a hug.

'Well maybe we have to focus on finding the Regent then, so we can do it all the time,' she said.

'That sounds good,' said Gabriel, bending to kiss her ear

lobe, sending a tingle along April's spine. *Let's find him quick*, she thought, *Please, God.*

Linking her arm through his, they walked away from the tomb.

'So how do you feel, honestly?' she asked.

'Honestly? I feel amazing. That month of feeling human – of feeling the cold and the rain and pain in my head, it feels like I dreamt it. But it was dangerous too, so seductive, feeling that vulnerable and exposed.'

'Not to me,' said April. 'I hate it.'

'Well I'm here to protect you now, aren't I?'

April looked around at the headstones, the dark trees.

'Can you really protect me?'

'I will,' he said, squeezing her hand.

'And who's going to protect me from you, Gabriel Swift?' She had meant it to sound jokey and flirtatious, but there was genuine fear in her question too.

'The way you looked at me on Primrose Hill …' she said. 'It was as if you wanted to kill me.'

He nodded gravely.

'Which is why you need to take this seriously, April. The Suckers are experts at putting on masks, on pulling you in with their lifestyle and friendship. But underneath the mask, that's how they all look. They all want to rip your throat out.'

'Is that what you want?'

'No, not any more. I'm different, April. Truly. I don't want to kill anyone.'

'Not even the Regent?'

'No. Not really. Yes, I have the vampire instincts and powers, but it gives me no pleasure to use them. I would much rather be like you. Be normal.'

'I'm about as far from normal as you can get.'

He smiled ruefully. 'I suppose. But I mean being human, worrying about exams and dates and what to wear to the next party, the everyday concerns of everyday people. I don't want to kill the Regent, but I will because it's the only way I can be released from this prison. And I want to stop whatever his scheme is.'

'What do you think it is? Miss Holden says ...'

'Miss Holden? Don't listen to that witch!'

April stopped and looked at him with a frown.

'Miss Holden is the only reason you're still here, Gabriel Swift. She swallowed her principles and risked getting drummed out of her weird sect for you.'

'No. She did it for you, April.'

'Perhaps. But she did it because it was the right thing to do. You could take a leaf out of her book. And that woman from the woods, too. All you people are going to have to start working together or we're never going to get out of this mess.'

He laughed out loud.

'You are unique, April Dunne.'

'I'd hope so.'

April and Gabriel walked up the path arm in arm. Something was nagging at April, tugging away at the back of her mind. Suddenly she realised what she was feeling: guilt. This was the first time she had felt properly happy since her father's death.

'You're quiet,' said Gabriel, sensing her unease. 'What's the matter?'

She shook her head.

'Nothing's the matter,' she said. 'Feeling happy.'

'Hey, don't make a habit of it.'

She remembered the last time she'd felt so close to Gabriel; they'd been here in the cemetery that night after Milo's party, before everything had started to unravel. She turned to Gabriel.

'Hey, do you remember that night we first came here?' she said. 'Can we go back? To the Circle of Lebanon?'

That night had been so romantic, so perfect. Gabriel had led her down into the circle of tombs which should have been terrifying, but she had only felt peace down there in the moonlight. Perhaps, she thought, it was because even then she'd been in love with Gabriel. It made her shiver.

'I've got a better idea,' said Gabriel, taking her hand and leading her up the hill. The shadows seemed longer up here, closer to the moon. They passed the circle with its huge cedar tree and saw the strange shape of the Beer tomb with the pyramid roof looming above it.

'Where are we going?'

'This way,' he smiled, pulling her up a flight of steps, bright white in the moonlight. There was a wide terrace at the top with a low balustrade, a little neglected with plants and moss growing here and there, but impressive nonetheless.

'What is this place?' asked April.

'We're on top of the catacombs. It was built to give a perfect view of London; people used to come here to promenade and pass notes to each other.'

'Seems a strange place to come.'

'No, it was wonderful back then, flowers growing everywhere, the paths swept clean and those trees ahead of us were cut back to make the view as spectacular as possible.'

April fought back a pang of jealousy, thinking of Gabriel coming here with other girls. *Be happy that he's here at all*, she scolded herself.

'You're right,' she said, 'it's beautiful.'

'No. *You're* beautiful,' said Gabriel. He leant in and kissed her neck, his nose pressing against her ear. His hands slipped inside her coat and she sighed with pleasure. *Oh God, I've missed this*, she thought, urging him on, pressing her body against his.

'I wish I could kiss you,' he murmured, 'you're so …'

She waited for more, but Gabriel had frozen. April looked up and flinched; Gabriel's teeth were bared, his eyes narrow, darker. His whole body seemed tense.

Oh God, he's not going to kill me, is he? she thought miserably. There was no terror, no fear for her life, just sudden misery that their romance had all been a sham, that Gabriel had simply been attracted to her Fury scent all along.

'Wha—' she began, but Gabriel put a finger to her lips.

'Shhh …' he said in a low whisper. 'Can you smell that?'

'What?'

He shook his head and led her back to the stairs. He was

moving like a lion stalking prey, his head turning from side to side, his eyes taking everything in. When April reached the bottom of the stairs, he turned back to her. 'Wait here,' he said. 'If anything comes for you, scream. And then run. In that order.'

'Bugger that,' said April, 'I'm coming with you.'

'No, April, there's something dangerous here.'

'What, and it's going to be less dangerous if you leave me by myself? I'm sticking to you like glue, hero.'

She followed Gabriel along the path. To their left was a long grey stone wall with arched doors let into the sides, the occupants' names carved above them: tombs for London's wealthiest Victorian families. April remembered coming along here on her tour of the cemetery; the main doorway ahead of them was the entrance to the Highgate Catacombs. It had been a pretty creepy place then, and that had been in full daylight. Gabriel stopped and crouched down, as if he were searching the ground for tracks.

'What is it? What can you see?'

He looked up and pointed ahead of him to the high black iron door set into a stone archway. The catacombs were open.

'Oh no,' whispered April. She remembered the tour guide making a big deal about how the catacombs were kept locked at all other times.

'Someone's been here,' said Gabriel.

'Someone or some*thing*?'

Gabriel turned to her, the moonlight catching his face. She didn't need an answer. He looked like an attack dog straining on the end of his lead. Whatever the something was, he wanted to get at it.

'Stay outside, April,' he said, moving towards the door. 'I'm serious.'

April watched as he stepped into the vault, staring at the entrance after he vanished inside. She turned around, her eyes darting from shadow to shadow, wondering if the something was out here watching her from behind a tree or a tomb.

Scrabbling in her pocket, she brought out the little torch

and began shining it at the tree line, back at the tomb, any-where. There was nothing – nothing she could see, anyway. There was a noise to her right and she whirled around, hold-ing the torch in front of her like a gun. What was that? All she could see were trees, but she was sure she'd heard something: a whisper? A chuckle? *God, not again.* 'Gabriel,' she hissed, backing towards the door. *'Gabriel!'*

She wasn't going to stay out here alone. She walked slowly towards the dark open doorway, her body tensed, hearing her heart thumping in her ears. Where was he? As she reached out to touch the stone archway, she immediately jerked back as Gabriel stepped in front of her.

'Dammit, Gabe, you scared me!'

'Don't go in there,' he said, putting his arms around her. It was a gesture of protection and sympathy, the same sort of embrace people had given her at her dad's funeral.

'Why not?' she said, trying to look around him, 'What's in there?'

'You don't need to see,' said Gabriel, his face grave. 'We should go.'

'No,' said April angrily. She didn't know why, but suddenly it was very important that she see inside the vault. 'Whatever's in there, I want to see it,' she said, trying to get around him. 'Don't tell me what to do, I'm sick of people telling me what's best for me.'

More than that, she was sick of not knowing what was going on, of half-glimpsing things, of constantly feeling that she was groping around in the dark. She could tell from the look on his face that she wasn't going to discover a box of fluffy kittens, but at that moment she wanted – she *needed* – to see, however horrible it was. She darted to the side and ducked under his arm.

'April, don't . . .'

But he was too late. There, in the entrance to the cata-combs, she could see a body. Hanging by the neck.

'Jesus, God . . .' said April, a hand over her mouth. Her heart was hammering and bile rose in her throat. Because she knew who it was; she recognised the dress, and the shoe hanging loosely from the toe of the left foot. She knew who it was, but still she couldn't help raising her torch beam towards the face. Because she *had* to see, she simply couldn't help herself. She had to be sure that what she was seeing was real. April let out a sob as she saw the horribly distorted face, her eyes mercifully closed, her blonde hair falling in waves, still perfect even in death. 'Layla,' she moaned. 'Oh Layla.'

Gabriel caught April as she staggered backwards, wrapping her in his arms and pulling her outside. He held her tightly as she shook, her breath coming in gulps. It was horrible, monstrous, unreal. She looked up into Gabriel's face, tears streaking her own.

'Why?' she asked. 'Why is this happening? God, Gabriel, why?'

Gabriel didn't answer. What could he say? 'Because creatures like me have come to destroy everything you know, to turn this place – to turn the world – into a living hell'? There was no way to explain this, to explain the endless horrors which kept coming again and again. Alix, Isabelle, her father, her own ordeals and now Layla. Who would be next, who was safe? No one was; April saw that clearly now. She had been floating in her naïve belief that the worst was over and all they had to do was catch the bad guy. But now she saw with sickening clarity that any one of her friends, her neighbours … anyone she knew could be next, anyone who stumbled onto the vampires' secret, anyone they felt could be a threat. And if she didn't do something about it, something very, very soon, then any day now, that vault would be piled high with bodies.

'We have to stop them, Gabe,' she said fiercely.

'We will, baby,' he said. 'We have to.'

Chapter Seventeen

The police examiner thought Layla had been dead for two days. Which placed her time of death on the night of the party at Davina's house.

'Are you okay, April?' DI Reece had found April in the kitchen where she was staring into a cup of tea which had gone cold ten minutes before.

She looked up. 'Not really.'

Reece nodded. 'Well, I think I'd have been more worried if you were doing cartwheels. Do young people still do cartwheels?' he wondered aloud.

April forced a smile: he was only trying to lighten the mood, but she really didn't feel up to swapping jokes. And to think only half an hour ago, she had been feeling so happy. Happy that her boyfriend had lived, happy that she hadn't killed him with her kiss after all. *Well, that didn't last long, did it?* she thought cynically.

Gabriel had taken her back to her mother's house, where they'd raised the alarm. They both agreed that having Gabriel find another body would prompt too many questions. It was bad enough that April was wrapped up in yet another violent death, but at least she had an excuse for being in the cemetery – even if it had involved some minor breaking and entering.

'I know you and Layla weren't exactly friends,' said Reece, sitting on the stool opposite her, 'but it's never pleasant to hear about a suicide.'

Suicide. It was all April had been thinking about. Could Layla really have committed suicide? Or had the Suckers forced her into the noose? She wasn't sure which was more horrible.

'But she just wasn't the type, Mr Reece,' said April urgently. 'She wouldn't have killed herself, she was too …' she trailed off.

'Too what, April?'

'Too arrogant.' She shrugged. 'Too full of her own self-importance. Layla loved herself, Mr Reece, there's no way she would have done that.'

'People do funny things sometimes. You think you've seen everything, but they will constantly surprise you. No one can really know what's going on inside someone else's head.'

He looked at April sympathetically.

'I'm sorry, she was your friend. You don't want to hear this right now.'

'It's okay, I want to work it out as much as you. Because if someone as self-obsessed as Layla can kill herself, then something's seriously wrong in Highgate.'

Reece nodded.

'Okay, well let's see if we can work it out. Her boyfriend's death could certainly have been a trigger, but is there anything else you can tell us?'

April hesitated. She wasn't sure how much she should tell him. She never was: that was the eternal problem.

'Well, there was one thing,' she said slowly. 'Layla said something to me the other day about how "they" were after her. She was acting really strangely.'

Reece noted it down in his notebook, then tapped the page. 'And who were "they"?'

'I don't know,' she said, avoiding his gaze, 'I assumed she was talking about some of the other girls in her clique, you know, that they were pushing her out of the group or spreading rumours about her or something, not that anyone was actually threatening her life. Especially since when I asked her about it the next day, she acted like I was talking rubbish. She was back to being the same cocky girl she was before.'

'So you think there could have been a bullying element to this? Something that pushed her over the edge?'

'Look … I don't want to speak ill of the dead, but Layla

was a bit of a bully herself. It's like asking if a shark could be attacked by another shark. I suppose it's possible, but ... I can't see how someone calling her names would make her do ... that. Like I said, it doesn't make sense that Layla would kill herself.'

'And yet she did.'

'Did she?'

Reece raised his eyebrows.

'What do you mean?'

'Well, are you sure it was suicide?'

Reece looked down the corridor towards the living room where DS Amy Carling was talking to April's mother and Mr Sheldon.

'Just between us, just in conversation – and I'm not saying she was killed, we're just talking hypothetically here, okay? – it's an awful lot of effort to go to, faking a hanging. Someone must have really wanted her dead. Given that people have been killed in much more bloody ways recently, as you well know, why would anyone bother?'

And suddenly it came to her in a rush. All at once, she knew who had done it and more importantly, *why* they had.

'Oh no,' said April, clamping her hand over her mouth. 'Oh God.' *Why didn't I think of it before?* She jumped to her feet, knocking her stool to the floor with a great clatter, and ran from the room, pushing through the kitchen door and out into the back yard, gulping at the cold air, her head spinning. *Stupid! So stupid. How did I miss it?* They had killed Layla because of *her*. Because they thought Layla was a Fury, rather than April. The vampires had watched Milo waste away, eaten away from the inside by disease, and they'd thought 'vampires don't get sick'. The only possible cause was a Fury. The only creature on earth which could destroy a vampire. As Milo's girlfriend Layla must have been their prime suspect. Perhaps he fed from her, perhaps not. Either way they had kissed. God, that was why they had killed her in such a horrible way – snap her neck, no blood, no danger to the vampires.

She squeezed her fingers into her eyes. *It was me, it was*

me, she thought, *I killed Layla. If I wasn't a Fury – if I hadn't accidentally killed Milo – they would have left her alone.* And ironically, Gabriel would have been the perfect cover for April. All the Suckers had seen them kissing and yet here he was, a picture of vampire health. Killing Layla had made her safe – for the moment, anyway. God, that just made her feel worse.

'April?'

Reece had come into the yard. He handed her a glass of water. 'Are you okay? Can I help?'

'No, no,' she said, taking a sip of the water. 'I'm just … it just suddenly hit me – what had happened, what I had seen. God, Mr Reece, she was just hanging there. It's just so … wrong.'

'You said it. And it hasn't gone unnoticed either.'

'What do you mean?'

'Layla's father is a well-connected businessman, something in telecommunications, I think. He has friends in high places, specifically the Home Office, the mayor's office, not to mention Ravenwood – which is why Mr Sheldon is here. All of which means that suddenly this case has become big news. We're going to be crawling all over this.'

'Well that's good, isn't it?'

Reece pulled a face.

'Not necessarily. Not for me, anyway.'

'They aren't taking you off the case, are they?'

'Not yet. But they will, believe me, if I don't come up with results quick smart. And they're bringing in some big guns.'

'Why do you look so worried about that?'

'I think you'll see why when you meet Dr Tame.'

'Who's Dr Tame?'

'A hot-shot police psychologist. Used to be an Oxford professor, written loads of books about how to tell if someone's lying, which is why they bring him in to work on difficult cases.'

'I take it you don't approve?'

'He gets the job done, I'll give him that. But I'd rather be working with coppers, not some jumped-up teacher. And his methods … are not to my taste. But it's out of my hands.'

'But you'll still be looking into my dad's case?' she said urgently.

'As long as they'll let me.'

The police wrapped up their questioning and April's mother showed them and Mr Sheldon out before she came to find April in the kitchen.

'Are you all right, darling?' said Silvia as she walked in.

Yeah, like you care.

'So what was Mr Sheldon doing here?' asked April.

'He came to offer his help. He has some connections in the force and they contacted him about the suicide.'

'I meant why did he come here instead of visiting Layla's family?'

'Because he's our friend, April. Don't start this again.'

'Okay, but how come he's so friendly all of a sudden? How come I'd never heard of him before?'

'Your dad and I were at university with him, you know that.'

'Do I?' said April. She shook her head. Maybe they *had* told her. She wasn't that sure about anything any more. She made her excuses and trudged up to bed. She'd barely slept over the past three days through worrying about Gabriel and she was drained from their reunion, especially when so swiftly followed by yet another body blow. She ran herself a bath and slipped under the bubbles. A really hot dunk sometimes helped her think, but April found she couldn't close her eyes without seeing Layla's face. She pushed the image away and concentrated her mind on something else: why had Sheldon been here exactly? She had a strong suspicion Sheldon was a vampire – why wouldn't he be, being the head of a school overrun by them? – so maybe he was spying. But that actually wasn't what was bothering her, it was the way he seemed to be sniffing around her mother and the way Silvia was reacting to him, like it was the kindest thing anyone had ever done. After all, why would her mother be interested in *him*? He even had funny eyes!

She dried off and clambered into bed, checking her mobile for texts. Caro, Fiona, Davina – of course. She couldn't deal with all that overwrought drama right now. There was nothing from Gabriel, although he was probably keeping a low profile. *God, why am I always making excuses for him?* she wondered. She was too weary to think about it. But as she lay down, she couldn't stop thinking about Layla. DI Reece was right; she hadn't really liked the girl, but she had seen the fear on her face – she was terrified. And what had April done about it? Nothing, that's what. But what *could* she have done, even if she had made the Fury connection earlier? Called the police? Confessed to the vamps that she was a Fury, not Layla? But how could she have known they were going to do that? She tortured herself, imagining Davina leading Layla away after the party. Had they tied her up? Or just used threats? Somehow the idea of being locked up in the catacombs was more horrible than having your throat ripped out. Alone in the dark, surrounded by corpses. Had they forced her into the noose, or simply left it for her? *God, that was the worst thought.* Locked in that windowless tomb, pressed in on all sides by whispers and grinning skeletons, facing starvation or a swinging rope. But no, that couldn't be right, the door was wide open, wasn't it? Perhaps the vamps had left it that way, so Layla's corpse would be found, like gamekeepers leaving snared rats and crows hanging to rot as a deterrent to the others. This is our territory, leave it alone or you will suffer the same fate. What sort of evil was surrounding her? She turned over, pulling the duvet up around her ears. It took a long time for April's mind to let go, spinning down to twitching, disquieting dreams of chase, darkness and a bird's yellow beak stabbing at her eye.

Chapter Eighteen

'Jack the Ripper was not a psychopath,' said Miss Holden. 'At least not in the classic sense. He wasn't committing his crimes because he was unable to control his urges – which is the usual definition of a psychopath – in fact he was acting deliberately and methodically.'

April and Benjamin exchanged glances across the history class. The serial killer was an especially gruesome choice of subject straight after Layla's death. Why was she talking about this now? The whole school was subdued, talking in whispers. April was getting used to the sideways glances and muttered conversations when she walked by. 'See that weird girl who got attacked by Marcus Brent? She found another body.' She wasn't surprised to see someone had set up a Wall of Layla outside the refectory, fast becoming a Ravenwood tradition. The first one had been a Wall of Milo in honour of Layla's late boyfriend and it had quickly been covered in pictures of Layla along with written tributes and poems. 'Milo and Layla – together at last' was a strong favourite.

April's mind jumped back to the lesson when Miss Holden's voice reminded her of her dreams, of being chased through dark streets.

'The Ripper was only out of control in the sense that he couldn't resist this urge he had to kill,' said Miss Holden. 'And he clearly wasn't that bothered about getting caught – in fact he wanted people to see what he had done. He laid his victims out carefully as if they were on display, and as if they were supposed to give people a specific message.'

Like a warning, perhaps? thought April.

Miss Holden was trying to use the Ripper case to show how something as commonplace as a handful of murders – which were a depressingly ordinary event in Whitechapel in the 1880s – could change society so much, leading to reforms in the police service, leaps forward in forensic techniques and a massive change in the way the media reported crime. But today, it had taken on a different meaning. After Layla, Marcus and the other murders, the long-ago terror of the East End felt very close to home, very easy to visualise for most of the students. April began to wonder about Miss Holden's real motivation. Surely she would know that they would all be thinking about Layla that morning?

'So how did he kill them, miss?' asked Carl Newton, a fleshy boy in a mohair sweater. He looked anxious, worried, as if he expected the Ripper to be waiting for him in the playground.

'Contrary to popular belief, Carl, he strangled them, then cut their throats. He didn't kill by cutting, he killed in order to cut. Which is why I emphasise my point that he was a hugely controlled individual. This wasn't a frenzied stabbing in a doorway. He took his time, making his incisions carefully.'

'Is that why people think he was a surgeon?'

'Yes, he removed organs and made incisions, which required a certain amount of anatomical knowledge.'

For some reason, April thought of Gabriel. He had medical knowledge, in fact he had saved April's life with it. But he had also spoken to her about the vampire's uncontrollable urge to kill. Had the Ripper been a vampire?

'Weren't the crimes random, just choosing girls who came his way?' asked a girl at the front.

'No, he killed them to cover up his marriage to one of the prostitutes,' said Carl, which brought on a ripple of laughter.

'Ah, that's the Johnny Depp film you're talking about now. There are no facts to back that theory up, I'm afraid. But we do know that Jack was deliberately trying to terrorise Whitechapel specifically. He sent a kidney in a letter to George Lusk, a local neighbourhood watch vigilante, rather than a newspaper editor. His focus was very specific: on causing terror in the Whitechapel area.'

'Why?' asked April.

'Again, that's unknown. But I think we can assume he had a grudge against the area. Something had happened there which he wanted to avenge, or someone lived there who he wanted to punish. Powerless people always seek to take the power back – I'd put Jack the Ripper in that bracket. Before he became a killer, he had been a victim.'

April stayed at her desk while the rest of the class filed out. She watched silently as Miss Holden put her files and papers back into her briefcase and wiped down the white board.

Finally, the teacher looked up at her.

'This isn't the time, April,' she said.

'Well, when is?' said April, glancing at the door. 'They killed Layla because' – she dropped her voice to a whisper – 'they thought she was a Fury. How do you think that makes me feel? I as good as killed her!'

'First of all, we don't know why Layla was killed. And secondly, you did not kill her. At best, it's a case of mistaken identity, April ... but if they thought Milo had been killed by a Fury, why would they wait so long to remove Layla? My guess is that she was killed for another reason entirely.'

'But what reason? Layla hadn't done anything.'

The teacher snorted.

'April, it may have escaped your notice, but Layla was one of the group you all call the Faces. I think she knew well enough what was going on. She'd made her bed, as they say.'

'How can you be so cold?' said April. 'She was only seventeen.'

'Not cold, April. Pragmatic. Sometimes you have to take a stand. Not so long ago, your great-grandparents stood up to the Nazis. A good thing, you think. But the Allies killed hundreds of thousands of people in the process, many of them innocent – was that acceptable just because they were stopping an evil regime?'

'I ... I don't know. Of course we should try and stop them, but if innocent people are being killed ...'

Miss Holden gave a cold smile.

'This is your dilemma, April. You have to weigh up the consequences and rewards. Is winning the battle worth the sacrifice?'

'So you're saying Layla is expendable.'

'No. I'm saying I think the vampires have to be stopped, and I'm asking how much you're prepared to pay to do it. Is Layla's death too high a price?'

'Yes, I think it is.'

Miss Holden spread her hands. 'Then you have your answer.'

'What's your answer, miss?'

'In war the price is always, always far too high. But you have to consider the alternative.'

'What's the alternative?'

'That we all end up like Layla.'

Dr Charles Tame was not what April had been expecting at all. Throughout the morning, students had been called out of lessons and taken up to Mr Sheldon's office for their interview with the police psychologist. Rumours were rife as they moved between lessons mid-morning. Davina said Chessy had seen him arrive before first bell and that he had been wearing a trench coat and carrying a sinister leather bag. Simon had already been called in and he described Dr Tame as 'pushy'. So by the time Mrs Bagly, the school secretary, had summoned April in the middle of her English lesson, she had built him up into some combination of a Cold War spy and a Nazi SS officer. It was some surprise to find that Dr Tame was neither of these things.

'Ah, April,' said Mr Sheldon as he opened the door. 'This is Dr Tame, he's here to ask you a few questions.'

'April,' said the man sitting behind the desk. He was thin, with pale skin and over-long snow-white hair. With his pink eyelids and invisible lashes, April guessed he was an albino.

He didn't get up, merely offering her a limp hand. April shook it: it was like touching a raw chicken breast.

'Mr Sheldon has told me so much about you,' said the doctor. 'I think we're going to get along just fine.'

He glanced quickly in Sheldon's direction and the head teacher almost jumped to attention. 'Well, I'll leave you two alone,' he muttered, shutting the door behind him. Odd, thought April, it wasn't like Hawk to behave so deferentially. But then it wasn't like Layla to commit suicide. Not much was making sense at the moment.

'Sit, sit,' said Dr Tame, flapping a hand at the chair in front of the desk. April perched uncomfortably on the hard wooden chair as Dr Tame stared at her. His eyes were watery and his curiously translucent skin was slightly blue. There was a slightly unsettling smile on his face. It was hard to look at him directly, so April gazed at the floor instead. Still Dr Tame just stared at her until, finally, she had to break the silence.

'Are you a psychologist?'

'Don't I look like one?'

'I don't know any. I heard you were an Oxford don.'

'I have worked at Oxford, I've been a teacher, I ran a school, but I've also been a fisherman. Which do you think is most important?'

April didn't like him. She hated the way he threw her question back at her, trying to unsettle her.

'I didn't think this interview was about me. Don't you want to ask about Layla?'

'Is there something you want to tell me about her?' said the doctor.

'No, I just thought that was why you were here. Inspector Reece said—'

'You're quite close to DI Reece, aren't you?' interrupted Tame. 'Quite … pally?'

'No, not really. He's just the officer investigating my dad's death.'

'Yes, yes, a tragic affair,' said the doctor, gazing up towards the ceiling. 'Raises a lot of questions.'

'Questions? What do you mean?'

'Oh, such as who killed him,' said Tame, meeting her gaze. 'I thought that's what you wanted to know.'

'Of course I do,' said April.

'Is that why you wanted to kill Layla?'

April felt all the air push out of her lungs. For a moment she couldn't speak.

'Kill her?' she finally spluttered.

Tame reached for a file on the desk and flipped it open. 'Yes, kill her. Those were your words weren't they? "I'll kill you"?'

She felt a huge rush of anxiety. They couldn't take that seriously, could they? People said things like that all the time. She hadn't meant she was actually going to kill Layla.

'Yes, I said it. We were having a fight, she had just said something bad about my father and I was angry. But I didn't mean I was actually going to kill her.'

'Powerful emotion, anger,' said the doctor. 'Can make ordinary people do things they wouldn't usually do. Like Layla, for example.'

April frowned.

'You think she was angry?'

The doctor sighed and pushed himself up. He seemed weary.

'Who can say? Her boyfriend died in tragic circumstances. The normal response to such tragedies is to become angry, to want to blame someone. Perhaps someone he was cheating on her with, perhaps?'

'Who? With me? No!'

'But that's what Layla thought, wasn't it? That's why you were fighting that day. Her friends have all told me. She said, "Stay away from my man." But you didn't, did you?'

Tame walked around the desk, perching on the front, right before April.

'Did you kiss him, April?' he asked, leaning in close.

'No!' she said, pulling away, her chair scraping on the floor. 'I didn't. Layla was paranoid.'

'Really?' asked Tame, that half-smile on his face. 'Are you telling me the truth?'

'Yes I am,' said April, pushing herself back in the chair as far as she could go. Having the man so close to her was giving her the creeps.

'Mmm ... I wonder,' said Tame, standing up and walking back around the desk. He sat down and began writing. April watched him for a moment, before he glanced up. 'Oh, you can go,' said Tame, waving his pale hand. Confused and upset, April quickly walked to the door.

'Just one last thing,' said Tame as she turned the handle. 'Who did Layla think was going to kill her?'

'Pardon?' stuttered April.

'Oh come now, don't look so shocked. Your chum Mr Reece wrote it up in his report.' Tame bent forward to read another paper in front of him. 'She said "they were after her". Who are "they"?'

'I don't know.'

'I think you do, Miss Dunne. I really think you do.'

Then he waved his had again, as if he was shooing a fly from the room.

'We'll speak again.'

Mr Sheldon was waiting for her outside his office.

'How was your little chat?'

April glared at him.

'Can I go back to class?' She'd had enough questioning for now.

'No, April, you cannot,' said Mr Sheldon, taking her by the arm and steering her towards an empty classroom. 'I need to speak to you too.'

Once inside, April sat on a chair and crossed her arms.

'Look, April, I know it's difficult but we must get to the bottom of this. There has been enough unpleasantness already.'

'Unpleasantness? Is that what you call it?'

Mr Sheldon looked as if he was about to shout at her, then seemed to think better of it.

'I'm sorry, April,' he said. 'It really must be hard for you. You've had to deal with so much since you came to Ravenwood and I can sympathise, I really can. But you need to understand that my responsibility is to all the students here.'

He glanced towards the office and lowered his voice.

'I'll be honest with you, I'm not entirely sure the police are on top of this and that's a worry when you are in charge of hundreds of young people.'

April nodded. It made sense, although she suspected he was more worried about his own neck than he was about the kids at Ravenwood.

'So is it all right if I ask you a few questions now?' said the headmaster with a slight smile.

'Only if you'll answer one first. What are you doing with my mother?'

Sheldon barked out a laugh.

'Is that what you're worried about? Heavens, April, your mother is still grieving over your father's death.'

'You could have fooled me.'

'People deal with loss in their own way, April. Your mother is a good woman and she only wants the best for you.'

Just then, there was a light knock at the door and Mrs Bagly put her head into the room.

'Sorry, Headmaster,' she said, holding up a mobile phone. 'Important call.'

'I'm in the middle of something, Mrs Bagly,' he replied.

She pulled a face. 'It's the *chairman*,' she said, widening her eyes for emphasis.

Mr Sheldon looked at April, then back at the phone. 'Very well. We'll continue this later April, all right?'

He took the phone and walked into a corner of the classroom. As Mrs Bagly ushered April out, she could hear him talking.

'Yes, I'm sorry … I know it's a school, of course, and Ravenwood's reputation is uppermost in my … yes, yes, I'll get it sorted as soon as possible, you have my word.'

'Is he in trouble?' asked April as the secretary escorted her back to her class.

'I don't think the governors are too happy that the police are using school facilities for their investigation. It wouldn't look good in the papers, would it?'

'No, no I suppose not,' she said.

'I don't know why you're so disappointed Hawk's not the Regent,' said Caro. 'Is it because he's after your mum and you wanted an excuse to kill him?'

'No! I don't want to kill anyone.'

'Well you could have fooled me. You look like you'd strangle the next person to ask you the time.'

They were sitting in the refectory eating lunch or, in April's case, pushing some rice salad around her plate. She was still unsettled by her encounter with Dr Tame and the way her mother and Mr Sheldon seemed to be playing some sort of elaborate game with each other.

'So if Hawk isn't the Regent, who is?' said Caro. 'I mean, he's in charge of the school, which makes him a suspect, but he's clearly answering to someone else. So we need to find whoever's behind the school. This plot to recruit the best kids in the country must be their idea.'

'Yes, but what are they planning on doing after that?'

'Take over the world, presumably. It's not as if they're breeding these kids to be kind and considerate, to build a better society, is it?'

'Miss Holden said something similar. They used to be experts in hiding from the world, now it's as if they're daring someone to see them, like they want to be discovered.'

'Well when we track down the Regent, we can ask him about his dastardly plan, just before you give him the kiss of death.'

'I wish you'd stop treating this like some sort of joke! Someone's *dead.*'

'I know, April!' said Caro, suddenly fierce. Startled, she looked at Caro and saw that she had tears in her eyes. 'Layla was my friend,' she whispered, angrily swiping at her tears with the back of her hand. 'Okay, so she had turned into a horrible bitch, but before that we were best friends. We grew up together.'

Her shoulders shook and April put her arm around her and led her to a corner where they wouldn't be overheard.

'I'm sorry, Caro, I didn't think,' she said, handing her some tissue from her bag.

'S'okay, I just want to find these scumbags and bring them down. So they can't recruit any more nice people and turn them into their bloody slaves. Layla was great before they got their claws into her. Before … well, you know.'

April narrowed her eyes. 'You mean "before me", don't you? You think if I wasn't here Layla would be fine?'

'Well if you hadn't come here with all your magical powers, then maybe … oh, I don't know!'

'Yes you do! You think if I wasn't here stirring the Suckers up, Layla might be alive. I know you're upset, Caro, but do you really think they'd be playing nicey-nicey if I hadn't arrived? They were killing people before I got here, remember?'

'But they thought she was you, April! They thought she was a' – she glanced around – 'a Fury. That's why they hung her like that, so they wouldn't get any of her blood on them!'

'Do you think I don't know that? Don't you think that's sitting on my chest like a five-tonne weight? But I didn't kill her, Caro. And Layla chose to play dress-up with the Suckers.'

'But she didn't know what she was getting into, did she?'

'I think she did. I think they all do, deep down. I don't mean it's their fault. They're being manipulated. But someone else killed her, Caro. Not me.'

Caro turned to April, her eyes pleading.

'We've got to stop them, A. We can't let this evil spread any more.'

'We'll stop them, honey,' said April. 'We will. We have to.'

Caro rubbed her face and tried to smile.

'Okay then, here's our chance …'

Davina swept into the room on Benjamin's arm, dressed entirely in black and wearing over-sized sunglasses.

People crowded around her, cooing.

'Come on,' said April, 'we're going in.'

'How are you, Davina?' asked April.

'I'll be okay,' she said, sniffing, dabbing at her eyes under the sunglasses. 'I just wish it would all stop. All these deaths. It's horrible. Layla ...' she broke off to give a loud sob. 'Sorry, it's just ... I can't bear to think of her being all alone like that.'

April glanced at Caro and saw a momentary flicker of hurt and anger in her eyes, then it was gone. April knew that her friend was screaming inside, that she wanted to grab Davina by the throat and shake her, but instead she gave Davina a hug. 'We know,' said Caro. 'It must be awful for you.'

'It is!' said Davina, looking at Caro as if she was the only person on earth who understood her. 'She was right there in my house, and then ... then she was gone. I keep thinking: what if I had kept her there, what if I'd insisted on a sleepover or something?'

'Don't beat yourself up,' said Caro. 'We all know you did everything you could for Layla.'

'God, you're so right Caro, thank you,' said Davina with another appreciative look. 'No one else seems to get it; I tried my best to help Layla. I mean, when I first came to Ravenwood she was just this geeky girl. I turned her into a woman.'

'Sometimes you can't help people,' said Caro. 'You can only do your best.'

'That's what I told the police.'

'Did they interrogate you, too?' asked April.

'Oh honey, you found her, didn't you?' said Davina, her hand to her mouth. 'That must have been so horrid. Were the police asking you hundreds of questions? They must have been. I had them round the house last night for hours. All these horrible little sweaty men asking the same questions over and over again. And then today that strange man, Dr Tame. At least he didn't keep asking what time Layla left the house.'

'I saw him this morning. He was creepy.'

'You can say that again.'

'What did he ask you?

'Oh, how long we'd been friends, what had been troubling her. I told them, she had everything to live for – the Spring Ball's coming up next weekend. We were talking about our dresses. She had this amazing McQueen outfit. Why would anyone pass up the chance to wear that?'

'You're so right,' said Caro.

Davina tilted her head and squeezed Caro's arm. 'I wish everyone was as perceptive as you, Caro,' she said and walked off. April whistled quietly.

'... And the Oscar for Best Actress goes to Miss Caro Jackson.'

'It's not me who should get the Oscar, it's her,' said Caro, her suppressed fury making her voice shake. 'Look at her, flouncing around like she doesn't know a thing about it.'

'Do you think it was Davina? You think she put Layla in the noose?'

'I'm sure of it. The last time anyone saw her was at Davina's party and she was still there when everyone left, so we only have Davina's word that she left at all. I think she and her coven led Layla down to the tomb.'

'God, that's horrible. But if they really thought she was a Fury, wouldn't they be worried she would attack them?'

'I don't want to worry you, A, but half a dozen fanged-up vampires swarming all over you, I don't think you'd stand much of a chance.'

April shivered. Caro was right, she'd seen how terrible one vampire could be with Marcus. If they decided to gang up on you, it'd be over before you could utter a sound.

'But Milo died weeks ago,' said April. 'Why did they wait so long?'

'I don't know,' said Caro. 'But I do know one thing: I will get even with that monster if it's the last thing I do.'

Chapter Nineteen

Layla's funeral was short and sweet: it had to be. The platitudes usually wheeled out at a young person's funeral: 'she had everything before her', 'she was cut down in her prime', didn't really work when someone had taken their own life. Suicide was the official line the coroner was taking, at least until the inquest was resolved, and that wouldn't be for months. April hadn't really felt good about attending, seeing as she and Layla hadn't been friends, let alone close, but Caro had wanted her there. She was in bits, weeping steadily during the service and sobbing at the graveside. April was going through her own pain, especially when she saw Layla's parents and cousins who were all grey with grief. She couldn't help agreeing with Caro: if she hadn't come to Highgate with her birthmark and deadly virus, Layla might well still be alive. Whatever Miss Holden said, that did lay some responsibility at her door. *I have to put a stop to this – and right now, before anyone else gets hurt*, she thought angrily as they filed out of the cemetery gates.

In many ways the wake, held at Layla's family home, was even worse. April and Caro had to endure Davina, Chessy and the rest of the Faces squeezing out their crocodile tears and treating the whole thing as one big monochrome catwalk. At least Gabriel hadn't come. It was a small relief not to have to worry about how she was supposed to act around him.

'You look how I feel,' said Benjamin. Caro had gone to repair her smeared make-up, so April had come through to the kitchen to find a bit of space. She had been staring through the kitchen window at the frozen lawns beyond, wishing she could just open the back door and run away.

'That bad, huh?' she said.

'Don't worry,' said Ben. 'Whatever my sister thinks, I think you're supposed to look unhappy at a funeral.'

'It's just …' began April, but Benjamin just stepped over and squeezed her arm.

'April, I know,' he said kindly. 'You don't have to explain. It can't be much fun coming to any funeral so soon after your dad's.'

She nodded. 'It doesn't make it easier. I mean, I'm the one who found her. I was only there to visit my dad's tomb, but people are looking at me like it's …'

'… like it's your fault?' he finished. 'Don't be silly, April. I think everyone's glad you did. No one likes to think of her, well, being up there any longer than she was. God knows Layla had her faults, but no one deserves to go out like that,' he said with feeling. 'It's not right to be alone like that.'

April was surprised by the passion of Ben's words. Did he know something? Was he saying he disapproved of the way the Suckers had murdered Layla? Was he trying to say he hadn't had anything to do with it? But of course that was stupid; that would imply that Ben knew that April knew that he was a vampire … *Arrrgh!* she thought, *this is all so complicated!* It was like juggling a hundred balls at once.

'Listen, I'd better go and check Davina's not trying to seduce someone's unsuspecting uncle or something,' said Ben. 'I'll come and see Caro before I go, okay?'

April poured herself a glass of water and wondered about finding Caro herself. *It's not all about you today, April*, she reprimanded herself. She should be there for Caro, she was the one really suffering.

'Were you a friend of Layla's, my dear?' asked an elderly woman shuffling into the kitchen with the aid of a stick.

'Well, yes … I suppose …' stammered April. 'I only joined the school last term, so I didn't know Layla that well.'

The woman offered a slim hand.

'I'm Grace, Layla's grandmother.'

April tried not to let her dismay show. The last thing she

needed right now was any more grieving relatives.

'So I suppose you didn't know her other friend, the boy called Milo?'

April shook her head slightly.

'I met him once, but not really.'

'I can be candid with you, then,' said the old woman in a conspiratorial whisper. 'I never really liked him. He was so arrogant and preening. He was always very charming, of course, but there was something unpleasant just below the surface, if that makes any sense? I didn't mourn his passing, let me put it this way.'

April smiled politely, not sure what to say.

'But Layla took it very badly,' said the woman, almost to herself. 'When he was in hospital, it was as if she was ill too. Whatever he had, it ate away at her. I forgot how strong love can be at that age. I think adults assume you teenagers are just playing at love, but for Layla it was real. Too real, I think.'

Oh Christ, thought April. *Now I have to feel bad for breaking her heart as well as killing her.*

The old woman was examining April's face.

'You're the girl who was injured at the Osbournes' party, aren't you?'

'Yes.'

'I hear you lost your father, too. I'm sorry.'

'Thank you,' said April quietly. The woman reached over and squeezed April's hand. 'I understand,' she said. 'I've been doing the same thing, looking around to find some reason, some explanation for what's happened. Nothing makes sense, does it?'

'No. Not really.'

'I don't have any answers for you, I'm afraid. Even at my age, when everyone seems to be dying.' The woman reached up and began fingering a silver cross hanging around her neck.

'I turn it over and over in my mind, but there doesn't seem to be any logic. The doctors still have no idea what killed Milo and in the end, it's not important. It was a terrible piece of bad luck, that's all. The problem is that we're all interconnected and you can never know how something so horrible is going to affect you. It hit Layla harder than she thought. Young love is too strong when it can make something beautiful turn black.'

The woman stood up and patted April's hand.

'If you'll take my advice, just let it go.'

'Let what go?'

'Trying to work out what happened to your dad. I know you think it will help if the police catch whoever killed him, but I'm not sure it will. He'll still be gone. I think the best you can do is try to remember all the things we have to be grateful for and be happy you had all that time together.'

April nodded sadly. She looked up at the woman, her eyes pleading.

'I'm sorry about Layla,' she said. 'I really am.'

Grace frowned.

'Don't be. It's not your fault. We have enough to deal with without adding guilt to the list. There was nothing you could have done.'

If only you knew, thought April.

'Maybe not, I just wish I …'

The woman shook her head.

'Wishing's not going to make a difference. We have to do things now. It's time to move on.'

April was left wondering if the woman had known more than she had been saying.

Chapter Twenty

April knew something was wrong the moment she opened the front door. Laughter echoed down the corridor from the kitchen; her mother and a man, she thought.

Please, not Sheldon again, she thought as she hung up her coat and walked down the hall.

'Oh darling, there you are,' said Silvia, her cheeks still flushed. 'Dr Tame came by to see you.'

The psychologist was sitting at the breakfast bar, a mug of tea in front of him. He waved at her.

'Nothing to worry about, just a few informal questions. Thought you might be more relaxed at home rather than at school or in my office.'

'Mum, I've just got back from a funeral,' she hissed.

'Oh don't be silly, darling. The doctor only wants to ask a few quick questions. How was it, by the way?'

'Lovely,' she said sarcastically.

'Well that's fine then, isn't it?' said Silvia. 'I'll leave you two alone, shall I?'

The doctor shot her a 'thanks for understanding' type look.

April's mother squeezed her shoulders. 'Be good,' she whispered in April's ear. 'He's quite dishy, isn't he?'

April rolled her eyes. *No*, she thought. *He's creepy*. And why do adults insist on using that old-fashioned language? 'Dishy', 'Hunky', 'the tops'. It was about time someone told them how ridiculous they sounded. Sighing, she sat down opposite Dr Tame, feeling his eyes on her.

'My mother's just the same,' said Dr Tame, his smile tight. 'Means well, but she can be so embarrassing.'

April smiled politely. *Don't think you can get more out of me by pretending to be my friend*, she thought. The doctor chuckled.

'Sorry,' he said. 'Force of habit. You're too smart to be taken in by my little tricks, aren't you, April?'

'What?' said April, unsettled. Was he reading her mind?

'So how was the funeral?'

'Okay, I suppose. They kept it short.'

'Yes, that's usual with a suicide. Difficult for everyone, isn't it?'

April shrugged. She had no intention of playing his little mind games.

Tame looked at her, his fingers steepled.

'Okay, April, let's stop pretending. You're a clever girl, and you know I'm a psychologist. A head-shrinker, like one of those fake psychics off the telly. But I can tell you're sharp – that's no trick, it's just the truth. I've spoken to most of your friends and they're not exactly Einsteins, are they? Davina, Chessy, Sara. They may be attending a posh school but I suspect that's got more to do with Daddy's bank account than their brains. And then there's Caro Jackson ...'

April looked up at him. 'What about her?'

'Well, Caro's intelligent of course, but she thinks everything is a conspiracy, doesn't she? Whereas you, April,' he said, pointing a finger at her, 'you know there's more to it than that, don't you?'

'Do I?'

He nodded confidently.

'Yes, and that's why I'm here. I think you know a great deal more about what's going on at Ravenwood than you're saying. It's my job to find that out.'

'I thought that was the police's job.'

'Oh, I *am* the police. I am here on the highest authority and let me tell you, the powers-that-be are very concerned by the body count in this area and they don't want the situation to get out of control.'

'Situation? Is that what you call a serial killer?'

'You think it's a serial killer at work?'

'Three murders. All have the same cause of death, all close to each other. I've seen enough cop shows to guess there's a link.'

Tame grinned.

'What's so funny?'

'I was right about you and DI Reece,' he said. 'Only Reece can have told you they all had the same cause of death. The Inspector's been a naughty boy, giving you privileged information like that.'

'Perhaps he thought that I might need more information, given that my father was murdered and someone tried to kill me too.'

'Ah yes, the Marcus Brent episode. So do you think he's the serial killer?'

'I don't know. He was certainly mad enough.'

The doctor nodded.

'But why didn't he kill you?'

'I think he was trying, don't you?'

'Hmm ... maybe.'

'Maybe?' she repeated. 'Do you want to see the scars?'

'No, I meant the serial killer theory. It's nonsense.'

'What?' said April, startled. 'Why?'

'Serial killers always do things the same way. They have very strong patterns. I won't bore you with the technical jargon, but you can take my word for it. Now that doesn't mean there's not a killer at work – clearly there is. But they don't quite fit the profile for a serial killer.'

April frowned. Was this the message Miss Holden was trying to get across with her talk of Jack the Ripper?

'So you're telling me there's a whole host of killers on the loose?' she asked.

'Again, maybe,' said Tame. 'But then where does Layla fit in?'

'You just said Layla committed sucide.'

'But that's not what *you* think, is it?' said Tame, stabbing his finger at her again. 'You think there was foul play involved in Layla's case too, don't you? Well, let's assume you're right for a moment, why didn't the murderer kill her in the same way? Why force her into a noose?'

She wasn't going to tell him the truth: they couldn't rip out her throat, because they thought she was a Fury and her blood was deadly. It would sound crazy and she had no doubt that Dr Tame would lock her up in a psych ward at the drop of a hat.

'I don't know.'

'Ah,' he said, waggling his finger again. 'But I think you do, April Dunne. I think you know – or *you* think you know – a great deal about this case. Clearly you have reasons for not telling me – misplaced loyalty, perhaps, or maybe you think you can crack the case yourself. But I know you want to tell me. I think you're desperate to. I can see it there inside your head, trying to get out. You want to unburden yourself. It's killing you that you can't tell someone.'

April tried to swallow, but couldn't. Her throat was dry and her heart was pounding. She had always been a lousy liar and Dr Tame seemed to know exactly what she was thinking.

'Okay, so why would I want to tell you all these supposed secrets?' said April.

'Because you know exactly what will happen if you don't.'

'I do? What's going to happen?'

'Now that,' he said, standing up. 'That much you do know.' Before she could move, the psychologist grabbed her hand and pulled her out of her seat.

'Hey!' she cried.

He strode out of the kitchen, dragging her behind him. 'I think you know exactly what's going to happen if you keep it to yourself,' he shouted over her protests, twisting her wrist and dragging her down the hall.

'Mum!' shouted April.

Stopping at the front door, Tame grabbed April's shoulders and looked into her eyes.

'Why don't we go in and see?' he said and pushed her backwards into her father's old study. 'Was it here?' said Tame, his voice rising. 'Was this where you found him?'

'Who?'

'Who? Your father of course! The great William Dunne!'

He seized her shoulder and pushed her down onto the floor.

'Don't be shy, April,' he said. 'Let's have a look where you found him, bleeding into the carpet.'

'No!' she shouted, 'MUM!' April twisted her head away, but Tame grabbed her face and made her look down at the floor, right at the spot where her father had died. 'Was it here? Was this where he died?'

'Yes!' she screamed, yanking herself free, pushing the doctor back against the wall. 'Is that what you want? I saw him die here! Is that what you want me to say?'

'What the hell is going on?' yelled April's mother as she ran into the room, stepping between April and the doctor. 'Who the bloody hell do you think you are?'

'Do you want to see more people die, April?' said Tame, ignoring Silvia. 'Or was one enough? Maybe the next one you will care about.'

'Screw you!' yelled April, lunging for Tame, her hands formed into claws. Silvia caught her.

'Stop!' she cried. 'Stop this at once! What on earth has got into you?'

'There's nothing to worry about, Mrs Dunne,' said Dr Tame calmly. 'I've just been using a psychiatric technique called Cognitive Re-alignment.'

'I don't care what you call it,' she said. 'Get the hell out of my house.'

'I merely wanted April to face up to her responsibilities, to see the consequences of her actions and of remaining silent. I think it's clear I succeeded. We understand one another, don't we, April?'

April glared at him.

'Get out!' said Silvia again, pulling the front door open. 'You can be sure your superiors will hear about this.'

The man laughed. 'They'll be glad to hear I'm doing so well.'

'OUT!' she said, pointing at the door.

The doctor smoothed his hair back and looked directly at April.

'I was right about you, wasn't I, April Dunne?'

April stuck her chin out defiantly.

'No, Dr Tame. I doubt you have the faintest idea.'

'Oh, I think I do. You're certainly not like all those other girls at Ravenwood. You're different.'

'You'll be different too, unless you get out of my house,' said Silvia. 'You've made a big mistake.'

'Have I? I think I got it exactly right. We'll talk again, April.'

'Not if I have anything to do with it,' said Silvia with ice in her voice. 'When I've finished with you, you'll be lucky if you can speak at all.'

She slammed the door behind him.

April lay on her bed, listening to her mother rant on the phone downstairs.

'Completely outrageous ... vulnerable girl ... just seventeen for Christsakes! I want him fired immediately.'

She knew that Silvia was well-connected and that her grandfather was even more powerful, especially among the levels of the police where they used funny handshakes, but she suspected that not even her mother's rage would get Dr Tame shifted from the case. What he had said about 'the powers that be' being concerned about the death toll in Highgate made sense. Whether he was talking about the police commission, the mayor's office or the cabinet, it was certain that no one wanted any more bad publicity. Reporters had been pouring into the area since the Alix Graves murder, fuelled by her father's death, and Layla's suicide had only given them more ammunition. The *Post* had already run a two-page story about the 'troubled girl with the tragic past', talking about Milo and giving a damning profile of Layla's father and his business dealings. April didn't know whether Layla had been 'troubled' – if anything, she had seemed unnaturally self-confident. Apart from getting Davina's approval on her new shoes, she didn't seem to have any problems. But then she had watched her boyfriend die. Milo might have been a rat, not to mention a vampire, but it still couldn't have been much fun. Her grandmother certainly seemed to think Layla had been serious about Milo, even if he hadn't exactly returned the compliment. Maybe she wasn't giving Layla enough credit. Maybe she'd had a soul after all.

She turned over and picked up her phone, speed-dialling Fiona's number.

'Hi darling, what's happening?' April felt a familiar rush of happiness to hear her best friend's voice. There was something reliable and constant about it.

'Major drama going on downstairs. My mother is trying to get the police psychologist fired.'

'Ooh! You have the most exciting life,' said Fiona eagerly. 'Tell me everything.'

April quickly filled her in on the day's events, particularly Dr Tame's attack in the study.

'God, that is weird. There's something not right about that Dr Tame. You sure he's from the police?'

'What do you mean?' April could hear her friend tapping away at her computer in the background.

'Well, the interviews were done at Ravenwood instead of a police station and that, especially unsupervised, doesn't sound like a standard interview technique.'

'Come on, Fi, I know you. What are you thinking?'

'I'm just looking up ... ah, here we are. Ooh! Seems you're not the first person Dr Tame has upset. "Expert witness causes case to collapse." And here ... it looks like he's pretty well connected. He's been a teacher and a headmaster at various public schools, before he started assisting the police. There are a few upsets, but he gets results. You remember that bomb on the Tube last year?'

'Why do you think I take the bus whenever I can?'

'Well, Dr Tame is the man who made the bomber confess. Gave up his whole cell. From this, it seems he gets results, but with suspect methods.'

'Suspect methods is right!' said April. 'How can someone like that be allowed to interview kids?'

'Well, that's what's worrying, isn't it?' said Fiona.

'How do you mean?'

'Well, if the police are prepared to unleash a "psychological attack dog" – the words of George Framley-Green, QC, not me – onto a load of kids, it shows they're pretty desperate for results. I think you're right about your mum. I wouldn't want to be on the receiving end of one of Silvia's tirades either, but I don't think even that will shift them. Layla's dad may well be an important man, but Highgate is full of them. I think someone's determined to put a stop to this.'

'That's not what bothers me; I want this stopped as much as anyone. I'm just worried Tame might be right. That if I don't help them more people will die.'

'So help them. Seriously, what's stopping you?'

'The fact that it sounds insane, Fi! Am I supposed to call him and say "Hey, I just thought you'd like to know, all those murders in the village are actually the work of vampires"?'

'But can't you call anonymously or something, give them a few pointers?'

'I don't have any evidence. I only have Gabriel's word for it that Davina and the Faces are recruiting promising brains for their evil scheme to take over the world. And then they'll ask why they should believe him. How am I supposed to answer that? "Because he's a vampire too. I know because I stabbed him"?'

'I see what you mean. But you could speak to that nice policeman, what's his name, Inspector Reece?'

'Maybe. I don't know. I wish I knew who I could trust. I feel so alone down here.'

'I know, honey,' said Fiona sympathetically. 'But you know you can trust me and Caro and all the rest of your friends. And your mum, she's down there sorting things out for you, isn't she?'

'I'm not so sure any more. She's been acting really strange since Dad died. She's never here, anyway.'

'Well, what about Gabriel?'

April sighed.

'That's the annoying thing about him. *One* of the annoying things about him,' she corrected herself. 'When he's here, he's all "I want to be with you," but then he'll disappear for days. It's not like he's adapted to the advent of mobile phones either.'

'April, he's a hundred years old. The *telephone* is probably a bit of a culture shock for him.'

They both giggled. It felt good to be able to laugh about it and it lightened the rest of their conversation. When April hung up she looked at the phone. She scrolled to Gabriel's number, hesitating for a moment. *Oh hell, why not?* she thought. *He's supposed to be my boyfriend isn't he? You can call them to chat, can't you?* She pressed 'call' and waited while it rang.

'Hello?' Gabriel sounded distracted, annoyed.

'Hi, it's me,' said April.

'Oh.'

Silence.

Oh? Is that all he's got to say?

'Just wanted a chat,' said April. 'Things have got a bit weird around here ...'

Gabriel didn't say anything for a moment, then: 'Listen, I'm with someone, can we talk later?'

'Oh, okay, I just wanted ...'

He ended the call.

'... to say I missed you,' she finished to dead air. April felt her stomach churn. *What was that all about? He's with someone? Someone more important than me? Hang on, aren't I the one who saved you from slipping into a coma and dying?*

'Bloody MEN!' she shouted, throwing her phone against her pillow.

Just then it began to chirp. *Ha! He called back! Well, he can grovel,* she thought.

'Yes?' she said icily. 'What do you want?'

'Oh, is this a bad time?' It was Davina, amusement in her voice.

'Sorry,' said April quickly. 'Not you. I was …'

'Let me guess. Mr Gabriel Swift, by any chance?'

'Yes, how did you know?'

'Sweetie, the only thing that makes a girl that mad is a man. And Gabriel Swift is a particularly maddening one.'

'God, he drives me crazy sometimes!' said April. Then suddenly, irrationally, she got a stab of intense jealousy: maddening? Why would Davina find him maddening? Was there some history there? Suddenly April realised that beyond his great lost love of Lily, she knew almost nothing about Gabriel's history, let alone his romantic history. Had he and Davina ever been a thing?

'All men are the same,' said Davina, oblivious to April's thoughts. 'I think this calls for an emergency girlie night in. I was calling to ask you over anyway – I'm having a crisis of my own.'

'What's up?'

'I can't decide on a gown for the Spring Ball.'

April shook her head. She should have known Davina's definition of crisis might well be different to everyone else's. She supposed that even the vampire world must be divided into girls who watched Sky News and those who obsessed over dresses. Just because she was one of the undead, who was to say she was any less shallow?

'Come on, I need a second opinion!' cried Davina dramatically. 'We'll drink left-over eggnog and bitch about why boys are useless.'

April had no idea if leftover eggnog would be any better than fresh eggnog, but she was in the mood for forgetting all about her problems. She just wanted to veg out and gossip about pop stars like any other teenager, even if it was with an untrustworthy vampire.

'I'll be right over.'

Chapter Twenty-One

Davina answered the door in a flowing bottle-green gown. Off-the-shoulder and cut from shimmering silk, it looked as if it cost more than her mum's car. *It probably did*, thought April.

'Sorry, sweetie,' said Davina, holding the door open while hopping on one foot. 'This bloody dress keeps getting caught on my heels. It's a living hell.'

'It looks amazing.'

'Thank you, darling, but I know you're just being kind. It's going straight back to Browns; I don't know why they sent it over anyway, it's a size *four*!'

April followed Davina down the hall and up the stairs as the girl kept up a constant stream of complaints about the personal shoppers at Harvey Nicks. 'You should have seen some of the things they brought out,' said Davina, her lip curling. 'I wouldn't have dressed a dog in them. They even brought out Armani diffusion. I mean, *diffusion*!'

April walked in to Davina's huge room, stifling a gasp. It was April's idea of a dream bedroom. Canopied bed, voile at the windows, polished wood cabinets. The carpet was so deep, April's feet sank into it as she walked across the room. It was hard to get the full effect of the interior design, however, as every surface was covered with clothes. Dresses, skirts, jackets, draped over drawers and chairs, plus a huge pile on the bed. There was even a scarf hanging from the light, as if it had been thrown there in a fit of pique.

'I know, it's such a mess,' said Davina, waving a hand at the pile. 'But I need a pair of fresh eyes, I've tried everything on twice and it all looks revolting.'

She went over to the dressing table and, moving aside a pillbox hat, poured April a generous measure of something that looked creamy and sweet. 'Here, have a belt of this,' she said, handing her the glass. 'You're going to need it.'

April took a tentative sip and sat down to watch the show.

Davina, of course, looked amazing in everything. The big surprise, however, was that she was also great company. Complimenting April on her figure as she tried on gowns too, giggling about boys, bitching about parents and teachers and reality TV, she was surprisingly witty and even wise about relationships. 'No boy, whatever he says, really wants a one-night stand,' she said as she forced her feet into a pair of silver sandals at least a size too small. 'They're all looking for "the one" just as much as we are, it's just they feel they have to conform to this Neanderthal Boy Code and never admit it. Now, take my brother for example ... '

'Did I hear my name?' said Benjamin, putting his head around the door. April squealed, clutching a dress to herself.

'Hey!' said Davina. 'Ladies only!'

'I can only see one lady in the room,' grinned Ben. 'And honestly, April, whatever she's been telling you about me, it's not true.'

'Don't flatter yourself,' said Davina. 'We've got better things to do than talk about you.'

'Well if you need any assistance with a zip or anything, just yell,' he said.

'OUT!' screamed Davina, flinging one of her silver sandals at him.

'I'm going, I'm going. See you in history tomorrow, April.'

Davina rolled her eyes. 'God, rather you than me,' she said, refreshing April's glass. 'I couldn't stand to be in the same room as that witch Holden, let alone listen to her chirp on for hours on end.'

'Why do you hate her so much?'

'Hate is rather a strong term,' smirked Davina. 'Dislike might be more accurate. It's that nose-in-the-air attitude, as if she's so much better than the rest of us. I mean, darling, not in those clothes. And an Oxford degree or whatever she's got? I mean, is that supposed to impress us? What has she ever done in her life?'

'I found some magazines she'd written for in the library.'

'Exactly,' said Davina. 'I mean, I'm guessing it wasn't *Vanity Fair*?'

April laughed. 'No, some boring old history journal.'

'See? When I'm as ancient as that old bag, I intend to be living the life of Riley, sitting on a yacht, fingers covered in jewels, being handed a Mojito by some gorgeous heir with a six-pack.'

'Sounds like a plan.'

'What about you? I suppose you're dreaming of running off with Gabriel Swift?'

April blushed.

'I mean, I get it, the boy does have heavenly cheekbones. But what else does he have? You should be setting your sights higher. Someone with a car, perhaps? Maybe I'll hook you up with some more eligible bachelors at the Ball.'

'There's no need.'

'Come on, we've got to get you over this crush. Trust Davina, okay?'

'All right, you're on,' said April. She needed to get in with the Suckers, didn't she? And anyway, why shouldn't she make new friends? Gabriel seemed too busy to talk to her at the moment.

'Listen, I'd better get back,' said April, standing up. 'My mum gets super-jumpy if I'm out of her sight these days.'

'Understandable, given what's happened,' said Davina picking up her phone. 'I'll get Miguel to drop you home.'

'No, no,' said April quickly, 'it's only ten minutes' walk.'

'Please,' said Davina seriously. 'I let Layla walk home that night. If I had insisted on getting her a car, maybe … maybe …'

A single tear rolled down her cheek.

'Hey, don't,' said April, walking over and rubbing her arm. 'Come on, it wasn't your fault.'

'Oh, I know,' sniffed Davina, brushing the tears away. 'It's just … I know people think I'm this ice queen, but Layla was my friend.'

She looked into April's eyes, her face a picture of misery.

'She really was and I wish … I just wish I could have stopped it.'

'Stopped it?' said April, looking at her more closely. What was she saying? Was this a confession? 'How could you have stopped it?'

'You know, asked her to stay the night, called her a cab, *anything*. Instead she went into that cemetery and I could have prevented it.'

April didn't know what to say. If Caro was right and Davina had been behind Layla's so-called suicide, then this was the coldest, most manipulative thing April had ever heard. *But then she's a vampire, a pure-bred killer, what do you expect?* she reminded herself. But there was something about Davina at that moment, a brittle vulnerability April had never seen before. She seemed genuinely broken-up about the death of her friend: April could have sworn the tears were real. Even if she was lying about being able to prevent Layla's death – surely if they believed she was a Fury, the vampires would *have* to kill her, whoever she was? – she certainly seemed racked with remorse.

'It's easy to think we could have done something afterwards,' said April. 'I've gone over my dad's death time and time again, wishing I'd done something differently: if only I'd run straight home, if only I'd told him I loved him, but "if onlys" are futile, I know that much. They only make you feel worse.'

Davina nodded and looked up at April gratefully. 'Thanks, honey,' she said. 'Maybe you're right, but it all seems so … so unjust. Layla wasn't perfect, but she was a good person underneath it all. Why is it always the good ones?'

April shook her head.

'I've been asking myself the same thing. There's no answer.'

Davina took a deep breath and stood up purposefully.

'Well one thing's for sure, I'm certainly not letting you walk home,' she said reaching for the phone. 'I'll get Miguel to come around.'

'Okay. Thank you.'

'No, thank you, April Dunne. I've had a lovely time.'

For once April almost believed her.

It was raining as the Bentley pulled up. The windows were misted and the street lights looked like hazy lollipops. 'Is this all right, miss?' asked the driver, opening her door and escorting her to her front door with an umbrella.

'That's fine thanks, Miguel, please don't wait,' said April, fumbling in her purse, wondering if she was expected to tip the chauffeur, but he moved off before she had a chance to make a faux pas. She hunched her shoulders against the drizzle, cursing as she failed to locate her front door key. Just then her phone chirped and she sent half the contents of her bag clattering down onto the step in her rush to answer it. Just a text from Caro.

Need to talk – urgent.

Not so urgent I can't pick up my stuff, she thought, bending down to scrabble it all back into her bag. It was then that April spotted the bouquet sitting propped against the step, looking a little bedraggled in the rain. Well, *bouquet* was stretching it a little far. It was an old-fashioned bunch of flowers: roses, daisies, chrysanthemums and the like, obviously picked from flower beds rather than bought from a florist. She picked the bunch up and saw that there was a small rain-smudged note attached.

Sorry for earlier, it read. *There's no one else I'd rather talk to. Gx*

April grinned and clutched the flowers to herself. He did care after all!

'I thought I should hand-deliver them,' said a voice behind her.

'Gabriel!' she gasped.

He was drenched: his hair was plastered to his forehead, the shoulders of his coat soaked through, but he still looked incredible.

'Have you been waiting here all night?'

'Not *all* night,' he laughed, pulling her into an embrace, kissing the rain from her nose and her eyelashes. 'I just wanted to make sure my apology was accepted.'

'Oh, it's accepted all right,' she said, closing her eyes and feeling his arms around her. It felt all kinds of good. 'Are you coming inside?'

'Not tonight, I wouldn't want to ruin your carpet. But I'll see you tomorrow night, okay?'

'Tomorrow night?'

'The Spring Fundraiser, remember? We do have a date, don't we?'

'Really?' said April, her heart fluttering. 'I didn't think we were allowed to be seen out together.'

'Not any more,' smiled Gabriel. 'No danger of me keeling over from Fury-itis, is there? Unless I give in to my urges and kiss you again.'

'I wish,' said April.

'Me too. But at least now we can walk into that party together – I can't wait to see the jealous looks of every man in that room.'

Reluctantly she watched him walk back across the square before she opened the door and ran inside, straight up the stairs, calling Caro as she went.

'What's up?' she said, looking around for a vase to put the flowers in. 'Your message said urgent.'

'You sound happy,' said Caro.

'Yes,' she said. 'For once, Gabriel has done everything right.'

She told Caro about the flowers and Gabriel's impromptu appearance.

'So what was the thing you wanted to tell me about?'

'Oh,' said Caro, 'er, don't worry, it's nothing that won't wait.'

'Okay, tell me tomorrow.'

April ran up to bed, sliding a rose from the bouquet under her pillow before she fell asleep.

Chapter Twenty-Two

Gabriel looked amazing. He was wearing a grey overcoat over his black dinner suit, his shoes were polished and there was a flower in his buttonhole.

'Wow!' said April, standing on her doorstep. 'Who are you?'

Gabriel smiled.

'Special delivery for Miss Dunne. Have I come to the right house?'

'Special delivery?' she grinned. 'What is it?'

'It's me,' whispered Gabriel with a playful smirk. 'I'm all yours.'

'Shhh!' said April, glancing behind her and hoping her mother wasn't eavesdropping. She stepped forward and kissed his cheek. Up close, she could see that his skin was radiant and his hair was sleek. He was like an airbrushed version of the man she knew. *The man I love*, she corrected herself, feeling butterflies in her stomach.

'You do look beautiful, you know,' he murmured, his lips close to her ear. Davina had allowed April to borrow one of her dresses, a long sheath of dark red that felt a little tight, but she knew looked pretty good. She had pinned her hair up to show off her long neck and her mother had lent her a gold Egyptian pendant; it was about as good as she got.

'And you smell good enough to eat.'

'Hey, you keep your fangs out of me,' she replied, giggling. 'Well, at least until you've met my mother.'

She took his hand and pulled him along the corridor and into the kitchen where Silvia was touching up her make-up.

'Good evening, Mrs Dunne,' said Gabriel formally. 'I hope

you don't mind my escorting April to the party.'

'Silvia, please,' she said, holding out a hand. 'It's so good to finally meet you properly. I never got the chance to thank you for saving her life.'

Gabriel gave a slight nod.

'It was nothing, Davina's father was the one who got her to the hospital.'

'Don't be so modest,' said Silvia. 'The doctors told me that without you, April would not have made it and for that I'm eternally in your debt. Do you understand?'

April looked from Gabriel to her mother and back. Their eyes were locked, as if something was passing between them.

'Mum …' said April, squirming. 'We've got a party to go to?'

'Yes, you're right,' said Silvia, still staring at Gabriel. 'And will you promise to look after my baby girl tonight?'

'Of course,' said Gabriel as April took his arm, keen to get him away from her embarrassing mother.

'You make such a lovely couple,' said Silvia following them out. 'I just hope those heels aren't going to sink into the ground in that park.'

'No, I understand there's a marquee with a proper ballroom floor inside,' said Gabriel.

'Oh yes,' said Silvia. 'But I know you youngsters, sneaking off to the bushes.'

'Mum!'

'Hey, I may look half-dead, but I had a life before you were born. Your father could get quite frisky …'

'Enough! Please!' cried April, putting her hands over her ears. 'I don't want to hear about it!'

Silvia rolled her eyes. 'Kids!' she tutted. 'You all think you invented sex. People have been managing to have babies for thousands of years, you know. Or don't they teach you about that in your fancy school?'

'Mum!' cried April. 'Come on, please, let's just go.'

'You sure you'll be all right on your own? I feel terrible I can't come, but I've got this thing with your grandpa and …'

'Waterlow Park is only about two hundred yards away, Mum. I think we can make it across the square without getting killed. Besides, the police are everywhere these days.'

As April pulled on her coat, Silvia flipped up the collar and kissed her on the forehead.

'You look after each other, okay? Remember what happened at the last party you went to.'

'Yes, Mum,' she sighed.

Silvia need not have worried. Waterlow Park had better security than a celebrity wedding. There were burly security guards with walkie-talkies stationed along the fence and a police van parked by the gate checking invitations.

'It's harder to get into than Glastonbury,' said Gabriel.

'You've been to Glastonbury?' said April with surprise.

'All of them,' he smiled.

'But didn't it start in nineteen seventy ...' April twigged she was having her leg pulled and gave him a nudge in the side. It was hard to come to terms with having a boyfriend who you couldn't even kiss, who had better hair than you and who really wanted to bite you. And on top of that he was hundreds of years old – that made her head spin.

'Can I ask you something?' she said as they passed through the gate and walked along a curving path lit by strange toadstool lanterns placed every few yards.

'Sure, as long as it's not about Woodstock – I couldn't make that one.'

'I mean it seriously. Haven't there been other girls? I mean, you've been looking this gorgeous for a hundred years. There must have been times when women have thrown themselves at you.'

He was silent for a moment.

'I mourned Lily for a long time. I wanted to die to be with her, but I couldn't. It was torture, real torture. But when pain finally fades, love stays. Yes, there were girls here and there. Feeders and others. You can't avoid mixing with women if you want to maintain a cover story.' He stopped and held her hands. 'But there was never anyone but Lily. Not until you. I promise.'

She knew she shouldn't ask, that it was paranoid and childish, but she couldn't help herself.

'What about Davina?' she said.

He threw his head back and laughed.

'Is that what this is about? Has she been dropping hints?'

'It's not funny. And you didn't answer the question. Seriously, I need to know.'

'Seriously then, I had to infiltrate the group, I needed to find my way to the recruiter. Davina was my way in.'

'So did you ...?'

He snorted again.

'I don't know what she's been telling you, but no. There was some flirtation, there was some messing about, but there's never been anything between us. Okay?'

'Okay,' said April uncertainly. What did 'messing about' entail exactly?

'So who is the recruiter? Who's in charge at Ravenwood?'

'Haven't you worked that out? Mr Sheldon, of course. We all report to him.'

'But I heard him on the phone to the governors, bowing and scraping. There was obviously someone way above him in the pecking order.'

'Oh yes, that's certain. But we only deal with Hawk. I guess we need to keep our eyes peeled tonight, see who he talks to.'

They were approaching the marquee now. They could hear the music and see the lights. There was another police cordon to pass through, manned this time by Miss Holden.

'April, Gabriel,' she said. 'How are you feeling now, Gabriel?' she asked, not meeting April's eye.

'Much better thank you,' he said. 'Just a bit of a bug going around I think.'

'Yes, I think a lot of people are going to get it.'

'Perhaps. Let's hope not.'

'Well, don't mind me,' said April, pushing past them. 'Just pretend I'm not here.'

'Hey,' called Gabriel, catching her by the marquee door as she handed over her coat to the cloakroom attendant. He pulled her to one side.

'What's the matter?'

'I don't appreciate being talked about like I'm some sort of bacteria you picked up off a dirty cup.'

'It wasn't like that, April,' he said. 'You have to read between the lines – I was saying thank you and telling her I owe her one.'

'Well why couldn't you just say that, then?'

He smiled.

'Because we're sworn enemies, remember? Anyway, what's really the matter? Is it the thing with Davina? Listen to me, April Dunne. I'm here holding your hand because I love you and I want to be with you right now – and I want to walk into that party with you on my arm, as the proudest and luckiest man in the world.'

'Oh. Okay.'

He reached up and straightened her hair, gently brushing it away from her face.

'Come on, beautiful, this is your moment.'

They walked in, April's hand on his arm. She could see all heads turn in their direction. She glanced up at Gabriel. He looked amazing. Handsome, strong, stylish – she felt glamorous just being with him. Caro ran up to them.

'Have you seen this place? It's huge,' she gabbled, 'There's a dance floor in the back with a band and a lounge and the doors open to the side onto the lawn next to the lake, it's amazing!'

'Well who is this lovely thing?' said Gabriel, putting on a look of mock surprise. 'You'll have to introduce me to your pretty friend, April.'

Caro looked suspiciously at Gabriel and fingered her hair. 'Does it look okay? My mum insisted on doing it and I'm never sure. She does all these hairdressing competitions, so I always think she's going to make me look like some sort of school craft project.'

'I think you look great,' whispered Gabriel before excusing himself to go to the bar.

'He's right, honey, you look fabulous,' said April. 'Honestly.'

'Not too shabby yourself, although I understand it's all down to Davina. She's been boasting about your girly night in – I suppose she's trying to make me jealous.'

'Did it? I know we usually get ready together.'

'Don't be silly. You're on a mission from God or Allah or somebody. You have to get yourself in with her. Not too deep though, okay?'

'Okay.'

'And is everything alright with Gabriel?'

'Yes, why wouldn't it be?'

'No reason.'

'Caro … what's the matter?'

Caro shook her head slightly as Davina approached, and whispered 'later'.

'I see you made up with Lover Boy then,' said Davina.

'He was very persuasive,' April smiled. 'And no one else asked.'

'That's only because my brother's such a dork. I'm pretty sure he would have loved to have brought you.'

'Really?' said April, looking over to the bar where she could see Benjamin sitting alone. 'He never said anything.'

'Like I said, he's a dork. Do me a favour and go over to say hello or he'll be unbearable. I'll keep Caro entertained. In fact, I think Ling wanted to show you her new tattoo. *So* cool.'

Caro rolled her eyes and mouthed '*So cool*' as she was led off. Gabriel was laughing with a group of older men, having been sidetracked while getting the drink, so April walked over to Benjamin, who was sitting at the bar, a cocktail in front of him.

'Hello stranger,' she said. 'Gonna buy me a drink?'

'You sure your boyfriend won't mind?'

'Hey, I'm sorry if I …'

'No, no,' said Ben, signalling to the waitress. 'I'm joking. You look great together.'

'Thanks.'

'But seriously, Gabe's one of my best friends and he can be a little flaky.'

'Tell me about it.'

'If you ever need someone to talk to when he's on one of his disappearing acts, or if you ...'

April put her hand on his.

'Thanks, Ben, I will.'

'Okay then,' he said, 'How about a bit of an eye-opener? They're not allowed to serve us youngsters booze for some reason, but I have an understanding with the waitress.'

'An understanding?'

'I slip her a twenty, she slips vodka into anything I order.'

'Sneaky.'

'My middle name,' he said, passing her a vivid orange and green confection. 'Here's to ... what shall we toast?'

'To happy endings.'

He looked at her, his blue eyes twinkling, and clinked his glass against hers.

'April Dunne, you do ask for the most difficult things.'

It was certainly an impressive turnout. Caro had identified half a dozen politicians and four or five heavyweight businessmen.

'See that guy over there talking to that horrid police psychologist?' she said to April.

'Dr Tame?'

'Yeah, the fat guy next to him in the awful grey suit. He's Conwin Briar. He's a Canadian oil and gas man, worth about ten billion.'

April stared at him. *Billion?* Why was it that super-rich men looked so shabby? Because they could, she supposed. Who was going to tell them to get a decent suit?

'How do you know who all these people are?' asked April.

'I read the business pages,' said Caro simply. 'Don't you?'

'I rarely get beyond the gossip pages.'

'Well, if it isn't my favourite Marxist agitator,' said a voice behind them.

April turned to see Nicholas Osbourne.

'Enjoying yourselves, girls?'

'Yes thank you,' said April. 'And I never did get a chance to properly thank you for saving my life last year.'

'It was my pleasure, April, really.'

'Wouldn't have looked good having a corpse on the lawn, would it Mr O?'

Mr Osbourne laughed.

'Good to see your cynical streak hasn't dimmed, Caro.'

'Oh, you know me, I like to get to the truth.'

'The truth can come in many guises, you know.'

'Talking of which, not out on the dance floor, Mr O?'

He laughed again.

'I'm a steady captain of industry tonight, Caro. So no *Boogie Wonderland*. I save that for my own parties.'

'So whose party *is* this?'

'Ravenwood school's, of course.'

'But who actually set it up?'

'Mr Sheldon sent out the invitations, I believe.'

'But it's funded by the governors?'

'Yes of course, the governors. But before you ask, they value their anonymity, so I'm not about to give you a list.'

Caro looked at him sideways.

'You're only postponing the inevitable,' she said. 'I'll find out eventually.'

'I don't doubt it, Caro,' he smiled, walking off. 'I don't doubt it at all.'

When he was gone, April gave her friend a playful little shove.

'Caro Jackson, I do believe you have a little crush on Davina's daddy,' she said.

Caro blushed slightly.

'Well, a girl has needs. I'm certainly not getting it anywhere else.'

'Yes, I saw Simon was here with Ling.'

Caro shook her head.

'I'm not interested in Simon any more, that's ancient

history. But I am interested in hitting that dance floor,' she said, making a tactful departure as Gabriel returned carrying drinks. He put them down on the table and turned to April, holding out his arm.

'And would you do me the honour?' said Gabriel.

'You can dance?'

'I'm very good at the waltz.'

'Hmm, I'm more of a Lady Gaga girl myself,' said April, watching as a beautiful woman in a red dress entered the marquee. April did a double take. It was Jessica, the woman from the Covent Garden bookshop.

'Gabriel, look! It's that woman from Redfearne's, you know – the witchy bookshop. She's the owner.'

She grabbed his hand and pulled him across the floor.

'Hi Jessica, do you remember me?' said April, 'Listen, I'm sorry I haven't brought the card back yet, I kept meaning to but things have been so mad ...'

Jessica smiled at her. 'Don't worry about it, April,' she said. 'As long as you get it back to me next week.'

'Of course, I'll do that, I promise.'

Jessica looked up at Gabriel. 'And how did it all work out?'

April grinned.

'It worked perfectly. I just wanted to come over and thank you so much from the bottom of my heart. If it hadn't been for you, things would have been completely different.'

'You're very welcome,' said Jessica. 'I was glad to help.'

'Oh!' said April. 'And this is Gabriel, he's the one I ...'

April glanced at Gabriel's face and was dismayed to see him looking furious.

'Gabe?' she said. 'What's the matter?'

'Nothing,' he said. 'I'm just surprised to see Jessica here.'

April looked from Gabriel to Jessica and the penny finally dropped.

'You ... know each other?'

'No,' said Gabriel immediately. 'Not really.'

'Our paths have crossed,' said Jessica, her eyes not leaving Gabriel's. It was as if they were having a conversation April couldn't hear, and it made her feel excluded and forgotten.

'Listen, I mustn't keep you two,' said Jessica suddenly. 'April, it was lovely to see you again. Don't forget that card though. And Gabriel, you have a great evening.' She moved off into the crowd.

'What was all that about?' asked April.

Gabriel shook his head.

'Someone I used to know. It's …'

'… complicated, I'm sure,' said April more sarcastically than she meant it to sound. 'Listen Gabriel, I don't know why she's got you so obviously wound up, but I do know that without her help I would never have found the White Book and we would never have been able to save you. So whatever's annoyed you, remember that.'

'Of course I'm grateful. It's not about that.'

'Well whatever it is, can't you forget about it for tonight? It's supposed to be us, hand in hand, remember? You're here, you're alive and we have each other. Or would you rather be with someone else?'

He looked at her intensely.

'Of course not, don't be ridiculous. It's you, April, it always will be.'

'Then start behaving—'

'Lovers' tiff?'

They turned as Mr Sheldon approached them, glass in hand.

'No, sir, just a conversation,' said Gabriel.

The teacher raised a sceptical eyebrow.

'Well do you mind if I cut in?'

Gabriel looked at April, but April looked away.

'He's a nice boy,' said Mr Sheldon as Gabriel walked off. 'A little misguided, perhaps, but I think he'll come round.'

April nodded. She didn't know what to say. Who wanted to discuss their love problems with their headmaster?

'I was disappointed not to see your mother here tonight,' said Mr Sheldon.

I bet you were, thought April.

'She had an important meeting with my grandfather.'

'Ah. An influential man, your grandfather, or so I hear.'

April shrugged. Why was he forcing conversation with her?

'Did he ever pursue that issue we were talking about?'

April looked at him. *God, is that why you've been hanging around my mum?* she thought suddenly. Maybe that's why he was flirting with her, why he came to see them instead of going to see Layla's family that night – he was hoping to get them onside so they wouldn't sue him or the school.

'You'll have to ask him about that,' said April. 'He did seem pretty upset about it though.'

They lapsed into silence again.

'Anyway,' said Sheldon finally, 'I just wanted to say how sad I was about your father.'

She looked at him, frowning.

'Sorry? You're sad about my dad?'

'Yes. I didn't really have the chance to offer my condolences after the funeral,' he said awkwardly. 'And then, well, there was all that unpleasantness at the Osbournes'.'

Unpleasantness? Someone tried to kill me, thought April, *and all you care about is a lawsuit.*

'Thank you,' she said lamely, hoping it would be enough to make him go away.

'If you ever need to talk, I'm here. Your mother is an old friend of course, so I feel doubly responsible.'

He was looking over her shoulder and had obviously spotted someone more important.

'Well, I must mingle,' he began, but April stopped him.

'So how did you meet her? My mother, that is. I never heard the story.'

Mr Sheldon looked uncomfortable. His strange hooded eyes searched hers.

'We were friends at university. A long time ago, of course.'

'It's just that she never mentioned you before. Not even when she knew I was coming to Highgate.'

April realised why the news that Hawk was supposedly a 'family friend' had made her feel so uncomfortable. She had been told that Grandpa Thomas had 'pulled a few strings' in order to get her into the prestigious Ravenwood, but if Sheldon and Silvia were such bosom buddies, then why didn't she just call him up herself?

'As I say, it was a long time ago.'

'And did you know my dad, too?'

The smile instantly left his face, those eyes searching hers again.

'We – ah – he and I didn't exactly move in the same circles.'

'But he was there?'

'Oxford is a big place, April. Something I hope you'll discover for yourself.'

April almost laughed out loud.

'You think I'm brainy enough to get into Oxford?'

'I think – a lot of people think – you can be whatever you want to be, if you channel your energies in the right direction.'

Just as she was about to ask more, a large fat man walked over, a tall thin woman trailing behind him. There was something dark and unpleasant about the man. He exuded anger and irritation.

'Good evening, sir,' said Mr Sheldon quickly, 'and the lovely Mrs Wilton too. I do hope you're enjoying yourselves.'

The man waved his champagne flute in disgust.

'I would be, Sheldon, if you weren't serving this revolting bubbly. All the money we shovel into your coffers and you can't spring for something decent?'

'I'll see to it at once, sir,' Sheldon said, almost bowing as he scuttled off. April watched in amazement. Clearly Caro was right; there were people pulling the strings behind Ravenwood. And they made Mr Sheldon afraid. April made a mental note to follow up on 'Mr and Mrs Wilton' as soon as she got home.

When April found Caro, all her friend's previous buoyancy had gone. She was sitting at a table next to the dance floor, taking big swigs from a cocktail. April leant over and sniffed it.

'One of Benjamin's specials?'

Caro shrugged.

'What's up?'

'Nothing, everything's just peachy. Nothing that a machine gun wouldn't sort out.'

April frowned.

'What is it? All these rich, smug people showing off? I thought you would have been infiltrating like nobody's business. In fact, I saw Hawk speaking to this horrible fat man ...'

'It's not all about you, you know,' snapped Caro. 'You and your perfect man. Who, I should point out, isn't as perfect as you think.'

'Hey! Don't have a go at me, I haven't done anything. And what's all the snide remarks about Gabe all of a sudden?'

Caro looked sulky and took another drink.

'Caro, what's going on? I thought you liked Gabriel.'

Caro avoided her gaze.

'I'm just sick of all this vampire business.'

'Shhh!' said April, waving her hands. The music was loud, but vampires had acute hearing, didn't they? 'Keep it down – remember where we are. Besides, I thought we were in this together.'

'It's all right for you with your destiny and your grand plot for revenge, but what's in it for me? Eh? I'm the sidekick who gets killed just before the end of the movie.'

April touched her hand.

'You're my friend, Caro. And no one is going to lay a finger on you. What's brought all this on?'

Caro pointed with her chin across the dance floor. Simon was sitting on the other side, holding hands with Ling.

'Oh, honey,' said April. 'I thought you said you weren't bothered by it.'

Caro turned to her, tears glistening in her eyes.

'Well clearly my heart thinks differently.'

'Simon's still Simon. It won't take him long to realise how shallow and horrible they are.'

'That's what I've been telling myself for the past few weeks, sure he'd come to his senses, but every day that looks less and less likely. He dresses like them, he talks like them. He even finds their jokes funny.'

April squeezed her hand.

'Come on, let's go over.'

Caro pulled her hand away. 'What? No!'

'Come on,' April said firmly. 'We're not going to save him from across here. And besides, we're supposed to be joining them ourselves, aren't we?'

Reluctantly, Caro allowed herself to be pulled from her seat. They threaded their way across the dance floor and into the seating area where all the Faces were gathered.

'A-ha!' said Benjamin, offering April a glass. 'The very girl. I knew you'd be back.'

'Couldn't drag me away.'

She glanced around at the Faces, watching them look her up and down. Chessy forced a smile at her. 'Nice dress,' she said with an air of sarcasm.

'And what have you come as?' said Caro. 'Is the circus in town?'

'Now, now, girls,' said Simon, 'let's not quarrel. I think you're looking lovely tonight, Caro.'

Caro blushed. 'Thanks, so are you.'

A look passed between them.

'I think your hair looks amazing, Caro,' said Ling. 'Very Roman, like something from the Trajan era.'

Caro looked at her in surprise, clearly having to remind herself that the vampires were recruiting these students for their brains. They might talk like airheads, but there was intelligence underneath. Which, of course, made them all the more dangerous.

'Thanks,' she said lamely, 'my mum did it.'

Chessy tittered. 'Yes, I heard she's a hairdresser,' she said. 'Do you think you could get me a discount?'

'I think you'd need one, the amount of work you'd need.'

Davina flashed a look at Chessy.

'Well, I think it's amazing,' said Davina, walking up and

touching Caro's ringlets gently. 'I wish my mother was useful for something.'

'I think your mother's perfectly charming,' said Simon.

Perfectly charming? thought April, *God, they have brainwashed him.*

'It's nice of you to say so, but she's not much use beyond the dinner party circuit and even then she only seems to sit around reeking of scent.'

'She does spend an awful lot of time abroad though,' said Benjamin with a smile. 'Usually in some clinic or other in a vain attempt to reverse the wrinkles. Which means we get the house to ourselves.'

April couldn't believe they were talking about their parents with such contempt. Silvia was hardly a model parent, but she was still her mother. She would never dream of running her down in public. But then, she thought suddenly, maybe that was what was required.

'I wish my mother would do the same thing. She's always hanging around. She could do with a clinic of her own,' she made a drinking motion with her hand.

'A woman after my own heart,' said Benjamin.

'I just wish they'd leave us alone – adults, I mean,' sighed April. 'Always going on as if they know better than we do, as if their own lives have been these massive successes. Drives you mad.'

Davina gave a sympathetic nod.

'I know what you mean. We have to do our best to cope without their interference.'

'But how do you do it? I mean, they're always interfering.'

Davina gave a smile, to knowing smirks from the rest of the group.

'Stick with us, honey,' she said. 'We'll show you how it's done.'

'What was all that about?' said Caro after they had gone back to the bar. 'Chessy starts off having a go at my mum, then you pile in complaining what a drunk your mother is.'

'Well, it's true. You should see the empties we put out on a Monday morning.'

'Maybe, but your mum has been through a lot over the past few months, you shouldn't be dissing her like that. She's not in the same category as Barbara Osbourne, not yet anyway. At least she's supportive.'

'Hey, I can understand you wanting to defend your mum,' said April, 'but mine happens to be driving me mad. Supportive? I don't know where she is from one day to the next, out on the town. Anyway, it wasn't about attacking my mum. It was about getting in with them. Didn't you see the way they reacted? They smell fresh meat. They're looking for the weak ones, and we've got to act weak.'

Caro shook her head.

'I'm not sure I can do it.'

'Well I can. If it's the only way I can find out who killed my dad, I'll do anything necessary. This is a race, Caro. We've got to get to them first. If they find out what I am and what we're doing, then we're all dead.'

She couldn't find Gabriel anywhere. She did a circuit of the dance floor and elbowed her way through the bar, but he had disappeared. Giving in to her paranoia, she changed tack and looked for Jessica instead, but quickly spotted the lady in red discussing wine with Nicolas Osbourne. She was just going to check the decking area outside when she ran into Miss Holden.

'Enjoying yourself?'

'Not much.'

'I see Gabriel's looking well.'

'Oh, God. Miss, I'm sorry, I should have come to thank you.'

'Don't be silly, April, there's no need. How's he coping with it, anyway?'

'What do you mean?'

'Well, it's going to be hard to go from human to undead. He may be the first to choose that path with full knowledge of the horror.'

'Horror?'

'He willingly died, April. He felt his life slip away from him, for the second time; and he did it for you. That's a pretty big thing.'

'Pretty big thing?' said a voice. April turned to see Dr Tame standing behind them. *How much did he hear?*

She glared at him, remembering the last time they had met, the way he had bullied and terrified her all in the name of 'the truth', but Tame didn't seem to notice or if he did, didn't seem to care, just standing there with that smug half-smile on his pale face.

'Oh, I was just talking to Miss Holden about applying for Oxford,' said April as smoothly as she could. 'Mr Sheldon says I can do it. Do you think I've got a chance?'

'I should think that is a question for the lovely Miss Holden,' said Tame. 'What's your verdict, Annabel?'

April could see that Miss Holden disliked him and she could also see she hated his using her first name in such a familiar manner.

'As I was saying to April,' she answered, 'it's all about how much work she's prepared to put in. She'll have to knuckle down this year and that's going to have a significant impact on every area of her life. It's quite an undertaking, should she choose it.'

I thought we were talking about my university prospects, thought April, *not the war on the vampires.*

'Well, I'm sure April is up to the task,' said Tame, squeezing April's arm and leaving his hand there a little too long. 'Do you mind if I steal her away for a moment? There's something I'd like to discuss with April if I may.'

'Actually, I've got to go over to …' began April, but Tame wasn't listening and steered April towards the terrace area.

'I'm glad Mr Sheldon brought it up, actually,' said Dr Tame when he had dragged April away from the main party. 'Because I've been meaning to ask you, April, what do you intend to do with your life?'

'I'm sorry,' she said, rubbing her arm. 'What do you mean?'

'Just trying to get a handle on the real April Dunne. Are you the sort to get a mundane job in an office? Do you want a high-flying career in the city? Or are you going to marry and become a yummy mummy?'

April looked around, searching for allies, someone she could wave over to save her. She didn't like being here with this man; he made her flesh crawl. No, it was more than that; all her instincts told her Dr Tame was actively dangerous.

'I don't know what I'm going to do yet,' said April. 'I'm still weighing up my options.'

'Weighing up your options,' repeated Tame. 'Yes, that's good. But do you really think you have that many? I mean, really? Surely it's all mapped out before you like a destiny.'

She went cold. Did he know something? He always seemed to know more than he said; it was unsettling. But then maybe this was another one of his nasty techniques.

'Destiny?' she stuttered.

'Destiny, April. A fate you cannot escape no matter what.'

'I don't understand.'

'Well, surely you're going to follow the old man into journalism?'

Relief flooded through her.

'Why do you say that?'

'Your interest in English and History,' he ticked the points off on his fingers, 'and on poking your nose into other people's business. Breaking into the headmaster's office, searching private houses. Even the odd bit of amateur chemistry.'

She gaped at him. How did he know all that?

'What are you talking about?'

'Oh you know exactly what I'm talking about, April Dunne,' he said, his eyes flashing. He reached out and grabbed her arm again.

'Leave me alone,' she gasped, but he pressed his fingers into her flesh, probing for nerves.

'No, April. I will not leave you alone, no matter how much you squeal, no matter how hard your mother and grandfather try to make me back off. You are the key to this case and I don't know if you're aware, but I have a reputation for getting results. I will keep pushing until I get what I want. And I *always* get what I want.'

She looked around for Caro, Gabriel, anyone. Where *was* he?

Suddenly Tame released her, a cruel smile on his face.

'Looking for your boyfriend? I think you'll find him down by the lake.'

April stood there, stunned, rubbing her arm. He was a madman. Someone must have seen them? She looked around, but everyone was engrossed in their own conversations, oblivious. And anyway, it was a school event – anyone seeing that scene would assume Tame was a teacher telling her off. She watched Tame go over to a group of besuited men including Nicholas Osbourne, shaking hands, laughing with them as if nothing had happened. And who would believe her, anyway? She thought about what she'd said about her mother only minutes ago and felt ashamed. Silvia wouldn't stand for this sort of thing. She would have protected her. Talking of which, wasn't she supposed to have an escort to look after her? Where *was* Gabriel?

She walked out onto the wooden terrace. There were chairs and tables with candles in the middle, but not many people out here despite the patio heaters. The decking went up to the edge of the lake which twinkled with the reflected party lights. It would be a romantic spot to be with your boyfriend – if only she could find him. April wrapped her arms around herself. God, it was cold. She was feeling it more since her injuries. They had healed well, but she still didn't feel completely whole, completely solid. She wondered if she ever would again.

Where is he? she thought with irritation. She stepped down off the decking and walked a little way along the path. She needed some air after her encounter with Tame, anyway. She wished her dad was here. She remembered her mother toasting him at the start of the Osbournes' Winter Ball. He'd loved a good party. *Where are you, Daddy? Are you watching over us? I hope so, because I could certainly do with some looking after at the moment.* Just then she stopped. She heard a scuffed foot on the path and hushed voices. Ahead, she could just make out a couple standing together. April stopped. She didn't want to disturb their intimacy, but something made her linger for a moment. The boy put his hand up to the girl's face, gently pushing a strand of hair from her eyes, then bent down to kiss her on the cheek. It was a tender moment and she felt as if she was intruding. Embarrassed, April stepped back quickly, her shoe scraping the path. In that moment, the boy looked up and April could see his face in the moonlight. It was Gabriel. With Jessica. Cool, pretty Jessica from the bookshop, the same Jessica Gabriel had said was just someone he 'used to know', someone whose relationship with him was 'complicated'.

Of course it was, she thought. *Of* course *it was.*

'April,' said Gabriel, but April was already running. She ran past the marquee, back along the path following the lake. She had to get away from him. From them – *was* there a 'them'? Of course there was, she'd been completely taken in. The way Gabriel had looked at her ... she could feel her heart shattering inside.

'April!'

Gabriel had caught up with her. He grabbed her arm but she pulled it away.

'Ouch!' she shouted. 'That hurts. Some bloody vampire tore it open, remember?'

Gabriel stopped and held his hands up in front of him.

'Sorry, sorry. I forgot, but ...'

'It's pretty obvious you forgot, isn't it? It obvious that a few things have slipped your mind, too, little things like the fact that you have a *girlfriend.*' She shouted the last word in Jessica's direction, but the woman had gone.

'Come on, April, this isn't what it looks like. Jessica is a friend.'

'A friend?' she shouted, incredulous. 'Is that what you call her? I *saw* you, Gabriel.'

'April, it's not what you think ...'

'Isn't it?' she shouted. 'It never is. So why don't you tell me? No, on second thoughts, don't. I've had enough of your explanations: "it's complicated" or "you won't understand". I don't want to hear your lies any more, Gabriel. In fact, I don't even want to see you again.'

She turned and began to stride away up the path, but Gabriel jumped in front of her. Without thinking, April balled up her first and punched him as hard as she could.

'Bloody hell, April,' said Gabriel, staggering backwards in surprise. 'Just give me one minute to explain.'

'And what are you going to say, exactly? "It's not you, it's me"? That you need space? You're not ready for a relationship right now? Spare me. You've always got an excuse and I'm sick of it.'

She tried to push past him, but he stood his ground, anger on his face.

'Get out of my way,' said April.

'No, not until you've heard what I've got to say.'

April gaped at him. 'How *dare* you!' she shouted. 'How dare you stand there and make demands of me. I've lied for you, covered up for you, I've listened to your ridiculous stories. I've given you everything.' April realised she was crying and angrily swiped away the tears. 'I risked everything – I risked my *life* – to save you. And what do I get in return? "It's not what it seems", when I catch you kissing another girl. Well I think it *is*, Gabriel. I think it's *exactly* what it seems. You've got your old life back and now you don't need me any more.'

Gabriel stepped forward, trying to put his arms around her, but she stepped backwards, turning her ankle over in her heels.

'Damn!' she shouted in frustration, bending over and angrily pulling the shoe off. She flung it at him. 'Here, a present for you. I won't be needing to look beautiful any more, will I?'

'April, you've got this completely wrong.'

'No, Gabriel. I haven't,' she said. 'All I wanted was for you to love me as much as I loved you, but no. That was too much for you, wasn't it? Your stupid destiny and your stupid' – she flapped her hands in frustration – 'your stupid *war* have to come first, don't they? It's never me, Gabriel,' she whispered. 'It's never me.'

'It is, April. You're everything to me.'

His face softened and he put his hand to her face, in exactly the same gesture she had seen him making towards Jessica only minutes ago.

'NO!' she shouted, slapping his hand away. 'Don't you dare!'

She bent down, pulled her other shoe off and, clutching it hard in her fist, ran up the path, away from the party, and away from him.

'April!' he shouted after her. '*April!*'

'Leave me alone!' she shouted. She could feel the cold stinging her feet as she ran, mud splattering her legs and soaking the hem of her lovely dress. She pulled it up and increased her pace around the lake and up the hill towards the top of the park. All she wanted was to get home, to get away from him, away from this whole mess. How had she got herself into this? Why had she fallen for his lies?

Finally her protesting lungs gave out and she stopped, looking back anxiously to make sure he wasn't following her. There was nothing there, nothing except the dark lawns and the trees bending down towards the path. Panting, feeling the frost in her scraped toes now, she pushed on up the hill, not sure where the path was leading exactly, but knowing that home – and with luck, her mother – were in that direction. She put her hand over her mouth to stifle a sob. *Why?* she thought angrily, looking up towards the starry sky. *Why me? Why do you keep heaping all this on me? All I try to do is be a good person, help people out. And then they turn around and unload on me from a great height.* She wiped her nose and shook her head. Maybe everything Gabriel had ever told her was a complete load of rubbish. The vampire recruiters, the birthmark, the destiny, maybe it was all part of his elaborate lies. Maybe the incident with the knife on the Embankment had been a conjuring trick or hypnosis or something. She had no one else's word for it. Well, Miss Holden's, but maybe she was another one of Gabriel's conquests, maybe they were in on it with him, leading her on a wild goose chase. She was walking through a wooded area now, bushes and flower beds on either side, the thick trunks of the trees bending in towards her, their arching fingers blocking out the moonlight. April suddenly shivered and wished she hadn't flung her shoe at Gabriel.

It had been funny though, she thought, remembering the look of surprise on his face. She let out a chuckle. Half detached amusement, half hysterical sob.

'Something funny?'

April's heart gave a bump and she whirled around, but she was too slow. She felt a stinging blow to her ear and she flew sideways, landing painfully on one knee. *Who? What?* she thought, turning her head to see. 'Gabriel ... ?'

Thud. Another thump to her back and she pitched forward face down onto the path, a crushing weight – *a knee?* – pressing her down into the cold tarmac, her palms scraping the gravel. She tried to raise herself, tried to fight it, but the weight bore down harder.

'Not Gabriel,' hissed a voice close to her ear. April's blood ran cold. She would know that voice anywhere.

'Marcus?' she whispered in disbelief, her mind scrabbling to cope. *How can he be here? How?*

A high-pitched giggle rang out. 'And here I was thinking you'd forgotten me.'

Marcus gripped her hair and yanked her head back painfully. 'Did you miss me, little rabbit?'

'Go to hell, Marcus,' she spat and instantly regretted it as Marcus slammed her head back down onto the path. She tried to roll over, but Marcus grabbed her wrist and dragged her backwards, pulling her across the path, grazing her arm and leg. A rage rose up in her. She'd had just about enough of people pushing – and pulling – her around for one night. She twisted her body around so that she was on her knees and, with all her strength, yanked herself backwards. To her surprise, she broke free and fell back onto her bum. April knew she had only seconds to act before he came flying at her again. There was no time to think, no time to run. He was a vampire; she was a mouse trying to escape a tiger. She sprang to her feet just as he loomed up at her.

'You want to kill me?' she yelled. 'You want revenge? Well come on, then! You'll be doing me a favour.'

She heard a bubbling chuckle from the dark and saw him step towards her.

'Oh, I want to kill you, little rabbit,' he said. 'But not for revenge, oh no.'

As he walked towards her a beam of moonlight lit his face and she saw him for the first time – and she understood immediately. His skin was grey, mottled, his eyes sunken, his cheeks hollow. Marcus Brent was dying.

'You see it, don't you?' he whispered, spite dripping from his lips. 'You see what you've done to me, don't you – *Fury*?'

Her heart lurched. He knew, *he knew*. Her worst fears had come to pass. They all knew she was a Fury and they would tear her apart. And once April was gone, the vampires would continue their plans unhindered, turning the world into a living hell. Gabriel would stay a vampire for ever, Caro and Fi would be turned into Suckers, her mother married to Sheldon ... and her father's death was all for nothing. Pointless. *Futile*. Marcus must have sensed her despair, because he laughed.

He took a step forward and April stumbled backwards, not wanting him to get any closer, but knowing she had no chance of escape if she ran.

'You know why we call you Furies, rabbit?' he hissed, his voice fully of quivering menace. 'I bet you think it's from Greek mythology, don't you? The three Furies,' he said sarcastically, 'the daughters of the night. I bet you'd like that, wouldn't you? All very superhero.'

April didn't say anything, couldn't say anything.

'No, we call you Furies because of the Romans. It's from *fures* – the Latin for "thief". That's all you are, Fury. A dirty little thief, sneaking in and stealing our glorious light.'

She could tell Marcus was enjoying this, gleefully drawing the moment out. Why? Why not just get on with it? And then she realised. Because this was his last act. There was no

Dragon's Breath for Marcus and if the vampires found him, they'd probably kill him. And it was then April decided she wasn't going to give him the pleasure.

'Didn't like it, then?' she whispered, trying to keep her voice from shaking.

Marcus frowned.

'Didn't like what?

'The taste of my blood.'

With a roar he leapt forward, grabbing April by the throat. His fingers squeezed viciously into her flesh and she flinched at the foul breath on her face.

'No, I did not,' he snarled. 'But that doesn't matter, does it? You've already infected me with your disgusting little disease. I can't catch it twice, can I? So now ...'

He ran a finger down her cheek until it was touching her neck. '... now when I drink you dry, we'll go to Hell together.'

He opened his mouth, pulling his cracked lips back to reveal bleeding gums and broken teeth. Horrified as she was, April felt some satisfaction at that: they were teeth she had knocked out during their battle in the snow last Christmas. All of her fear and pain and loss rose up inside her and she let out a scream. Marcus flinched in surprise and April used that moment to bring down the heel of her shoe like a hammer, hitting him square on the temple. He cried out in pain and fury, but April didn't wait to see if she'd done any real damage. She turned and ran.

Stay down, stay down, she repeated over and over in her head, hoping she'd hurt him enough to at least slow him a little, but knowing he was a vampire and that a little tap like that would barely register. With every step, every heartbeat, she knew he would reach out for her and pull her down like a tiger falling on a fleeing deer. She could almost feel his fingernails digging into her skin. Yet still she ran, faster than she had ever run, tearing along the path past the tennis courts and out through the gate onto Swain's Lane.

'Hey!' shouted a security guard, but she didn't even pause, her feet pounding, her only focus getting home to safety.

Safe? she mocked herself, *Safe at home? The place your father was murdered? You call that safe?* But there it was, looming in front of her, the tall windows, the friendly yellow door. She tore across the road, crashing through the gate which clanged back and forth behind her. And there was the door. Closed. Locked. *Ohmygodohmygod*, she thought, hammering on the wood. *I left my key in my coat. I left the key in my coat!*

'Mum!' she shouted, knowing full well that she was out. 'Mum! Please!' she shouted, the flat of her hand stinging as she banged it on the door. 'Help me! Please!'

But who would help her? She was cornered like … like a rabbit. Then she heard him coming for her, the footsteps running across the square straight for her.

'No!' she shouted, crying. 'No!' She turned to face him. But it wasn't Marcus. It was a man in a black coat. A uniform.

'It's okay, love,' said the man, holding up his hands. 'You're all right now. You're okay.'

Then there was another man and a woman, also in uniform. Uniform? For a moment, her brain didn't register, then she was flooded with relief. *The police! The police were here!*

'April!' shouted DI Reece as he ran up the path. 'It's okay, love, it's okay,' and she fell into his arms.

'Marcus!' she sobbed, 'Marcus is back.'

'I know, April. It's okay, we've got him. We've got both of them.'

She looked up at him. 'Both? Who else have you got?'

He looked grim.

'Gabriel, April. We've arrested Gabriel. I know he was only trying to help, but …'

'What? Why have you arrested Gabriel? Why haven't you arrested Marcus?'

Reece looked across at the female officer who shook her head.

'We can't arrest Marcus, April. Marcus is dead.'

Chapter Twenty-Three

April walked through the open gates and up towards the house. She gently pulled her scarf higher up her bruised throat. It seemed colder today – perhaps it was, it was coming up to midwinter – or perhaps it was just how she was feeling. The gravel crunched under her shoes and she came down through a line of trees. There it was: Kenwood House. She had been meaning to come here for ages – after all, the Georgian mansion was all of ten minutes' walk from the square – but she had never managed somehow. It was the pull of the cemetery, the pull of the past.

It had been three days since the police had charged Gabriel with Marcus's murder. With unintentional dark irony, they were calling it manslaughter. April still had little idea of what had happened, but she guessed that Gabriel had followed her after their argument and caught Marcus just as she was running away. That was evidently the police's theory too – they had made her go over and over the events in detail, until she had felt she was going mad, but at least they hadn't made her speak to Dr Tame again. Her mother had, of course, gone completely ballistic that the police had allowed a crazed killer to attack her daughter for a second time. She said she would have their jobs, and from the look on DI Reece's face, April guessed he agreed with her. Of course, the story had made the papers, the tabloids lapping up this juicy new twist to the story of murder in Highgate: *'Daughter of slain journalist is attacked for second time in weeks, police are powerless'*. Poor DI Reece. It wasn't as if his panda cars and house-to-house inquiries ever had much chance against a nest of vampires, was it?

She walked slowly along the back of the house, peering in through the glass doors, winding in and out between its white marble columns. She almost had it to herself; Kenwood was a summer place, picnics on the lawns by the lake and all that. It meant that she could take her time. Apart from a few cuts and grazes, she had escaped injury – 'this time', as Silvia had reminded the police commissioner down the phone at high volume, but the main damage was to her feeling of well-being. April was scared and she didn't mind admitting it – and her fear had nothing to do with having been a hair's breadth from getting her throat torn out. The thing which still frightened her was the fact that Marcus had known she was a Fury. Obviously it hadn't taken much for him to work it out, considering that her blood was slowly killing him. But who else knew? Had he told anyone else? Had other vampires seen him in his grey-faced, hollow-eyed state and made the connection? Marcus had never been close to Layla and they all knew he'd drunk April's blood in the cemetery at Christmas. But then, if any of the Suckers had seen Marcus, they would never have let him live. He had committed the cardinal sin: he had risked uncovering them all. April shivered again, tugging at the scarf. The funny thing was, she was far more scared of being hunted than she was of being killed. Facing Marcus last night she had been frightened – terrified, in fact – but it hadn't been anything like as bad as the graveyard chase and fight during the Winter Ball. Maybe she was becoming a super-powered arse-kicking vampire killer after all. Or maybe you just got used to being beaten up after a while. But she couldn't get used to the suspense, the not knowing, the sense that she was being watched and hunted, killers waiting for her around every corner. Certainly Marcus had tracked her like an animal and if it hadn't been for Gabriel's timely arrival, she could well have been torn apart on that lonely pathway. *Gabriel! Bloody Gabriel!*

'And bloody men!' she whispered to herself. How dare he come steaming in on his white charger to rescue her? It was so typical. She could just imagine him sitting there in his cell feeling smug and thinking he was the big hero, when she wouldn't have been walking home alone in the dark if it hadn't been for him and his bloody secrets.

She headed down the sloping pathway towards the lake, wondering if it would be frozen solid. There had been a pond near the house where April had grown up, out in the countryside – she wasn't sure where exactly – they had collected frogspawn there and sailed little boats in the summer. In winter it had frozen so hard that April could walk out on it and see the fish swimming under her feet.

DI Reece had explained that her scream had alerted the police waiting by the lower gate. When they had arrived, they had found Gabriel standing over the body, his hands covered in Marcus's blood. He was being charged with Marcus's murder and they were once again looking into his connection with both Isabelle and Alix Graves's murders, maybe even Layla's death. April knew in her heart that it was rubbish, but she was so angry with him, she didn't care. He could rot in prison for ever for all she cared.

Her heart gave a leap as she remembered his betrayal. How could he? She had given him everything, saved his life, and he had repaid her by grabbing the first girl who came along.

She cursed out loud, then felt bad about it. *God, why can't I just find a nice, simple, straightforward boy who just wants to love me instead of all this destiny, vampires, good versus evil crap?* she thought.

The truth was, however angry she was with Gabriel, she still felt a bit guilty. Gabriel had been trying to save her. Or perhaps he was just angry after the argument and found Marcus in his way. Had she brought about Marcus's death? Obviously, Marcus had been planning to kill her: *he* wouldn't have felt bad afterwards, but that didn't stop April from feeling that perhaps she could have done something to prevent it. She obviously wasn't cut out for this Fury business.

April was disappointed to find that the ice on the Kenwood lake was thin and had already been broken. Kids had thrown rocks and sticks at it, turning it into a patchwork of giant ice cubes. Shame. She checked her watch: five to two. She turned and walked briskly back towards the house, where she was pleased to see Miss Holden was early.

'What's all this about, April?' asked the teacher as she walked up. She was wrapped in a long coat and a woolly hat and her cheeks were bright pink from more than just the cold. 'You can't just call me up for a meeting without giving me more of an explanation.'

'I didn't think I needed to give an explanation, Miss Holden. I was almost killed the other night, and I supposed you'd heard.'

'I did, April, of course I did.'

'Well Marcus seemed to know I was a Fury.'

'That makes sense. I imagine he was in a pretty bad way.'

'You knew?'

'It's logical, April. He was covered in your blood at the Winter Ball; I'd have been surprised if he hadn't been infected.'

'But if he knows, other people probably know I'm a Fury too.'

'It's possible,' said Miss Holden.

'"It's possible"? What about some reassuring speech about how we're going to handle this?'

Miss Holden didn't answer, just crossed her hands over her stomach, rubbing her wrists. Now April could see that there were red rings under her eyes, like she had been crying.

'Miss? What's the matter?'

She looked at April with a mixture of anger and pity.

'The Guardians visited me last night. They took a dim view of my helping you make the Dragon's Breath.'

'They ... visited you?'

'A "hearing" they call it. Like getting called to the head-master's study, I suppose, only slightly more serious. I have been expelled from the order.'

She held out her wrists and April gasped. The skin was bright red, rubbed and torn.

'God, what happened?'

'They tied me down and "put me to the question". They suspected I'd gone over to the other side.'

April felt sick. Her teacher had been tortured and all because of her.

'But that's just crazy!' she said.

'Is it?' snapped Miss Holden. 'Guardians are sworn to fight the vampires, to wipe them from the earth. I not only saved Gabriel's life, I actively – knowingly – turned him from human to vampire. Whatever the reasons, it goes against everything we stand for. I was lucky they didn't kill me!'

'Didn't you tell them why you did it? That you decided it was the right thing to do? What about all that stuff you said to me about Gabriel being different from the other vampires?'

'They don't care about any of that, April!' said Miss Holden. 'They're fighting a war! In war you can't stop to think if a particular enemy is good or bad, you just keep killing them until they're all gone.'

'That's horrible! That doesn't make them any better than the Suckers!'

Miss Holden didn't reply. She just turned to stare out at the lake.

'But you can still help me, right?'

'No, April, I can't. I have been told to stay away from you.'

'What? You're kidding me! What am I supposed to do?'

'I don't know, April,' she said, her voice weary. 'Carry on with what you have been doing, I suppose. Nothing has changed, has it? Ravenwood is still recruiting your friends, you still want to find out who killed your father, don't you?'

April couldn't believe her ears. She had come here for some reassurance and advice and instead she was being abandoned.

'But I can't do it on my own, Miss!' she said desperately. 'Why can't you just help me on your own?'

'Why? Because I'm sick of it, April!' shouted Miss Holden. 'I'm sick of the whole bloody thing. Don't you understand? I devoted myself to the cause completely – no friends, no relationships, they weren't allowed – I've spent my entire life fighting this war. And now, because I helped you, the Guardians have cast me aside. I have nothing left!'

'*You* have nothing left?' spat April, suddenly furious with her teacher. 'What about *me*? The vampires came into my house and tore my father's throat out – or don't you remember that? This is *your* bloody war, Miss. I don't want to be involved, but it seems I don't have any choice. You've spent the last few months telling me how special I am and how important it is to get involved with your crusade against the vampires. But now all of a suddenly you're "sick of it", so I'm all on my own against a tidal wave of undead serial killers. Well, cheers for that.'

'I'm sure they'll replace me, April,' said Miss Holden bitterly. 'I'm sure another Guardian will be in touch.'

'Screw the bloody Guardians!' shouted April. 'There's no way I'm helping them any more. I thought *you* were going to teach me how to use this so-called "gift", I thought you were going to help me. What do I do now?'

'You are a strong girl, April. Stronger than you know. You will find your own path.'

'Bollocks to your path! I need help! People are being killed. It's not just me – my dad, Isabelle, even Layla.'

'Layla? Layla wanted to be a vampire!'

April gaped at her.

'Listen to yourself! She was seventeen years old and she just wanted to fit in at school. You can't condemn people for wanting to have friends. Layla was never my favourite person, but she didn't deserve to die. Especially not like that.'

Miss Holden's expression said she clearly thought differently.

'If that's the way you think, then I'm better off without you.'

'April, you have to understand my point of view ...'

'I think I do. We're all just pawns in this eternal war you're fighting, where anyone is expendable. But when it gets too difficult, you just step away from it. That seems to be the way all adults work. So forget it. I'll do it on my own.'

April turned on her heel and began walking up the hill. 'Don't worry, I won't bother you again.'

'April please, listen ... *Please!*'

But April kept walking.

Chapter Twenty-Four

'I can't believe you gave it to her with both barrels,' said Caro, leaning back on the bench in the playground and laughing. 'God, I'd give anything to have seen her face.'

'Well, you can see it later in class, we've got History this afternoon. I'm not exactly looking forward to it.'

'Why not? What can she do? She can't exactly say, "Sorry children, I'm in a bad mood today because I've been kicked out of this secret society and then April told me where to get off."'

'No, but she can give me a hard time about the work. I'm expecting to suddenly start getting Ds.'

'It must have been worth it though. God, I wish I'd been in your shoes.'

'You wouldn't, Caro, honestly. It was horrible – it *is* horrible. You should have seen her wrists.'

'The Guardians sound as bad as the Suckers, if you ask me,' said Caro, wrinkling her nose.

April nodded.

'But it leaves us exposed, doesn't it? What if we need another Dragon's Breath thing or something?'

'We'll be all right, we found the book ourselves, remember?'

'I know, but it's one less person we can rely on. It feels like the Suckers' army is getting bigger and bigger, while ours is shrinking.'

'Don't be stupid. You've still got me and Fiona and …'

April looked at her, her eyebrows raised. 'And who, Caro?'

'Sorry, I didn't think, I was going to say Gabriel.'

April pulled a face.

'I can't believe I was so stupid. I'd convinced myself that he was somehow different, but boys are all the same. Shallow, stupid and unreliable.'

'Aren't you worried that he's in prison, though?'

April picked at the wood of the bench with her nails. The answer was yes, of course. She hated the idea of him being cooped up in a cage, but she couldn't get past the betrayal. She kept seeing that image of him reaching up to touch Jessica's face – the way he used to touch her.

'He's only getting what he deserves,' said April, sticking her chin out.

'Well, don't beat yourself up about it,' said Caro soothingly. 'He had me going too. I thought he was this upstanding, decent type. I couldn't believe he'd go off with some other woman.'

Some other woman.

Without knowing it, Caro had hit the nail on the head, cut to the heart of April's anger. The betrayal had been bad enough of course, especially after all the risks she'd taken. But Jessica was a *woman* and cheating with her played into all of April's insecurities about Gabriel. He might look like a seventeen-year-old boy, but he was actually much older, much more experienced, and April found that, more than the fact that he was technically undead, disturbing.

'Do you think it's because I'm a terrible kisser?'

Caro laughed, then saw that April was being serious. 'Come on, of course not. You two seemed to be playing tonsil tennis enough before he went back to being a Sucker. I don't think he would have put up with it if he didn't like it.'

'Well what is it, then? I know I'm not as pretty as her and she's got this amazing body, but …'

'Hey, hey!' said Caro, putting her hands up to stop the flow. 'It's nothing to do with you, A. Don't start thinking that way. Men are dogs, end of. They're all pathetic.'

April raised her eyebrows.

'So you didn't have much fun at the party either?'

Caro snorted.

'Not much. At least you loved and lost, April Dunne. I couldn't get anyone to even look at me.'

'You seemed to be dancing with Simon for ages,' smiled April.

'Ha! Simon? You're joking. I wouldn't be interested in him if he were the last man on earth. Anyway, he and Ling are joined at the hip.'

'I think the lady doth protest too much.'

'It's "the lady doth protest too much, methinks," idiot. This is Ravenwood, you can't go around misquoting Shakespeare here.'

'Don't change the subject. I still think there's a spark between you.'

'Well, when it all went mental after you disappeared – cops running in, people screaming – Simon did come straight over to me to check I was all right.'

'See?'

'Yeah, but then Ling came and dragged him away.'

'Oh well, maybe we're both fated to be alone.'

'Better than being dead, honey. How are you bearing up?'

April shrugged.

'Miss Holden's right about one thing. I'm on my own now, so I've got to toughen up. I've been thinking about it: if Marcus told anyone else I'm a Fury, then they're coming for me and there's nothing I can do about it. I might have this magic virus inside me, but I can't fight a whole ...' April paused. ' ... what do you call a collection of vampires, anyway?'

Caro pouted. 'Good question. Umm, a coffin of vampires? A belfry?'

'Anyway, I got lucky with Marcus, but I can't fight all of them. All I can do is carry on trying to find out who killed my dad and hope I get to the Regent before he gets to me.'

'And find out who's behind Ravenwood.'

'Oh, don't go on about that again. I don't even care about that any more.'

'Why not? It's important.'

April shook her head. She was tired of people telling her

what was important and what she should do. 'No it's not. Not to me, anyway. All I care about is finding the Sucker who hurt my family.'

Caro frowned.

'But look around you, A. All these kids, half of them geeks who can't get dressed in the morning, let alone protect themselves. You said the very same thing to me only about a week ago. Unless we find out who's recruiting them and what for, they're going to end up dead like your dad. Like Layla.'

'I know Layla was your friend, but I can't be responsible for everyone. I've got enough on my plate with staying alive.'

'The only way you're ever going to be safe is to get to the source of the vampires. As long as there are any here, you're a target. We need to take them all down.'

'This isn't a game, Caro. Your fixation with conspiracy theories is blinding you.'

'They're not theories, April! It's real! You know that better than anyone.'

'If the Guardians won't help me, then I won't be part of their war. I'm looking out for number one.'

'Then you're as heartless as they are.'

'Heartless? Haven't I suffered enough? I want this over with. Why should I have to look out for all these kids?'

'Because you're the only one who knows what's going on! Don't take it out on them just because your boyfriend is a dog.'

April suddenly felt defensive.

'Don't talk about him like that.'

'Why not? He *is* a dog. Everyone else could see it, but you were too busy playing Barbie and Ken to see him for what he was.'

'Hang on, you *knew* about this?'

'I saw him and that Jessica woman the night you were hanging out at Davina's. They were coming out of Americano together.'

'You *saw* them? How could you not tell me?'

'I tried to, remember? But it was all lovey-dovey for you that night – Prince Charming had brought you flowers, probably out of guilt as it happens – and you seemed so happy, I didn't want to spoil it for you.'

April put her hand over her mouth. Was that why Gabriel had been short with her on the phone that night? Had he been with Jessica when she phoned? April could feel bile rising in her throat.

'You should have told me!' she said, turning all her anger on Caro. 'I thought you were my friend!'

'What was I supposed to do? Tell you your boyfriend was disappearing off behind your back? You already knew that. I didn't want to hurt you.'

'So instead you let him humiliate me in front of the whole school?' April said, standing up. 'You know what, Caro – *you* look after them. You take down Ravenwood. I'm going to find my dad's killer – and that's it.'

'Then you really are alone, April.'

April walked strode up Swain's Lane. *Screw Caro, screw school, screw everyone*, she thought. She glanced through the railings into the East Cemetery. Probably full of vampires watching her, hunting her, sniffing after her blood. *Yeah? Well, bring it on, Suckers*, she thought. *I'm way past caring.*

She was furious with Caro. Who was she to tell her what to do? Caro had no idea of the burden on her shoulders. Save the geeks, she had said, look after the freaks. Forget it; she was going to find out who had killed her dad and then it would be over. She could wash her hands of all of it. It was only as she reached Pond's Square that April realised she should have been in Miss Holden's class right now. For a moment, the old April surfaced and she felt a pang of stress: *God, I'm going to get in trouble for skiving*. She almost laughed out loud. Here I am being hunted by vampires and I'm worrying about my school attendance record. No, she'd let Miss Holden explain her absence away. And if anyone asked about it, she'd plead stress. She had been attacked in the dark by a known, and now dead, psycho. Who wouldn't expect her to be a little emotional about it? Right now she was free, so she decided to go and get a magazine from the newsagent on the high street. Hey, maybe she'd go really crazy and get one of those coffees with the whipped cream on the top.

'Oh no.'

Her heart sank as she spotted DI Reece. The policeman was standing on the other side of the road, hands in his pockets, she could tell he had bad news from a hundred yards away.

'Fancy a walk?' he asked, walking over.

'It's a bit cold.'

'Come on, it will do us both good.'

They walked in silence, April praying that he wouldn't point out she should be in school, until they were down the hill by the ponds.

As they crossed the road, April's phone buzzed in her pocket. A text:

I think we need to talk. Miss Holden

God, was everyone watching her? April turned the phone off.

'How are you feeling?' Asked Reece.

'Okay, I suppose. I'll cope.'

Reece shook his head.

'You shouldn't have to "cope", April. All this, it's not normal for a seventeen-year-old girl, you know.'

'Can I ask you something, Inspector Reece?'

'Ask away.'

'You once said you buried someone. Who was it?'

'My wife,' he said quietly.

'Was she—?'

'They're taking me off the case,' said Reece, changing the subject .

'What? No, they can't. You've been in charge from the start.'

'They can and they are. There are a lot of very influential people who live in this area and they're very upset by these incidents. Can't say I blame them. I wouldn't want to pay a king's ransom for a house up here, then have a murder on my doorstep every night.'

'But it's not your fault, Inspector Reece. You've done your best.'

'Well, it's not good enough. It's gone way over my head now. I suspect I'll be offered a job somewhere else.'

'Are you going to take it?'

Reece shrugged. He didn't look like he cared much one way or the other.

'I'll think about it. Anyway, I just wanted to tell you in person. One of my superiors, DCI Johnston, is taking over.'

'What's he like?'

Reece pulled a face. 'I wish I could tell you he's the man for the job, April, but I can't.'

'What's that mean?'

He took a deep breath.

'In the modern force, there are two types of copper. There are those who do their best to get things done despite all the red tape and the paperwork and government targets, and there are those who should have been on *The Apprentice*. They just see the job as any other management role, every case as a way of furthering their career or winning brownie points with their boss. They are hunting criminals, yes, but they might as well be selling baked beans for all they care about the job. And they will do anything to get the job done. Anything.'

'And this new Chief Inspector is one of those?'

'Exactly. He's also been ordered to work more closely with Dr Tame.'

'Oh no!'

'Now that's a sensible reaction,' said Reece. 'I don't mind telling you I don't like him. But he has connections at the very top. You need to watch yourself.'

'What do you mean?'

'They need someone to pin this on, April. They've already got your friend Gabriel, but they can't blame everything on him.'

She looked at him wide-eyed.

'You think they might blame me? I haven't done anything!'

'That won't matter to them, April. You have connections to the case, and if they can make a case they won't care if you're guilty or not.'

'God. What can I do?'

'Stick to your story, don't lose your temper. And wait.'

'Wait? What for?'

'I think you know as well as I do. There are going to be more killings before this is over.'

They walked back up to the High Street, where Reece had left his car.

'Thanks, Inspector Reece. For telling me in person. You didn't have to, I know that.'

Reece reached into his pocket and pulled out his notebook, scribbled something down, then tore the page out.

'Here,' he said, handing it to her. 'That's my phone number. If you need anything, even to talk, give me a call, okay?'

'You're worried about me, aren't you, Inspector Reece?'

'Who wouldn't be, April? I don't know exactly how you're mixed up in this whole mess, but I do know one thing. Death seems to be following you.'

'And who's this I see? Is it April Dunne?'

I'm hopeless at truancy, thought April. *First I bump into a policeman, then into a sucker.*

'Hello, Davina.'

She glanced at her rose gold watch.

'Shouldn't you be in school?'

'Shouldn't *you*?'

'I get special dispensation. Mr Sheldon and I have an understanding.'

'An understanding?'

'Let's just say he relies on my father to keep his job. I don't think he'll be giving me a hard time about truancy. You on the other hand ...'

'Yeah well, I don't really care what Hawk or anyone else thinks at this precise moment. I'm sick of Ravenwood.'

'That's the spirit!' said Davina. Her eyes twinkled with mischievousness.

'What's the point of doing all that boring schoolwork? Why bother when we could all be dead tomorrow?'

'Oh, I know.' Davina touched her arm. 'How are you doing? Who would have thought Marcus would come back for you? Were you terrified?'

'No, funnily enough. Well, I was scared, but he pissed me off more than anything.'

'You're so brave. And Gabe coming to your rescue! It's like a fairy tale.'

'He did not come to my rescue,' said April petulantly. 'I'd already got away from Marcus, I didn't need Gabriel Swift to rescue me.'

'But I couldn't believe it when I heard he'd –' she glanced around her at the passing shoppers '– *killed* Marcus. I mean, I know Gabriel has a bit of a temper, but killing him? That's mental, isn't it?'

April shook her head.

'I don't know. I don't know what Gabriel thinks or why he does anything.'

Davina pouted.

'Yes, I heard you'd had a bit of a row. I never knew what you saw in him – I mean, he's sexy, but after all this I think you're better off without him.'

'I couldn't agree more.'

Davina glanced around again.

'Listen, we can't talk here, do you want to come over to mine? Daddy's away again and Ben will be at rugby practice all afternoon so we've got the place to ourselves.'

For all her rebelliousness, April was still nervous about being spotted in the street by a teacher or, even worse, by her mother.

'Okay,' she said. 'Let's go.'

April barely recognised Davina's bedroom. On her previous visit, it had been buried under piles of clothes, but today it was like something from the 'décor' section of a swish magazine. The cream carpet was spotless, the ironed bedcovers barely had a wrinkle on them and apart from a few copies of foreign fashion magazines artfully tossed onto a side table, nothing was out of place, not a speck of dust or a coffee-mug ring anywhere.

'Your room is incredible,' said April. 'In mine, you can barely see the floor for clothes and books and stuff. How do you live in it? I'd be scared to move anything.'

'Oh it's okay I suppose, but it's so poky, isn't it?' said Davina. 'I've been lobbying Mother to get her to let me have their room, I mean it's not as if they're ever in it, but all she would do was add the dressing room.'

'You have a *dressing* room?' gasped April, thinking of her own crammed Ikea wardrobe, with socks and knickers poking out of the wonky drawers. 'I didn't see that the last time I was here.'

'Ah, that's because it's hidden.'

Davina walked over to her floor-to-ceiling mirror and gave it a push. It slid aside to reveal a doorway into another room almost as large as April's living room. On either side were hanging spaces full of shimmering gowns and dresses and shelves piled with neatly folded jeans and tops. But it was the far wall of the room which really made April gasp. It was a honeycomb of shelves, each slot housing a pair of shoes, displayed like museum exhibits.

'God, I've never seen so many shoes in one place before.'

'I can't help myself,' laughed Davina. 'Mummy's got an account at Browns, you see. Plus I have a few friends in the press offices of some of the fashion houses. I should really send some of them back.' She giggled.

'Hey, you know what we should do?' she said suddenly. 'Let's give you a complete make-over. Hair, make-up, clothes, everything.'

'Oh, I don't know,' said April, glancing nervously at the rails and then back at Davina's super-slender figure. 'I don't think I'd fit into any of your dresses.'

'Nonsense!' said Davina, 'You wore that gown at the fund-raiser and you looked fabulous. Come on, it'll be fun!' She took April by the hand and led her through another door into her ensuite bathroom.

'First things first, we're going to give this lovely hair some shine.'

'Davina, I'm not sure,' protested April as she was pushed down onto the edge of the bath.

'Well I am,' said Davina, turning on the shower head. 'We're going to condition and then wash in a gentle colour. It's going to look amazing, trust me.'

Suddenly April panicked. The Fury birthmark behind her ear! She couldn't have Davina staring at the back of her head – that would be suicide. The paranoid thought struck her that Davina might have offered to wash her hair for that exact reason.

'Okay, but let me do that,' said April, reaching for the shower head and turning Davina around. 'You go and rummage through that massive wardrobe of yours. I'm going to need shoes and bags and earrings, everything.'

Davina looked surprised.

'Are you sure? I do a great Indian head massage.'

'Stop stalling, you just don't think there will be anything that fits a whale like me.'

'Don't be ridiculous, just leave it to Auntie 'Vina.'

April let out a long breath. Bending over the bath, foam running into her ears, water splashing her face, she began to laugh. She was still grinning when Davina walked back in.

'What's so funny, young lady?' Davina said with mock severity.

'Just all this,' said April, wrapping her hair up in a towel. 'It's nice. I always had you down as a bit of a selfish cow.'

'Oh that's nice!' said Davina, flicking some water into April's face.

'No, but seriously, Davina, this is nice of you. Better than any therapy. It's just what I need, so thank you.'

Davina looked away. If April hadn't known better she

would have thought she looked embarrassed. Did vampires get embarrassed? Gabriel had said that the lack of connection to the real world through pain, fear or discomfort had robbed them of their humanity, their ability to empathise. But here was Davina, head vampire, with a full-on blush. Maybe Gabriel didn't know everything. He certainly didn't know how to treat girls properly, that was for sure.

'It's all an act, you know,' said Davina quietly.

'What is?'

'The selfish cow thing,' she said. She pulled a cleanser pad from a packet and began to swipe it across April's skin in a soothing circular motion . 'Shock news: I'm just like everyone else, April. But because my dad's rich and I live in this nice house and have nice things, everyone assumes I'm sort of a bitch. After a while you get sick of all their "well it's all right for you" comments and start playing the part.'

'But you could be nice, like this.'

'Believe me, I've tried. But people don't allow you to show weakness. I mean, we've got pots of cash, how could we have any problems, right?'

'What problems?'

'Oh, don't worry about it.'

'No, tell me.'

'Well I suppose everyone has a father who's never there and when he is flies into vicious rages or whose mother is like a zombie on prescription drugs and is only interested in her tennis pro. I suppose having a big lovely house is perfect, unless you'd rather have a small cosy one like yours.'

April would have laughed if Davina's face hadn't been so sad.

Remember she's an evil vampire, she said to herself. *Remember she's an evil vampire*. But then couldn't vampires have problems? It was hard enough being a teenager at the best of times, but imagine being trapped there, living with your mum and dad for ever with no prospect of getting out. Being a vicious killer must get wearing after a while.

April let out a giggle.

'What?' said Davina, stiffening. 'What are you laughing at?' April could hear the hurt in her voice. She stood up and strode back into the bedroom.

'No, sorry Davina,' said April running after her. 'I didn't mean to upset you. It's just ...'

'What?' Davina turned around, her hands defiantly on her hips, but there were tears in her eyes, just like when she had talked about Layla. Maybe Gabriel really had been wrong. Maybe vampires could feel pain.

'It's just I was thinking about my Dad's funeral. You know, when you came to my house? I was cringing, worrying about what you thought of our tiny little terrace, when in real life you would rather live there.'

Davina grabbed a tissue and wiped her eyes.

'Oh, it's okay living here I suppose and I know I shouldn't grumble, but it's so ... so dark and cold sometimes. I know it sounds mad, but after a while you get sick of hiding out, cowering, scared of being found out.'

'Found out?'

'That you're not what everyone thinks you are. That you're a fraud.'

She blew her nose.

'I see you, April. You never pretend to be anything you're not and your family, your house, seemed so warm and cosy and full of life. And I know your mum's a bit unusual ...'

'You can say that again.'

'But that's great! She gets drunk and goes out to clubs and does her own thing. I wish my parents would dare to deviate from the posh person's handbook once in a while.'

'Your dad seems to like bad disco tunes.'

Davina laughed sadly.

'Yes, but that's so embarrassing. It's as if he's developed this one thing he'll do in public that makes him seem human. "Hey look! I dance badly to Duran Duran, I can't be all bad." I just wish I had a relationship like yours with your mum and dad.'

April could feel the tears start in her eyes now.

'Oh God, now I've got you started,' said Davina, plucking another tissue from the box and handing it to April.

'Don't worry, it's just it's not so long since he died. Somehow it seems to get harder, not easier. I miss him. And I suppose my mum's okay, I just wish she could open up. Since Dad died she's been so wrapped up in her own grief, it's as if I'm an embarrassment or that I remind her of him or something.'

'Maybe you should give her more of a chance.'

'Look who's talking.'

'Ah, well I've tried again and again with my mum. I don't think she's ever going to be an apple-pie-and-knitting sort of mum.'

'Mine either.' April blew her nose and laughed. 'See? I told you this was better than therapy.'

'Yeah, but it was supposed to be for you, wasn't it?'

After April had dried her hair, she sat patiently with her eyes closed while Davina did her make-up for her, more subtle and natural than she would have done it herself. Then she pushed her into a wrap dress which accentuated her curves and added some insanely high heels.

'Wow!' she said looking at herself in the mirror. 'Is that really me?'

'It's all you, honey,' said Davina.

It was a transformation. She looked more grown up and mature. The colour Davina had given her had darkened her hair and made it twice as shiny. *Maybe vampires aren't supernaturally beautiful*, thought April, *maybe they just have good beauticians.*

'Well, I think you're too good to waste,' said Davina, reaching for her phone. April gave her a questioning look, but Davina only smiled and held up a finger. 'Hi Miggy, are you free?' she said into the phone. 'Excellent. Can you be out front in fifteen? We're going to the Dorch. Could you ring ahead for me? You're a star.'

She hung up and grinned at April. 'Come on, if you're going to ditch lessons, then we're going to make the most of it. I'm taking you for tea.'

'No really, I can't, I've got to …'

'You've got to what? Do homework? Not dressed like that you haven't. Come on, Mummy doesn't need Miguel at the spa so he's only going to waste. Plus he's gorgeous. And since you've got to eat at some point, you might as well do it in style.'

April was about to raise another objection, but Davina held up a hand.

'No time,' she said, pulling her cashmere sweater over her head and heading for the dressing room. 'I've only got fifteen minutes to make myself as gorgeous as you. I need all the help I can get.'

Despite the fact that she was sitting across the table from a vampire who might have killed someone she knew, April was having a pretty good time. Away from all the other Faces, Davina was actually quite funny and self-deprecating. There was none of her usual showing off and one-upmanship, even when it became obvious that the tea room at the Dorchester was somewhere she visited often. April hadn't even known it existed.

'Hello again, Jamie,' said Davina as a gorgeous waiter approached their table. He had chiselled features and even under the crisp white shirt it was obvious Jamie was no stranger to the gym. The waiter smiled in recognition.

'Hello, Miss Osbourne.'

'How many times must I tell you to call me Davina?'

He shrugged those powerful shoulders.

'Sorry, Miss Osbourne,' he said. 'Hotel policy. Thanks for the in with Guido, by the way.'

'Not a problem,' she said, touching his hand. 'Just bring us two more of these, okay?'

She raised her glass. Davina had insisted on them both having a glass of champagne when they had arrived. 'We're celebrating, remember? The real April Dunne has finally emerged.'

When he had gone, Davina leant over the table. 'I put him

in touch with an agent at W2 Models. He's too pretty to be waiting tables for ever.'

'See what I mean about you being nicer than your reputation?'

Davina waved the compliment away. 'Maybe I've got other plans for Jamie,' she smiled.

April wondered. Was she just referring to dating the gorgeous waiter, or was she planning on feeding from him? Or had she plans to turn him into the male Kate Moss *and* use him for the vampire cause? Maybe it was the booze bubbling through her veins, but April couldn't see Davina as a one-dimensional blood-sucker any more. She was vulnerable and funny and real. Plus she was at home in places like this. She looked around at the pillars and the gilt and velvet. It was all a bit old-fashioned and silly but at the same time it was glamorous and brilliant. She bit into a tiny pastry and sat back.

'I could get used to this.'

Davina pointed at her.

'I knew you'd like it. Underneath that reserved British shell, there's a diva fighting to get out.'

April giggled and sipped her champagne.

Davina glanced at her watch. 'Now, do you want to go back to computer club or whatever it is you normally do after school, or shall we go and get our nails done?'

'Oh, I think the nails.'

Davina smiled her approval.

'I'll call Miguel. By the end of the day you will be more fabulous than me and that's saying something.'

April was feeling pleasantly fuzzy and happy. She was enjoying the feeling of being naughty and decadent. There was certainly no way she wanted to go home to the disapproval of her mother and the inevitable shouting that would follow. April was sure that Mr Sheldon would have gleefully rung Silvia about April's disappearance under the guise of 'concern for her well-being'. Really he was just creeping around her, trying to get in with her mother to avoid a lawsuit. She pulled a face.

'What's up?'

'Just thought of Hawk and my mum.'

'What about them?' asked Davina, clearly sensing some intrigue.

'Oh, he's been nosing about, turning up at the house at weird times, having little chats with my mum. I think he's after her.'

'Eww! That's horrible. And what's your mum thinking of? Your dad's funeral was only a few weeks ago.'

'Tell me about it. He gives me the creeps.'

'Oh, Hawk's harmless. He'd like you to think he's in charge at Ravenwood, but he's just a lackey.'

Now it was April's turn to be interested.

'Really? Who is in charge then?'

Davina looked evasive.

'Oh, some fat cat billionaires. The way my dad talks about them, they're pretty powerful. I certainly wouldn't want to be in Hawk's shoes right now anyway.'

'What's he done?'

'More what he hasn't done, I think. The school's not producing as many geniuses as it's supposed to or something. Daddy's upset with him, anyway. And the governors are definitely not going to be happy about all the scandals in the papers, with both Marcus and Layla. So I wouldn't worry, he's probably going to be fired long before he can get anywhere with your mum.'

Davina obviously knew a lot more than she was saying. Which was another reason for April to stick with her. Maybe she could squeeze out some more information. Caro would be pleased. Not that she was doing anything for her, she reminded herself. She'd had enough of Caro Jackson and her holier-than-thou attitude. No, April had been through enough for that stupid conspiracy cause and it was about time she had a bit of fun. Paying the bill with Davina's shiny black credit card ('Well, technically it's Mummy's, but if she will leave her PIN lying around …'), they click-clacked through the lobby and out to the car where they fell back into the white leather seats. Davina picked up her phone and started tapping away.

'Who are you texting?'

Davina tapped the side of her nose. 'All in the name of fun, don't you worry.'

She leant over to Miguel and said, 'Slight detour, Miggy darling. Zip up to Selfridge's, would you?'

Waiting for them on the kerb were Chessy and Ling. April's heart sank. She'd been enjoying her day of liberation with her new-found friend Davina. She'd been warm and open and surprisingly sensitive, but she knew how she got when she was around the rest of the Faces: like some sort of fashion-conscious ringmaster, cracking the whip to get everyone to jump her way.

'Don't look so worried,' said Davina as she opened the car door for the girls. 'It will be fun, I promise you.'

'Hi April!' trilled Ling and Chessy together as they squished into the back seat, Ling sitting on Chessy's knee. 'This is such a stroke of luck, isn't it?' gushed Chessy. 'We were just shopping for a watch for Ling.' The other girl proudly held up a gem-encrusted disc of gold on her wrist. 'Is it too much?' she pouted.

'Just a little,' smiled Davina. 'But then you can pull it off, honey.'

They drew up at a nail bar in Mayfair, piling out and going inside, chattering and laughing. Ling immediately latched onto Davina, chattering about her new watch, so April sat down next to Chessy. She'd rarely spoken to the girl, but she was always there at the edge of the Faces group, a smart-arse smile on her face. If she was honest, April was a little intimidated by Chessy. She seemed so aloof and otherworldly. Plus she was the prettiest of all the Faces, which didn't help.

'So how are you feeling after all the drama?' said Chessy as the technicians, inscrutable behind their face-masks, began to buff their nails.

'Oh, not as bad as you'd think. After all the knocks, it's almost as if I'm getting used to it, you know?'

'You're very brave,' said Chessy. 'I mean, I'd have gone to pieces. I wish I had your strength.'

April looked at the girl, searching her expression for hints of sarcasm, but there was none. Chessy seemed to be saying what she meant. April was taken aback.

'Oh, well I wouldn't say I was strong ...' she muttered.

'Don't be so modest,' said Chessy. 'Look at all you've been through: moving to a new school which, let's be honest, is full of weirdoes.' She leant forward and hushed her voice. 'And I do include present company. It can't have been easy fitting in at Ravenwood.'

'No, it wasn't, but there are some pretty cool people.'

'Even so, it's hard. Then you get mixed up with that horrid thing with that girl Isabelle, then your dad ... well, who wouldn't be knocked by that? I would have ended up in a loony bin if I was you. And then on top of all that, you get attacked by a maniac. Twice! Honestly, April, I don't know how you coped.'

'Like I say, people have been really nice. Davina's been great.'

Chessy smiled wickedly and lowered her voice, glancing over to where Davina and Ling were gabbling about some club in Mayfair. ''Vina's brilliant, of course. But don't you think she's a bit, well, full of herself?'

April put a hand over her mouth to stifle a giggle.

'Well, sometimes perhaps.'

'Most of the time, you mean,' smiled Chessy. 'Always bossing people around like she knows everything. And she's always doing these makeovers on people. She wants to get a bit of advice herself.'

April had to pinch herself to stop from laughing out loud.

'Personally I think she's a bit jealous of you.'

'Of me? Why would she be jealous of me?'

'Because you're so in control. You take everything in your stride.'

'Me? No! Besides, I never thought Davina had any problems with self-confidence.'

'Ah, but arrogance usually masks insecurity.'

April blinked at her, then Chessy smiled. 'I read about

it in *Glamour*,' she giggled. 'But still, it's true, isn't it? She's sophisticated and beautiful and everything, but cool she is not. Uptight is more like it.'

This time April couldn't hold it in and burst out laughing.

'What are you two gossiping about?' asked Davina.

'Those two out there,' said Chessy promptly, pointing to two girls walking past on the opposite side of the street. Their clothes were a mish-mash of high fashion and vintage edginess. They had ridiculous Geisha-style make-up and back-combed hair, tottering along in mini-skirts and platforms.

'April was just saying how it looked like the circus was in town.'

Davina laughed.

'Art students, it's the only explanation,' said Davina.

'Maybe a Japanese mime troupe,' said April. Everyone laughed and April felt something wonderful: belonging. She felt accepted and wanted. No one was asking her to be some great superhero or spend every waking moment searching for the answers to conspiracies. She could just relax and have fun. She realised she hadn't really done that since she had left Scotland.

'What do you think Marcus had against you?'

April shrugged. 'Maybe he didn't like my talking to Benjamin so much.'

'Yes, I've noticed Baby Ben's been following you around a lot,' smiled Chessy. 'And there was I thinking you were a one-man woman.'

'Not any more,' said April, 'if I ever was. I mean, I suppose Gabriel was only trying to protect me and I hate that he's in prison because of that, but ...'

Chessy nodded sympathetically.

'Well you could do a lot worse than Ben, but I think we can show you a lot better.'

'What do you mean?'

Chessy's nails were finished and she turned around to Davina and Ling. 'I think we need to show our friend from Scotland what London's all about, don't you?'

'The Saturn?' said Davina with a wicked smile.

'Yes! The Saturn!' said Ling, clapping her hands together. 'Oh do come, April, it will be so much fun!'

'What's The Saturn?' asked April.

'The Saturn Club,' said Davina. 'It's only the celeb hangout du jour.'

Chessy smirked and mouthed 'Du jour' to April.

'Say you'll come, April,' said Ling. 'It's always filled with gorgeous men.'

'How can I refuse an offer like that?'

April felt a buzzing in her bag and scrabbled her phone out. A text from Caro. She clicked the button.

Sorry, me and my big mouth again. And I'm sorry I didn't tell you.
Forgive me over ice cream? CJxx

No, not tonight, thought April, snapping her phone closed. *I think I've got somewhere better to be.*

Chapter Twenty-Five

The club was like a spaceship; high-tech and dangerous at the same time. As they descended down a long silver staircase lit by red neon bars it felt like the whole building was about to take off. It was furnace hot and April was feeling the bass from the music pounding in her ribcage.

'This way,' shouted Davina as they pushed into the main room. 'You're gonna love it!' She led the way through the dancing crowd to an elevated booth where a burly security guy immediately lifted the red-velvet rope to let the girls pass through. The VIP area was more intimate than the main room, with booths finished in white padded leather and modernist perspex chairs.

A hostess showed the girls to a booth and April huddled up next to Ling, admiring her long legs and impeccable make-up as the waitress handed them champagne.

'I have to say you've changed since we first met,' said April.

'I know. 'Vina's changed my life. When I think of the boring geek I was before, it's so embarrassing.'

'Don't say that. Just because you weren't up to the Faces standard of ...'

'Oh no, they're not like that at all. I know everyone thinks they're a bunch of bitchy cows who spend all their time putting everyone else down, but they're actually great when you get to know them. I think they're misunderstood.'

'Well, I have to admit you've all been very nice to me today. Davina's been especially nice.'

'She's wonderful, isn't she?' said Ling, looking across at her with shining eyes. 'I love her so much. I'd do anything for her.'

'Anything?'

'Pretty much. I mean, I've always found it quite hard to make friends. I'll be honest, I've never really had a best friend. But Davina's done everything for me. She did my hair, make-up, showed me how to dress, she's completely restored my confidence. I feel like a new woman.'

April thought about her day with a sinking sense of worry. Wasn't that exactly what Davina had done for her today? Given her a makeover then brought her into her circle of friends, made her feel wanted and lovely? *Is this just the recruitment process? Is this how she draws people in?* As the cocktails and champagne flowed, April realised with a twinge of guilt that she hadn't thought about Gabriel once. She was actually having real fun.

'Come on girls,' said Davina, 'I want to introduce you to someone.' She pulled them over to a handsome, tanned boy.

'Is that Jamie George?' whispered April. 'I love him.'

The actor was tanned and fit, having just finished filming a romantic comedy where he'd played a lifeguard. The gossip magazines were full of pictures of him strutting about in his trunks.

'I saw him first!' said Chessy with a flirtatious smile.

'Do you really know him?' April asked Davina, her eyes wide.

Chessy rolled her eyes. "Vina knows everyone,' she said, just a hint of mockery in her voice.

'Not everyone,' said Davina. 'Just the people who matter.'

She walked over and bent down to air-kiss the actor.

'Hey, Vee,' he drawled. 'I haven't seen you since that party at Alix's. Mad scenes, eh? Shame about the big guy.'

April looked at her. Davina had known Alix Graves? This was huge news.

But he can't be a vampire, can he? she wondered. *God, April, stop being so paranoid, of course he isn't.* Vampires couldn't have their photographs taken, she knew that much. A man who spent all day in front of cameras wouldn't be much use if he just came out as black smudge.

'This is our new friend, April,' said Davina. 'Say hello.'

'Hi April,' said Jamie, offering her a hand to shake. 'You're as pretty as your friends.'

'You're such a sleaze,' said Davina. She was talking to a Hollywood star as if he was an old friend. No wonder Ling looked at her with such hero-worship.

'No one's going to believe I've met him,' April whispered to Ling. With her phone in her hand, making sure she turned the flash off, she clicked off a shot. But immediately someone grabbed her arm.

'Don't do that.'

She turned. 'Benjamin!' she said, surprising herself by hugging him, 'What are you doing here?'

'Oh, the party usually ends up here at some point, so it's always worth popping by. Plus I need to keep an eye on Davina. She can get herself into trouble.'

She looked at him, squinting slightly. Ben really was very good-looking. She felt bad thinking that way, but then remembered why she was so angry with Gabriel. And why shouldn't she find other men attractive, especially when they were as nice as Benjamin Osbourne? He looked at her phone.

'I think you've got his best side. But it's better not to take photos in the VIP section.'

'What? Why not? He has his photo taken all the time.'

'Exactly. But not here. There's a lot of people here who don't want to have their photo taken.'

'Why not?'

'Because there are a lot of people here doing things they shouldn't,' said Ben with a wink. *God, he's nice*, thought April. She felt bad for even thinking it, but then she thought of Gabriel, his hand tenderly stroking Jessica's cheek, and her guilt faded. She took another swig of her cocktail and sat down on the banquette next to Ben.

'So how's it feel to be the girl everyone's talking about?'

'Am I?'

He laughed: throaty and suggestive.

'You can't go getting yourself attacked by a maniac twice in a month, April, and expect to slip under the radar.'

'Ah. I suppose not,' she said, aware that she was slurring a little, but not really caring. 'I think it's getting to be a habit.'

'Perhaps,' nodded Ben, his bright blue eyes on her. 'I can see what made Marcus go crazy for you though.'

April blushed, covering her embarrassment by sucking on her straw and looking out at the crowd. She could feel Ben's eyes on her, but she was determined not to wilt under the power of his gaze.

'Do I make you uncomfortable, April?' he asked, a hint of amusement in his voice.

'No, not at all. It's just after all that's happened ...'

Ben shook his head. 'Nah, I don't think so. I think you're the sort of girl who can take anything in her stride.'

She shrugged and looked at him sideways. He was interesting, that was for sure. Oh, and handsome. And nice. But there was something about him she just couldn't put her finger on.

'You look quizzical, April,' said Ben. 'Like you're trying to work out a difficult problem. Is it me?'

'No, you're easy to work out. You're a predator.'

Ben laughed.

'How have you come to this shocking conclusion?'

'It's like watching one of those nature programmes. Sitting in your cave, waiting for the prey to come to you. Let them get close and *snap*! You've got them.'

Ben looked down to where April's leg was pushed right up against his.

'Aren't you sitting dangerously close, then?'

'I probably am,' said April. 'But I'll take the risk.'

Slowly, wonderfully slowly, Ben turned to her and kissed her on her neck.

'Oh,' she said as his warm lips trailed down over her bare shoulder. His hands circled her waist and stroked down her thigh. *Oh, yes*, she thought, instinctively moving her own lips down towards his.

You can't kiss him, said a voice inside her head, *he's a vampire.*

But it was a quiet voice and she was enjoying the moment too much to listen too hard. Then suddenly, Ben stopped and pulled back.

'Hey! What's the matter?' she protested. 'Don't you want to kiss me?'

'Of course. It's just … I don't want to take advantage of you. Not while you're confused about Gabriel. I'd feel bad.'

'I don't mind things which are bad for me,' she said, raising one eyebrow. Ben laughed.

'Okay, here's the deal. You get home tomorrow. If you decide you still want nothing to do with Gabriel Swift – and you're still interested in me when you're sober – then give me a call. I will be there in three minutes flat, okay?'

'Three minutes?'

'Two minutes then. But do call me, okay?'

'Oh I'll do that all right,' said April. 'Just you wait.'

Chapter Twenty-Six

It wasn't until the moment she put the key in her front door that April remembered she'd played truant all day. She'd been so swept up in her perfect day that she'd forgotten all about her mundane, everyday life. She knew it was past midnight, and she'd been out since morning. Surely her mother would be passed out, star-shaped by now? She winced at the clunk-click as the door closed, then tiptoed into the hall, hanging up her coat as quietly as she could. She paused, cocking her head. The house was silent and there were no lights coming from the kitchen. Maybe she'd got lucky. She gingerly pulled off Davina's borrowed heels and put a bare foot on the first step, bracing herself for a creak.

'It's past midnight, April.'

April nearly hit the roof.

'God, Mum,' she breathed, clutching her chest. 'Don't scare me like that.'

Her mother walked out of the shadows. There were bags under her eyes and her face was drawn, as if she'd been given some bad news.

'What's up?' said April, suddenly concerned.

'What the hell do you think is "up"?' snapped her mother. 'You walked out of school this morning and disappeared off the face of the earth. Where the hell have you been?'

'I ... I went into town with Davina.'

'Putting aside your truancy for a moment, why haven't you answered your phone all day?'

'It didn't ring.' She pulled out her phone and looked down at the screen: she had left it on silent. There were twelve

263

voice messages, and twice as many texts, all from Caro and her mother. April felt a sudden rush of guilt. Of course they would be worried, especially after Marcus and Layla.

'I'm sorry,' she said, looking at the floor, 'I just wanted a bit of time to myself.'

'After all that's happened? How could you be so thoughtless? We've been sitting here thinking the worst.'

'What do you mean "we"?'

There was an awkward cough and Mr Sheldon walked out from the living room.

'What's he doing here?' said April.

'Don't talk about Mr Sheldon like that!' snapped Silvia. 'In this house you will show him some respect. Mr Sheldon was concerned about your sudden disappearance and he came to me.'

April glanced at the teacher and noticed that his tie was undone and his shirt untucked..

'Oh yeah, I'll bet he was *concerned*,' she said sarcastically. The alcohol had loosened her tongue and, more than anything, she hated the way her mother felt the need to ruin her brilliant day out by shouting at her, especially when she appeared to have been cosying up to her headmaster!

'April!' shouted Silvia. 'How dare you?'

'How dare I? Dad's hardly cold in his grave and you're inviting fancy men around for a cosy chat? How's that meant to make me feel?'

'I don't like that tone, young lady,' said her mother, but Mr Sheldon stepped forward and touched her arm.

'It's okay, Silvia, April's right. I should be going. I just wanted to make sure she was all right.'

April snorted, glaring at them both, swaying slightly so that she had to reach out to hold on to the banister.

'Don't move,' said Silvia coldly. 'We haven't finished, not by a long chalk.'

April sat down on the stairs while Silvia saw Hawk to the door. When their backs were turned, she surreptitiously took a picture with her phone, making a mental note to look at it later.

'What the hell has got into you, April?' said Silvia as she walked back, her tone more weary than angry now. 'You used to be such a lovely straightforward girl, now look at you. Drunk, disrespectful – and what are you wearing?'

April pulled a face. She couldn't be bothered with arguing any more. All she wanted was to get to bed. 'It's Davina's.'

'Well I don't want you seeing that girl any more. She's obviously a bad influence.'

'I thought you liked me hanging out at the Osbournes',' said April defiantly. 'I thought it helped your pathetic plan for social climbing.'

In a flash, Silvia darted forward, her face inches from April's. Her eyes were narrow, her teeth clenched. April jerked backwards, thunking her head on the banister. She'd seen her mother turn her fury on other people, but she'd never seen it this close, or turned on her. It was terrifying.

'Do not speak to me like that,' Silvia whispered. Her eyes bore into April's, cold and vicious. *Good God*, thought April. *I'd rather face that loony Marcus than this.*

'No more Davina Osbourne, no more nightclubs, and you are grounded until you are thirty. Are we clear?'

April nodded, quickly.

'Get. To. Bed,' said Silvia. April didn't need telling twice. She turned and ran up the stairs.

Chapter Twenty-Seven

At about eight in the morning, roughly three seconds after her bedside alarm clock began to squawk, April decided that she would never drink again. Her mouth was as dry as the inside of a vacuum cleaner and every time she moved, her head felt like it was being pushed on a swing. That was without the pain behind her eyes, which was like kebab skewers being pushed through her brain.

'Feeling good?' said Silvia, yanking back the curtains. It was only a murky grey morning but the dull light was enough to give her another stab of pain through her head.

'Not especially.'

'Well I've made you eggs, that should make you feel better. Downstairs in five minutes.'

April groaned and pulled her duvet over her head, but she knew she had no choice. She crawled out of bed, jumped in the shower and threw on some clothes, all the while doing her best not to make any sudden movements.

She could smell frying fat as she came down the stairs and it almost made her retch. She sat carefully at the breakfast bar and watched as her mother bustled about, popping brown toast from the silver toaster and spreading butter over it, making tea in a teapot, a picture of domesticity. April couldn't remember ever seeing her mother make anything in the kitchen apart from a gin and tonic. And even then, she'd made April slice the lemon.

'Is this supposed to be some sort of bizarre punishment?' croaked April. 'Because if it is, it's definitely working.'

Silvia pushed a plate of scrambled eggs and bacon in front

of her. 'Eat,' she said. 'It will make you feel better. Believe me, I'm an expert at this sort of thing.'

Reluctantly, April shovelled a few forkfuls of egg into her mouth with a shaking hand and washed it down with some fresh orange juice. For one horrible moment she thought her stomach was going to rebel and throw it all up, but slowly it stopped grumbling and April even managed to force down a slice of toast. To her annoyance, she did feel a little better.

'I'll give you some water and a banana to take to school,' said Silvia. 'Potassium and hydration, works wonders on a hangover.'

'Oh no, do I really have to go to school?' moaned April, putting her head down on the bar.

'Yes, April, you do. Just because you've behaved like a spoilt brat doesn't mean the rest of the world has to stop.'

'A spoilt brat?' said April. 'Mum, some maniac tried to kill me – twice! I thought I was entitled to let off a little steam.'

'You are, April, but not at the expense of everyone else. If you were feeling shaky, you should have come to see me or one of your teachers. Disappearing isn't going to solve anything. I was terrified something had happened to you.'

'I was only getting my nails done!'

'Maybe so, April, but you could have sent me a text. I know you're never more than three feet away from your phone, so when you didn't answer – when you were almost killed two nights ago – you'll excuse me if I'm worried you were lying bleeding in a ditch somewhere.'

'Mum, I was fine,' said April, knowing she'd screwed up.

'I'm glad. But I was so scared, darling.'

Tears appeared in her eyes.

'There's been enough trauma around here, with your dad and then with you in hospital. God knows how the police can live with themselves letting that bloody maniac get into the party …'

'Mum, I'm okay.'

She went over and hugged her mother.

'I couldn't stand to lose you. Not now.' She took a long

ragged breath. 'But you understand why I was so angry?'

April nodded, feeling terrible. She'd been so angry herself, felt so isolated and alone, she just had to get away. And it had been fun, one of the best days she'd had since she'd arrived in London. But she hadn't for one moment considered how her mother would have taken it. Of course she would assume something bad had happened – no wonder she had called Mr Sheldon. Trouble just seemed to follow her around.

'Sorry, Mum,' she whispered.

'Okay. It's over now. Don't do it again. It wasn't just me worried either, your friend Caro was calling every half-hour.'

'And Mr Sheldon, apparently.'

Silvia gave her a severe look.

'Don't take that attitude. Robert – Mr Sheldon – was concerned for you.'

'Concerned for his job, more like.'

'April,' she said in a warning tone. 'You may not like Mr Sheldon, but he is the headmaster of your school.'

'I doubt most headmasters would show up at a pupil's house at midnight just because she'd skipped class.'

Silvia pursed her lips and looked away.

'Come on, Mum, what's going on?'

She turned towards the fridge. 'I don't know what you mean.'

'Yes you do. Why is "Robert" always round here? I know it's your house and everything, but I … well, I don't like it.'

'He's an old friend of mine and your dad's.'

'So how come you never mentioned him to me before? I'd never heard of him before I got to Ravenwood. Surely that would have been the first thing you said to me in Edinburgh: "Don't worry darling, at least you're going to Uncle Robert's school"?'

Silvia sighed.

'Your dad didn't really like him.'

'Well Dad always did have better taste than you.'

Silvia pulled a face. 'April, I've told you …'

'All right, so tell me the story then! Tell me about "Robert".

How do you know him? Was it at Uni? I asked Hawk about it ...'

'Hawk?'

'Oh ... that's what the kids at school all call him. Because of his eyes.'

Her mother gave her a curious look, as if she were searching her face for more information, then seemed to change her mind.

'Yes, we met at Oxford.'

'Well, I asked him about that and he didn't seem to know Dad very well.'

'Oh, they knew each other, but they weren't in the same social group. We were at different colleges, you see.'

'So why didn't you ever mention him?'

'You know how it is, you have friends at a certain time, then you drift apart.'

April thought of Caro. She didn't think that you gave up friends without a really good reason.

'Why didn't Dad like him?'

'If you must know,' Silvia said reluctantly, 'Robert was a little more than a friend. We went out before I met your dad.'

April pushed away from the table, pain flashing in her head at the sudden movement.

'Urgh! No! But he's horrible!'

'April! Don't be so mean. He was a lot younger then.'

'Eww, Mum! That's ...' she shivered. 'How could you?'

Silvia laughed.

'He had a car. I was easily impressed.'

'God,' said April, letting it sink in. 'So what happened? Did you dump him for Dad?'

'No, it was all over by the time your dad arrived. But you can imagine that they were never going to be best friends. No one likes to be confronted with their partner's ex, do they?'

No, they don't, thought April, her mind drifting back to the horrible moment she'd seen Gabriel with that Jessica woman. She'd thought around it, hoping for some other explanation: perhaps she was coming on to him and he was pushing her away? Perhaps she was she his long-lost sister? No, that only happened in romantic comedies starring Jennifer Aniston.

'But I don't understand why you didn't tell me when I came to the school. You must have known I'd have found out eventually.'

Silvia shrugged.

'I know you assume adults all have some kind of secret handbook on how to behave in the proper manner, but we don't. We make bad decisions, just like everyone else. In hindsight, we should have mentioned it, but you'll remember that your dad and I were preoccupied with the move and his new job.'

'You were arguing all the time, you mean.'

Her mother nodded.

'That too. I suppose we both knew it would just trigger more rows and just avoided the subject. I'm sorry.'

April got up, feeling that some of the jellyness had left her legs. She hated to admit it, but her mother had been right about breakfast. She still felt sick, but nowhere near as bad as before.

'It doesn't matter now. But I don't like having him in the house. Honestly, I know he's my teacher and everything, but he gives me the creeps.'

Silvia smirked.

'That's exactly what your father used to say.'

Suddenly April had a horrible thought.

'Oh God, I've got Philosophy with Mr Sheldon today!'

'I'm sure he'll be discreet.'

'But even so, it's going to be awful seeing him there. Do I really have to go?'

'Yes. In fact I'm going to drive you there.'

'Aww, Mum.'

'No arguments, April.'

She looked at her seriously.

'Listen to me, April. I don't know what's going on, but I'm really worried. It doesn't look like the police have a clue what they're doing, and after everything that's happened, I don't want you wandering around. I was serious about no more nightclubs and I mean it about the grounding. I want to know where you are.'

'I can look after myself, Mum.'

'I'm not asking! Just humour me, okay? Come straight home after school. And no more disappearing acts.'

April's mother was right, Mr Sheldon didn't say anything. In fact, he barely looked in April's direction throughout the entire hour he was standing in front of the class. The only person who looked her way was Benjamin Osbourne, who gave her a secret smile, but April was too preoccupied with her thoughts to pay much attention.

It was nice that her mother was concerned, of course. And April had to admit it had been selfish to run off like that without telling anyone. But there was something bothering her about her mother's sudden protectiveness and she couldn't quite put her finger on it. Obviously, her woolly head wasn't exactly firing on all cylinders today, but something didn't ring true. Yes, April had been attacked twice and yes, anyone could see that there was an escalating level of violence in Highgate, but that had been going on for months and Silvia had never so much as raised an eyebrow before. So why was she suddenly talking about curfews and driving her to school? Was it something Hawk had said to her? Did he know something about the vampire activity? Maybe he wasn't top dog at Ravenwood – Davina had made that pretty clear the day before, and otherwise there was no way he would let her walk in and out of school whenever she felt like it – but there was a good chance he had a hotline to whoever was in charge. So had he given Silvia some inside information about the vampire threat? Were they on the rise, as Mr Gill had said? And how did Hawk know, anyway? God, there were so many things she didn't know she felt like her head was spinning.

Silvia had been out with him, how could she not know he was a vampire? But then, until she'd seen the knife sticking out of Gabriel she hadn't believed it either. She had kissed Milo and he'd seemed like a normal boy too. Vampires just didn't wear capes or turn into bats like they did in the movies. It was lucky Hawk didn't ask her any questions about the lesson – she hadn't listened to a word. He actually seemed to be ignoring her by the end, rummaging in his briefcase when she walked by his desk on the way out. Perhaps he was as embarrassed as she was. *Why be embarrassed*, she wondered, *if he really did come over because he was concerned?* Maybe she had been right the first time, and she had caught them doing something when she stumbled in. *Oh God*, she thought. *Maybe they were at it.*

'Hi, April,' said Ben, catching her arm. 'I wanted to talk to you about last night …'

Oh no, she thought, it all coming back to her in a flash. *We almost kissed last night, didn't we?*

Her already unsteady stomach turned over.

'Sorry,' she said, covering her mouth and bolting in the opposite direction.

Pushing her way through the thronging students crowding the corridors, she barged into the ladies and bent over a toilet, but nothing came up.

She flushed, banged the seat down and sat down heavily. Was she feeling sick because she was hung-over? Yes, partly. Was she feeling sick because she was thinking about her mother and Hawk fumbling about on the sofa? Probably. But she was also nauseated by her own behaviour. *I'm a bloody Fury!* she thought angrily. *My kiss is deadly to a vampire.* She covered her eyes in shame as she remembered almost kissing Ben. *I would have killed him and would probably have made myself a target for the entire vampire nation. How could I be so stupid?* She turned around, about to heave again.

'April? Is that you in there?'

It was Caro tapping on the door.

Oh God, the last thing she needed right now was another argument about responsibility.

'Are you okay?'

April wiped her mouth and opened the door.

'I'm fine,' she said, trying to stay steady on her feet.

'You sure? You don't look too good.'

'I said so, didn't I?'

Caro flinched and April immediately felt bad. Caro was her friend, it was just that she had become too wrapped up in the vampire empire conspiracy. Frankly, April didn't give a monkey's about any of that right now.

'Look, I'm sorry, Caro, but I've got a lot on my mind at the moment, okay?' she said, moving for the door.

'Okay, sorry,' said Caro. 'Listen, what happened yesterday? Did you get my texts? I'm sorry about our argument, it was stupid.'

'Yes, it was,' said April.

'I'm glad you said that,' said Caro looking relieved. 'I've had an idea ...'

'Oh no,' said April putting her hands up. 'I didn't mean to upset you, but I meant what I said. I'm not taking part in your stupid conspiracies and investigations any more. I'm sick of it.'

Caro glanced around at the passing students rushing for class.

'But April, you are involved,' she whispered. 'More than anyone. You can't pretend ...'

But that was exactly what she wanted to do right now. She wanted to blot it all out, forget about everything, just be normal – well, as normal as she could be. This huge weight of responsibility being a Fury and knowing that the vampires even existed was too much for her right now.

'I can pretend, Caro,' said April. 'I can do whatever I like.'

She walked out of the ladies with Caro right behind her.

'April, please. I just wanted to apologise ...'

April spun around.

'Apology accepted,' she said. 'But I haven't got time for this any more, Caro. Honestly. I just want to forget it, okay?'

She turned and pushed through the refectory doors. Davina and the Faces were sitting in their usual place.

'April ...' said Caro, but April waved to Chessy and walked over, leaving Caro standing at the door.

'Hi, girls,' said April as loudly and cheerily as she could. 'How are you feeling after our night of sin?'

They all laughed and started chattering about their hang-overs and their journeys home. When April turned to check that Caro had seen her sitting with her new friends, there was only an empty space where her friend had been. April wished she felt better about it.

April walked up Swain's Lane and then into Waterlow Park. She knew it wasn't the smartest move to be walking through a lonely open space – especially after her promise to her mother – but she was so drained, so sick of it all, she would almost welcome death as long as it was quick. Besides, it was cold and this was the shortest route to Americano, where she had arranged to meet Davina and the other girls after school.

Her phone buzzed and she pulled it out. Two messages … one from Miss Holden – *Please April, can we talk?*

'No, we can't,' said April, deleting it as she had all the teacher's other messages.

… and one from Benjamin.

Want to finish what we almost started last night? B x

She smiled to herself. It made her queasy to think about how close she'd come to infecting him with a deadly virus, but it was still nice to have a handsome boy ask her out. An image of Gabriel's face jumped into her head, but she shook it away. That was over – it *had* to be. April could see a girl sitting on a bench up along the path, but it wasn't until she got closer that she realised it was Ling, her face pale with cold, her short wool coat wrapped around her.

She stepped forward the moment she saw April, looking around her nervously.

'Ling, what are you doing here?'

'I needed to talk to you,' said Ling. Her cheeks were white and her face drawn. 'I made an excuse to the others. I thought you might come through here.'

'What is it? Are you in trouble?'

Ling looked about again and took April's arm.

'Can we go somewhere else?'

'Sure, let's walk back to my house.'

'No! I don't want to risk being seen by anyone.'

April hesitated for a moment. 'I know, we'll go to the church.'

'The church?'

'It will be empty, especially at this time of day. It'll be a bit warmer, too, and we can talk.'

They walked back up towards the Square, then turned left towards the spire with its fox, lazy today without any wind. As April had predicted, when they went inside it was deserted, the stone floor echoing as they walked over to a pew and sat down. April couldn't help but glance up at the stained-glass window with the picture of the fox and the sword. *I think I could do with a sword myself, foxy*, thought April. *But then I'd probably only cut my hand off.*

'Thanks, April,' whispered Ling, clearly intimidated by the grand church, but at least they were out of the cold and could speak freely. 'You were so nice yesterday, I knew I'd be able to talk to you about this.'

April waited.

'You know that time?' said Ling softly. 'That time you found me in the toilets?'

'When you were bleeding?'

Ling waved her hand. 'Shhh!' she said. 'I asked you not to tell anyone about that.'

'I didn't! I haven't told anyone. But what about it? Is it something to do with Davina and the other girls?'

At the mention of Davina's name, Ling looked terrified.

'I don't want to talk about it.'

'I know, but ...'

'I *can't*,' she said. Her face was a mask of horror. 'I can't talk about it.'

'Listen,' April said softly. 'I know it feels like it's the worst thing in the world right now and that you can't even bear to say it, but believe me, I've been through some really weird stuff over the last few weeks and nothing you say is going to surprise me. Really.'

Ling still looked unsure.

'It's a church, remember. It's like confession. I really won't say anything.'

'The thing is, I'm glad to do it,' said Ling in a half-whisper, her hunted eyes darting towards the church entrance.

'Glad? To do what?'

'This.'

She pulled back her sleeve to show April her arms. They were covered in what looked like scrapes and scratches, as if she had been caught in a thorn bush. As she looked closer, April could see they were little cuts.

'I use a blade,' said Ling, her eyes searching April's. April tried hard not to betray her disgust. 'Just little cuts, it hardly hurts at all. It's just that sometimes they ...'

April touched her knee and nodded encouragingly.

'Sometimes what?'

'Sometimes they take too much.'

'Who's they, Ling?'

Ling looked at April like she had asked where the sun was. 'You know.'

'No, I don't,' lied April. 'Tell me. You mean someone else does this to you?'

Ling shook her head and made to stand, but April stopped her.

'Please, Ling, I'm just trying to understand. I've heard about self-harm but ...'

'I'm scared they won't stop,' she whispered. 'They didn't stop with Jonathon.'

'Jonathon?' said April. 'What do you mean? I thought he moved to Somerset?'

Ling barked out a hollow laugh.

'That's what they want you to think. I've seen the look on Davina's face. At first it looks like love. And you want them to feed. It feels good. Oh, God, it feels good. But after a while it hurts, it's like they can't stop, they have to force themselves away.'

'But what happened to Jonathon?'

'I don't know. All I know is that one day he was there, the next he was gone. And I think ...'

'You think it was because of ... this? Because he was a feeder?'

'Who knows,' shrugged Ling. 'But I don't think any of us is safe. Layla wasn't a feeder – she told me she wasn't having anyone marking her skin, not even Milo – but she still ended up dead, didn't she? I think they're starting to get jumpy about something, it's like they could turn on anyone, even me.'

'But why would they kill Layla?' asked April, wondering if Ling had overheard the Suckers talking about the Fury, but Ling just shook her head.

'One day she was part of the gang, the next they turned against her, started bad-mouthing her. Saying horrible things. Awful. And then she was dead. That's all I know.'

Ling put her hands over her face and started crying.

'Come on, Ling,' said April, putting an arm around her. 'It's not that bad, you have no reason to think ...'

'But I do,' said Ling, looking up, her frightened eyes searching April's. 'Something's spooked them and they're paranoid, edgy. Any one of us could be next. Any one of us.'

April stayed in the church long after Ling left. She made sure she texted her mother first – she didn't want Silvia in her face on top of all the other worries – then sat back in the pew looking up at that window with the fox wrapped around Jesus's ankles. To April, that window seemed a little like her life right now. As she got closer to the mystery, she could see all the little pieces, but they were distorted and unclear and when she stood back, they all looked like they came from completely different pictures. It was horrible to see what was happening to Ling. It was one thing to hear Gabriel talking about 'feeders', talking about it as a victimless crime, just something the vampires had to do to keep going. But to see it there in front of her, Ling's arms covered in cuts and bruises ... and more importantly to see the terror in her eyes. Ling was just a geek who had wanted to fit in. But now she was scared because other people who had joined that particular gang were dying. Davina had struck a devilish bargain with her: she had given Ling confidence and freedom, the ability to mix with people she idolised. But at what cost? And what was April supposed to do now? How could she help Ling without revealing that she knew what was going on? She stood and walked back down the aisle. That wasn't her only problem, of course. There was her mother and her thing with Hawk. She knew Silvia had a selfish, needy side, but that was just horrible so soon after her dad dying. And then there was the thing with Ben. He was obviously very keen – and he was nice – but she'd almost done something stupid, something unfixable. And should they go out, how could she avoid kissing him? How long would she *want* to avoid kissing him? Yes, he was a vampire, but he didn't deserve to die for it. She thought of his sweet text – what was she going to do about that? *Oh well, I suppose I'll figure that out when—* She was just opening the door, when an arm shot out and grabbed her.

'Don't scream,' whispered a voice in her ear. 'I just want to talk.'

'Gabriel!' April's eyes were like saucers. 'You aren't in jail?'

Gabriel put a finger to his lips, glancing out through one of the small windows either side of the main door.

'Escaped,' he said simply. 'They were taking me to court and ... well, let's just say I'm hard to keep locked up.'

'Well maybe they should have taken more care,' said April. 'Maybe it's the right place for you.'

He took a step towards her, his face creased.

'I did it for you, April, you must know that.'

She stepped backwards.

'For me? What the hell are you talking about?'

He looked towards the window again.

'I know you didn't have any choice, but I couldn't let you take the blame for it.'

'What – me? You think I had something to do with Marcus's death?'

His face was a mask of confusion.

278

'Yes. April, you're a Fury …'

'So? I just whacked him with my shoe and ran. I'm not exactly Wonder Woman.'

'April …'

'Jesus! You really do think I killed him, don't you? I mean, which one of us is the vampire exactly?'

'April, I followed you up the path. I heard you scream, and I ran. But when I got there, Marcus was lying there with his throat ripped open.'

'Well it wasn't me!'

Gabriel looked at the floor, frowning. 'That's why I let the police take me. I was so sure you had killed him, and I wanted to protect you. I didn't kill Marcus, April. He was dead when I got there.'

She looked at him. He looked so genuinely concerned, she immediately believed what he was saying. *Oh no*, she thought with a wave of guilt, *I've spent the last few days thinking the worst things about you – I've even come within a hair's breadth of kissing another boy – while all the time you were prepared to go to prison for me.* April felt like being sick again.

'But I was sure you had killed Marcus,' she said.

'No April, I didn't.'

'So who did – and why? I assumed it was you, swinging in on your white charger and playing the hero.' *Oh Lord, that just makes things worse, doesn't it?* she thought. *I've been a stroppy cow, thinking he was just some arrogant show-off when he was actually sacrificing himself for me.*

She wanted to jump into his arms, to thank him for what he had done, but she still couldn't. There was still one huge barrier between them: Jessica. Okay, so Gabriel had been trying to protect her, but he had still been kissing another girl.

'April, I would have done anything to protect you. I love you.'

'Well that's all very nice, Gabriel,' she said, thinking of that awful moment when he had tenderly stroked the hair away from Jessica's face. 'But it's a bit late for all that now.'

'I know how you're feeling and that's why I'm here. I couldn't go another day with you thinking I'd let you down.'

'Well yes, that's exactly what I think, as it happens.'

'Well, you're wrong.'

'Oh yes? When I clearly see my boyfriend – or at least, the person I thought was my boyfriend – kissing another girl, just after I've saved his worthless life, I think I'm entitled to feel a little betrayed.'

'April. Please – you have to believe me, it's not what you think.'

'I'll bet it's exactly what I think.'

'I was kissing her goodbye.'

'It looked a little more than that to me.'

He looked away.

'Uh-oh, I can feel another one of Gabriel Swift's "you wouldn't understand" moments coming on.'

'Don't joke about it, April!'

He grabbed her arm and looked urgently into her eyes.

'I never told you about Jessica because …'

'Because what? Because you're a typical man?'

'Because I was *ashamed*.'

There was something about the look in his eyes that made April stop.

'Ashamed?'

'Jessica was the reason I turned away from the darkness,' he began quietly. 'She was my first feeder. I met her in a tavern, and she was drawn to the life. She wanted to be turned, but she had no idea what she was asking for. And after my promise to Lily, that I would never take a life, I refused. But … then I was feeding from her and I couldn't stop. It was too much. It was such a terrible urge, she wanted it so much, and I couldn't stop. She wouldn't let me.'

'What do you mean "couldn't stop".'

Gabriel turned away, but she grabbed his arm, spun him back around.

'Tell me!'

'I couldn't stop! I drank until there was no more to drink.'

April felt sick.

'You *killed* her? You turned her into a vampire? But you told me you'd never done that!'

'I know. And I couldn't stand it. I've spent decades trying to atone for that one moment.'

'How could you do that? Jesus, Gabriel.'

'You can't be any more angry about it than I am. I've tortured myself a thousand times, reliving that night.'

'But to take someone's life. I thought you were different!'

'I am! I've tried to be. I've worked so hard since then trying to make up for it.'

'How?'

'I took her to the witches.'

'Witches?'

'Don't sound so surprised, you saw them in the woods. They took her in. They have spells, herbal ways to suppress the vampire urge. She's been a witch ever since. I helped her set up her bookshop, I've tried to look after her. But I've stayed away from her – I can't stand the shame of seeing my own victim. But after you went to see her, Jessica came to me. She wanted to tell me what she had seen in your eyes.'

'What?'

'Love, April.'

April felt butterflies in her stomach, but she was still angry.

'Well it's a fine way to repay me, by kissing your ex.'

'She's not my ex, April. We were never lovers. She's a reminder of what I am and what I did. I am fond of her, she's a better person than I am, and that's all. That's what I was saying to her when you saw her. I was asking for her forgiveness, something I haven't been able to do for a hundred years.'

'So why the kiss?'

'I told her we were together. It was a kiss goodbye.'

April didn't know what to think. Should she believe him? He'd told her so many lies before – if he could lie about not killing someone, he could lie about anything.

'You told me you hadn't killed anyone.'

'I know.'

'So why should I believe this new story?'

He took her by the shoulders.

'Because it's true. Because I never want to be with anyone but you, because if I can't have you then I may as well go to prison. But we could run away together! Let's forget all about this and just go somewhere we can be alone.'

'Gabriel, I … I want to believe you,' said April. 'But I can't just—'

'You can,' he said urgently. 'Because I am telling you the complete truth right now. I love you, I want to be with you – there's no one else. There never was, there never will be.'

Suddenly there was a hard banging on the door.

'Gabriel! Gabriel Swift! Come out, we know you're there!'

Immediately, Gabriel reached out and grabbed April, holding her around the neck from behind.

'What are you doing?' she gasped.

'I'm getting you off the hook,' said Gabriel, dragging her to the window, making sure the police outside could see him holding her.

'Back off or the girl gets it!' he shouted, before ducking back into the church. As soon as they were out of sight, April pulled away from him and kicked him in the shin.

'What the hell was all that, Gabriel?' she hissed.

'I want them to think you're a hostage,' said Gabriel, rubbing his leg. 'Otherwise they might think you're willingly involved. Plus …' He took her hand and ran towards the back of the church. '… it will give us a bit of time to find a way out.'

'There's no way out,' said a voice. The vicar stepped forward across the altar. 'So you might as well let her go.'

Gabriel pushed April behind him. 'Get out of my way, old man.'

'Don't threaten me in the Lord's house!' shouted the vicar. 'Come to me, April. You'll be safe here.'

'No, please,' said April, 'I want to go with him,' suddenly knowing it was true. Gabriel looked at her and they exchanged a smile.

'My child, you don't know what you're saying. You don't know who he is – what he has done.'

'I do, Reverend. I really do,' said April.

'Please Reverend,' said Gabriel, 'can't you help us?'

The vicar looked back and forth between them, seeming to struggle with it, then he nodded.

'Maybe I can, but April will have to stay here.'

'But—'

'No arguments, April. The police have blocked the road at the front, there's no chance you'll both get out.'

He looked at Gabriel and pointed to an arched wooden door to the left of the altar.

'If you go through there and up the stairs, you will come out on the roof. Cross to the end nearest the cemetery, and a fire escape will take you down. There's no other way to the back of the church, so unless they've surrounded the whole cemetery you should find a way out.'

'Why are you helping me?'

'For the girl and her father. Not for you.'

Gabriel opened the door and, with a last look at April, ran up the spiral stairs.

'Gabriel!'

April ran after him. At the top of the stairs, he turned and she ran into his arms, feeling his strong body next to hers, squeezing him for all she was worth. Suddenly, definitely, April knew that she believed him. She couldn't say for certain why, but if her time in Highgate had taught her anything, it was that nothing was ever completely clear-cut: some things had to be taken on faith.

'You be safe, you hear?' she said.

'Don't worry about me,' he said, smiling down at her. 'I'll be okay.'

'But what about me?'

He grinned.

'You'll be fine too. I'll be in touch, don't worry. In the meantime, do what you can to find the Regent. That's our best – our only – hope.'

'I will! I will!'

He opened the door and a sudden wind blew his hair back. It was fully dark now and April could see the dull moonlight reflecting off the slates.

He bent and kissed her tenderly on the cheek. 'I'll be back, my love.'

Then he ran across the roof. Suddenly there was a huge roar of wind and a beam of light swept across it, after him. April looked upwards just in time to see the helicopter swing around, narrowly missing the church spire.

'Leave him alone!' she screamed at them, her voice lost in the roar of the engines.

'Come back inside,' yelled the vicar, putting his arm around her shoulders. 'We have to go and open the front door. Don't worry, he's got a good head start.'

'But what's going to happen to him? He didn't kill Marcus. He told me and I believe him.'

'Leave it to the police, April. You can't help Gabriel now.'

As they walked down the stairs and through the church, they could hear pounding on the door and shouts from outside.

'Come on, we must hurry,' said the vicar.

But just as they crossed the Coleridge plaque in the centre of the aisle, April stopped and looked at him. 'Did you know about this?'

'About what, April?'

'About Gabriel and the others. About what they are?'

'What they are?' he repeated.

'Don't pretend you don't know what I'm talking about.' She pointed down at the plaque. 'That.'

There was a muffled bang from outside.

'April, the police!' said the vicar, trying to get past her, but April stood in his way.

'Please, Reverend Gordon, this is important.'

The vicar looked at her, then back at the door.

'I've lived next to the cemetery for twelve years, April. I'd have to be blind to have missed it. Now we really need to—'

'Did you talk to my dad about it?'

284

There was a loud thud against the church doors.

'April, this is not the time ...'

'Answer my question!'

'He asked me about what was happening in the village, yes.'

'So he knew!' she said dejectedly. 'He brought us here, knowing Highgate was bristling with the undead. He put us all in danger.'

'April, it's not—'

The doors burst open and officers in dark uniforms ran in.

'Down on the floor!' shouted a man in a black cap. April realised with horror that he was pointing a rifle at her. 'Get your hands where I can see them.'

The vicar took April's arm and pulled her to the side where they sat down in a pew, their arms raised.

'Gabriel Swift!' shouted another officer. 'Where is he?'

'He went through that door at the back,' replied the vicar and the men rushed past.

'Are you all right?' barked another policeman in black boots and what looked like body armour. 'Has he hurt you?'

April and the vicar both shook their heads and the man gestured that they could put their hands down. He led them out towards the main entrance, the doors now splintered, one hanging on its hinges. *Why so much fuss for poor Gabriel?* thought April, but then she supposed they didn't know him as the beautiful boy with the dark eyes who brought her flowers in the rain. To the police, he was an escaped felon, a vicious murderer who took hostages, a desperate criminal who was capable of anything. April slipped her hand inside her pocket and crossed her fingers. *Please get away, Gabe*, she thought, *please don't let them catch you.*

April and the vicar walked out together, into the glare of car headlights pointing at the church. April hoped to see the familiar face of DI Reece, but instead she was confronted by a short man in his fifties with grey hair. He was, inevitably, standing next to Dr Tame.

'Sorry about the door, Reverend,' said the first man. 'I'm

DCI Johnston and this is Dr Tame. You'll be April Dunne, I take it.'

'She is indeed,' said Tame before she could speak.

Two uniformed officers stepped up to take April, but the vicar waved them away. 'I don't think that's necessary, is it?' he said with authority. Johnston nodded.

'Let's get you to the station where we can have a proper chat.'

'Why?'

'We have plenty of questions for you, April. I'm sure we'll find something.'

Chapter Twenty-Eight

April felt a sinking sense of déjà vu as she sat in the interview room waiting for her mother to arrive. Four walls, a bare table and chairs, nothing else. It was horribly plain. Maybe that was the idea. Nothing for violent offenders to smash up, nothing for people like her to look at. *People like her: suspects.* If it was meant to be unsettling, it was working. April knew they thought she was involved somehow. When Gabriel had escaped, they must have started watching her, and if she'd been followed they would know she spoke to DI Reece, then met Ling and went to the church. Poor Ling, maybe they were questioning her too.

But she didn't care. One bright shining thing pushed all the bad things into shadow: Gabriel was back in her heart. He loved her, wanted to be with her and he hadn't cheated on her. All he'd wanted to do was protect her, look after her – he'd been prepared to go to jail for her! Sitting here in this grubby police station she should have been frightened, but she felt elated – and a little guilty, of course. She had treated Gabriel terribly, acted like a brat and had even considered going off with Benjamin. But Gabriel loved her and that was all that mattered. Yes, he was on the run and yes, she was still surrounded by people who wanted to drink her blood, but she felt better equipped to deal with it. Right now, in fact, April felt she could face anything.

'April!' her mother burst in, throwing her arms around her, squeezing her tight. April relaxed into the embrace, savouring it. She might be angry with her mother, but she was tremendously relieved to see her and a hug from her was such a rare occurrence that she had to make the most of it. All too soon, Silvia stepped back.

'Have they done anything you?' she asked. 'What have they said?'

'Nothing, Mum,' said April. 'They stuck me in here to stew, hoping the nerves would get to me or something.' She saw her mother's expression and shrugged. 'Well, that's how it works on the TV cop shows.'

'This is real life, April. It's serious.'

'They haven't charged me with anything yet. Maybe they were waiting for you to come.'

'They haven't charged you *yet*? You think they might? What could they possibly think you've done?'

'I haven't done anything!' she said. 'I was in the church talking to Ling, then Gabriel turned up and it turned into this massive police siege.'

'But the police told me you'd been taken hostage.'

'That's rubbish. They just wanted a reason to bash down the door. Gabriel would never do anything to harm me.'

'What makes you so sure? I know you liked this boy, but he killed Marcus Brent, April.'

'I thought you would want to thank him for that, Mother, or have you suddenly gone all Buddhist?'

'It's one thing wanting to strangle that monster for what he did to my baby, it's quite another thing to actually murder him in cold blood. He told me he'd protect you …'

'And that's exactly what he did!' cried April. 'You can't have it both ways, Mum. Would you rather Marcus had torn my throat out?'

'Don't be ridiculous. I'm simply saying it's naïve to assume Gabriel is as innocent as he says.'

'Mum, he told me he didn't kill Marcus and I believe him, all right?' Silvia looked at her for a long moment.

'Okay,' she said finally, sitting down. 'Let's not get too het up until we hear what they've got to say. Gramps' lawyer is on the way. We don't have to say anything until he gets here.'

'Why not? Do you think I'm going to incriminate myself? I haven't done anything!'

'Of course you haven't, darling, but we don't want them twisting your words.'

'Mum! I don't have anything to hide.'

'Are you sure? There's nothing you haven't told me?'

'You're a fine one to talk.'

'What's that supposed to mean?'

'It means that I'm not the one sneaking out at night, having secret meetings with old boyfriends.'

'Don't start on that again.'

The door opened and in walked DCI Johnston, quickly followed by DS Amy Carling, the detective who had often visited her with DI Reece. *They didn't waste much time finding that one a new partner, did they?* thought April. She had never liked the plain-looking woman in the clumpy shoes, there was something of the bully about her.

'Mrs Dunne, I presume,' said Johnston, offering her his hand. 'I'm the officer in charge of the case. I believe you already know DS Carling.'

'Where's Inspector Reece?' asked Silvia.

'He has moved on,' said Carling tonelessly.

'I am in charge of this investigation now, Mrs Dunne,' said Johnston.

'Well you're going to have to wait for our lawyer before you start investigating,' said Silvia.

'That is of course your right, but this isn't a formal interview, Mrs Dunne. We just want to ask April a few questions about what happened tonight.'

'So I'm not under arrest?'

'No, no,' said Johnston, as if it was the last thing on his mind. 'You are free to go at any time.'

Silvia immediately stood up. 'You didn't think to tell me this when I arrived?' she snapped. 'Come on, April, this is a disgrace.'

The inspector held up a finger. 'You will however still need to answer a few of our questions. We can of course organise a formal interview for the morning if you'd prefer?'

Silvia narrowed her eyes.

'So free to go in the sense of "stay where you are"?' said Silvia, the fury in her voice obvious. 'Is this usually the way police go about their business, Inspector? You drag me to a police station, giving me the impression I will be picking up my daughter, who has been the victim of another crime the police seem powerless to prevent. But no, it seems my daughter has been held here for hours without charge because you "have a few questions"? Is this your idea of professionalism?'

'I assure you, Mrs Dunne, we never had any intention of …'

Silvia pulled a sour face and sat down again.

'Spare me your assurances, Inspector,' she said. 'They're clearly not worth a great deal. Let's get this over with – assuming they *are* "just a few questions" and not something our lawyer will need to advise us on?'

'Just questions,' said Johnston.

'Fine. But I want it made clear that my daughter has done nothing wrong and I resent the implication she is in any way mixed up in this business.'

'Noted,' said Johnston. 'So perhaps you can start by telling us what happened after you left school this afternoon, April?'

Slowly April told them about walking through the park, meeting Ling and going back to the church.

'Why the church?' asked Johnston.

'Why not the church?' said Silvia, narrowing her eyes.

'Well, it seems a strange place for a seventeen-year-old girl to go, especially a non church-goer. Why not a coffee bar or your house?'

Silvia was about to reply when April put a hand on her arm.

'Mum, please,' she said. 'It's a simple enough question. We went into the church because Ling wanted to talk about something personal, so we wanted to go somewhere quiet.'

'Personal?' said Johnston.

'Personal,' repeated April. 'Girl's stuff.'

'Girl's stuff like meeting boyfriends?' asked Carling.

'No!' said April. 'I had no idea Gabriel was going to be there. And he's not my boyfriend.'

'Really? We were under the impression that you and Gabriel Swift were dating.'

'No. Well, yes we were for a while. Not dates as such, but ...'

'You were intimate?' said Carling, an oily smile on her face.

'No,' said April, blushing and glancing at her mother. 'I liked him, that's all. But it's all over now.'

'Yes,' said Johnston, looking down at his notes. 'You quarrelled on the night of the party in Waterlow Park? What did you argue about?'

April shrugged. It must be common knowledge by now – it had been a pretty public argument.

'He was with another girl.'

'Oh, I bet that made you angry,' said Carling.

'Yes, it did. Of course it did. That's why I left the party.'

'Is it?' said Carling.

'What? Of course it was! I saw him kissing another girl.'

'What's all this about?' said Silvia. 'What are you getting at?'

'Well, it seems rather strange,' said Johnston.

April frowned. 'What do you mean?'

'Well, that your boyfriend, the man who saved your life only weeks before, would suddenly arrange an assignation with another woman. In public, after he has arrived with you. That's rather odd, wouldn't you say?'

'Not really. It was actually a misunderstanding. I thought he was messing me about but I got the wrong end of the stick.'

'This is ridiculous,' said Silvia. 'What exactly are you accusing my daughter of?'

'Nothing at this time,' said Johnston, 'I'm simply trying to establish what happened the night of the party.'

'I thought that was obvious even to you: Gabriel Swift killed Marcus Brent – and good riddance too.'

Johnston nodded.

'That would seem to be the story, yes.'

'Well, what other story is there?'

'We don't dispute that Gabriel Swift killed Marcus: we pretty much caught him red-handed.'

'Literally, actually,' said Carling, drawing a weary look from Johnston.

April was desperate to defend Gabriel, point out that they had simply assumed he was the killer instead of looking for the real culprit, but she had a horrible feeling that would only get her into more trouble. She thought back to her last meeting with DI Reece. 'Watch yourself,' isn't that what he'd said? 'They need someone to pin this on, and they can't blame everything on Gabriel.' She knew they were under pressure to wrap up the Highgate murders as soon as possible, but surely they couldn't blame her? April became aware that Johnston was staring at her as he spoke.

'Unfortunately we only have April's version of events for what happened that night. No one saw Marcus Brent attack her, we have no idea why he was there …'

'Possibly because he was a psychopath?' said Silvia impatiently. 'Do I need to remind you that he almost tore my daughter's arm off a few months ago?'

'Perhaps,' said Johnston. 'As I said, it all seems rather strange and I don't feel I'm being told the complete truth.'

Silvia pushed her chair back and stood up.

'All right, April, seeing as we're free to leave, I think that's exactly what we'll do.' She glared down at DCI Johnston. 'Rest assured your superiors will hear about this.'

'Don't threaten us, Mrs Dunne,' said Johnston. 'I really don't think they will be interested in your complaints this time. It has become a priority at the highest level to stop the violence in Highgate. The plain facts are that your daughter has been present at four of these incidents, which leads me to believe she knows more than she's telling us. We are therefore perfectly entitled to ask her as many questions as we see fit, and we will continue to do so until these murders stop.'

'Well next time, you will be asking your questions with a solicitor present.'

'I look forward to it. One last question, April. Where is Gabriel Swift?'

'Don't answer that, April,' said Silvia, then turned back to Johnston. 'You don't want to make an enemy of me, Inspector,' she said, her voice icy cold. 'You really have no idea who you're dealing with.'

Johnston sat back in his chair, unperturbed.

'Quite a temper there, Mrs Dunne,' he smiled. 'I wonder if your daughter has inherited it?'

Silvia didn't answer, instead she took April's arm and steered her towards the door.

'We'll be in touch, April,' said the policeman as they left. 'Don't go leaving town.'

Chapter Twenty-Nine

April's mother had been so furious, she hadn't spoken a word all the way home. It wasn't until they got inside the house that she turned to April, her lips white. 'Well?' she said.

'Well what?'

'What exactly aren't you telling me?'

'You're saying you believe them?'

'No, but I know you, April. You may not think so, but I do. And you know more than you were saying in that police station.'

'I don't! I can't believe you think there's anything to that rubbish. Do you really believe that I had anything to do with Marcus's death?'

'No! But it does worry me that you've been so close to these events. You were there when Isabelle Davis was killed, then your father ...'

'I wasn't there then!' she objected. 'I wish I had been.'

'But you were close. Then there's Marcus's attacks and that poor girl Layla – you were at that party.'

'So were a lot of other people!' said April, exasperated. 'Come on Mum, you can't believe I had anything to do with any of this!'

'No, darling, I don't. But I agree that perhaps you know something.'

'I don't know anything!'

'I think you do. You're a clever girl, April, and so are your friends. I can't imagine you've just sat back and let all this wash over you.' She paused, looking at April searchingly. 'Why don't you tell me, love? Maybe I can help.'

'Honestly, Mum, don't you think if I knew who was behind it, I would tell the police? Nobody wants to catch Dad's murderer more than me. I want to see them pay.'

'I know that, April. But it's not just about finding out who took your dad away from us, is it? I have no confidence in these policemen at all. But if they don't get to the bottom of it, people are in danger. More importantly, *you're* in danger. You've been attacked twice in a matter of weeks – and tonight you were involved in a siege! Those policemen had guns. I don't know what's happening, but you seem to be a magnet for trouble at the moment and it's too dangerous out there.'

'So, what, are you grounding me again?'

'Darling, I just want to keep you close while this all dies down.'

'That could take ages! Am I supposed to stay indoors for the rest of my life?'

'We'll sort something out. But I want you to come straight home after school, do your homework, and no roaming around the village.'

Her heart turned over as whatever slim chance she had of seeing Gabriel again began to fade.

'But that's so unfair! It's not my fault some loony tried to kill me!'

'Straight home, April,' said Silvia. 'I mean it.'

'God!' she cried. 'You might as well have let the police lock me up!'

And she stormed upstairs.

If April had thought she might get sympathy from her friends, she was quickly corrected: even Fiona was against her.

'I can't believe you're siding with my mum,' said April sulkily.

'I'm not, honey. But look at it from my point of view. Here I am stuck five hundred miles away from my best friend, who is being attacked by vampires and witches and armed policemen. From where I'm sitting, your mum's idea of locking you in a tower seems a great notion, actually. Better that than see you dead.'

'But if I don't get out there and find out who's behind all this mayhem, I doubt keeping me locked in a tower's going to do much good. And other people are going to get killed. Marcus threatened to come up there and kill you too, remember?'

'Hey, don't go trying to scare me,' said Fiona. 'I'm scared enough as it is.'

'I'm sorry, I just feel so frustrated. How am I supposed to figure this out if I'm not allowed out of the bloody house?'

'Well you're not completely locked up, are you?'

'What do you mean? I can't sneak out past my mother again. She'd go mental.'

'But you can do a bit of Marple-ing without leaving the house, can't you?'

'How?'

Fiona tutted impatiently.

'You drive me mad sometimes, April Dunne. Your dad was a journalist, right?'

'Yes. Obviously.'

'Well, journalists make notes, they have big stacks of papers in piles next to their desks, they're always rattling away on their keyboards.'

'Duh. And?'

'Well, surely there will be clues in there. Like when you found his notebook.'

April sighed.

'No, the police went through all of that looking for clues when he was killed.'

'And since when have the Highgate police impressed you with their efficiency and world-class detection skills? I bet they had some lowly PC have a half-hearted flick through and anything not in big capitals with the words "Murderer" written next to it was ignored. Where are his notes now?'

'In the cellar along with all his other stuff. But I'm not going down there again, it gives me the creeps.'

'That's compared to sneaking around graveyards and spooky woods in the middle of the night, is it?'

April laughed.

'I suppose not.'

'Well, what are you waiting for? You've been running about with vampires breathing down your neck, now you can do a bit of snooping in the comfort of your own home. Come on, chop-chop. I've got homework to do.'

'Slave-driver.'

April hung up and dragged herself up from the bed. It wasn't the spiders and the musty smell that were putting her off. It was the idea of digging around in her dad's stuff. She felt as if she was intruding somehow, like she was looking at stuff she shouldn't, secret stuff he was hiding. *But how else are you going to find things out?* she thought to herself.

Still, as she walked down the stairs, April had a sense of foreboding. Since her dad had died, she had managed to compartmentalise him, put him in a little box. She could go to the cemetery – when she wasn't grounded – and talk to him through the door, but doing that felt like he wasn't dead. Opening up his boxes, though, it meant that he was gone, like she was sorting through his effects, deciding what to keep and what to throw away. And she wasn't sure she was ready for that.

But Fiona was right, there could well be clues there. She walked down the stairs and into the hall, pausing at the cellar door. She had the strangest feeling that there was something in those boxes she didn't want to find.

Mostly, April found newspapers. Old cuttings of her father's features, presumably filed to paste into a scrapbook at some point in the future, were mixed in with endless pages torn from broadsheets and magazines: yellowing pages of ideas for books that would never be written. It all made April feel incredibly sad. So many things he'd planned to do, and none of them would come to be. So many books he'd bought to read, to research things or just for pleasure. Now they were all just crammed into a box along with press releases and subscription offers and all sorts of random stuff like a postcard from Ibiza ('Having it large, love Iggy' – who was Iggy? – April would probably never know). But slowly April began to enjoy what she was doing, sorting all the detritus into ordered piles: books in one, bank statements in another, personal stuff in a third. Because in amongst all the never-was ideas and brochures for holidays he would never take, were hundreds if not thousands of pieces of proof that William Dunne had been there. Not just the words he'd written and picture by-lines, the little postage-stamp-sized photo they'd put next to his articles, but in everything else: the bills paid and unpaid, receipts for meals, an invoice for getting the car serviced just before their drive south from Scotland. Each one, she realised, was a reminder that her father had been here and had made a mark. She found a framed certificate: 'Young Journalist of the Year, 1994' and a strange chunk of Perspex in the shape of an upturned icicle etched with the words 'British Press Awards, 2000. Best Feature, Reportage'.

She had no idea her dad had won these. He'd never mentioned it to her. Why would he? In 2000, she'd have been six.

The thought of it made tears spring into her eyes. 'Oh, Daddy, I'm so proud of you,' she whispered. 'I wish you were here.'

She wished that more than anything. Not only because she wanted him safe and happy and alive again, but also because she felt sure William Dunne would have known what to do next. He wouldn't have given up on everything just because it was all getting a bit much.

'Right, let's get serious,' she said, rubbing the dust from her jeans and pulling a black bin bag from a roll with a flourish.

Over the next hour, April filled five rubbish sacks, ruthlessly dumping anything not directly relating to Ravenwood, anything that looked like it might offer a glimpse into what he had been investigating and who he had spoken to in those last weeks of his life. When she had emptied the last box, she threw all the 'important' material into a suitcase she'd found shoved under the stairs. The bulging bin bags she bumped up the stairs and left in a line in the hallway, ready to take into the yard.

'What's all this in the hall?' shouted Silvia down the stairs.

'I'm having a clear out. Making myself useful, seeing as I'm not allowed out.'

'What is it?' asked her mother suspiciously

'Dad's stuff. All that stuff the police went through. I've kept all the important things, but most of this is old magazines and papers.'

Silvia looked at it like it might scuttle up the stairs and bite her.

'Did you want to look through it? There might be something you want to keep.'

Silvia shivered. 'God no, I'm glad you're getting rid of it. I hated having all that stuff down there. His study was always full of junk.'

She turned to go.

'But don't just leave it there, April. I don't want to come down in the night and cripple myself tripping over a pile of *What Car* magazines.'

'You could have offered to help me carry it out,' whispered April to herself as she hoisted the bags into their wheelie bin out the back. 'What if I get attacked on the doorstep?'

That done, she took the suitcase of stuff she had designated worth reading back up to her bedroom and opened it on the bed. First, she went through the packets of photographs she had found. They were nearly all of her. April on her scooter, April in a swimming pool wearing duck-shaped armbands, April sitting under the Christmas tree looking delirious with excitement as she tore the wrapping paper off a Barbie doll. There were hardly any of the rest of the family, but she had found one of her with her dad, sitting on a rock by Loch Ness, one of the last happy holidays she could remember. The photo was old and a bit foggy, the way old photos get sometimes. But it was April and her dad next to a board advertising 'Nessie Funland'. She couldn't really see the background, but it looked like they were by the lake. Her heart soared as she looked at it. It was the only photo of him she had, beyond those inky by-lines, and it was certainly the only one of them together.

They didn't take photos, they weren't that sort of 'all in a line, now say cheese' family. But obviously he'd had his arm twisted by some photographer. She could just see the scene now, her mum, one hand on her hip, saying 'Go on, Will, give him the money,' like he never did anything fun for us. But her dad *had* been fun. She remembered their long walks along the cliffs by the Loch, Silvia crying off claiming hay fever or something. It had been a happy time, before her parents had started arguing. She and her dad had walked for miles, occasionally stopping to search the waves with his binoculars. They never did see Nessie, but William Dunne had remained open-minded. 'You never know what's out there,' he'd said to her. 'Most of the time we only see what our minds will let us.' *You got that right, Daddy*, thought April sadly.

She went back to the suitcase. Inside a brown envelope was a collection of sticky notes she recognised as the ones which had been tacked to the wall next to her dad's desk. None of them made much sense. She looked at one she remembered. It read 'Call FG, ask to find Ott. Text' – Could that be Mr Gill? Yes, it must be, hadn't he called himself Frances the other day? It wasn't exactly a breakthrough, as April already knew that her dad had been planning to visit Griffin's bookshop just before he was killed, but it was encouraging that she was on the right track. Then there was that one she had puzzled over the night she had sneaked down to his study. '23.11.88 – 14.02.93 – signif?' She had noticed it because the second date on the note was her birthday. But what was the first date? Five years before – the day of something that had happened to him? Was it the date he'd met her mother? No, that was silly, why would he write that down? She shook her head. She didn't know. But then she had a thought. She went over to her wardrobe and dug around in the back, pulling out a shoebox. Inside was her dad's notebook and the diary she had found hidden on the cellar stairs. She flicked to the fourteenth of February, but all it said was 'April's Birthday!!!', then a number with the word 'Pelargonium'. She went over to her computer and quickly typed it into Google.

'Come on, come on,' she muttered, trying to contain her excitement.

Her heart sank. The phone number matched a branch of Interflora and Pelargonium was the name of a type of flower. Of course – it wasn't just her birthday, it was also bloody Valentine's Day, wasn't it? Why couldn't she have been born on an ordinary day, so her birthday would be special? She always went off to school wanting everyone to make a fuss, but instead she would find all her friends breathlessly discussing how many cards they had got and speculating who had sent what to whom.

April tapped in the other date – 23rd of the 11th – but nothing came up. Maybe it didn't mean anything, she thought dejectedly. She went back to the sticky notes, but nothing else seemed to make sense. 'Find at Ux dig', 'Remember 2nd rule', 'Golders Green?'. Without knowing their context, it was all just gibberish. Maybe none of it was of any importance; maybe there was nothing here that could help her.

She picked up the diary again and turned to the twenty-third of November. 'Publishing meeting 10 a.m.' was all it said. But then he'd never got that far. He'd been killed before the twenty-third of November, hadn't he? She was overcome by another wave of grief and anger. It was all so unfair and so unreal. Murder was something that happened to other people – and vampires didn't happen to anyone. Because they didn't exist, right?

But they did – they'd happened to her. *Gabriel* had happened to her. Where was he now? Hiding in some damp wood somewhere? No, hadn't he always talked about how vampires were excellent at staying under the radar? If he could drink blood and avoid detection, she was sure he could check into a hotel without being found. She picked up her phone and started tapping out a text … but then she stopped and deleted it. For one thing, his phone was probably with the police after they arrested him. And even if he had it, he wouldn't reply – she was sure she had seen something on *Crimewatch* about how they could track mobile phones even if it was only switched on. Plus she had to protect herself from the likes of DCI Johnston. She threw down the phone in frustration. Why couldn't she have fallen in love with a normal boy, one who was obsessed with football? They could go to the pictures and eat popcorn or something. Maybe get Chinese. Instead, her undead boyfriend was on the run, wanted by the police who were clearly prepared to shoot him if he didn't give himself up. *They don't talk about that sort of thing in the advice columns, do they?*

She rummaged further in the suitcase and pulled out a cancelled passport – her dad with an embarrassing 1990s haircut. A sort of half-mullet. There were a lot of stamps for Romania. Had they been going back to see her mum's family? Why hadn't April ever gone? There was also an envelope with birth certificates inside – hers, her mother's. One with the name Hamilton, the other as Silvia Vladescu. April knew that name, because it was written on the tomb her father was buried in. But why would her mum have it on her birth certificate? Didn't Grandpa tell me he'd changed their name when he came over in the sixties? Suddenly something clicked in her mind. She leafed back through the diary to the days before her dad was killed. She was sure she had seen that name before. And there it was: 'Vladescu – Rom?' and a phone number. One she recognised. Her grandfather's.

April frowned. Was there something about her family which they were keeping from her? Duh, stupid question – of course there was. Every time she'd ever asked anything about the family's background, her mother and grandfather had changed the subject. Well, it was about time she found out what they were hiding from her.

She leafed through a few more invoices and receipts. A lawnmower, a flight to Edinburgh. Then she pulled out a glossy brochure: a Ravenwood prospectus. Inside were sheets of information – educational standards, exam records, safety procedures (ah, the irony), policy on bullying (double irony – she wondered if it covered being recruited into a vampire cult) and endless pictures of the happy smiling faces of students messing about with test tubes and soil samples. Nothing of interest to April. On the back of one of them, her dad had scribbled some notes – a scribbled calculation about fees which made April's jaw drop, and some details about the history of the school. She was about to turn over when she noticed he'd written on the inside cover of the folder too.

She looked at it again and her heart started beating harder. It was easy to see why the police had ignored this, if indeed they'd ever bothered looking inside the prospectus – why would they? It was a perfectly normal thing for a student's father to have in his possession. There was a diagram of the governors hierarchy which her dad had circled in blue, with the note scribbled underneath: 'Dean of admissions is key', then 'Speak to Peter D, AM'. April felt a rush of excitement. He *had* been investigating the school, Gabriel was right! She grabbed her bag and pulled her purse out, spilling all her cards and cash point slips onto the bed.

'Come on, come on,' she muttered, 'Be in here, be in here …'

And there it was, the business card Uncle Peter had given her at the funeral. Her father's old friend, the one who had offered him a job on *The Sunday Times*.

'Bingo,' she said and snatched up her phone.

Chapter Thirty

The newspaper offices were exactly as April had imagined they would be. Or rather, they were just the way she had seen them in films and on TV: a huge open-plan space covering the whole floor of the high-rise office building, divided up into smaller booths containing desks, computers and endless ringing phones. People rushed about carrying piles of paper or shouted across the room about having 'a break on the city desk' or needing to get things 'subbed a-sap'.

Caro would have been over the moon to be here. April felt bad she hadn't invited her along even though they weren't really speaking. She also felt guilty for having snuck out of the house again despite having promised her mum she would tell her where she was at all times. But this was too important – to April, anyway. Clearly Silvia didn't care much about her dead husband any more, let alone finding out who killed him, but to April it was everything. A girl led them down a corridor to a line of glass-fronted offices where a familiar-looking man stood. He had white hair and a beard. He was dressed in a creased shirt and grey trousers.

'Hello, April,' said Peter warmly, shaking her hand.

'It's very exciting here, isn't it?'

'Sadly not as glamorous as the movies would have you believe. Sorry for all the mess,' he said, leading her into his cramped office. It immediately gave April a pang of longing and sadness: it was cluttered and chaotic, with piles of papers and books on every surface, his tatty computer screen covered in Post-its. It was so like her dad's study – it even smelled the same: of coffee and newsprint and the dry dusty smell of computer fans.

'So, what can I do for you?' said Peter. 'It sounded urgent on the phone.'

'It is. Well, I think it might be,' said April. 'I found some of my dad's notes and they said he'd talked to you about his Highgate investigation.'

'That's true.'

'So what was it? The investigation, I mean? Can you tell me?'

He paused.

'I know you're a bright girl, April, and it's only natural that you want to find out who killed your dad, but this really isn't something you can get involved with. Leave it to the police.'

'But the police aren't getting anywhere. They're not even looking in the right places.'

Peter raised his eyebrows.

'And you think you have a better idea where to look than they do?'

'Perhaps, yes.'

So why haven't you told them?'

'Because it sounds … well … a bit mad.'

'The vampires, you mean?'

'You know about it?' said April, shocked.

Peter shrugged.

'I know what Will was like and I know he loved a crazy conspiracy theory. If he could connect it to some sort of mythical beast, all the better. So it wasn't a big surprise when he told me that vampires were over-running Highgate cemetery. He still believes the Loch Ness monster is eating Scots fishermen. Or, well, he did.' He looked down at his hands. 'Sorry April, it's still hard to think of your dad in the past tense.'

'It is for me too. So what did he tell you, exactly?'

'It was some wild story about an army of vampires, how he had proof they were secretly recruiting people and planning to take over the world. I had to point out that we were a newspaper – we need to retain some kind of credibility.'

'He said he had proof?'

Peter shook his head.

'Maybe he did, maybe he didn't. Look at it from my point of view, April. Your dad was one of the most respected investigative reporters in the business. If he said he had seen something with his own eyes – Weapons of Mass Destruction, crack dealers in Buckingham Palace, whatever – that would be enough for me. But this? Well let's just say this kind of investigation was always his Achilles heel. I knew your dad for twenty-five years and I can't remember a time when he wasn't chasing some sort of marauding mummy or werewolf. It was what he did instead of going to the football or collecting stamps.'

April could see his point. Even if her dad had dragged the Vampire Regent into Peter's office, the paper's readers would still be highly sceptical about the story. If they had realised the same William Dunne had published umpteen books about the Yeti and flying saucers, and there was no proof to back up his story, the paper could become a laughing stock. After all, how likely was it? Suddenly April understood that it was this very scepticism which had allowed the vampires to carry on killing people undetected for centuries. Gabriel was always saying how great they were at hiding, but how well did you have to hide when no one would believe it even if you pushed a vampire in front of them?

'So why didn't you tell me? At his funeral you said you hadn't seen him for years.'

'To be honest, I was a little worried about it; about your dad. I mean, I know he was enthusiastic about his ghouls and ghosties, but he was so ... well, so persuasive about this. I had no doubt he genuinely believed what he was saying, which was why I was reluctant to tell you about it. I didn't want to say I thought your dad had lost it.'

April nodded sadly. She knew Uncle Peter meant well, but she couldn't help feeling disappointment. She had been harbouring a small hope that he might take the whole thing seriously. Instead, he was just another person who knew the story, who knew that vampires had overrun a village in London, but who didn't – or wouldn't – believe it.

'But *had* he lost it?' said April. 'I mean, *something's* wrong, isn't it? People are dropping like flies. Even if you don't believe the vampire thing, there's definitely something going on in Highgate. Maybe there's a serial killer at work. You can't dismiss the whole thing, can you?'

'Yes, of course it's crossed my mind,' said Peter with a touch of irritation. 'Will was my friend. I want to see his murderer brought to justice more than anyone. I even sent a couple of our best reporters up there to investigate, but they didn't get anything except the official police line that the deaths are unconnected.'

'And you believed that?' said April.

Peter looked at her with a smile. 'I know what you're saying, April: your dad was killed and there have been two attempts on your life, which suggests a strong link between the victims. But this Marcus Brent, the boy who attacked you? Surely if you're looking for a serial killer, he's a strong front runner. He clearly had a grudge against people in your family.'

'No, but Marcus—' April began to protest, but Peter held up a hand.

'I'm not saying this Marcus *did* kill your dad or anyone else, I'm simply saying that if you're looking for a link between the murders, Marcus Brent is a much more believable solution than a nest of vampires.'

'I know it sounds crazy – I *know*!' said April. 'But if my dad said he had proof, then maybe there is something out there to find.'

Peter looked at her, rubbing his chin.

'Do you know something the police don't?'

April shrugged. What could she say? *Yes, I've seen vampires with my own eyes. I've kissed two, killed one, stabbed one and had my arm half torn off by another*. It sounded hysterical. Besides, she had to assume the police were watching her – there was a very good chance they would come straight into Peter's office the moment she left. DCI Johnston was already questioning her reliability as a witness – what would be make of her claiming the undead were walking through his crime scene?

'It's not that I know anything the police don't,' said April, hoping he wouldn't see through the lie. 'It's more that I'm seeing things they can't. Yes, my dad's theory sounds crazy, but when weird things keep happening right in front of you and people keep being killed, there comes a point when it starts to make sense. I was almost torn apart, Uncle Peter.'

Peter nodded. 'I know it must have been disturbing, but the police psychologist, Dr Tame? He seems to think the boy was deranged or on drugs or both. That doesn't make him a creature of the night, does it?'

'Dr Tame?' said April, looking at him sharply. 'He interviewed you?'

'Other way around. *I'm* the one trying to get the story, remember? Dr Tame is very press-friendly.'

April sighed. What hope did she have when Peter was talking to people like Tame?

'Okay. Well thanks anyway,' said April sadly. She supposed she had hoped he would say 'Vampires? This is sensational! I'll put my best people on it – we'll have this case cracked in a week!' But that wasn't any more realistic than expecting the police to take her seriously. She began to get up, but then had a thought.

'What if Dad was right about the conspiracy, just wrong about the blood-suckers?' said April.

'What do you mean?' asked Peter.

'Well, I've been through all his notes and it seems that, along with all this vampire stuff, he was right in the middle of writing an exposé about Ravenwood.'

'Really?' said Peter. 'What sort of exposé?'

'Something to do with the school governors,' said April. 'No one seems to know who's behind Ravenwood, but they do seem to be using the students to do all sorts of high-level research for companies like Agropharm.'

'Agropharm?' said Peter, suddenly interested. 'The pharmaceutical conglomerate?'

'And Ravenwood has strong links with Nicholas Osbourne, he's the CEO.'

'Oh, I know who he is, he was at your Dad's funeral, remember? But this is interesting,' said Peter, beginning to scribble down notes on a pad. 'And they're using Ravenwood pupils as unpaid researchers?'

'They're selling students' work. Mr Langdon, the head of science, has just sold a camera sensor to a Japanese electronics company. He's admitted that the pupils came up with the idea – you should talk to a student called Jonathon, he's just left Ravenwood, so he might be prepared to talk.'

April wanted to tell Peter everything – that Jonathon 'left Ravenwood' because he was dead, his blood drained by Davina and the Faces – but she suspected it would be more effective if he discovered Jonathon's disappearance on his own. Let him make the link between the Ravenwood students and the murders himself.

'This is interesting, April,' he said enthusiastically. 'Do you have any other evidence?'

'An email from Nicholas Osbourne to Mr Sheldon giving him a hard time for not producing enough geniuses for the conveyor belt.'

'Mr Sheldon? You mean Robert Sheldon?'

'Yes, he's the headmaster. Do you know him?'

'A little,' said Peter quietly, thinking for a moment. 'Well, this certainly seems more printable. And how did you get this email?'

'Research,' said April, turning red.

'Well, maybe it is worth looking into after all. Do you think you can find out anything else for me?'

'So you do need someone on the inside to help?' said April.

'I'm not putting you on the pay-roll if that's what you're asking,' smiled Peter. 'But it's certainly better than having you running around in the dark by yourself.'

Chapter Thirty-One

How bad can it be? thought April, staring at the shop across the road. *I mean, I've faced homicidal vampires. It can't be worse than that, can it?*

She took a deep breath and forced her feet to move. One step, two steps ... cross the road. Eight steps, nine steps ... open the door. The crystals tinkled as she stepped into the cramped little bookshop and April had to remind herself to breathe. Jessica was sitting behind the counter, just as she had been that first time April had walked in. She looked up and raised her eyebrows.

'Hello, April,' she said. 'I'll be honest, I didn't expect to see you again.'

April walked over to her desk and held out the library card.

'I said I'd bring the card back and so I thought I should and ... well, say thank you.'

Jessica took the card, but didn't speak.

'And I'm sorry about that night at the party,' said April, rushing on to fill the silence. 'I – I think I over-reacted a bit. Well, a lot actually. Anyway, it wasn't your fault, so I'm sorry if I dragged you into my drama.'

Finally Jessica smiled. 'It's okay, April,' she said, gesturing to a chair next to her desk. 'I think I would have reacted in exactly the same way. Gabriel has many fine qualities, but tact isn't one of them. Anyway, it sounds as if you had bigger problems to worry about that night.'

April nodded as she sat down. 'It was a memorable evening, I'll say that much.'

Jessica leaned forward and touched April's hand.

'I hope Gabriel convinced you that there was nothing going on between us? Truly, April, there never has been any romance between us. I'm very fond of him, but well, we have history.'

'Oh yes, I know,' said April quickly. 'Gabriel explained it all.' She paused. 'Well, not that I believed him for a long time,' she added with a laugh.

Jessica smiled. 'As I say, I think I would have reacted the same way. But really, it's as much my fault as his. I think I knew you were talking about Gabriel the moment you told me about the vampires in Highgate. I really should have said.'

'But how ...?'

Jessica waved a hand.

'Oh, call it intuition if you like. But he's never very far from that damned cemetery and ... well, there was something in the way you talked about him. There aren't that many men who inspire that sort of emotion and you were taking an awful risk for him, so I knew it had to be someone special. That was why I wanted to see him, to make sure he appreciated that he'd found someone pretty special in you too. Unfortunately it rather back-fired, didn't it?'

April looked away, afraid that if she spoke she might burst into tears.

'Oh no,' said Jessica, stepping out from behind the desk to put her arm around April. 'Is it Gabriel?'

April nodded.

'He took the blame for the murder thinking he was helping me, but all I could do was give him a hard time about kissing you. And now he's being chased by armed police.'

'Don't worry, Gabriel will be fine,' said Jessica. 'Really. Those idiotic policemen have no chance of finding him, not if he doesn't want to be found.'

April fought back the tears. *You've got to toughen up*, isn't that what Miss Holden said to her? She was right. What use would a Fury be to anyone if she kept bursting into tears at the first sign of trouble?

'I'm okay,' said April, refusing the tissue Jessica offered her.

'Honestly. It's just I've got a lot on my mind at the moment. Yes, I'm worried about Gabe, but it's not just that.'

'You're trying to find the Regent,' said Jessica matter-of-factly.

'Yes! How did you ... ? Oh.' But *of course* Jessica would know about the Regent. She knew everything about Gabriel. And if she was honest, that was what was upsetting April more than the memory of Gabe kissing Jessica. She believed – she *had* to believe – they were telling her the truth when they both denied they had any interest in each other, but she still hated hearing someone talk about her boyfriend with such familiarity, such intimacy. Jessica had known Gabriel for *a hundred years*, how could April ever compete with that?

'Oh, I knew about the Vampire Regent before I even met Gabriel,' said Jessica, perching on the edge of her desk. 'He was spoken of in whispers in the taverns and the rookeries. He was evil, but he was elusive – and that was his power. A real person, a real figurehead can be killed or overthrown, but an unseen presence like the Regent becomes more of an idea, a symbol of whatever people want him to be.'

April frowned.

'What, are you saying the Regent doesn't exist?'

'He's real, all right. I've got his infection in my blood, remember? He turned Gabriel, Gabriel turned me. And that means he can be found.'

'But where do we look?'

'Ravenwood, of course,' said Jessica.

'You make it sound so obvious.'

'It is. Being obvious is *the point*. The Regent – all the vampires, in fact – have always stayed hidden, creeping about in the night, taking feeders, killing those foxes, but never leaving any bodies to alert anyone that they're there. But Ravenwood is different, it's *obvious*, visible to anyone who wants to see. And pretty soon I think a lot more people are going to see.'

'Are they planning on taking over the world?' said April.

Jessica smiled. 'I don't know, April, maybe. But for now you'd probably better concentrate on Highgate.'

'So how do I find the Regent? Is he the one behind Ravenwood?'

Jessica looked at April with her big green eyes.

'Maybe you should ask your grandfather.'

April had never liked Stanton. Grandpa Thomas's butler had always looked ancient to April – ancient and a little bit creepy, like a servant in a gothic novel. More than that, the old man seemed to look down his nose at her whenever he answered the door at her grandpa's Covent Garden house, like she was bringing in the plague or something.

'Your grandfather is in his study,' intoned Stanton. 'If you would just follow me …'

I know the way to the study, thought April, following him through the grand pillared entrance hall, walking at the speed of a sleepy tortoise. Still, it gave April time to rehearse what she was going to say. She couldn't very well come out and say 'So what do you know about Ravenwood, Gramps?' could she? – he'd get suspicious and defensive. She'd seen enough cop shows to know that much. *I wish this was a cop show*, she thought. Then at least you'd have a fair idea that the good guys were going to win. April looked up at the dark portraits of her ancestors hanging in the hall. They didn't seem to approve of her any more than Stanton. Maybe that would be a good place to start – to ask about her mum's side of the family and about that birth certificate she had found in the cellar. Not that Gramps had ever been particularly keen to talk about the past. He was a typical immigrant: he'd get all misty-eyed about the 'old country' with its half-remembered forests and mountains, but suggest he go back and he'd start talking about blood feuds and typhoid and how they only have electricity on Sundays.

As she walked down the corridor towards her grandpa's study, she could hear voices. It sounded like her grandfather was talking to another man. Suddenly April wished she had phoned first. She couldn't really grill her granddad about family matters with some stranger there. But it wasn't a stranger.

'Uncle Luke!' said April with surprise as she walked through the door.

'Hey there, niece,' said Luke, embracing her. 'Great to see you safe and well,' he added meaningfully, looking over at Thomas.

'And just where the hell have you been, April?' boomed her grandfather, a scowl on his face. 'Your mother has been on the phone all afternoon. She thinks you have been attacked or abducted or something worse. I shouldn't be surprised if she's called the police by now.'

'I had something important to do,' said April defensively. She had expected her usual warm welcome, but she should have known Silvia would ring Gramps the moment she failed to come home from school.

'Something so important you couldn't send her a message?'

'No, I suppose not, but—'

'No "buts", April,' interrupted Thomas. 'Your mother said she told you to come straight home after school. No wonder she is frantic. It's irresponsible, April. Damned irresponsible.'

April was shocked by Thomas's outburst. She had often heard her grandfather shouting of course; he and Silvia spent most of their time barking at each other like a couple of dogs trapped in a cave. But she couldn't remember her Grandpa ever shouting *at her*. It was always 'Princess' or 'my beautiful Prilly' as he squidged her in a huge bear hug and showered her with compliments. He had never so much as raised his voice to her before.

April glanced at Luke, who just shrugged. 'He's got a point, cuz,' he said. 'We've all been worried. Why didn't you tell someone where you were going?'

'I didn't think—'

'Think? You think of no one but yourself,' snapped Thomas. 'Your mother is suffering enough as it is.'

'Suffering?' laughed April. 'She's having the time of her life.'

'How dare you!' shouted Thomas. 'She is in mourning – her husband was murdered on her doorstep and you're all she has left.'

'I *know* he was murdered, Gramps,' shot back April. 'I was there, remember? I couldn't get the blood off my hands ...' she said, her voice beginning to shake. 'He was my dad too, you know.'

'I'm sorry, Prilly,' said Thomas, softening his tone, 'I didn't mean to upset you, but you have to understand we've been thinking the worst.'

'Yeah? Well that's all you adults ever think, isn't it?' cried April angrily. 'I know it's dangerous. I *know*. I've been attacked and chased and terrified – no one knows more than me how horrible it is out there. But what am I supposed to do? Lock myself in a tower?'

'Your Grandpa's not saying that, April,' said Luke. 'He's just saying that you could have let us know you were okay.'

'Well I'm not bloody okay!' she shouted. 'I'm sick of being frightened all the time. I just want all this to stop – and having you lot shouting at me isn't helping.'

'April, we just want you to be safe,' said Thomas, coming over to hug her, but April pushed him away.

'And where am I safe, exactly? At home? The place my dad had his throat torn out? Fine, I'll go straight back there if that's what you want.'

She turned and ran down the corridor, through the hall past a startled Stanton and out into the street. She plunged into the tangle of alleyways and back streets, not bothering to look where she was going, just taking turns at random. Finally she stopped and leant against a wall, her chest heaving. Why did they all have to make her feel like it was her fault? She hadn't asked for any of this – she'd have gladly gone back to her boring old life in Edinburgh, no question. April knew Gramps and Silvia were terrified that something else might happen to her, but they really seemed to think that staying in her bedroom would keep her 'safe'. Staying at home hadn't kept her dad safe, had it?

She looked up to see that she was on a narrow street of tall grey stone buildings, possibly Victorian, like something you might see on a Christmas card. But it didn't feel jolly and cosy, it felt abandoned and impersonal. Even the street lights looked old-fashioned. She heard voices and turned to see two men behind her, laughing loudly. She moved off, increasing her pace. Turning left again, she came out into a wide street with shops and restaurants and she felt a little safer. To her right, she could see a large church with a tall spire, and in front of that, there was a bus stop. She had no particular desire to go home and face the wrath of her mother, but where else was she going to go? Sighing, she crossed the road, and as she approached the church, April was struck by the unusual architecture.

At the top of the steeple, there was a strange pyramid surrounded by pillars. *How odd*, she thought, *doesn't look very Christian.*

'Egyptians!' shouted a voice. April turned to see an old man on the church steps. He had a tatty beard and a dirty coat and he was gesturing towards the spire with a bottle.

'The Egyptians knew the power of the pyramid!' he cried. 'They knew it's the only thing that will keep the darkness out!'

April quickly walked away, worried that the old man might follow her. She glanced around, but he had gone. No, there *was* someone, but it wasn't the tramp. This man was tall and dark and walking quickly, like he wanted to catch up with her. Unnerved, April turned a corner into a narrow street of terraced houses, hoping to lose him, but the tall man followed.

Who the hell is that? she thought with alarm. *Is he really following me?*

She quickly walked to the next corner before she looked back again. To her horror, the man was just standing there watching her, a horrible smile on his face. April didn't need to see any more: she turned the corner and ran, twisting left then right, trying to lose the man and double back towards the main road, but she quickly became disoriented. She spotted a gate in a high wall and ducked inside, closing it behind her. She flattened herself against the wall and waited, holding her breath, straining her ears for the sound of following footsteps, but all she could hear was the whoosh of cars on the main road.

Maybe it was just someone walking home, she thought to herself. *Maybe.*

It was only then that April looked around and saw the arched stones silhouetted against the night sky. She was inside the grounds of the church.

Great, trapped in another graveyard, she thought, sliding down behind a headstone and pulling her phone out. She stared at the screen, wondering who to call. Gabriel was off the grid, she had been abandoned by her supposed protector, Miss Holden, and she couldn't call her mother: she would just yell at her. She scrolled down to the mobile number DI Reece had given her for emergencies. *Does this count as an emergency?* She shrugged and pressed 'call'.

'Inspector Reece, it's April Dunne,' she said to the answerphone. 'I … well, I think I'm being followed. I know I sound paranoid, but can you call me back?'

Why was there never anyone there when you needed them? Where were her *friends*? Her best friend was in Scotland and, at the moment, her closest friends in London were vampires. She almost laughed out loud.

'Screw this,' she whispered, calling Caro's number. She wouldn't blame her friend if she didn't ever want to talk to her again, but April really needed to speak to her. She was the only one who really knew what she was going through, the only one who could understand why she was squatting in a cemetery when most normal people would be safely at home watching the soaps.

'Please pick up,' she whispered, 'Please …'

'April?' said Caro guardedly. 'I thought we weren't talking.'

'We weren't. Listen, I know you're angry with me because … well, because I've been an idiot, but I need your help. Again. Like I always do.'

There was a frosty silence down the line.

'What about your new friends?' said Caro finally. 'I thought they were more important to you now.'

'Please, Caro, I'm sorry I've been a daft cow, but I really, really need your help.'

Caro heard the desperation in April's voice.

'What's going on? Where are you? And why are you whispering?'

'I'm stuck in a graveyard and I think someone's following me.'

'Bugger. Is it a vamp?'

April glanced around.

'Probably.'

'Well then you need to get among real people, they're not going to attack you in public, are they?'

'Let's hope not. What do I do?'

'Well you must be near a main road, can't you flag a taxi or jump on a bus?'

April felt a chink of hope: she could head for the bus stop she'd seen in front of the church. If she skirted around the building, it should bring her out on the steps where she had seen the crazy old tramp. Not ideal, but better than being cornered by some semi-mortal.

'Okay, thanks, Caro. I'll try that,' whispered April. 'Can you meet me at Americano in half an hour? Assuming I get out of this alive.'

'Sure. But keep your phone on, okay?'

'It's never off,' said April. 'And Caro? Thanks.'

'Thank me with a hot chocolate. And some cake. Just get yourself over here safely, okay?'

'Okay.'

As quietly as she could, April got to her feet and began walking along a path curving around between the headstones.

'You're beautiful in the moonlight, you know.'

Jesus!

Her heart leaping into her mouth, April whirled towards the voice, every muscle in her body tense.

'Who said that?' she said, trying to sound brave.

There was a chuckle. 'I don't know whether to feel insulted or not. No, actually, I do.'

'Gabriel!' she gasped as he stepped out of the shadows. She

jumped up and wrapped herself around him, hugging him tightly.

'Hey, steady on,' he laughed. 'I'm an old man, remember?'

She kissed his neck and his hair. 'What are you doing here? How did you find me?' she asked all at once, then stepped back and looked at him.

'Gabe, I think someone was following me.'

'Well we'd better get out of sight, then,' he said, pulling her into the shadows, wrapping his coat around her.

'I'm serious,' she said. 'Do you think it was one of the vampires?'

'Possible, although I doubt you'd have lost them by coming into a graveyard. More likely it was the police hoping you'd lead them to me.'

April looked up in alarm.

'Don't worry, I'm pretty sure no one followed me. And anyway, I needed to see you.' He bent his head to kiss her neck. 'Mmm ... it's definitely worth the risk.'

She laughed and squeezed him tight.

'But I've been so worried. Where have you been?'

April couldn't help the note of accusation in her voice. She hated herself for it, but it had been almost impossible not to wonder where Gabriel had been hiding. With some pretty feeder, some old girlfriend? She had imagined all sorts of scenarios and none of them were good.

Gabriel smiled. 'I've been laying low thinking about you, worrying that you'd forgotten all about me.'

'Well, it's hard to forget when your boyfriend is wanted by the police for murder.'

She was trying to make light of it, but April was genuinely frightened for him, especially after Inspector Reece's warning that the powers-that-be desperately wanted to close the case – and they needed someone to pin it on.

'You forget that I know I didn't do it,' said Gabriel.

'But that doesn't matter to them, Gabe ...'

He put a finger to his lips.

'Shh,' he said soothingly, 'I'll just prove it to them.'

'But how?'

'By catching whoever *did* kill Marcus, of course. Trust me, I've been keeping my ear to the ground.'

'Have you found out something?'

He shook his head.

'Not exactly, not yet anyway, but things are gathering speed. There are ever more signs that something's changing, that something new is coming.'

'What do you mean, something new?'

'I'm not sure, but I can feel the shift. The change in the rules, the way the vampires seem to be gathering. There's almost an excitement in the air, but not in a good way. It's almost as if some darkness is spreading, infecting them.'

'Do you think it's to do with the school?'

'I think it's bigger than that. I think I'm onto something myself – it's another of the reasons I came to find you. One of my contacts thinks he can put me in touch with the Regent.'

She opened her eyes wide.

'What? How? Who is this?'

'Just a small-time thug. Teddy the Toad.'

April wrinkled her nose. 'Do they really have names like that?'

'I'm afraid so. You get a lot of them hanging around the fringes of The Life. They're in awe of the money and the violence. The vamps use them as go-betweens and runners.'

'Can you trust him?'

'No. But he would never have dared to mention the Regent's name unless he could deliver. I think the Regent wants to meet me.'

April frowned.

'But why now? I mean, you've been chasing him for years, how come he's suddenly interested?'

Gabriel gave a wry smile.

'Because I've never been wanted for murder before. I'm guessing he wants to offer me some sort of deal; maybe he has contacts in the police who can drop the murder charge in return for a favour he needs doing.'

'What sort of favour?'

Gabriel shrugged.

'He probably wants me to kill someone.'

'What? No! You can't!'

He laughed softly.

'Don't be silly,' he said, stroking her hair from her face. 'It's just a meeting, remember? I'm not going to kill anyone.'

'Except the Regent. You need to kill him to be free ...'

'Yes, but that's not all we need from him. There are bigger questions to answer here – like what's the big plan for the vampires and why he killed your dad. I'm not going to get any of that if he's dead, which is why I need this meeting.'

'But wasn't he looking for you? For the time when you wounded him?'

'There's no way he can connect me to that incident. It was a hundred years ago and I've stayed off his radar since then. Don't worry about me, you concentrate on staying safe.'

'I will. But only if you do. Promise me you'll be careful.'

Gabriel grinned.

'I always am.'

Chapter Thirty-Two

It was good to have Caro back. She had the same enthusiasm for catching vampires as she did for a chocolate eclair. She threw herself into it with excitement and energy and she was fearless about the dangers.

'So tell me again about this Teddy the Toad,' said Caro as she hoovered up the pastry and got stuck into a slice of Black Forest gateau.

'Don't you worry about your arteries?' asked April.

'I've got to keep my strength up, haven't I?' said Caro as she wiped her mouth on her napkin. 'Who knows when something might leap out and grab my throat.'

April's face fell.

'Not funny, Caro,' said April in a low voice, not wanting to be overheard by the waiters. 'I don't know how you can be so flippant about it. I was really scared earlier on.'

'I know, honey, I know it's real, but you've really got to lighten up. All this weight on your shoulders, it's going to snap you in two.'

'How can I lighten up when people – things – are trying to kill me?'

'I'm not saying you should whistle a happy tune, I'm just saying you need to accept what's going on and roll with it. It's not doing anyone any good for you to be walking around with a face like a wet weekend.'

April laughed despite herself.

'Thanks for pointing out I'm such a misery.'

'I'm just saying you look nicer when you smile.'

'Now you sound like my mum,' said April, feeling a stab

of guilt. She guessed that Grandpa Thomas would have told Silvia about her visit, but that wouldn't have stopped her from worrying herself sick – with good reason as it happened.

'Your mum's not always wrong,' said Caro, pointing at April with her fork. 'Anyway, the point is, the Suckers are here, they're not going to disappear just because you go all mopey. We've got to pick ourselves up and come out fighting.'

'Funny you should say that ...' said April, and filled Caro in on her meeting with Uncle Peter earlier that day. Caro's eyes lit up at April's description of the newspaper office.

'Wow! And Peter's serious about looking into Ravenwood?'

'Well, the conspiracy part of it – he's not buying the idea that there are vampires here, but he was certainly into the idea of finding out who's behind the school.'

'So we're all chasing the Vampire Regent really,' said Caro thoughtfully.

April pulled a face. 'Sadly we still have no idea who he is.'

'So let's work it out,' said Caro, putting down her fork and pulling out a notepad. 'Who are the prime candidates?'

'Well, you thought it was Davina's dad, didn't you?'

'We know Nicholas Osbourne's not a vampire, but that doesn't mean he's not involved in this. And it's got to be someone like him, someone with power. Agropharm's still in the frame too. Just because Davina's dad isn't one of the undead, doesn't mean there aren't Suckers behind it.'

'Mr Sheldon?' said April, then stopped dead. 'Oh my God ...'

She turned and scrabbled in her coat pocket, pulling out her phone.

'What is it?' asked Caro.

'Hawk – Mr Sheldon. The other night I took a picture of him and my mum.' She clicked to her pictures file and looked for the date.

'There it is.'

April could feel her heart beating as it opened. It had been a snatched photo in a dark corridor and the camera on her phone wasn't exactly cutting-edge, but it was clear enough.

They could see the front door and the coat-rack and the freshly painted walls, but where Mr Sheldon should have been, there was only a weird dark smudge, as if a child had taken a black crayon and scribbled him out. You couldn't even see April's mother standing behind him. It was like she was being obscured by thick fog.

'No *way* ...' whispered Caro, her eyes wide. 'I mean, we pretty much knew Hawk was a vamp, but to see it ... it's like – wow!'

April nodded.

'Imagine how I feel, to think of him smarming up to my mum.'

'Eww,' said Caro, wrinkling her nose. 'Still, it's no big surprise, is it? Gabriel told you that the Suckers all report to him. He had to be a vampire – but does it make him the Regent?'

April shrugged. 'Probably not. We've seen that he answers to other people, haven't we? The Regent's not going to let people push him around.'

'Dr Tame?'

'Don't think so. He's evil, but in a different way. Besides, Fiona checked him out, and she found photos of him everywhere.'

'That new police inspector? What's his name?'

'No way. He's hardly going to be able to do a press conference. He might be a vamp disciple, but he's not a vampire.'

'Maybe we're not looking in the right places,' said Caro. 'Didn't Gabriel say he was great at hiding? If that's true, there's a good chance we've never even seen him.'

April slumped back in her seat.

'It's hopeless, isn't it?'

'If only we'd found some sort of guidebook on getting rid of vampires at the V&A,' said Caro. 'You know, like, *How To Get Rid of Ants From Your Kitchen.*'

April didn't laugh.

'Hey, how do you get rid of ants, anyway? You follow them back to their nest and pour boiling water down the hole, don't you?'

Caro shivered. 'Really? Is that what you do?' She pushed her plate away. 'Ugh, I don't much feel like eating all of a sudden.'

But April was still thinking. 'So where is their nest?' she said. 'Where are they all crawling about at the moment?'

Caro looked confused.

'The cemetery?'

'*Duh*,' said April. 'Where's the one place you can be sure to lay your hands on a vampire? Ravenwood.'

Caro gave a grim smile.

'Better put the kettle on, then.'

Inspector Reece was waiting for April outside the café. He was standing by his car wearing a rumpled trenchcoat. He had bags under his eyes and looked like he could do with a decent night's sleep. Caro gave a little wave and moved off back up the High Street. 'I promised I'd meet my mum by the hairdressers,' she said. 'See you tomorrow, A?'

'Yeah, see you. And thanks.'

'No,' said Caro, patting her stomach, 'thank *you*.'

Reece gave April a wan smile.

'I assumed you weren't being attacked in the coffee shop, so I let you finish,' he said.

'Oh God, sorry,' said April, blushing. 'I forgot all about ringing you. How did you find me?'

'We can find anyone within a few hundred metres if their phone is on, April,' he said. 'Even faster if they're making calls.'

'Oh. Well I really did think someone was following me, honestly Inspector Reece.'

'Who was it?'

April hesitated. DI Reece might have been taken off her case, but he was still a policeman. She didn't want to have to lie to him about her meeting with Gabriel.

'I ... I don't know. Maybe it was no one. I didn't wait to find out – I just jumped on a bus and came back here.'

Reece looked at her shrewdly. April had the unsettling feeling that he knew exactly where she'd really been.

'Well you're safe now, that's the main thing,' he said.

'I'm really sorry, I didn't mean to worry you.'

'That's okay, I wanted to talk to you anyway.'

'Why is it that whenever we talk you end up giving me some bad news?'

Reece snorted.

'Part of my job, I'm afraid,' he said, walking slowly up the hill away from the café. 'No one ever asks the police to give good news. Hence the dark uniforms, I suppose.'

They walked in silence until they reached Pond Square and sat down on a cold bench.

April looked at him sideways.

'So what is it this time? I'm not sure I can take any more shocks.'

'I'm sorry it's been so hard for you, April,' he said. 'You've been asked to deal with an awful lot since you came here and I hesitated to add this to your burden.'

He paused to rub his eyes, as if he were suffering from a migraine.

'But I still think you should see this.'

He reached inside his coat and pulled out a brown envelope. Inside were two date-stamped photographs. She peered at them for a moment, a look of confusion slowly turning to disbelief and anger.

'Why didn't you tell me?' she whispered.

The photographs were from a traffic camera. They were grainy and the driver's face was a blur, but you could see the car and the registration number as clear as day. Her mother's car; she had been caught speeding. There was nothing particularly strange about that, but it was the date and time stamped on the pictures which was making April's heart thump: the day, the time, her father died. The precise time when Silvia had sworn she was with April's grandfather.

'But this proves she was lying, doesn't it?' said April. 'It changes my mum's alibi.'

'Not really,' said Reece.

'Why not? She lied! Aren't you going to question her?'

'You're not getting it, April. This photo was taken at the exact time your father died, so your mother *couldn't* have killed him. Okay, so she lied, but it doesn't alter the fact that she has a water-tight alibi. Anyway' – he shook his head – 'I'm off the case. Not that there is really a case any more.'

April's mouth opened.

'My dad's case is closed?'

He shrugged.

'Not officially – officially it's an on-going investigation, but off the record, all the manpower has been reassigned. Someone at the top doesn't want it looked into any more. I don't know if they're just trying to sweep it under the carpet or ... well, it's not like we're swamped with leads.'

'That's not fair! How can you let it happen? There must be someone you can speak to, get it reinvestigated?'

'On what grounds, April?' said Reece, anger in his voice. 'I mean, if you have some compelling new evidence, then I'd be pleased to pass it on, but otherwise it appears as though my colleagues have their hands full with all the other deaths in Highgate!'

Reece rubbed his chin, the stubble rasping.

'I'm sorry, April, I shouldn't take this out on you. None of this is your fault and I can imagine you feel pretty let down by this investigation.'

April gave him a sad smile.

'I don't blame you, Inspector Reece. It just seems so wrong that the police can just give up on this.' She looked across to the yellow door of her house, remembering that night, the police cars with their spinning lights, the paramedics ... the blood. If the police – or whoever was in charge – could make something like that go away, then surely there was *nothing* they couldn't hide.

'Can't you do anything?'

'What do you expect me to do?' said Reece wearily. 'Give it all up, take a moral stand? Say "Either the case is re-opened or I'm walking?" It's been tempting, I will say that much, but ... there are elements in the police who would like all these cases closed down. Maybe they're corrupt, maybe there's someone behind the scenes telling them what to do, I don't know. But call me naïve, I still believe that the force needs decent people doing real police work. If we all left, what hope would there be?'

April nodded. 'Sorry. I didn't mean that you ...'

He shook his head.

'No, it's fine. It's not as if I haven't had this same argument with myself dozens of times. But I do know that people who try fighting it too hard find themselves transferred to traffic duty. And people who shout too loud, who threaten the wrong people, they find things get dangerous. Very dangerous.'

April couldn't take it all in.

'But what does this mean, Mr Reece?' she asked, holding up the photos. 'Does it mean my mum is involved in all this?'

Reece shook his head.

'Not at all. This proves she wasn't there.'

He handed her the envelope.

'But if I was you, I would want to know why she's not telling you the truth.'

Chapter Thirty-Three

April slammed the front door and threw her coat on the banister.

'Mother!' she shouted, craning her neck up the stairs. 'Mother, are you here?'

'Yes, I'm here,' said Silvia, stepping out of the living room. 'And where the bloody hell have you been? I've been worried sick since your grandfather rang. How could you be so selfish?'

April walked over and thrust the paper at her mother.

'What's this?' she frowned.

'It's a photo from a traffic camera showing you speeding. Look at the date.'

'That's the day ...'

'Yes. It's the day Dad was killed.'

Silvia looked up.

'So what's the big fuss? The police must have called me and I was rushing home.'

'No,' said April, stabbing her finger at the photo. 'Look at the time. That was the time you told the police – you told *me* – that you were with Gramps. You lied to me.'

Silvia stood there, not speaking, which only angered April more.

'Is that it?' she said. 'No denial? No "you've got it wrong, April"?'

'Deny what, April?' she snapped. 'What am I supposed to have done? So I wasn't exactly where I said I was. I don't tell you everything I do, and I don't *have* to.'

'But this was important! This isn't about you sneaking off

for a facial, this is your alibi, the thing that proves you didn't kill Dad.'

'Is that what you thought? You really believed I could have killed him?'

April shook her head.

'No, and that's not what this is about. This is about trust. If you can't even tell me the truth about where you were at the moment my dad was being murdered, how the hell am I supposed to believe anything else you say?'

'As if you ever did.'

'Oh grow up!' yelled April. 'I'm sick of you behaving like a teenager – no, in fact most of my friends are more mature than you.'

'So what do you want from me?'

'I want the *truth*, Mother! Where were you?'

Silvia looked away.

'You don't want to know.'

'I do, of course I do! Because if you can't give me a decent explanation, what can I do but think you're hiding something?'

'Like what?'

'Like having something to do with Dad's death.'

'April, that's ridiculous, I loved your father so much—'

'Loved, past tense. You were such a bitch to him before he died.'

'Don't speak to me like that!'

'Why not? It's the truth and you know it. So why can't you tell me where you really were that afternoon?'

Silvia looked at her hands.

'Because I am ashamed,' she said quietly.

'What of?'

She looked up at April and her eyes were shining with tears. 'Because I let your father down.'

April felt a sudden clenching of her stomach. Like she had some premonition that she wouldn't like what she was about to hear, that it would change everything. But she couldn't stop now, she had to know, however bad it was.

'Let him down how?'

'You have got to understand, April. It wasn't easy living with your father, he was obsessed with his work, he'd be away for a week living in some horrible squat in Moscow or somewhere, I'd have no idea where he was, if he was alive or dead ...'

'That was his job,' said April impatiently. 'Don't use that as an excuse.'

'There were other ... issues between us too.'

'Oh God,' said April, her hand over her mouth. 'You had an affair, didn't you?'

Silvia didn't need to say anything, April could see from her face that she had guessed correctly.

'It was when you were little. I felt so alone. I had no one to talk to, you have to understand what it was like. Robert was a shoulder to cry on.'

'Robert?' She felt sick. 'Robert *Sheldon*? You had an affair with Mr Sheldon.' Of course. She'd suspected something, but had never allowed herself to believe that it was true.

'I never meant to hurt your father,' said Silvia. 'But it was as if he was punishing me.'

'*He* was punishing *you*? You were the one who jumped into Hawk's bed! You're disgusting.'

'April,' said Silvia, moving towards her.

'Don't touch me!' she cried, jumping away. 'How could you do that to Dad? And with someone he hated.'

Suddenly April understood why her parents had spent so much time screaming at each other. When she was a little girl, she remembered them as happy and loving, but then something had changed, just before they had moved to Edinburgh, and ever since they had snapped and sniped at each other. April had assumed it was her; that she had simply grown up and noticed the tension she hadn't seen before. But no, her mother's selfishness had driven a wedge between them.

'Darling, please try to understand. Love makes you do strange things sometimes.'

'Love? How dare you talk to me about love? You must have hated him.'

'I never hated your father, April. He was wonderful, but

we had problems in our marriage. They were there from the beginning, but we thought we could overcome them. Maybe we never could.'

'Don't start blaming him. You were the one who had the affair.'

Another thought hit April like a blow to the stomach.

'Were you still seeing him? Is that why you came down here? So you could be close together? God, this is horrible ...'

'No, April,' said Silvia fiercely. 'Absolutely not. I would never have come within a hundred miles of Robert Sheldon, but ... we came here because your father wanted to.'

'That's rubbish! You want me to believe Dad insisted I went to a school run by your lover? Pull the other one. You were still seeing him and you tricked Dad into coming here. I wouldn't be surprised if you got him fired from the *Scotsman* on purpose!'

'How dare you!'

'How dare I? You're the one running around behind Dad's back, lying and cheating! Is that why you lied about where you were when he died? Because you were off having your affair?'

'No! The thing with Robert was years ago, one drunken night, a horrible mistake.'

'That's such rubbish. As soon as Dad died, Hawk was around here all the time.'

Silvia ran a hand through her hair.

'Robert was only trying to help. I think he feels guilty about ... about what happened between us. Yes, he wanted me back, that much is true, but I swear to you, April, I never cheated on your dad ever again.'

'Why should I believe you?'

'Because it's true.'

'Is it? You've lied to me so many times. For all I know you and Robert Sheldon plotted to have Dad killed, to get him out of the way. Dad was so stupid.'

Like lightning, Silvia stepped forward and slapped her.

April stood there, her mouth open, holding her stinging cheek. Silvia stepped towards her, but April turned, trying to run from the room. Her mother grabbed her and held her.

'Think what you like about me, April. But never think about your father that way. He was a fine, brave, principled man. Yes, I cheated on him once, yes I was selfish and weak, but he was strong enough to stay with us. Any other man would have walked out on us, but he put his own hurt to one side in order to protect you. And because, despite it all, he still loved me.'

'He loved you?' yelled April, wrenching herself free and running for the door. 'He *loved* you? Then he really *was* stupid!'

Chapter Thirty-Four

'How could she?' April stood sheltering under a tree as the rain swept down. She hoped it wouldn't get into her phone, that would really cap her day off.

'I don't know, honey,' said Fiona soothingly. 'But I know she didn't do it to upset you.'

'What do you mean?' said April. 'You can't imagine how much she hurt my dad.'

'I can, actually,' said Fiona. Her own family had split in two when her mother ran off with the local golf pro a few years earlier. 'And I know what your mum means when she says it took incredible strength for them to stay together. But whatever happened back then was between your mum and your dad. Yes, she was selfish and stupid, but no one ever knows what goes on inside someone else's relationship. Try not to judge her. I know that sounds like useless advice, but believe me, I've been through the same thing and it gets you nowhere trying to hate your parents, however idiotic they are.'

'I suppose,' said April, but she was still too angry to listen to reason, even if her friend was talking from bitter experience. 'Why can't adults behave like adults? They spend so much time telling us how to behave and getting all worked up about the way we look and speak and all the time they're sneaking off to do horrible things. Are we going to turn out like them?'

'We've got to be better than they are, if we can,' said Fiona sadly. 'I know you're angry at your mum, but shouting at her isn't going to help. Like I say, I have experience.'

'Sorry, Fee, I don't mean to reopen old wounds.'

'Oh, don't be silly. I've got over it, as much as I can. The

334

tricky part is grasping that your parents are human too. You want them to have all the answers, and it turns out that they're as clueless as we are. That's pretty scary the first time you work it out.'

'It's no excuse though, is it?'

'No, of course not. But the bottom line is your mum is your mum and she always will be. You might not want to see her right now, but you will one day.'

'I can't stand the sight of her.'

'Well then avoid her for a while. You'll only say something you can't take back. Or rather yell something.'

April shook her head. All she wanted to do was yell. At this very moment, she wanted to strike out at someone. Mr Sheldon in particular.

'Well if I can't yell at my mum, maybe I should yell at Hawk. God, I'd like to wring his neck,' she said, kicking at a tree root.

'Obviously. But again, just avoid him. You don't want to get expelled from Ravenwood just when you've got Peter helping you on your investigation.'

April thought for a while, watching the rain dripping off the leaves of the tree.

'Do you think my mum was meeting him that day?' she asked. 'I mean, she swears she wasn't having an affair with him any more, but she's not exactly told me the whole truth so far, has she?'

'Possibly,' said Fiona. 'But does it really matter?'

'Of course it matters!' said April, 'If she was going off to have some sort of horrible rendezvous, that makes it even worse!'

'But weren't you with Mr Sheldon just before it happened?'

'Yes, he drove off in his stupid sports car. He could have gone straight there and killed my dad. And …'

'What is it?'

'Well, maybe that was why my mum wasn't at home. Maybe Hawk arranged to meet her to get her out of the way so he wouldn't have any witnesses. And maybe that's why she lied about where she was.'

335

Fiona was silent for a moment.

'It's possible, but that's an awful lot of maybes.'

'Yes, I guess. But someone out there knows.'

'Mr Sheldon for one. Perhaps you should ask him.'

April laughed.

'I can't just go up and say "Hey Mr Sheldon, I hear you were screwing my mother and I was wondering, did you also murder my dad?"'

There was a pause at the other end of the line.

'What?' said April. 'Do you think I should?'

'April, you're my best friend and it's terrified me hearing all about the things you've gone through over the past few months. The last thing I want to do is put you in more danger ...'

'But? I can feel a big "but" coming on.'

'But they do say attack is the best form of defence. You and Caro have spent months sneaking around, reading books, doing research and where's it got you? Maybe it's time for a more direct approach. At least then you won't be sitting around waiting for one of the Suckers to jump out at you.'

April felt a weird mixture of thrill and fear. She knew Fiona was right, she just wished someone else could go and do it for her.

'So what do I do?'

'Go and see Mr Sheldon tomorrow. Ask him about it straight out. He'll probably deny it, but you'll be able to see how he reacts, won't you?'

It sounded crazy, but right now, April was so angry, she felt she could have walked into a lion's cage and come out unscathed.

'You know what? I'll do it,' she said. 'I'd certainly love to see his face when I tell him I know everything.'

'Good for you. So what are you going to do right now?'

April looked at the time. Eight-thirty. She knew she'd have to go back some time, but she couldn't face seeing her mother right now. Let Silvia worry for a while – this time, she deserved it. April so wished she could see Gabriel, but she knew there was no way he could come back to Highgate.

'I suppose I'll call Caro. She's been texting me since I met up with DI Reece. I'll go to hers and we'll see if we can plot our next move.'

'Keep safe, okay?'

Just then her phone beeped in her ear.

'Speak later, Fee,' said April. 'I think that's Caro now.'

She quickly flicked through her phone's menu, but the message wasn't from Caro.

It was from Miss Holden.

I need to speak to you, it's urgent. Can you come to school? Mr Sheldon's office, I've found something I think you should see.

April frowned. Had Miss Holden finally seen sense and decided to help her out?

'I hope so,' she whispered to herself. 'I could do with some help right now.'

April walked straight up the path to the school, feeling a new sense of purpose. Fiona was right; there was a time for gathering evidence and looking for clues, and there was a time to take action. She needed to take the bull by the horns, even if it meant the risk of being gored, because the longer April sat around and waited for something to happen, the more time she gave the Suckers to work out who she was and close in on her. April needed answers, and she was only going to get them by asking the right people – Miss Holden and Mr Sheldon were excellent places to start.

April walked up the steps and pushed in through the main doors: they were unlocked. Maybe Miss Holden had left them open, or perhaps they were always unlocked, she'd never been here this late. As she walked inside, April was immediately struck by how quiet it was, her shoes tapping on the stone floor. Empty buildings always had a neglected, unhappy air and Ravenwood's high-ceilinged passageways added to the unsettling sense that she was both alone and being watched.

337

She was just turning into the corridor housing the headmaster's office when her phone buzzed, echoing in the silence, and she pulled it before it could ring again.

'Caro,' she whispered, covering the mouthpiece with her hand. 'Can't talk right now.'

'Where are you? I've been trying to call you. And why are you whispering again?'

'I'm at Ravenwood, I had a message from Miss Holden to meet her here.'

'Miss Holden? What's she doing there?'

'She's found something in Hawk's office. I can't talk now, I'll call you when I get out.'

'April—'

'Speak later,' April hissed urgently and hung up, turning her phone off. She didn't want it going off again and alerting some caretaker or security guard.

She tapped gently on Mr Sheldon's door and could see there was a light on inside, so she pushed it open. There was a strange smell in the air, like burnt meat.

'Miss Holden?' she said, peering around the door.

'Oh no!' she gasped as she saw what was happening inside. April moved fast, but not quite fast enough. A hand shot out and grabbed her hair, pulling her sideways into the room. She fell to her knees, grazing them on the carpet, then someone kicked her over and she felt a foot on her neck, pinning her to the floor.

A trap! her mind screamed. It was a trap! *So stupid.* Anyone could have sent that message using Miss Holden's phone. And, from her position on the floor she could see exactly who had done it.

'Good evening, April,' said Benjamin, bending down so she could see his smiling face. 'I'm sorry to have deceived you, but I thought it was time we finally had that date we've been talking about. It's a sort of double-date actually.'

Suddenly she was jerked up off the floor and her arms were twisted up behind her back.

'I think you've heard of my associate, Teddy the Toad,' he said, nodding to the giant holding her.

Oh please no, thought April. Had they caught Gabriel too?

April tried to twist around, but she was held in a cruel grip. 'Let me go,' she said, trying not to show her pain.

'Oh, is he pinching you a little?' mocked Ben. 'I'm so sorry, Teddy *can* get a little zealous. Seems to enjoy inflicting pain for some reason. Ask Miss Holden if you don't believe me.'

Teddy spun April around to face Mr Sheldon's desk. The table top had been swept clear and Miss Holden had been tied over it, facing the ceiling. Her face was covered in blood.

'What have you done to her?' screamed April.

'Isn't it obvious?' said Benjamin. 'We've been torturing her. I thought she'd appreciate the irony,' said Ben. 'It's long been a tradition of the Guardians to put people "to the question" – to torture them until they confessed to their crimes. So far, she hasn't said much except your name. Now why do you think that was? Hmm?'

He walked over and flicked a Zippo lighter open, the orange flame jumping out. Then he held it to Miss Holden's feet. She screamed, jerking against her ropes.

Benjamin leant in close to the teacher's ear. 'Where is the White Book?' he whispered. 'Tell us where you've put the *Albus Libre* and it will all stop.'

She looked at April, then shook her head.

'Have it your way,' said Benjamin, his voice heavy with regret as he applied the flame to her feet again.

'Stop! For God's sake stop it!' shouted April, struggling against Teddy. 'Ask me, I'll tell you!'

Benjamin was across the room in a flash, his face right up against hers. 'Yes you will, April Dunne,' he hissed. 'By the time I've finished with you, you will beg to tell me every last little secret in your tiny head.' He pressed the lighter against her cheek and she flinched at the touch of the hot metal.

'Now tell me what you know about the White Book.'

'What white book?'

Benjamin curled his fist around the lighter and punched

April hard on the jaw. Pain exploded in her mouth and spots danced in front of her eyes.

'I'm getting impatient, April. I know you've seen that book. I know *everything*.'

How? How did he know? Had Miss Holden told him? April had a feeling she hadn't told him very much at all, otherwise why would he have summoned her?

'What do you need it for?' she asked, trying to stall him.

'There's a revolting little virus going around, I don't know if you've heard? This book contains a cure. But then you know that, don't you, because you used the Dragon's Breath to save your hero boyfriend. Not that it'll do him any good now.'

'Where is he?' she shouted. 'If you've hurt him I'll kill you!'

'Oh, now, that's not very nice, April. I thought you liked me.'

In the blink of an eye, Ben's handsome face twisted into a horrific leer, his sharp teeth bared, his eyes yellow, like a wolf standing over a wounded deer. It was the same face she had seen on Gabriel when the Dragon's Breath had taken hold, the same hellish mask she'd seen on Marcus that night in the cemetery, his pale skin spattered with her blood. April closed her eyes and turned away.

'What's the matter?' he whispered, his words dripping with spite. 'Don't you fancy me any more?'

'You're disgusting,' she said.

'Now you've hurt my feelings,' said Benjamin. He grabbed her hand and held the naked flame to the sensitive web between her finger and thumb. She screamed.

'Tell me where the book is or I swear you will end up like Layla!'

'You killed Layla?' she gasped.

'Not technically,' he said. 'Okay, so I put her head in the noose, but she jumped off the ladder herself. Well, I may have wobbled the ladder a tiny bit.'

April lunged at him, but Teddy the Toad held her.

'Bastard!' she spat.

'Yes.' yelled Benjamin, 'Yes I *am*, has it taken you this long to work it out? Now tell me about the book. I've already torn her worthless little cottage apart and it's not there. If you don't tell me where it is, I'll burn this shit hole school to the ground with both of you inside.'

April didn't know why, but she sensed that she was more valuable to Benjamin alive than dead. Why else would he be so keen to get the Dragon's Breath recipe? If he'd barbecued the Fury, there would be no need for it.

'Screw you,' she said.

Benjamin nodded to Teddy the Toad. 'Bring her,' he said.

The gorilla behind her dragged April over to the desk, holding her hair so she couldn't look away. Miss Holden flinched as Benjamin bent down towards her.

'So pretty …' he said, touching her face. 'For a witch, anyway.'

April could see the fear in Miss Holden's eyes.

How long had he been torturing her? Longer than was necessary, that was for sure. April knew that her inbred Guardian hatred of the vampires would have allowed her to resist for a while, but what chance did a history teacher have against an undead killer?

April gasped as Benjamin pulled out a knife, twisting the blade so it caught the light. 'Now, what do you think I'm going to do with this, Fury?' he asked.

'Slit your wrists?' said April, trying to sound defiant, feeling anything but.

'Funny,' said Benjamin – and pushed the knife against Miss Holden's throat.

'Okay, I'll make this simple,' he said. 'Either you tell me what I want to know or I'll slit her from ear to ear and make you watch as I drink her dry.'

He pushed the knife down harder and April could see a thin line of blood appear.

'All right, all right!' said April quickly. 'I know where the book is and I have the Dragon's Breath recipe. I have it all, so you can let her go – please, Ben? *Please.*'

Benjamin nodded to Teddy the Toad, who immediately let go of her arms.

Surprised, April began to turn – and then suddenly it went dark. It took a moment for April to realise that a bag had been pulled over her head.

'No!' April screamed, but her cries were choked off by an arm around her neck.

'Shut her up, Teddy,' said Benjamin. 'If she's got the book then I have no more need for this witch.'

Suddenly, she heard Miss Holden's voice.

'Fight them, April,' she said urgently, 'fight them all the way. You have the power. Send them back into the darkness!'

'Quiet!' snapped Benjamin and Miss Holden's voice was cut off.

'NO! DON'T …' April tried to scream, but something hit her head. And then all she saw was darkness.

Chapter Thirty-Five

It was as if April was waking from a dream she didn't want to leave, those short seconds of cosy oblivion just before the real world seeped in. Then it came at her in a rush: Miss Holden, the flame, Benjamin, his twisted smile. April knew she wasn't about to wake up under her duvet. She kept still, her eyes shut, her breathing even. She wanted to work out where she was before anyone knew she was conscious. She could feel the ropes holding her to a chair, could feel the wooden arms digging in to her back. *Kidnapped and tied up?* – not a good situation, especially having seen how it had turned out for Miss Holden. Her heart leapt as she thought of the teacher. 'I have no more need for this witch,' Ben had said. Had he *killed* her? It was more than possible. April had glimpsed the beast behind his mask: Benjamin Osbourne made Marcus Brent look like a fluffy kitten.

April became aware of raised voices; it sounded as though they were in the next room. 'Why did you bring her *here*? Are you insane?' shouted one, muffled through the wall. 'As if my office wasn't incriminating enough!' It had to be Sheldon, thought April with a sinking stomach. 'She wanted to see her boyfriend,' said another voice. There was no mistaking the cruel arrogance in that one: Benjamin Osbourne.

'Don't get smart with me,' said Sheldon. 'Don't you think the police will be watching her, trailing her wherever she goes?'

'I thought you could control the boys in blue?' replied Ben.

April supposed that if they were both outside the room, she was okay to open her eyes. She squinted against the light and found that she was in a large drawing room – and she wasn't alone. Her heart leapt: Gabriel! He was tied to a chair to her left, and although his head was slumped forward on his chest, he seemed to be breathing. *Thank God, thank God*. It wasn't a good situation, but at least they were together – and he was *alive*.

'Hey there, beautiful,' he said in a gravelly voice, opening his eyes.

'Gabriel! Oh my God, I thought I'd lost you!'

'You can't get rid of me that easily,' he said with a crooked smile. 'I'm already dead, remember?'

'Not yet,' said April. 'Not if I have anything to do with it.' She strained against her ropes, but she was stuck tight. 'If only I can ...'

'Quiet,' said Gabriel urgently as the volume of the argument in the next room rose. 'We don't want to end up like him.'

He gestured backwards with his head and April twisted around. She gasped in horror. There was a body lying on the floor between their chairs.

'Teddy the Toad,' said Gabriel. 'Outlived his usefulness, apparently.'

'Oh God,' whispered April, looking away. 'How did—'

But Gabriel cut her off.

'They're coming,' he hissed. 'Stay still and play dead.'

April immediately closed her eyes and feigned unconsciousness.

'You've brought danger to my house – I won't tolerate that,' said Sheldon, his voice moving towards them.

'Relax, *sir*,' said Benjamin in a mocking voice, 'I have some information about your favourite student.'

April squealed as Benjamin grabbed her hair, yanking her head up.

'Wakey-wakey, lover,' he said as she opened her eyes. 'I think it's time for some formal introductions. You've met my friend Teddy, of course,' he said, poking the body with his foot. 'So first I'd like to introduce my master. April Dunne, meet Mr Sheldon ...' He gave her a mock-bow.

'... and Mr Sheldon, meet the Fury.'

Sheldon snorted impatiently. 'Don't be ridiculous,' he said. 'April is not a Fury.'

Benjamin nodded.

'Oh yes she is. She killed Milo and Marcus.'

'No, Ben,' said Sheldon. '*You* killed Marcus. On my orders, as I recall.'

'Well, it wasn't the hardest kill you've sent me on,' said Benjamin, staring at April. 'He already had one foot in hell, didn't he, Fury? He drank too much of your blood in the cemetery that night. When I got to him, he already looked like a corpse.'

'*You* killed Marcus?' said April incredulously.

'You didn't think lover boy here was up to it?' said Benjamin. 'I don't think so. The poor lamb's frightened of blood. I followed you after your little tiff at the party and I killed Marcus where he stood.'

'And I'll do the same to you,' said Gabriel in a low voice.

'Oh, you're awake now, are you?' said Ben, walking over to Gabriel and punching him in the side. 'I don't think you'll be doing anything today except *dying*.'

'Enough!' said Sheldon impatiently. He walked over to April, examining her closely. 'Is this true, April?' he said, talking to her as if she was a naughty schoolgirl caught talking in class. 'Speak up, girl, or would you rather the traitor spoke for you?'

'Traitor?'

Sheldon gestured towards Gabriel.

'You really think Gabriel was fooling anyone? He wouldn't drink blood, wouldn't kill, it was all very transparent. And then he comes here saying he's desperate to work for the Regent as his assassin ... such sweet irony, isn't it, Ben?'

Benjamin chuckled. 'Sure is, boss. Shall I ...?'

Sheldon nodded and Benjamin disappeared into the corridor.

'Are you a Fury, April?' repeated Sheldon. 'You'd better give me an answer or I won't be able to stop Benjamin doing to you what he did to your beloved Miss Holden.'

'What have you done to her?'

'I cut her pretty little throat,' said Benjamin casually as he walked back in carrying a heavy metal jerry can. He unscrewed the top and took a sniff.

'Ah, I love the smell of petrol in the morning,' he smiled.

'It's evening, you idiot,' said Gabriel.

Without a word, Ben turned and poured the liquid over Gabriel's head, making him splutter and cough. The sharp smell of fuel filled the room.

'What are you doing?' said April, suddenly terrified. 'No! You can't!'

'Can't I?' asked Ben, sloshing more over Gabriel's body and legs. 'But I am.'

'All right, stop. Stop! I am the Fury, okay? I'm the Fury!'

'So it's true.' Sheldon laughed. 'Now it all makes sense. Gabriel thought you had killed Marcus and that was why he took the blame for the murder. I had assumed it was simply a convenient case of mistaken identity. I really should have known.'

Sheldon walked over to April and, without warning, slapped her hard across the face, splitting her lip.

'Your kind disgust me,' he said.

'I'm not too fond of you lot either,' said April, spitting out blood.

He grabbed her hair and yanked it back so that her birthmark was exposed. April squealed from the pain, but Sheldon was oblivious.

'Look at it,' he said with contempt. 'The mark of the North Star, the bringer of light. Are you the best they can do?'

'I've killed two of you already,' said April, sticking her chin out.

Sheldon snorted and pushed her away.

'Oh yes, well done,' he said. 'That will make us even, then, won't it? We killed Isabelle Davis and now we're going to kill you.'

'Isabelle? What's she got to do with it?'

'Apparently your history teacher hasn't been doing her job,' said Sheldon. 'There are *three* Furies a generation. Isabelle

Davis was the first. Like you, she thought she could bring us down. Like you, she was wrong.'

'Dead wrong, wasn't she, Gabriel?' giggled Benjamin. 'You put her straight though, didn't you?'

'Ben,' said Sheldon, a warning in his voice. 'Not now. Let's concentrate on the job in hand.'

Ben nodded. 'All right then,' he said, patting his pockets. *Oh God, he's looking for his lighter*, thought April.

'Regent!' she shouted out suddenly, desperate for anything that would slow their executioners down.

Sheldon looked at her sharply.

'What did you say?'

'You're the Vampire Regent, aren't you?' she said, hoping she sounded more confident than she felt. 'You're the one in charge of recruitment at Ravenwood. You ordered Marcus's death, you're the one they all listen to.'

'Finally,' said Ben. 'Finally she gets it.'

'You?' roared Gabriel, jerking forward in his chair. '*You* are the Regent? How can that be? How can you have been so close all this time ... NO!'

Benjamin flicked his lighter open, waving the flame in front of Gabriel's petrol-soaked face.

'Be quiet, Romeo,' he said. 'Or I'll turn you into charcoal.'

'But what about the governors at Ravenwood?' said April quickly. 'I mean, I saw, you were bowing and scraping. You were scared of them.'

'Once again, my so-called students disappoint me,' said Sheldon shaking his head. 'We are *vampires*, April. The ultimate predators. We excel at two things – the hunt and the kill. And to be a hunter you need to be able to hide in plain sight, to make your victims believe you pose no threat – until you strike.'

'So you let the governors believe they're in control, while lining them up as your pawns when you take the throne?'

'Throne is right, sweetness,' said Ben.

April frowned.

'What do you mean?'

'Jesus, don't you Bleeders ever listen in school?' said

Benjamin with irritation. 'Doesn't anyone read the dictionary any more? A Regent only steps in to rule while the king is absent. But soon Robert will be crowned as king,' he said, looking over at Sheldon with something like hero-worship in his eyes. 'And he will lead us to glory.'

'That's enough, Ben,' snapped Sheldon. 'Now is not the time.'

'Now *is* our time, Robert. It's time to stop hiding, to stop cowering in the dark, always terrified of being discovered. No, when the throne is ours, we will live like kings and humans will live in the eternal darkness, begging to be our slaves.'

'Like Alix Graves?' said April.

'Ah, you're not quite as dim as I supposed, April,' said Sheldon. 'Alix Graves thought he could be our equal, he thought he could muscle his way to a position of power. When he found out what we really wanted, he tried to back out – he even threatened to tell the media about our little scheme.'

Sheldon wagged his finger. 'Never try to blind-side a vampire, April. You may find someone tears your throat out.'

'Like my father?'

Sheldon looked at his watch and shook his head. 'Sorry, April, I wish I could stand here answering all your questions, but it's time we got on with this.'

He gestured to Ben.

'No!' shouted April. 'If you kill me, you'll have no chance with my mother!'

Ben and Sheldon looked at each other, then burst out laughing.

'Have a *chance* with her?' said Sheldon. 'Is that what she told you? Oh, she's good.'

'But she said ... she said you'd had an affair and now you wanted her back.'

'*She* wanted to be with *me*,' he spat. 'Your precious mother always was a little tart, even at university. She'd go wherever the most popular boys were. Anyone with a title, teachers, anyone cool, she had to have them. So she hooked up with me for a while, then cast me aside when her precious William came along. Look how wrong she was about him. But now she sees I'm in charge, so she's back, crawling after me like a dog on heat.'

'Don't talk about her like that.'

Sheldon looked at April with contempt.

'I can see you don't believe me. Why do you think your family moved to Highgate?'

'Because my dad had to get a job. He talked her into it.'

Mr Sheldon laughed.

'William Dunne hated me. Your *mother* persuaded your father to come to London, not the other way around. She wanted to be with me. She *begged*, April.'

Shock ran through April's body.

'Is that why you killed my father?'

'He didn't kill your father, you stupid little bitch,' said Benjamin.

'Don't you speak to her like that!' growled Gabriel. 'I'll kill you!'

'You're not going to kill anyone, Gabriel,' said Benjamin. 'You think it's beneath you.'

'I'd make an exception for you.' He looked at Sheldon. 'And for you too, Regent.'

Sheldon laughed.

'I am a born vampire, Swift. You know the difference, don't you? I would crush you like a bug.'

'Oh really?' said Gabriel, straining at the ropes. 'You over-estimate your power.'

'Do I? I don't think so, Gabriel,' said Sheldon, a smirk on his face. 'Ask yourself what really happened in the cemetery on the night Isabelle died.'

'I fought off her killer,' said Gabriel. 'The killer you sent.'

Sheldon raised an eyebrow. 'Half right, boy,' he said. 'Think harder.'

April looked at Gabriel. He had a faraway look as if he was seeing the scene in front of his eyes. 'I know what happened,' he said, frowning as if he was trying to remember something that had been bothering him. 'I tried to help her—'

'But you're not sure, are you, Gabriel?' said Sheldon. 'You don't even know why you were there, do you?'

'I was there to visit Lily's grave—'

Benjamin laughed, a mocking, delighted laugh.

'And who did you fight with that night?' sneered Ben. 'Who were you struggling with?'

'What do you mean?' said Gabriel, his face a mask of confusion. 'The vampire with the strange eyes …'

Sheldon laughed and clapped his hands in delight.

'He really has no idea,' he said. 'Even after all this time. Truly amazing.'

'You leave him alone!' shouted April. 'Don't listen to them, Gabriel! You helped Isabelle and saved my life, remember?'

'Yes, Gabriel's such a hero isn't he?' mocked Sheldon. 'If you knew the truth, I doubt you'd be so comfortable being in this room with him.'

'Don't think you can play your mind games with me,' said April. 'I know who he is.'

'But look at him, April!' said Sheldon. 'He doesn't even know himself! Do you really think it was chance that Gabriel was there in the cemetery that night – the touching anniversary with his fiancée which just happened to fall on the night Isabelle was killed? Quite a coincidence, isn't it?'

'Not if you were trying to frame him for the murder,' said April.

Sheldon shook his head. 'It really is remarkable how much love blinds people to the truth,' he said. 'If we really wanted to connect him to a murder, there are plenty more bodies with his bloody fingerprints on them, believe me.'

Then, seeming to tire of the conversation, he turned to Benjamin.

'Enough talking,' he said. 'Let's get on with it.'

He pointed to April. 'Her too.'

Benjamin frowned. 'But I thought you wanted to keep her? If we have her blood and the White Book, we can—'

'Do as I say,' said Sheldon impatiently. 'While the Fury lives, we are all in danger. It goes deeper than her blood.' April watched in horror as Benjamin picked up the jerry can and began soaking the furniture and walls with the petrol, moving towards her, a smile on his face.

'Wait,' she shouted. 'I thought you wanted the *Albus Libre*. I know where it is.'

Ben looked at her, then over at Sheldon. 'Where?' he said guardedly.

'I have it here,' said April.

'Where?'

She nodded downwards.

'My inside pocket.'

Ben glanced at Sheldon for permission, then put the can down and cautiously reached inside her jacket.

'Mind your nose,' April whispered. Ben frowned and leant in closer. 'What did you say?'

The moment he was close enough, April lunged towards Ben, the front legs of her chair pivoting and catapulting her forehead hard onto the bridge of his nose with a crack. Her momentum carried her forward and she landed on top of him, splintering the wood of the chair. April pulled her hands free from the ropes, expecting Ben to leap at her, but instead he stayed on the floor, clawing at his throat. As she looked on in horror, Ben's neck began to swell and twist, the arteries beneath the skin turning black, his eyeballs bulging as if there were some great force pushing from inside his skull. What the hell was happening? April reached up and felt the wound on her forehead – and straight away she understood. Her blood had mixed with his, immediately infecting his system.

'Help me… !' Ben screamed, his voice rising to a wail and then a shriek as his legs thrashed uselessly against the ground. Suddenly, dark blood poured from his nose, ears and the corners of his eyes. His hands dropped from his throat and he lay still.

'April! Behind you!' shouted Gabriel, but he was too late.

As fast as a snake, Sheldon grabbed her around the neck and dragged her backwards out of the room.

'Try and follow us and I'll snap her neck like a twig,' he

growled. As he reached the door, Sheldon kicked the petrol can over, spilling a lake of petrol towards Gabriel, still tied to his seat.

'No!' shouted April, trying to twist away. Sheldon slammed her against the door frame, dazing her as he opened his lighter, flicked the wheel and threw it into the fuel, instantly sending an orange-white sheet of flame across the floor.

'Gabriel!' April shouted, as Sheldon dragged her backwards out of the room and up the stairs. *Gabriel*, she thought desperately. *I've got to get to Gabriel.*

'Let me go!' she screamed, kicking out.

'Oh no, I've got other plans for you, Fury,' he hissed into her ear, locking his arm around April's throat, making her struggle for breath. She clawed at his arm, but he didn't seem to feel it as he hauled her up, step by step. Facing backwards, she could only look with despair as the door of the drawing room filled with flame, black smoke pouring up towards the ceiling.

'No, no, no ...' she moaned. How could Gabriel have survived such an inferno?

Just as they were about to turn onto the first landing, there was a loud crash from the front of the house. April watched in amazement as the front door burst open, slamming back against the inside wall.

'Sheldon!' came the shout as Detective Inspector Reece charged into the hallway, then immediately fell back, throwing his arm up to shield his face from the flames.

'Let her go, Sheldon,' he shouted up at them. 'We've got you surrounded.'

Sheldon laughed.

'You want her?' he called. 'Come up and get her.'

The policeman started along the corridor, but the heat from the front room was already too fierce and he was forced back.

'I'm coming, April!' he shouted, his voice cracking as the swirling black smoke reached his lungs. 'We'll get you out.'

'Don't count on it,' said Sheldon, increasing his grip on April's throat and dragging her along a corridor, throwing her down on the cold tile floor of a bathroom. Finally released from her stranglehold, April tried to suck in air, but already the room was thick with smoke and she began to cough.

'Come up here,' said Sheldon, yanking her up and pushing her against a sink. He lowered his mouth to her ear.

'Don't worry, April,' he whispered. 'This won't take long and you won't feel a thing – well, not much, anyway.'

'What … what are you doing?' she said, terror rising in her throat.

'Oh, I need a sample of your blood,' he said. 'If our scientists can grow your virus in the labs I'm sure they'll be able to create an anti-venom. Then you and your kind will no longer pose a threat to the true elite and I will be the most powerful king in the history of our people. But you don't need to worry about that, April …' he pulled an old-fashioned cut-throat razor from the cabinet above the sink. '… when this sink is full, I doubt you'll care one way or the other.'

But April did care, she cared very much. Not about herself, but about the boy who had risked everything for her, the boy who had wanted to be with her so much, he had embraced death. She cared about the boy lying in the front room surrounded by smoke and flame more than anything in the world. And all the pain, all the anger, all of the hurt, all of the *rage* she had felt since she had come to this Godforsaken corner of the world, it all rose up in her chest like a ball of fire.

'Get off me!' she screamed, pushing herself up off the sink and throwing Sheldon back against the wall. She turned, punching and kicking at him, her teeth bared, pushing him further backwards until he was in a corner.

'Stupid little girl,' said Sheldon, back-handing her across the face, sending her sprawling against the bath, stars popping in front on her eyes. 'You think you can take on a true-born vampire – a *king*?'

'You're not a king!' screamed April. 'You're just an errand boy!'

Lying on the floor, her fingers had found a glass knocked from the sink and she threw it at Sheldon with all her might, hoping it would smash into his head, but instead it shattered uselessly against the mirror behind him.

'Now we're going to have some fun,' said Sheldon, his voice low. As April looked up she could see his face had twisted into the vampire mask: the burning eyes, the upturned nose, the dragon smile. But April didn't scream as she was supposed to.

Instead she began to laugh. A hiccuping giggle that grew in her throat until her shoulders were shaking. Sheldon stopped in his tracks.

'What's so funny?' he said.

'You should see your face,' laughed April. Frowning, the Regent turned to the cracked mirror, his eyes widening as he saw his reflection. Some shards of the broken glass had cut his cheek, leaving two bloody fingers trailing down to his neck.

Immediately, Sheldon took a step backwards and April could see the uncertainty, the fear in his eyes.

'Where are you going, sir?' said April. 'I thought you wanted some of my blood?' She put her hand up to the wound on her forehead, her fingertips coming back red. She held them out to him.

'Here it is, don't you want it?'

Sheldon was stumbling back now, his back against the door, fumbling with the lock. The vamp-mask had gone now, replaced by the face of a frightened man. Finally April understood the power of the Fury. When Miss Holden had talked about her 'abilities', she had imagined high-kicking kung fu moves or some sort of magical wizardry. But the true power of a Fury was in the fear it could instil in the vampires. That was what Sheldon had meant: it went deeper than her blood. She was a symbol, a rallying point, a blazing light in the darkness they wanted to bring to the world, and that was a far more potent weapon than the virus she carried inside her.

'Come on now, April,' said Sheldon. 'Why don't we think about this?'

'Think about it?' said April, taking another step forwards. 'Like you thought about killing Alix Graves and Isabelle and Layla? Like you thought about killing my *father*?'

354

She jabbed her fingers towards his head and Sheldon jerked backwards, falling through the doorway and scrabbling across the corridor until his back was hard against the wall. The smoke was getting so thick, she could only see him as a grey outline.

'Please, April,' he said, holding up his hands in surrender. 'What do you want? What can I do?'

'You can tell me who killed my father!' she shouted.

Sheldon gave a low chuckle.

'I don't think you want to know that,' he said.

'Yes I do!' yelled April, jumping forward and grabbing Sheldon's shirt in one hand, holding her blood-smeared fingers in front of his face.

'Tell me,' she hissed. 'Tell me who killed my father or I will send you to hell.'

'Oh, I'm not going anywhere, April,' said Sheldon, bringing the cut-throat razor up in a slashing arc towards her neck, everything moving in perfect slow-motion.

'*REGENT!*'

To April, it seemed as if the smoke had solidified and rushed towards them like the down-swing of a wrecking ball. Sheldon was torn from her grip, his blade missing her by inches while April was sent sideways, spinning back into the bathroom. She looked up and Sheldon had gone, swallowed by the fog. She heard a terrible cracking sound, like a ship's mask breaking in a storm, followed by a scream that suddenly cut off.

'Gabriel?' she whispered. It had to be, it *had* to be.

And then he was there, beautiful and terrible, his face covered in soot and blood, his arms around April, lifting her from the floor.

'Come on,' he said, 'if we don't get out of here we're going to roast.'

'But what about Sheldon?' she said, looking up into his dark eyes.

'He's dead,' said Gabriel. 'For ever this time.'

April stopped, her hand on his arm.

'Did you ...' she hesitated. 'Did you drink his *blood*?'

Gabriel nodded, his face grave.

'So what's happening?' said April, 'Have you gone through some change like with the Dragon's Breath?'

Gabriel shook his head, then doubled over, coughing. 'No.'

'What do you mean, no?'

'I mean, *no*!' shouted Gabriel, anger flaring in his eyes. 'I mean nothing's happening! I can't feel anything!'

April felt panic fluttering in her chest.

'But aren't you supposed to be cured?'

'It's only a legend, remember? No one said drinking blood is an exact science.'

They were both coughing now and black smoke was rolling up the walls.

'Come on, we've got to get out of here,' said Gabriel, pulling her towards the stairs. At the landing, there were flames licking up through the banisters and the air was full of burning cinders.

'We have to go up,' shouted April, pointing to the narrow staircase that could only lead to the attic. Gabriel was moving slower now, his footsteps on the stairs heavy and ponderous.

April reached out to support him and her fingers touched scorched leather; his jacket had been completely burnt away on one shoulder. And there was a wound to his neck.

'Jesus, Gabriel, you're hurt.'

'I'll be okay,' he coughed.

He tried to stand but stumbled, going down on one knee, his chest heaving.

'Leave me,' he said. 'I'm dead anyway.'

'Not if I have anything to do with it,' said April. She grabbed his wrist and pulled his arm around her neck, yanking him to his feet. 'Come on! We're going up.'

She staggered sideways, but the stairway was so narrow, they didn't fall. At the top, April kicked the door open and they fell to their knees. The smoke was thinner up here and she gulped for air.

'Honestly, April, leave me here,' said Gabriel.

'Oh shut up,' she said, 'this isn't a war movie.'

She stood up and felt along the wall until she found an

opening – a small door that gave into the eaves, but flames were already shooting up between the beams.

'Oh crap,' she said, running back to Gabriel. 'All right, soldier, on your feet. You still reek of petrol and I don't want to be standing next to you when you turn into a Roman candle.'

Gabriel just shook his head.

'I can't stand. You go.'

April rolled her eyes.

'God, why are men such girls all the time? Get up or I'll carry you.'

She grabbed a handful of his blackened jacket and pulled him to the end of the room, then taking a few steps back, kicked out at the roof. With a splintering sound, the tiles gave way and a rush of cold air pushed the smoke aside. The relief was only temporary as the flames shot up higher.

'The oxygen is feeding the fire,' she panted. 'Come on, big guy, you're going to have to help me.'

Together, they threw their weight against the hole. *Once ... twice ...* then mercifully the tiles gave way, making a big enough hole to clamber through. The night sky was magical and wonderful to April as she lay back on the rough tiles, drinking in the cold air.

She crawled to the edge and almost wept with relief as she saw Caro down in the street. April could see she was with Reece, but above the roaring flames, she couldn't hear anything they were shouting to her. She could see where they were pointing though. April shuffled back to Gabriel.

'Uh-oh,' he managed between coughs. 'What now?'

She pulled him up one last time. 'Trust me, okay?' she said, looking into his eyes, tears streaming down her blackened face. 'Just hold my hand.'

'What? Why?' he coughed.

'Because you love me.'

He gave a laugh which turned into a coughing fit, but even so, he held out his hand, black with blood and soot. April leant over, kissed his cheek and then with a yank, pulled him off the roof.

Chapter Thirty-Six

'I wasn't sure you'd seen the firemen's blanket,' said Caro. They were sitting in a private room at the hospital, waiting for April to be seen by a doctor. April only really had a few cuts and bruises and a hacking cough from smoke inhalation, but the doctors had decided to keep her in overnight.

'You really think I'd just jump off a burning roof? I'm not an idiot,' said April, her voice gravelly. She had pulled Gabriel onto the firefighters' escape pad just in time. The roof had collapsed in a shower of flame and sparks moments after their leap.

'It was quite fun though.'

Caro laughed, then bent over coughing. April reached out and rubbed her back.

'Ooh, honey, sounds like you got a lungful too.'

'I tried to get in through one of the windows, but it was just too hot, the flames beat me back.'

April put out her hand and squeezed Caro's.

'If you hadn't called Inspector Reece, I think I'd be dead. So would Gabriel.'

'More dead than usual, you mean?'

'Don't duck the compliment! You saved my life.'

Caro shrugged. 'S'what friends are for, isn't it? If you can't run into a burning building when your best friend has been kidnapped by vampires, what use are you?'

'Thank you, anyway,' said April.

'You're welcome,' said Caro bashfully. 'But what the hell happened with Gabriel? I mean, why isn't he back to being human? Isn't that why we tracked down the Regent? Or wasn't Hawk the Regent after all? I'm confused.'

April shook her head.

'Oh, he was the Regent all right, he was boasting about it like some crazed Bond villain. But we made a big, big mistake – the Regent isn't the top man. There is at least one vampire above him.'

'Oh God. And that's who turned Gabriel?'

April looked down at her hands.

'I don't know. We only know it wasn't Sheldon.'

Caro's eyes widened.

'You mean you know because he drank Hawk's blood? That's disgusting!'

'Not as bad as what Mr Sheldon had in store for us. Or what they did to Miss Holden.'

Caro shook her head.

'I still can't believe Benjamin killed her.'

'Can't you? I think we managed to forget they're vampires, full-on killing machines. They hide behind this well-groomed mask of humanity, but underneath they're terrifying.'

Caro nodded sadly.

'I liked Miss Holden. I'm not sure it was mutual, but at least we knew which side she was on.'

'Well, we're on our own side now. No teachers, no Guardians, just us.'

'You mean we go on?'

'Of course we go on, Caro. We have to – there's about a million things we still don't know: who's behind Ravenwood, what their big plan is – we don't even know for sure who killed my dad. The Regent might be dead, but there's someone much worse out there. Someone far more powerful. And for them, a few bodies is just a minor irritation.'

'But you almost got yourself killed. Again!'

April laughed.

'Well that's exactly why we need to press on. I didn't put myself and everyone I care about on the line for nothing. Seriously, Caro. I saw them torturing her. It was … horrible. They're not human and we have to stop them.'

'But when you say "stop them", you really mean "kill them", don't you?'

April nodded. 'I know. But it's time to grow up and face up to what we're doing here. It's them or us. They killed my dad, they killed your friend – who else has to die before we decide enough is enough?' April picked at the edge of her hospital dressing gown. 'And there's another reason we need to press on too. Ben knew I was a Fury.'

'What? No! How?'

'The "how" was he saw that Marcus was dying of the virus and put two and two together.'

'So why was he all over you after that? He must have known you were a Fury when he almost kissed you.'

'I think he was trying to recruit me,' said April. 'Imagine how powerful a vampire would be if he had control of a Fury. It'd be like having nuclear weapons when everyone else has spears. But that didn't work out because Gabriel came back into the picture, so he decided getting his hands on the Dragon's Breath would be the next best thing: it'd make him immune.'

'But who told him about the potion?'

April pulled a face.

'That I don't know. It seems there's a leak somewhere.'

Caro shivered. 'God, we can't trust anyone, can we? I wish I could stay here inside the hospital where it's safe,' she said. Police guards had been posted in the corridor, although April suspected that was less about security, more about keeping her where they could see her.

'I'm not sure you're safe with the police either. Isn't the whole point that the vamps are infiltrating every level of society?'

'Oh, thanks for making me feel better.'

'Talking of which ...'

Detective Inspector Reece peered in through the door and April waved him in.

'Where's Gabriel, Inspector Reece?' she said urgently. 'Have you seen him?'

Reece shook his head. 'Shouldn't you be worrying about yourself? You have just fallen off a burning building.'

'She jumped,' said Caro helpfully.

'Well, Gabriel's been taken to a secure hospital unit attached to the prison to be treated for his burns and wounds. But he didn't look too bad, considering.'

April didn't say it, but she was fairly sure Gabriel's wounds would be completely healed by the morning and that he would have disappeared from the prison hospital before they had time to ask him any questions.

As if reading her thoughts, Reece's face turned serious.

'Now to less pleasant business. I'm afraid you're going to have to talk to DCI Johnston. He's on his way up.'

April's heart sank.

'Just stick to the story you gave me and you'll be fine,' said Reece. 'That *is* what happened, right?'

April and Caro had decided on the 'cover story' in the ambulance on the way to the hospital. It was an edited version of events which created a reasonably plausible explanation for the strange goings on. It stretched the bounds of credibility, but then the real story was even more fantastic. They had stuck to the facts where they could, beginning with Caro's phone call to April as she was entering Ravenwood for her bogus meeting in Mr Sheldon's office. Suspicious and worried, Caro had called Inspector Reece, who had rushed to the school and found Miss Holden's body. Together Reece and Caro had driven – at high speed, Caro was keen to point out, 'sirens and everything' – to Sheldon's home and, even from the street, they could smell the reek of petrol. Reece broke into the house just in time to see it go up in flames and Mr Sheldon dragging April up the stairs, giving credibility to her story. The fire fighters had found three bodies in the wreckage, all of them burnt beyond recognition, so with Gabriel on oxygen in the prison hospital, April was the only witness to the rest: that Ben had confessed to Marcus Brent's murder, Sheldon had quarrelled with him about killing Miss Holden and knocked him unconscious, then set fire to the house to destroy the evidence.

'That's how it happened. Apart from the bit about heroic Gabriel Swift carrying April to safety,' said Caro. 'April dragged *him* out.'

'Yes, well I'm happy to bend the truth a little there,' said Reece. 'The Crown Prosecution Service is more likely to look kindly on him if he comes across as a hero. Benjamin's confession and his fingerprints in Miss Holden's blood may be enough to get Gabriel off the hook for Marcus's murder, but he did assault a couple of constables when he escaped from custody.'

'But he was innocent! Surely he was justified?'

Reece smiled.

'I'm not sure the Police Federation will see it that way.'

DCI Johnston was sitting at a desk in a borrowed hospital office when April was shown in. The inspector gestured towards the chair in front of him, but didn't look up from April's statement. Finally, he stacked the papers neatly, took off his reading glasses and fixed April with a baleful stare.

'It's rubbish, isn't it?' he said.

April swallowed, trying to keep her expression neutral.

'What's rubbish, Inspector?' she said.

'The whole story,' said the policeman, leaning back. 'I don't believe a word of it, frankly.'

'But it all happened exactly as I said there, Inspector Johnston. How could I make something like that up?'

'A very good question, Miss Dunne,' said Johnston.

'What, are you suggesting I *did* make it up?'

The detective let out a long breath.

'Let's ask a more fundamental question, shall we? Why you? Why are *you* always involved?'

April shook her head.

'I don't understand.'

'You were at the scene of a murder, you've been seriously attacked twice, you personally knew both Milo and Layla – who both died in mysterious circumstances – and now someone has tried to set you on fire. Now why would all that happen to an innocent girl of seventeen?'

'And I suppose you're suggesting I made up those other two times I was half-killed? Times when the police were supposed to be protecting me, actually.'

'No, April. I don't think you made those events up. In those cases, we have witnesses, evidence, a plausible time-line. It's just that this ...' he tapped the statement in front of him. 'This particular story doesn't quite add up.'

'What do you mean it "doesn't add up"?'

'Well, why would Benjamin kidnap you?'

'How am I supposed to know?' said April. 'He put a bag over my head, he didn't discuss why he was doing it! Maybe he was jealous of Gabriel and I – I don't know.'

'Okay, but why take you to Mr Sheldon's? What was the headmaster's involvement?'

April looked away.

'I don't know that either. How could I?'

April was of course aware that there was little about the previous night's events which made sense in the cold light of day. Unless you had the key fact: that Robert Sheldon was a high-ranking vampire preparing to wage war on humankind, it did look strange. Really, *really* strange.

'Here's the problem, April,' said Johnston. 'We have Robert Sheldon, a respected academic, educated at Oxford, running a top private school, never been in trouble, never had so much as an overdue library book as far as we can tell. And then we have Benjamin Osbourne – intelligent, straight-A student from a prominent family, also with an unblemished record. Then out of the blue, Sheldon and Benjamin hook up together and decide to kill your teacher, Miss Holden.'

'Look, I don't know ...' began April, but Johnston held up a hand.

'Now, that's crazy enough, but put that to one side for the moment. Now let's ask this: why did Mr Sheldon try and burn you and Gabriel alive? And why, in doing so, did he deliberately set fire to his *own house*?'

'Maybe he wanted to kill us and make it look like a suicide pact.'

Johnston gave her a wintry smile.

'Suicidal lovers don't tie themselves to chairs, then set fire to the house.'

The policeman massaged the bridge of his nose and sighed.

'Try not to insult my intelligence, April,' he said. 'Clearly you know more than you're telling us. Maybe you're trying to protect someone, maybe you have something of your own to hide, who knows? But we have a small problem don't we?'

'What's that?'

'People keep getting killed, don't they, April?'

Suddenly Johnston banged his hand on the desk.

'People *keep* dying! And I won't have that on my patch, do you hear me?'

April just stared at him, gripping the sides of her chair.

'I can't help it if I keep getting caught up in these situations, Mr Johnston,' said April. 'Maybe I'm just unlucky.'

Johnston snorted.

'Unlucky,' he repeated, a twisted smile on his face. 'What's that Oscar Wilde quote? "To have someone try to kill you once may be considered unlucky, to have someone try to kill you three times looks like carelessness"? Perhaps it's all just coincidence? Hmm? Well one thing's for sure, Miss Dunne,' he said, walking over to the door and opening it. 'You certainly seem to have nine lives.'

He paused for a moment, his hand on the door knob.

'Although I think you might be running out.'

'The police tell me you've refused to see your mother.'

Grandpa Thomas was sitting at the side of April's bed, his face disapproving.

'Do you know what she did, Gramps?' said April. 'Do you have any idea what she's like?'

'April, I know you're angry with her, but she's different,' replied her grandfather. 'She might not be the best mother in

364

the world, she makes mistakes, yes, but she loves you the best she can.'

'And Dad? Did she love him the best she could? Is that the get-out clause? "Sorry for sleeping with other men, I'm a bit rubbish at this. Doh! Silly me!"?'

'Everyone makes mistakes, April. No one gets the life they want.'

'And that's supposed to justify what she did to Dad? I know you hated him, but he was a kind, gentle man. He was nice. He didn't deserve her.'

Thomas shrugged.

'Maybe, maybe not. And you're right, I didn't see eye to eye with your father, but I am sure of one thing: he loved her very much, and she loved him back.'

'What about me, Gramps? What about my love? Why do I always get the feeling she's disappointed in me?'

'It's not that. I think you remind her too much of your father.'

'Isn't that a good thing?'

'The wound is deep, April. She blames herself for his death. Everything that happened ... she just thinks things could have been different.'

'Well, she's right!' said April. 'And my wound is deep too.'

'If you could just talk to her ...'

'No, Gramps,' said April fiercely. 'I can't. I've heard everything she's got to say. All the excuses, all the lies. I'm not going back there. Maybe I can go to Caro's for a few days while I look for a flat ...'

'Nonsense!' said Thomas. 'You will come and live with me. Your room is there. We are family, we look after each other.'

'I wish that were true.'

'What do you mean?'

'You covered for her, Gramps. When she said she had come to see you the morning Dad died, you gave her an alibi.'

'She did come to see me.'

'But you let the police – and me – believe she was somewhere she wasn't.'

'I know it was wrong, but when your mother asked me to say she was with me, I supposed she had a good reason. Never for a moment did I think she had anything to do with your dad's death. She loved that man – too much, I think.'

'She had a funny way of showing it.'

Thomas stood up and walked over to the window, gazing out.

'As I say, Princess, we all make mistakes. I wish I could say I was a saint, but I'd be lying.'

'You cheated on Grandma?'

He turned to face her.

'No, not that. But I made bad mistakes. Some may say worse things. I was never there for my kids, we fell out. I regret things in my life. You must never regret anything, April. Live for now, because you never know what's waiting for you around the corner.'

April pulled a face.

'You really don't have to tell me that, Gramps.'

Chapter Thirty-Seven

When April woke in the morning, Silvia was sitting by her bed. She sat up with a start, pulling the covers around her and reaching for the nurse alert button.

Silvia put her hand on April's.

'Darling, please. I won't stay long.'

April sank back on her pillows and glared at her mother.

'What are you doing here?'

'Your grandfather told me you were here. I wanted to check you were all right.'

'It's a bit late for that, isn't it?'

Silvia sighed.

'You're going to have to speak to me sometime, you know.'

'Am I?' said April.

'Darling, I know you're upset, but—'

'Upset? Is that what you think? I'm furious! No, furious doesn't even begin to cover it. All those years I watched you giving Dad such a hard time about everything, sniping at everything he did, belittling his whole life, and now I find out the reason. You'd been having an affair ... and with a man who tried to kill me! I don't know how you can live with yourself.'

'It wasn't all one way, April,' said Silvia. 'Marriage is a complex thing, when you're older you'll understand.'

'Don't patronise me! I might only be a child,' she said sarcastically, 'maybe my brain isn't fully developed, but it seems pretty simple to me: keep your hands to yourself. And you couldn't even manage that, could you?'

'I'm still your mother, April.'

'No!' she yelled, 'No, you're not. A mother is supposed to

guide, nurture and support her child. You're supposed to give me affection and love. When have you ever given me any of those things?'

Silvia pulled out a handkerchief and began to sob into it.

'If you only knew ...' she said.

'Oh, don't give me those crocodile tears, I'm sick of your lies. Why can't you just look me in the eye and tell me the truth? You and Sheldon were always together behind Dad's back. Your tears are for him, not for Dad.'

Silvia said nothing, standing up and smoothing her skirt down.

'Aren't you even going to deny it?' said April with a sinking feeling. Even if it had been true, April wasn't entirely sure she wanted to know. She didn't think she could stomach the thought of Silvia carrying on with Hawk while her dad was alive – the truth was, April was desperate for her to deny it.

'You've obviously made up your mind, April. Nothing I say is going to change that. I wish I could explain why I kept it from you, but ...'

'You don't have to explain, I already know – because you're selfish and you always have been. You think about no one except yourself.'

Silvia pressed her lips together.

'Whatever you think, April, I do care. I care deeply about you and I always will.'

April looked out of the window.

'I think you should go.'

Silvia nodded.

'Do me one favour? Stay close to your Grandfather. I know you hate me, but it's dangerous out there. I want you to be safe.'

April glared at her.

'Maybe you should have thought of that a little sooner.'

She struggled out of her bed and crossed to the door, holding it open.

'Just leave me alone,' she said.

'April ...'

'No. Just go. *Go!*'

When Silvia had gone, April quietly closed the door, pulled down the blinds, then slid down the wall, curling up on the floor, her shoulders heaving with sobs.

Chapter Thirty-Eight

April sat down on the cold steps and hugged her knees.

'Hi, Daddy,' she said. 'You okay in there? I'm fine. Well ...
I'm not so fine, actually. I've left home. It's not going well with
Mum, and I've moved in with Gramps. So I guess I won't be
seeing you quite as often.'

She shook her head. Here she was, worrying that a cadaver
behind an iron door would be upset by a change in her routine.
He's dead, April, she said to herself. *Let him go.*

April blew on her hands and shifted her bum, hoping she
wasn't getting chilblains or haemorrhoids or something from
sitting on the cold steps.

'I think Gramps will be able to protect me from the police,
too. They seem to have it in for me now. Not that I can blame
them really.'

If she was investigating this, April had to admit she would
have been hugely suspicious of April Dunne. A witness to four
murders and one suicide, victim of three murder attempts herself, and now discovered in a burning house which contained
the bodies of one of her teachers and one of her supposed
school friends. She seemed to be a death magnet.

Even so, April wasn't all that worried about the police. She
was worried about the vampires. Two of them had worked out
she was a Fury. How long was it before the others realised?
And, crucially, would April manage to solve the Ravenwood
mystery before that happened?

She saw the vicar long before he spotted her. He was wandering up the main path, his cheeks pink, stopping every now and
then for a breather. April decided to walk down to meet him.

'Is there a funeral today?' she asked.

'Ah, April,' said the vicar, a little flustered to see her. 'No, no. They don't have many funerals in the West Cemetery any more – but then I suppose you know that. No, I come here to walk sometimes. I like being among the graves, I find all the faith and love soothing. Does that sound strange?'

'No, not at all.'

They carried on walking up the hill together.

'So how are you, my dear?' he asked. 'I heard you were in the hospital again.'

'Nothing too bad this time, just a bit of smoke inhalation. But you're right, the nurses all know me by name now.'

The vicar smiled.

'Trouble does seem to follow you, doesn't it? I suppose you wouldn't be your father's daughter if it didn't.'

'What do you mean?'

'He could never let anything lie either. He had to know the answer to whatever story he was working on, however much danger it put him in.' He stopped, his hand on his hip, catching his breath. 'Maybe he was too curious.'

'Do you think I should stop looking for answers, Mr Gibson?'

He shook his head.

'I fear that would be like asking a fox to stop trying to steal chickens. If it's in your nature, you'll never be happy until you find what you're looking for. The trouble is, when you lift up a rock, you often find more than you bargained for underneath.'

April gave a thin smile. She thought of her mother and what she'd done. She thought of Benjamin, clutching at his neck. And then she thought of Layla, so alone.

'I think I've already lifted that rock,' she said. 'And you're right, I didn't much like what I saw.'

The vicar fixed her with a serious look.

'The darkness is rising, April, and I think it's only going to get worse.'

'Then we've all got to do what we can, haven't we?' she said.

371

'I mean, even if you know it's going to hurt you and the people around you? You've got to follow the path you think is right, don't you?'

The vicar looked at his feet, scuffing at a loose rock on the path.

'It's at this point I'm supposed to quote a passage of scripture, I think,' he said. 'But I'll be honest with you, April, I think you're on your own now. Off the edge of the map, so to speak. Faith will only take you so far, and after that you have to trust that you're acting for the best.'

She squinted at him.

'I think I am,' she said. 'Or at least I try to.'

He reached out and squeezed her shoulder.

'Then perhaps you're already on the right road.'

At the bottom of the path, they could see a tall figure dressed in a dark overcoat climbing the steps and making his way up towards them. April didn't need to see his face to know it was Gabriel. There was something in his walk, the set of his shoulders, the way her heart began to beat faster when he was nearby.

'I can see you love him, and that's a good thing,' said the vicar.

'But? I can feel a but coming on.'

'He's not all he seems, April.'

She began to protest. 'You don't know him ...'

He touched her hand.

'Oh, but I know *what* he is. They were here when I came to this parish, I've always known about them.'

'Can't you do anything? Some good versus evil thing to cure him?'

The vicar smiled.

'As I say, I'm a great believer in the power of prayer, but there are some things it can't deal with. Sometimes we have to rise up and do God's work ourselves.'

'Am I doing God's work?'

'Only you can say. I know you love him and that's good, but

remember what he is. They're never completely in control of themselves. They can't be tamed.'

'He's a good man, Reverend.'

He nodded and began to walk back towards the church.

'Just be careful.'

Gabriel looked amazing. Considering he had been scorched, cut, blackened with soot and barely breathing when she had seen him two days before, he looked perfect. His skin was flawless, his hair sleek and his eyes sparkled as he grinned at her.

'What are you doing here?' she asked, wrapping herself around him. 'Aren't the police watching the cemetery?'

'I had a call from DI Reece,' he said. 'All charges against me are being dropped. In fact, I got the impression that the police want nothing more to do with us or the case. If they had their way, they'd prefer to pretend the whole thing never happened. They've managed to keep the deaths out of the papers and obviously Benjamin's father is as keen as they are to keep his death a private matter.'

'I'll bet he is. Agropharm shareholders wouldn't welcome another scandal involving the family.'

'I think they're drawing a line under it and hoping that's an end to it. And DCI Johnston's a career copper. If his bosses tell him to drop the case, he'll do it.'

'Do you think it will all go away now? The vampire recruitment at Ravenwood, I mean.'

Gabriel shook his head.

'I doubt it. We may have rid the world of the Vampire Regent, but you heard what Sheldon said: there's someone else out there, someone meaner and stronger. A vampire king. Sheldon obviously had his own agenda, but I'm convinced he was only following orders at Ravenwood. So I can't imagine the king, or whoever's behind it, will abandon their plans. In fact, we've probably made things easier for them.'

'How?'

'Politics, honey,' he said, stroking her hair. 'The way they were talking, I think Sheldon and Benjamin were planning an uprising, a sort of vampire rebellion. Sheldon was the Regent, a stand-in for the king. Maybe he heard the king wanted his throne back.'

April felt a sinking feeling.

'So you think we've actually *helped* the Ravenwood conspiracy?'

Gabriel smiled.

'We've destroyed a key part of their operation and removed two ruthless killers, I'd say that's pretty good going. But no, I don't think it's over, not by a long way.'

'And it's not over for us anyway, is it? You're still … well, still you.'

Gabriel smiled and ran a finger down her cheek. 'No, but I'm still here, thanks to you.'

April thought for a moment.

'Gabriel, can I ask you something?'

'Anything.'

'What Sheldon was talking about that day? How you didn't know yourself and how you were involved with Isabelle's death and maybe even other murders? What was all that about?'

'They are – they were – vampires, remember? They're masters at manipulation, mind-games. None of it meant anything. I think they hoped if they framed me for Isabelle's murder then I'd be out of the way, no more trying to infiltrate their organisation – and Isabelle and her investigations would come to an end as well. Two birds with one stone. I have to admit, I had no idea they were on to me.'

He pulled her closer.

'I'm so sorry, April, I put you in danger, I should have seen it sooner. I was so convinced it was the Regent who turned me, I wasn't looking at it properly. I guess we have to keep looking.'

'We have to. I can't stand not kissing you for much longer.'

He kissed her cheek.

'It won't be long.'

They walked up the hill hand in hand. As they reached a corner, April stopped.

'Listen,' she said nervously. 'There was something else.

When I was angry with you over that Jessica thing, I went with the Suckers to some club and …'

'… and Ben made a move on you. I know.'

'What? How did you know?'

'He boasted about it, April. Never forget, Benjamin Osbourne was a monster hiding behind this mask of charm. Don't ever feel bad for falling for that. And anyway, I was asking for it, I should have told you about Jessica before that. I just … I was feeling guilty too, and I suppose I didn't want anything to ruin what we had.'

'No more secrets?'

'Never.'

'Although I do feel bad. I've been giving my mum such a hard time about her cheating on my dad when maybe I'm no better.'

'You know, it doesn't get any easier as you get older. All the time I've had on earth, and I still make mistakes. Maybe you shouldn't be so hard on her.'

April glanced up the hill towards her father's tomb.

'But it's not just the cheating and the way she treated Dad. It's the fact she lied to me about it. That's what I can't forgive.'

Gabriel nodded.

'So what are you going to do?'

'I'm going to stay with my Granddad. I can't go back to Highgate right now.'

They walked a little further, finally sitting down on a low tomb covered in green moss. They were hidden from the path, but they had a wonderful view of London, spread out under the white sky before then. He kissed her then. Not on the lips, but on her neck, on her fingertips, her cheek. He stroked her hair from her face and looked into her eyes.

'Are you happy now?' he asked her.

'Happy? I'm always happy when I'm with you,' she said.

'Don't duck the question,' he laughed. 'Remember all that stuff about living in the moment, savouring the beautiful feelings when they're there?'

She pushed him on the shoulder.

'I've given you my undying love, what more do you want?' she smiled.

'Un*dying* love?' he asked. 'Is that a joke?'

'Well, you know what I mean.'

Gabriel wrapped his arms around her.

'Hmm, I'm not sure,' he said with a grin, 'Why don't you show me?'

Acknowledgements

Thanks to Avril Horner, Emeritus Professor of English at Kingston University for taking the time to give a one-person tutorial on the gothic and to Dr Ann Rowe for the introduction and her own invaluable feedback (along with Poirot-style guesswork on what's in store in book three). Thanks also go to Dr Jim, as always, for his road map to the dark side and 'Minty' Johnston (no relation) for police procedure and intrigue in Pat Val.

Big love to Eugenie Furniss – so lucky to have someone with such passion and commitment in the Ravenwood corner. Thanks also to Cathryn 'M' Summerhayes for stepping into the breach and to Claudia for tea and efficiency. Special thanks go to Gillian Redfearn whose world class editing made this book ten times better (NB. it's not really her bookshop, although I suspect she'd like to own one just like it). Equal thanks to the rest of the Orion team: marketing guru Mark Rusher (and his teen Eclipsers), Jon and Jon, Louise and Nina at Indigo and especially Jennifer McMenemy for her tireless mousework.

Double thanks to JK, Dr Alan Thompson, Kathryn Rowe, Scott and Tom, Will and Far, Ted for actually reading it, Lucy Fleming Brown for keeping it real and Diggo for 'judo moves' when deadlines loomed. And last but definitely not least love and gratitude go to Linda Butt for her limitless kindness and generosity just when it's needed the most.